Edward Stanwood

A History of Presidential Elections

Edward Stanwood

A History of Presidential Elections

ISBN/EAN: 9783337404185

Printed in Europe, USA, Canada, Australia, Japan

Cover: Foto ©Andreas Hilbeck / pixelio.de

More available books at **www.hansebooks.com**

A HISTORY

OF

PRESIDENTIAL ELECTIONS

BY

EDWARD STANWOOD

BOSTON

JAMES R. OSGOOD AND COMPANY

1884

STEREOTYPED BY

C. J. PETERS AND SON, BOSTON.

THIS History of Presidential Elections professes to be little more than a record of the circumstances of such elections, and of whatever had an appreciable influence upon the result of each election. But as in this category is comprehended almost every important incident of the domestic and foreign relations of the United States, the book will be found to contain references, with or without comment, to most of the events in American political history.

The materials have been gathered from a great variety of sources. The newspapers, — for the long period from 1812 until 1848, chiefly Niles's "Register," — the political almanacs, Mr. Greeley's "Political Text-Book," published in 1860, and Mr. Edward McPherson's biennial "Political Hand-books," have been drawn upon freely for facts and documents; but in all cases the author has endeavored to verify each fact, and to correct the text of documents, particularly of party platforms, by a comparison of authorities.

E. S.

BROOKLINE, MASS., September, 1884.

CONTENTS.

A HISTORY

OF

PRESIDENTIAL ELECTIONS.

I.

THE ELECTORAL SYSTEM.

"The mode of appointment of the chief magistrate of the United States," wrote Alexander Hamilton, in No. 67 of the "Federalist," "is almost the only part of the system of any consequence which has escaped without some censure, or which has received the slightest mark of approbation from its opponents." And it was also true, as was said by James Wilson, in advocating the Constitution before the Pennsylvania Convention, "The Convention, sir, were perplexed with no part of the plan so much as with the mode of choosing the President of the United States." To these assertions must be added, after a century of practice under the Constitution, that no other part of the great charter of the country has failed so completely to fulfil the intentions of the fathers; has, by its ambiguity of language, given rise to more, or more perplexing, disputes; or has been the occasion of more numerous and varied attempts at amendment.

It is, however, not the purpose of this work to criticise, but to record, — to exhibit the electoral clauses of the Constitution in their practical working, without the slightest attempt to cause the events of twenty-four presiden-

1

tial elections to emphasize the need of a change of system, nor even to indicate where, in the opinion of the writer, the failures have occurred. The people of the country have grown fully accustomed to the plan, and their patriotism has, on occasions quite as perilous as are likely to occur in the future, been equal to the demands upon it. The system has not ended in anarchy, as more than once it logically should have done, simply because the people did not wish for anarchy. That it is the part of statesmanship fully to consider the numerous evils which have been developed by a part of the Constitution faulty in what it enjoins and in its omissions, and unsatisfactory in its results, no one can deny; but that a failure to take up the question and to settle it will result in civil war or other disaster, past experience at all events contradicts.

The history of presidential elections begins with the evolution of the system by the Convention of 1787. On the 29th of May, Edmund Randolph submitted a plan of a national government, in which he proposed "a national executive to be chosen by the national legislature for the term of —— years," "and to be ineligible a second time." Charles Pinckney, at the same time, proposed "that the executive power be vested in a 'President of the United States of America,' which shall be his style; and his title shall be 'His Excellency.' He shall be elected for —— years, and shall be re-eligible." The first decision of the Convention was that the term of the Executive should be seven years. On the 2d of June, James Wilson proposed that there should be "certain districts in each State which should appoint electors to elect outside of their own body." In these three propositions were the germs of nearly all the features of the plan as ultimately adopted.

The Convention first adopted a resolution that the Executive should be chosen by Congress; next that the executive power should be vested in one person. A few days later Elbridge Gerry proposed that the Executive should be elected by the governors of the several States. This was negatived. On the 18th of June, Hamilton presented his draft of a constitution, according to which the choice of a single executive officer, a President, was to be made by electors chosen by the people very much as they are now actually chosen; and in case there was no choice by a majority of such electors, then an election from among the three highest candidates was to be made by a body of "second electors," two for each State, to be chosen by the first electors at the time of voting for a President, — who were to meet in one place and to be presided over by the Chief Justice. The perplexity of the Convention upon this subject is shown by the long discussions and the frequent reversals of decision. Having already decided that Congress should choose the President, the Convention rejected, on the 17th of July, an amendment providing for his selection "by electors appointed by the legislatures of the several States," and two days later adopted one almost in the same words: "to be chosen by electors appointed for that purpose by the legislatures of the States." Moreover, having fully determined that the term of office should be seven years, it voted, on the 19th of July, to make the term six years; and rejected an amendment that the President should not hold office more than six years out of twelve. The next day the Convention adopted Mr. Gerry's proposition regarding the number of electors. Massachusetts, Pennsylvania, and Virginia were to have three each; Connecticut, New York, New Jersey, Maryland, North Carolina, and South Carolina, two each; New Hampshire, Rhode Island, Delaware, and Georgia, one each; making twenty-five electors in all. Once more, on the 26th of July, the Convention reverted to the seven years' term, with the provision of ineligibility for re-election. The whole subject was referred, on the same day, to a committee of five, which made a draft of a constitution in conformity with the resolutions of the Convention, and reported this clause with the rest on August 6 : —

ART. X., SEC. 1. The executive power of the United States shall be vested in a single person. His style shall be "The President of the United States of America;" and his title shall be "His Excellency." He shall be elected by ballot by the legislature. He shall hold his office during seven years, but shall not be elected a second time.

This article, combining Mr. Randolph's and Mr. Pinckney's plans, and rejecting the electoral plan which the Convention had approved, was the basis of future discussions. On the 24th of August many proposed amendments were voted on. The Convention refused to give the election to the people, and, in two different forms, to entrust the choice to electors. It also rejected amendments to give each State one vote for President, and it negatived a proposition to give a casting vote to the President of the Senate. It adopted two amendments, which made the third sentence of the article above quoted read as follows : "He shall be elected by joint ballot by the legislature, to which election a majority of the votes of the members present shall be required."

It will be noticed that up to this point no proposition for the choice of a Vice-President had been made. But on the 4th of September the committee of eleven, to whom, on the last day of August, "the questions not yet settled" had been referred, reported an entirely new scheme for an Executive of the United States. It was proposed to strike out all of Article X., Section 1, after the word "Excellency," and insert the following : —

Each State shall appoint, in such manner as its legislature may direct, a number of electors equal to the whole number of senators and members of the House of Representatives to which the State may be entitled in the legislature. (A)

The electors shall meet in their respective States, and vote by ballot for two persons, of whom one at least shall not be an inhabitant of the same State with themselves; and they shall make a list of all the persons voted for, and of the number of votes for each, which list they shall sign and certify, and transmit, sealed, to the seat of general government, directed to the President of the Senate. The President of the Senate shall, in that house, open all the certificates: and the votes shall then and there be counted. (B) The person having the greatest number of votes shall be President, if such number be a majority of the whole number of electors; and if there be more than one who have such majority, and have an equal number of votes, then the Senate shall choose by ballot one of them for President; but if no such person have such majority, then, from the five highest on the list, the Senate shall choose by ballot the President. And in every case, after the choice of a President, the person having the greatest number of votes shall be the Vice-President; but if there should remain two or more who have equal votes, the Senate shall choose from them the Vice-President.

The legislature may determine the time of choosing and assembling the electors, and the manner of certifying and transmitting their votes.

On the following days a great number of amendments were offered to this plan. Those which were adopted were few, and of these a still smaller number were material. At the place marked (A) was added the provision that "no person shall be appointed an elector who is a member of the legislature of the United States, or who holds any office of profit or trust under the United States." At the place marked (B) was added the phrase, "in the presence of the Senate and House of Representatives," — an important clause, as showing that the intention was that the President of the Senate should count, and that the two houses were present only as witnesses. The word "immediately" was first inserted in the direction that the Senate should choose the President, and then the whole clause was struck out, and this was substituted : "The House of Representatives shall immediately choose by ballot one of them for President, the members of each State having one vote." The last paragraph was amended by adding words, so that it read as follows : " The legislature may determine the time of choosing and assembling the electors and of giving their votes, and the manner of certifying and transmitting their votes; but the election shall be on the same day throughout the United States."

On the 8th of September a committee was appointed " to revise the style and arrange the articles agreed to by the House." This committee reported on the 12th, and on the following day the articles were " read, debated by paragraphs, amended, and agreed to," and the Convention adjourned on the 17th. The article, as finally adopted and ratified, under which the first four elections were held, is, in full, as follows : —

ART. II., SEC. 1. The executive power shall be vested in a President of the United States of America. He shall hold his office during the term of four years, and, together with the Vice-President, chosen for the same term, be elected as follows : —

Each State shall appoint, in such manner as the legislature thereof may direct, a number of electors, equal to the whole number of senators and representatives to which the State may be entitled in the Congress; but no senator or representative, or person holding an office of trust or profit under the United States, shall be appointed an elector.

The electors shall meet in their respective States, and vote by ballot for two persons, of whom one at least shall not be an inhabitant of the same State with themselves. And they shall make a list of all the persons voted for, and of the number of votes for each; which list they shall sign and certify, and transmit, sealed, to the seat of the government of the United States, directed to the President of the Senate. The President of the Senate shall, in the presence of the Senate and House of Representatives, open all the certificates, and the votes shall then be counted. The person having the greatest number of votes shall be the President, if such number be a majority of the whole number of electors appointed; and if there be more than one who have such majority, and have an equal number of votes, then the House of Representatives shall immediately choose by ballot one of them for President; and if no person have a majority, then from the five highest on the list the said House shall in like manner choose the President. But in choosing the President, the votes shall be taken by States, the representation from each State having one vote; a quorum for this purpose shall consist of a member or members from two thirds of the States, and a majority of all the States shall be necessary to a choice. In every case, after the choice of the President, the person having the greatest number of votes of the electors shall be the Vice-President. But if there should remain two or more who have equal votes, the Senate shall choose from them by ballot the Vice-President.

The Congress may determine the time of choosing the electors and the day on which they shall give their votes; which day shall be the same throughout the United States.

II.

THE FIRST ELECTION.

It was provided by the Constitution of the United States that the "ratification of the conventions of nine States shall be sufficient for the establishment of this Constitution between the States so ratifying the same." New Hampshire was the ninth State to signify its adhesion to the new form of government, on June 21, 1788; Virginia followed on the 26th of the same month; and New York yielded, after a memorable and bitter struggle, on July 26.

It then became the duty of the Congress of the Confederation, in obedience both to the advice of the Convention of 1787 and to its own resolution, to fix the time for the new government to go into operation. But Congress wasted time in a dreary discussion where the seat of government should be fixed. A decision was at last reached in favor of New York; and on the 13th of September, 1788, Congress passed a resolution, reciting in a preamble that a sufficient number of States had ratified the Constitution, and directing that the choice of electors of President and Vice-President should take place on the first Wednesday of January, 1789, that they should meet in their respective States on the first Wednesday in February and give in their votes, and that the new Congress should meet in New York on the first Wednesday in March. The people had begun to be very impatient at the long delay of Congress, and they hailed this resolution with great satisfaction.

The interval of time before the appointment of electors was to take place was short. No preparations whatever

8

had been made for an election in any of the States. It would have been idle, so many of the people must have thought, to pass laws for the choice of representatives and electors under a Constitution which was so bitterly opposed as was that of 1787, and which might never go into effect. Accordingly it was necessary to begin with the preliminaries for an election only four months distant, after the resolution of Congress was adopted.

In those days communication was very slow. It would have been nearly impossible, in the time allowed, to have made full preparation for such an election as is that of electors to-day in some of the States. The news of the resolution of Congress would hardly reach some of the distant State capitals in two weeks. The governor must then issue a proclamation summoning the legislature, and again, an allowance must be made for the slowness of the mails. Then would follow the meeting of the legislature and a discussion, perhaps prolonged, as to the manner in which the electors should be appointed; the passage of a law conferring upon the people the right to choose them; and the further preparations for the election. The general impression seems to have been that Congress intended, when it made the time so short, that the legislatures themselves should make the choice. "It is evident," wrote a newspaper correspondent at Philadelphia, on Oct. 1, 1788, "that Congress construe the Constitution that the legislatures of the several States, not the people, are to choose the electors, as that body has ordered the choice of said electors to be on the first Wednesday of January, and their meeting for the choice of President four weeks later. For if the people, as hath been asserted, are to choose the electors, is it possible that in the large States of Massachusetts, Virginia, etc., the returns can be made for the choice, notice given to the persons chosen, and the persons thus chosen have time to meet together in the short space of one month? No, it is impossible, and can only be remedied by the legislature, who, in fact, are 'the States' making the choice."

Nevertheless, even at that first election, an attempt was made in several States to give the people the choice of electors. Rhode Island and North Carolina had not ratified the Constitution, and of course did not appoint electors. In Connecticut, New Jersey, Delaware, North Carolina, South Carolina, and Georgia, the governors did not summon the legislatures in season to provide for popular elections, and the appointment of electors was made on the designated day by the legislatures themselves. The proceedings in the other States are interesting.

In New Hampshire an act was passed under which the people virtually nominated the electors, but the actual appointment was reserved for the legislature. Under this law an election took place and the votes were returned to and counted by the legislature. On the day fixed by Congress, the 7th of January, 1789, the legislature being in session, no agreement had been reached as to the manner in which the appointment should be made. The Senate claimed equal power with the House of Representatives in the appointment. The House proposed a joint ballot. The contest was prolonged far into the night, the House stubbornly refusing to admit the pretension of the Senate to a full negative upon its action. At last, shortly before midnight, in order that the vote of the State might not be lost by a delay beyond the time fixed by Congress, the House yielded, under protest, and concurred in the appointment of the electors chosen by the Senate. They were all Federalists.

A somewhat elaborate scheme was devised and put in

operation in Massachusetts. The State having been divided into districts for the choice of representatives in Congress, the people were directed to bring in their ballots for two candidates for electors in each district. On the first Wednesday in January, the votes having been previously canvassed, the legislature chose one of these two for each district, and also two electors at large.

The vote of New York was lost. A contest similar to that in New Hampshire took place, but one much more bitter than the latter. The Assembly was willing to elect by a joint ballot of the two branches, or to divide the electors with the Senate. The Senate would assent to nothing short of a complete negative upon the action of the Assembly, which was not yielded, and the time for election passed.

Pennsylvania, Maryland, and Virginia passed laws providing for popular elections, which took place without great excitement. Not only in these States, but in Massachusetts and New Hampshire, the vote was very light. The two parties were made up of those who favored the Constitution on the one hand, and those who opposed it on the other. Political sentiment seems to have been largely one way or the other in each community. Here the Federalists comprised nearly the whole population; there, scarcely a Federalist was to be found. There were thus present none of the elements necessary for a great political contest. The majority cast perhaps a half of their possible vote, the minority hardly appeared at the polls; in fact, they often had no candidates in the field.

Meantime, who were to be voted for when the electors should meet? Washington, of course, was to be one of the two persons equally to be voted for by the electors, — he who had the highest number, being a majority of all

the electors, to be President, and the candidate receiving the next highest number to be Vice-President. But
there was no formal nomination and no agreement among
the electors, even among those belonging to the Federalist
party, that Washington should be chosen. It was simply
regarded as the obvious and proper course to make him
the first President. Nor did the Anti-Federalists at any
time come to the point of deciding to oppose him. Probably they never even seriously considered the propriety
of so doing. It was charged that they did so, but the
accusation was never supported by any evidence. For
example: it is said in the life of Alexander Hamilton, by
his son, that "for a time the pretensions of Franklin
were discussed in private circles. But the incomparably
superior claims of Washington silenced this purpose,
which there is no evidence was encouraged by Franklin,
whose extreme age would alone have presented an in-
superable objection." As a matter of fact, there is no
evidence that Franklin was even aware of any such purpose, if it ever existed. There is too good reason to
believe that the alleged disposition to pass by the claims
of Washington was a figment of the imagination, — an
invention for the purpose of forming the basis of an
intrigue either to control the vice-presidency, or to make
the vote for John Adams so small as to exhibit him to the
country as a most unpopular candidate.

Public opinion had, indeed, concentrated itself upon
Mr. Adams as Vice-President almost as decidedly as
it had fixed upon Washington for the first place in the
new government. The propriety of taking the Vice-
President from New England was recognized by all
Federalists. The names of Governor Hancock, Samuel
Adams, John Adams, and General Knox, were canvassed.
The last named was a soldier, like Washington, and he

was speedily rejected. It was deemed necessary that Hancock should remain in the position of Governor of Massachusetts. Samuel Adams had been opposed to the new Constitution at the outset, and although he had subsequently advocated it, his early position rendered him an unsuitable candidate. John Adams, on the other hand, had written a book in defence of the Constitution, and it was deemed on many accounts best that he should be chosen. Yet his relations to Washington had been such during the Revolutionary war that there were doubts whether he would be acceptable to the latter. In answer to an inquiry on this point, Washington had cautiously replied that, —

Having taken it for granted that the person elected for that important place would be a true Federalist, in that case he was altogether disposed to acquiesce in the prevailing sentiments of the electors, without giving any unbecoming preference, or incurring any unnecessary ill-will.

Both Hamilton and Madison were doubtful about taking Mr. Adams, but the former wrote, after full consideration, that, "on the whole, I have concluded to support Adams." The people had decided that before him. Most of the newspapers, in the Northern States at least, which were friendly to the new government, expressed themselves strongly in favor of him. One extract from a Philadelphia paper, under date of Oct. 8, 1788, will suffice for all: —

The electors of President of the United States on the part of the Commonwealth of Pennsylvania are to meet in the borough of Reading, where it is universally hoped and expected that one more tribute of merited approbation will be given to George Washington, Esq., by their unanimous suffrages. Of the several respected candidates in nomination for Vice-President, circumstances seem most in favor of John Adams, Esq. While the conciliating talents of Governor Hancock, and the attachment to him that prevails in

Massachusetts, render him necessary to the peace of New England, Mr. Adams is perfectly at leisure to fill a seat for which nature, education, and the experience of several years and various courts in Europe have eminently and peculiarly qualified him.

Under such circumstances the choice of electors took place. There was an understanding for whom they were to vote, but probably not one of the electors in any State had given a pledge. Then occurred an incident which has given rise to much discussion, and widely different views of it have been taken by the partisans of Mr. Adams and of Mr. Hamilton. It is to be remembered that at that time the electors voted for two persons for President. He who had the highest number, being a majority, was to be President, and the second highest was to be Vice-President. There is little doubt that the Anti-Federalists inclined at one time to concentrate upon George Clinton for one of the two places, in the hope of making him Vice-President. It is doubtful if they ever conceived of the possibility of choosing him a President, if they desired to do so, and there is no evidence that they intrigued to compass that end. But Hamilton either believed that they did so, and feared they would succeed, or he saw in the situation a chance to injure Adams. His conduct may be explained on either hypothesis. He seems to have intimated in various quarters a fear that Washington would fail to receive some votes, and that the unanimity in favor of Adams would make the latter President and Washington Vice-President. It was said, too, that the New York electors — as it turned out, New York chose none — would support Clinton and Adams, in the hope that Massachusetts and New England generally would do the same.

Whatever Hamilton's motive may have been, there is no doubt that he did send special messengers to two or three of the States which would have given a unanimous vote to Washington and Adams, advising that one or more votes be withheld from the latter so as to ensure Washington's election for the first place. The acceptance of his advice is the explanation of the scattering votes in Connecticut and New Jersey at least. The result was the election of Washington by a unanimous vote, and of Adams by less than a majority. The detailed vote was as follows : —

STATES.	George Washington.	John Adams.	Samuel Huntington.	John Jay.	John Hancock.	Robert H. Harrison.	George Clinton.	John Rutledge.	John Milton.	James Armstrong.	Edward Telfair.	Benjamin Lincoln.
New Hampshire . .	5	5	–	–	–	–	–	–	–	–	–	–
Massachusetts . . .	10	10	–	–	–	–	–	–	–	–	–	–
Connecticut	7	5	2	–	–	–	–	–	–	–	–	–
New Jersey	6	1	–	5	–	–	–	–	–	–	–	–
Pennsylvania . . .	10	8	–	–	2	–	–	–	–	–	–	–
Delaware	3	–	–	3	–	–	–	–	–	–	–	–
Maryland	6	–	–	–	–	6	–	–	–	–	–	–
Virginia	10	5	–	1	1	–	3	–	–	–	–	–
South Carolina . . .	7	–	–	–	1	–	–	6	–	–	–	–
Georgia	5	–	–	–	–	–	–	–	2	1	1	1
Total	69	34	2	9	4	6	3	6	2	1	1	1

It may be well to repeat here that Rhode Island and North Carolina did not vote, not having ratified the Constitution, and that the vote of New York was lost in a quarrel between the two branches of the legislature. The popular vote in the few States where the people chose the electors signified nothing, and no attempt has been made to collect the returns.

The counting of the electoral vote took place on the 6th of April, 1789, more than a month later than the time fixed by the Congress of the Confederation. On that day, a quorum of senators having appeared in their seats, John

Langdon, a senator from New Hampshire, was elected "president for the sole purpose of opening and counting the votes for President of the United States." A message was sent to the House of Representatives, notifying that body of the facts above recited, "and that the Senate is now ready in the Senate Chamber to proceed, in the presence of the House, to discharge that duty; and that the Senate have appointed one of their members to sit at the clerk's table to make a list of the votes as they shall be declared, submitting it to the wisdom of the House to appoint one or more of their members for the like purpose."

The House appointed two tellers, and, having notified the Senate of its readiness to join that body, proceeded to the Senate Chamber. The President of the Senate opened and counted the vote. The Journal of the Senate reads that : —

The Speaker and the House of Representatives attended in the Senate Chamber, and the president elected for the purpose of counting the votes declared the Senate and House of Representatives had met, and that he, in their presence, had opened and counted the votes of the electors for President and Vice-President of the United States, which were as follows: [The table given above is here inserted.]

Whereby it appeared that

George Washington, Esq., was elected President, and

John Adams, Esq., Vice-President, of the United States of America.

Notification of their election was given by the Senate, and the President and Vice-President elect were sworn into office on the 30th of April.

III.

WASHINGTON'S SECOND ELECTION.

Party spirit did not run very high until almost the close of Washington's first administration, but parties were in a process of formation. The antagonism between Jefferson and Hamilton, the two leading spirits of the cabinet, was strong at first, and became more decided as the latter, supported by the great influence of the President, carried one after another of the measures which have given form and character to the government even to the present time.

As the time for a fresh election drew near, General Washington expressed a wish to retire; but his withdrawal was not desired even by the Anti-Federalists, who now began to take the name of Republicans. The opposition concentrated their strength in an effort to defeat Mr. Adams, and to place George Clinton in the chair of Vice-President. It does not appear that there was any caucus or meeting, public or private, to agree upon this course; but it was a matter of general understanding that those who were opposed to Hamilton's policy would support electors favorable to Mr. Clinton.

At the last session of Congress before the second election, the following act was passed, which, with certain modifications to be noted hereafter, is still in force: —

An Act *Relative to the Election of a President and Vice-President of the United States, and declaring the Officer who shall be President in case of Vacancies in the Offices both of President and Vice-President.*

Section 1. *Be it enacted*, etc., that, except in cases of the

17

election of a President and Vice-President of the United States prior to the ordinary period, as hereinafter specified, electors shall be appointed in each State for the election of a President and Vice-President of the United States, within thirty-four days preceding the first Wednesday in December, 1792, and within thirty-four days preceding the first Wednesday in December in every fourth year succeeding the last election, which electors shall be equal to the number of senators and representatives to which the several States may by law be entitled at the time when the President and Vice-President thus to be chosen should come into office: *Provided always*, that when no apportionment of representatives shall have been made, after any enumeration, at the time of choosing electors, then the number of electors shall be according to the existing apportionment of senators and representatives.

SEC. 2. That the electors shall meet and give their votes on the said first Wednesday in December, at such place in each State as shall be directed by the legislature thereof; and the electors in each State shall make and sign three certificates of all the votes by them given, and shall seal up the same, certifying on each that a list of the votes of such State for President and Vice-President is contained therein, and shall, by writing under their hands, or under the hands of a majority of them, appoint a person to take charge of and deliver to the President of the Senate, at the seat of government, before the first Wednesday in January then next ensuing, one of the said certificates; and the said electors shall forthwith forward, by the post-office, to the President of the Senate at the seat of government, one other of the said certificates; and shall forthwith cause the other of the said certificates to be delivered to the judge of that district in which the said electors shall assemble.

SEC. 3. That the executive authority of each State shall cause three lists of the names of the electors of such State to be made and certified, and to be delivered to the electors on or before the said first Wednesday in December; and the said electors shall annex one of the said lists to each of the lists of their votes.

SEC. 4. That if a list of votes from any State shall not have been received at the seat of government on the said first Wednesday in January, then the Secretary of State shall send a special messenger to the district judge in whose charge such list shall have been lodged, who shall forthwith transmit the same to the seat of government.

SEC. 5. That Congress shall be in session on the second Wednesday in February, 1793, and on the second Wednesday in February succeeding every meeting of the electors, and the said certificates, or so many of them as shall have been received, shall then be opened, the votes counted, and the persons who shall fill the offices of President and Vice-President ascertained and declared agreeably to the Constitution.

SEC. 6. That in case there shall be no President of the Senate at the seat of government on the arrival of the persons entrusted with the lists of the votes of the electors, then such persons shall deliver the lists of the votes in their custody into the office of the Secretary of State, to be safely kept and delivered over as soon as may be to the President of the Senate.

SEC. 7. That the persons appointed by the electors to deliver the lists of votes to the President of the Senate shall be allowed, on the delivery of the said lists, twenty-five cents for every mile of estimated distance by the most usual road from the place of meeting of the electors to the seat of government of the United States.

SEC. 8. That if any person appointed to deliver the votes of electors to the President of the Senate shall, after accepting his appointment, neglect to perform the services required of him by this Act, he shall forfeit the sum of one thousand dollars.

SEC. 9. That in case of the removal, death, resignation, or disability both of the President and Vice-President of the United States, the President of the Senate, *pro tempore*, and, in case there shall be no President of the Senate, then the Speaker of the House of Representatives, for the time being, shall act as President of the United States until such disability be removed, or until a President be elected.

SEC. 10. That whenever the office of President and Vice-President shall both become vacant, the Secretary of State shall forthwith cause a notification thereof to be made to the executive of every State, and shall also cause the same to be published in at least one of the newspapers printed in each State, specifying that electors of the President of the United States shall be appointed or chosen in the several States within thirty-four days preceding the first Wednesday in December then next ensuing; *provided*, that there shall be a space of two months between the date of such notification and the said first Wednesday in December; but if there shall not be the space of two months between the date of such notification and the first Wednesday in December, and if the term for which the President and Vice-President last in office were elected shall not expire on the third day of March next ensuing, then the Secretary of State shall specify in the notification that the electors shall be appointed or chosen within thirty-four days preceding the first Wednesday in December in the year next ensuing, within which time the said electors shall accordingly be appointed or chosen; and the electors shall meet and give their votes on the said first Wednesday in December, and the proceedings and duties of the said electors and others shall be pursuant to the directions prescribed in this act.

SEC. 11. That the only evidence of a refusal to accept, or of a resignation of, the offices of President and Vice-President, shall be an instrument in writing declaring the same, and subscribed by the person refusing to accept or resigning, as the case may be, and delivered into the office of the Secretary of State.

SEC. 12. That the term of four years, for which the President and Vice-President shall be elected, shall in all cases commence on the fourth day of March next succeeding the day on which the votes of the electors shall have been given.

Fifteen States took part in the election of 1792. Rhode Island and North Carolina had ratified the Constitution; and Vermont had been admitted March 4, 1791, and Kentucky, June 1, 1792. Electors were chosen by the legislatures in Vermont, Rhode Island, Connecticut, New York, New Jersey, Delaware, South Carolina, Georgia, and Kentucky, — nine States; by the people in New Hampshire, Massachusetts, Pennsylvania, Maryland, and Virginia, — five States. A very peculiar system was adopted in North Carolina, which it is believed was never practised anywhere else, or at any other time. The apportionment, in accordance with the census of 1790, under which North Carolina was entitled to ten members of the House of Representatives, did not become law until April 13, 1792. The legislature was not then in session, nor did it meet again until the 15th of November. The electors were to meet, under the law of 1792, on the 5th of December. There was not time in the interval to provide for a popular election. Accordingly the legislature passed a law dividing the State into four districts, and directing the members of the legislature residing in each district to meet on the 25th of November and choose three electors. This was a mere hasty makeshift, and the legislature made permanent provision at the same session for the choice of electors by the people by districts.

It may be mentioned, as illustrating the extreme jealousy of State rights that prevailed at this time, that Governor Hancock sent a special message to the Massachusetts legislature, in the nature of a protest against the right of Congress to require the executives of the several States to certify the lists required by section 3 of the act of 1792. He was willing to perform the duty, but he did not believe Congress could direct him to do it.

The election passed off without excitement or serious contest anywhere. The result, by States, is indicated by the following table : —

STATES.	Washington.	Adams.	Clinton.	Jefferson.	Burr.
New Hampshire	6	6	–	–	–
Vermont	3	3	–	–	–
Massachusetts	16	16	–	–	–
Rhode Island	4	4	–	–	–
Connecticut	9	9	–	–	–
New York	12	–	12	–	–
New Jersey	7	7	–	–	–
Pennsylvania	15	14	1	–	–
Delaware	3	3	–	–	–
Maryland	8	8	–	–	–
Virginia	21	–	21	–	–
North Carolina	12	–	12	–	–
South Carolina	8	7	–	–	1
Georgia	4	–	4	–	–
Kentucky	4	–	–	4	–
Total	132	77	50	4	1

The counting of the electoral vote was for the first time a matter of previous agreement between the two houses of Congress, and the system pursued in 1793 was, with occasional slight but sometimes significant modifications, that which was followed for a great many years. The House of Representatives proposed, Feb. 5, 1793, the appointment of a joint committee " to ascertain and report the mode of examining the votes for President and Vice-President, and of notifying the persons who shall be elected of their election, and to regulate the time, place, and manner of administering the oath of office to the President." The Senate agreed, and the committee reported to the two houses, Feb. 13 : —

That the two houses shall assemble in the Senate Chamber on Wednesday next at twelve o'clock; that one person shall be appointed a teller on the part of the Senate (two on the part of the House), to make a list of the votes as they shall be declared; that the result shall be delivered to the President of the Senate, who shall announce the state of the vote, and the persons elected, to both Houses, assembled as aforesaid, which shall be deemed a declaration of the persons elected President and Vice-President, and, together, with a list of the votes, be entered on the Journals of the two Houses.

This mode was observed.

The two Houses having accordingly assembled, the certificates of the electors of the fifteen States of the Union, which came by express, were, by the Vice-President, opened, read, and delivered to the tellers appointed for the purpose, who, having examined and ascertained the votes, presented a list of them to the Vice-President, which list was read to the two Houses, and is as follows: [Here follows the above table.]

Whereupon

The Vice-President declared George Washington unanimously elected President of the United States for the period of four years, to commence with the 4th of March next; and

John Adams elected, by a plurality of votes, Vice-President of the United States for the same period, to commence with the 4th of March next.

It will be observed that in this case the Vice-President both opened *and read* the certificates, and that the tellers did no more than verify and tabulate the returns. The exclusive power of the Vice-President to count the votes was thus asserted and exercised in a marked manner. On the next occasion, as we shall see, the use of this power might have been a matter of some importance.

IV.

JOHN ADAMS.

BEFORE the end of Washington's second administration, party spirit reached a degree of acerbity which has been seldom equalled, and never exceeded, in this country. Mr. Jefferson had resigned his office as Secretary of State at the beginning of 1794, and was recognized as the leader of the Republican party, and the representative of opposition to the policy of which Hamilton had been the proposer, and which was fully accepted by the President. But foreign affairs, even more than domestic, divided parties. Jefferson and the Republicans generally were open partisans of France, advocates of the Revolution, and haters of the French monarchy and of England, the enemy of France. No doubt a very large majority of the people of the United States shared in these sentiments, which the long war with England, the intolerable relations with that country, the assistance France had rendered during the Revolutionary War, and the adoption of republican forms by the French on acquiring their liberties, all combined to render popular.

The only question, however, was, how far this sympathy with France should be allowed to carry the country. The French Republic claimed most insolently the active help of America; and her ambassador, " Citizen Genet, " had openly organized the friends of France for active operations. The calm but firm opposition of Washington to these plots and schemes had brought down upon him a storm of personal abuse to which the political vitupera-

24

tion of to-day is mildness. The anger of the opponents of the administration was transformed into uncontrollable rage by the Jay treaty, which they denounced as a most cowardly surrender of American interests to Great Britain. It was only the confidence which the people had in Washington's wisdom and patriotism, whatever opinion of him their words indicated, that saved the treaty from indignant rejection. It was ratified, however, and the House of Representatives was persuaded to agree to make provision for carrying it into effect, in the early part of 1796, a few months before the election was to take place.

Although there were no formal preparations of opposition, — for the elaborate political machinery of to-day was not then invented, — the Republicans were resolved to make a great effort to defeat the Federalists. In all probability they would not have endeavored to prevent the re-election of Washington if he had consented to be a candidate, and they would not in any event have succeeded. So late as the beginning of September, 1796, it was not known, though it was rumored, that Washington would refuse a third term in the Presidency. And even then, before the Farewell Address was issued, without any caucus or convention, the candidates were already designated by popular agreement. "It requires no talent at divination," it was said in the "Boston Gazette," a Republican paper, in September, 1793, "to decide who will be candidates for the chair. Thomas Jefferson and John Adams will be the men, and whether we shall have at the head of our executive a steadfast friend to the rights of the people, or an advocate for hereditary power and distinction, the people of the United States are soon to decide." Mr. Thomas Pinckney, who had not long before resigned the position of minister to England, was, by common, but not universal, consent, associated with Mr.

Adams. The prevailing sentiment was likewise in favor of Aaron Burr as the associate of Mr. Jefferson on the Republican ticket.

The appointment of electors took place at various times during the month of November, 1796. Sixteen States took part in the election, Tennessee having been admitted to the Union on June 1, 1796. The electors for that State were chosen by the legislature. Those for North Carolina were elected by the people. No other State changed its system, and there were, therefore, six States where there was a popular election, while in the other ten the choice was made by the legislature.

Attempts were made, while the elections were taking place, and after the electors had been chosen, to influence the result. They were of two classes. There was an effort in more than one quarter to represent that Mr. Adams was not faithful to the principles of Federalism, and that he could not be depended upon to follow out the policy which had guided Washington in his administration. Of this class was a communication signed "A Federalist," originally printed in a New York paper, but widely copied into the newspapers of other States, — chiefly those favorable to Mr. Jefferson's pretensions, — in which it was asserted that Mr. Adams was never taken into the confidence of the President; that he was not accustomed to reside at the seat of government except during the sessions of Congress; that he was regarded only as the President of the Senate; and that he had privately expressed himself in terms of decided hostility to many of the measures of Washington's administration. The object of this was, of course, to draw away from Mr. Adams a part of the votes of electors appointed as Federalists.

The other "bombshell" was cast by the minister of

France, M. Adet, probably at the instigation of his government. In the midst of the election he addressed a note to the Secretary of State, and also caused it to be published in all the newspapers which would print it, reproaching the administration with having violated its treaties with France, and with conducting itself in a most ungrateful manner toward a country which had rendered important assistance in the Revolutionary struggle. He also announced that he was directed by his government to suspend his diplomatic duties. The interruption of relations was, however, not to be interpreted " as a rupture between France and the United States, but as a mark of just discontent, which was to last until the government of the United States returned to sentiments and to measures more conformable to the interests of the alliance, and to the sworn friendship between the two nations."

This manifesto, if it had been able to exercise any influence at all upon the election, would have increased the vote for Mr. Jefferson, who was believed to be the fast friend of France, even to the extent of engaging in war in her support, if necessary; though it does not appear that Mr. Jefferson himself gave France any reason to expect him to adopt such a servile policy. But no effect of M. Adet's letter can be traced in the elections.

The popular vote in those States where there was a contest, real or nominal, is not preserved in a form to indicate the strength of the two parties. The minority usually refrained from voting altogether. The result by electoral votes is given on the next page.

The proceedings in preparation for the count of the electoral votes were in all respects similar to those of four years previous, except that the proposition for a joint committee originated this time in the Senate. The count itself is interesting on account of the fact that Mr.

STATES.	John Adams, Mass.	Thomas Jefferson, Va.	Thomas Pinckney, S. C.	Aaron Burr, N. Y.	Samuel Adams, Mass.	Oliver Ellsworth, Conn.	George Clinton, N. Y.	John Jay, N. Y.	James Iredell, N. C.	George Washington, Va.	Samuel Johnston, N. C.	John Henry, Md.	Charles C. Pinckney, S. C.
New Hampshire .	6	–	–	–	–	6	–	–	–	–	–	–	–
Vermont . . .	4	–	4	–	–	–	–	–	–	–	–	–	–
Massachusetts .	16	–	13	–	–	1	–	–	–	–	2	–	–
Rhode Island . .	4	–	–	–	–	4	–	–	–	–	–	–	–
Connecticut . .	9	–	4	–	–	–	–	5	–	–	–	–	–
New York . . .	12	–	12	–	–	–	–	–	–	–	–	–	–
New Jersey . .	7	–	7	–	–	–	–	–	–	–	–	–	–
Pennsylvania . .	1	14	2	13	–	–	–	–	–	–	–	–	–
Delaware . . .	3	–	3	–	–	–	–	–	–	–	–	–	–
Maryland . . .	7	4	4	3	–	–	–	–	–	–	–	2	–
Virginia	1	20	1	1	15	–	3	–	–	1	–	–	–
North Carolina .	1	11	1	6	–	–	–	–	3	1	–	–	1
South Carolina .	–	8	8	–	–	–	–	–	–	–	–	–	–
Georgia	–	4	–	–	–	–	4	–	–	–	–	–	–
Kentucky . . .	–	4	–	4	–	–	–	–	–	–	–	–	–
Tennessee . . .	–	3	–	3	–	–	–	–	–	–	–	–	–
Total	71	68	59	30	15	11	7	5	3	2	2	2	1

Adams himself presided, opened and read the certificates,
and declared himself elected, when the rejection of four
votes which had been called in question would have defeated him and elected his opponent. The legislature of
Vermont had appointed electors, but had not previously
passed a law directing how they should be appointed. It
was contended, privately, by some persons, that the appointment was invalid. But the question was not raised
in Congress, or at the joint meeting for the count of the
votes. Mr. Adams's opponents did not feel sure of their
ground, and probably did not know how to proceed to
make their objections effective. Mr. Madison wrote to
Jefferson, Jan. 8, 1797, "If the Vermont votes be valid,
as is now generally supposed, Mr. Adams will have

seventy-one and you sixty-eight, Pinckney being in the rear of both."

Mr. Adams could certainly not raise the question himself, but he seems to have given an opportunity for objections if anyone should see fit to raise them. The record shows this. When the tellers had reported the result, Mr. Adams thus addressed the assembled senators and representatives : —

Gentlemen of the Senate and House of Representatives,—By the report which has been made to me by the tellers appointed by the two Houses to examine the votes, there are 71 votes for John Adams, 68 for Thomas Jefferson [and so on to the end of the list.] The whole number of votes are 138; 70 therefore make a majority; so that the person who has 71 votes, which is the highest number, is elected President, and the person who has 68 votes, which is the next highest number, is elected Vice-President.

At this point Mr. Adams sat down for a moment. No person having interposed any remarks, he arose again and said : —

In obedience to the Constitution and laws of the United States, and to the commands of both Houses of Congress, expressed in their resolution passed in the present session, I declare that John Adams is elected President of the United States for four years, to commence with the fourth day of March next; and that Thomas Jefferson is elected Vice-President of the United States for four years, to commence on the fourth day of March next.

And may the Sovereign of the Universe, the Ordainer of civil government on earth, for the preservation of liberty, justice, and peace among men, enable both to discharge the duties of these offices conformably to the Constitution of the United States, with conscientious diligence, punctuality, and perseverance.

V.

ALTHOUGH the administration of Mr. Adams began with a bare majority in his favor, alike among the people and in Congress, it became increasingly popular during the greater part of his term of office; and it was only as the election of the year 1800 drew near that his choice for a second term became even improbable.

The one overshadowing question during the whole administration was the relations with France. Notwithstanding the long-standing friendship between the two countries, the treatment of the American embassy appointed in 1797, consisting of Messrs. Elbridge Gerry, John Marshall, and C. C. Pinckney, and the insolent depredations of France upon our commerce, turned public sentiment strongly against that country. Congress approved military and naval preparations for war with France by strong majorities, and the people were heartily in favor of the administration, though the minority which protested was fierce and vehement. During the long session of 1797–98, which lasted more than eight months, the Alien and Sedition laws were passed. These two laws concentrated the opposition, and made the rallying cry for the Republican party at the ensuing elections. They are referred to in numerous Democratic platforms to be found in other pages of this volume, where hostility to foreigners is deprecated, and a promise is made to defeat any attempt to abridge the rights of naturalized citizens " with the same spirit which swept the Alien and

Sedition Laws from our statute-book," which embodies a historical blunder; for as a matter of fact the Sedition Law was temporary and expired by its own limitation, as did also the greater part of the Alien Law: the rest of the latter act is still the law of the land. No act of repeal of either was ever passed. Opposition to these two acts, however, was very bitter in 1798 and the following years. But in spite of it the elections of new members of Congress, which took place in the autumn of 1798 and the following spring, were very favorable for the administration.

The measures of Congress having consolidated the opposition, Mr. Adams's own act alienated a large body of his friends. In spite of the insults to which the former embassy to France had been subjected, and in the face of his own assertion that he would make no more attempts at negotiation, he determined, in 1799, to send other agents to France and renew the efforts to make a treaty. He reached this determination without consulting his cabinet, and deeply offended Mr. Pickering, the Secretary of State, and Mr. McHenry, the Secretary of War, who were strongly opposed to the step. The Federalists were still disposed to support him in the election which was to take place the next year, but they had lost their enthusiasm for him.

As most of the electors were to be appointed by the legislatures, the contest for the Presidency virtually began with the election of the members of those bodies, and the contest was really decided when the legislature of New York, chosen in May, 1800, was found to have a Republican majority. New York had voted for Mr. Adams in 1796. Had it continued to support him in 1800 he would have had six more electoral votes than he received in 1796, and sixteen more than were given to Jefferson and Burr.

Mr. Charles Cotesworth Pinckney, a brother of Thomas Pinckney, who had been the candidate most voted for with Mr. Adams in 1796, was associated with Adams on the Federal ticket. Aaron Burr was second on the Jefferson ticket. The manner in which these tickets were formed is involved in much obscurity. Mr. Hezekiah Niles, whose " Weekly Register " is a treasury of facts for students of our early political history, tried to clear it up, but acknowledged his failure. Very early in the year 1800 a meeting of a few Federalist members of Congress, for the purpose, as was said at the time, of influencing the Presidential election, was held in the Senate Chamber. No account of its proceedings, so far as is known, was ever printed, but it was probably called for the purpose of strengthening Mr. Adams's cause; for Mr. Niles says in another place ("Register," vol. 24, p. 277) that " it was well understood that many of the Federalists were opposed to the taking up of Mr. Adams for the Presidency, — that they had nearly fixed on another person;" and it may be also for naming a candidate for Vice-President. But it is all a matter of conjecture and uncertainty. Whatever may have been its object, it excited the wrath of the Republicans, and was denounced in the Philadelphia " Aurora " as a " Jacobinical conclave," — for which and other insulting remarks the editor of the paper was arraigned before the bar of the Senate.

The Republican members, however, held a caucus somewhat later, — probably in February or March, 1800; also a secret meeting, and attended by a small number of members, not so much for the purpose of nominating Mr. Jefferson, who was designated by the unanimous voice of his party as the natural candidate, as with the idea of causing a union upon Burr, as well as upon Jefferson.

Burr's friends complained that in 1796 he had not been supported, particularly in the South, as he should have been. But, as the Constitution then stood, Burr was nominated and voted for as the equal of Jefferson on the ticket, and it was the basis of the claim which was set up in his favor a year later.

Pending this election, a serious, and at one time a most promising, attempt was made to remedy the deficiencies in the Constitution in the matter of the electoral count, by a law. As the legislation then proposed subsequently formed the basis both of the "twenty-second joint rule," so famous in the counts of 1869 and 1873, and of the electoral commission law of 1877, it becomes necessary to notice the proceedings at some length. A resolution introduced in the Senate Jan. 23, 1800, by Mr. Ross of Pennsylvania, directed the appointment of a committee "to consider whether any, and what, provisions ought to be made by law for deciding disputed elections of President and Vice-President of the United States, and for determining the legality or illegality of the votes given for those officers in the different States." The committee reported a bill, February 14, of which the provisions were, in brief, as follows: —

On the day before the second Wednesday in February of any year when there was to be a count of electoral votes, each House of Congress was to choose by ballot six of its own members, who, with the Chief Justice of the United States, or, in case of his disability from any cause, the next senior justice, were to form a "grand committee," with "power to examine, and finally to decide, all disputes relating to the election."

Each House was next to elect two tellers, to whom the certificates of the electors, after they had been opened and read, were to be delivered; and the tellers were to note the dates of the certificates, the names of the electors, the time and place of their meeting, and the governors' certificates accompanying, — these minutes to be read to the two Houses and entered on the two Journals.

After the certificates had been opened, read, and minuted, the President of the Senate was to administer to the members of the grand committee an oath to examine the certificates impartially, "together with the exceptions and petitions against them, and a true judgment give thereon, according to the evidence." All the certificates, papers, petitions, and testimony were then to be delivered to the chairman of the grand committee, which was to meet every day, sit with closed doors, have ample power to send for persons and papers, compel attendance of witnesses, and punish contempts. The powers of the grand committee were stated in the following section : —

SEC. 8. That the grand committee shall have power to inquire, examine, decide, and report upon the constitutional qualifications of the persons voted for as President and Vice-President of the United States; upon the constitutional qualifications of the electors appointed by the different States, and whether their appointment was authorized by the State legislature or not; upon all petitions and exceptions against corrupt, illegal conduct of the electors, or force, menaces, or improper means used to influence their votes; or against the truth of their returns, or the time, place, or manner of giving their votes: *Provided always*, that no petition or exception shall be granted, allowed, or considered by the sitting grand committee, which has for its object to dispute, draw into question the number of votes given for an elector, or the fact whether an elector was chosen by a majority of the votes in his State or district.

The committee was to make a final report on the 1st of March, stating the number of legal votes for each person, the number rejected, and the reason for rejection; such reasons to be signed by those who agreed to them. A majority of the committee was to decide finally all questions submitted, and on the day after the report was made the two Houses were to meet again in joint convention, when the result was to be declared, and, if no person had been chosen President, the House was to proceed immediately to make a choice according to the Constitution.

When the bill came under discussion, a motion was made to strike out the first ten sections of the bill — being all which contained any reference to a grand committee — and to insert instead of them a single section, providing that when the two Houses should be assembled for the purpose of having the certificates of electors opened and counted, the names of the States should be drawn in order by lot; that all petitions and exceptions should be read as well as the certificates themselves; that, if no objection should be made, the votes should be counted; but that "if the votes, or any of them, shall be objected to, the members present shall, on the question propounded by the President of the Senate, decide, without debate, by yea or nay, whether such votes are constitutional or not;" and so on, each question being decided before the name of another State was drawn. This proposition was rejected. Various other amendments were offered, some of which were adopted, and the bill was passed substantially as it was reported, except that the constitution of the grand committee was changed so as to relieve the Supreme Court from any duty in connection with the electoral count. Each House of Congress was to choose six of its members for this service, and the Senate was also to select three others of its members, of whom the House was to choose one by ballot as the thirteenth member of the grand committee.

The whole subject was considered with extreme care by the House of Representatives. After much debate

upon it in Committee of the Whole, the bill was referred
to a select committee, of which John Marshall, afterwards
Chief Justice, was chairman. The committee reported
back the bill, in a wholly new draft, on the 25th of April.
It provided for a joint committee of four members from
each House, with "power to examine into all disputes
relative to the election of President and Vice-President
of the United States, other than such as might relate to
the number of votes by which the electors may have been
appointed." To this committee all petitions, exceptions,
and memorials against either the electors or the persons for
whom they had voted, were to be delivered. The committee was to meet daily from the time of its appointment
until it made its report; it was to have the same powers
for reaching witnesses and compelling the production of
papers which the Senate had given to the grand committee. The report of the committee was to contain all
the facts ascertained in the investigation, but no opinion.
The count was to be made in presence of the two
Houses immediately after this report was made — tellers
having been previously appointed in the manner already
established by precedent — in the following method : —

The names of the several States shall then be written under the
inspection of the Speaker of the House of Representatives, on
separate and similar pieces of paper, and folded up as nearly alike
as may be, and put into a ballot-box, and taken by a member of the
House of Representatives, to be named by the Speaker thereof; out
of which box shall be drawn the paper on which the names of the
States are written, one at a time, by a member of the Senate, to be
named by the President thereof, and so soon as one is drawn the
packet containing the certificates from the electors of that State
shall be opened by the President of the Senate, and then shall be
read also the petitions, depositions, and other papers concerning
the same, and if no exceptions are taken thereto, all the votes contained in such certificates shall be counted; but if any exception be
taken, the person taking the same shall state it directly and not

argumentatively, and sign his name thereto; and, if it be founded on any circumstance appearing in the report of the joint committee, and the exception be seconded by one member from the Senate and one from the House of Representatives, each of whom shall sign the said exception as having seconded the same, then each House shall immediately retire, without question or debate, to its own apartment, and shall take the question of the exception, without debate, by ayes and noes. So soon as the question shall be taken in either House, a message shall be sent to the other, informing them that the House sending the message is prepared to resume the count, and when such message shall have been received by both Houses they shall again assemble in the same apartment as before, and the count shall be resumed. And if the two Houses have concurred in rejecting the vote or votes objected to, such vote or votes shall not be counted; but, unless both Houses concur, such vote or votes shall be counted. If the objection taken as aforementioned shall arise on the face of the papers opened by the President of the Senate in presence of both Houses, and shall not have been noticed in the report of the joint committee, such objections may be referred to the joint committee to be examined and reported on by them in the same manner and on the same principles as their first report was made; but if both Houses do not concur in referring the same to the committee, then such objections shall be decided on in like manner as if it had been founded on any circumstance appearing in the report of the committee. The vote of one State being thus counted, another ticket shall be drawn from the ballot-box, and the certificate and the votes of the State thus drawn shall be proceeded on as is hereinbefore directed, and so on, one after another, until the whole of the votes shall be counted.

The bill was carefully considered, and various amendments were proposed and negatived. It was passed on the 2d of May by a vote of 52 to 37. On being returned to the Senate, the bill was referred to a committee which reported several amendments, of which only one was adopted, but that was one of the greatest importance. The word "rejecting" was struck out of the passage quoted above, and the word "admitting" was inserted in its stead. The effect of this was to provide that,

unless the two Houses concurred in *admitting* any disputed vote, it should not be counted. This was precisely the principle of the twenty-second joint rule of
1865, and the Senate adopted it in 1800 by a vote of 16
to 11. The House non-concurred, and a vote in each
branch to adhere to the disagreement defeated the bill
altogether.

To return to the election: The contest was waged with
acrimony all through the year 1800, although there was
scarcely a hope for the election of Mr. Adams. The old
hostility between Mr. Adams and Mr. Hamilton had
something to do with this result. Mr. Hamilton wrote a
letter attacking Mr. Adams, which was probably intended
for Southern circulation only, but which was published
at the North also. His idea seems to have been to
get more votes for Mr. Pinckney than for Mr. Adams,
and so to make the former President, or at least Vice-
President. It was hoped at that time that the vote of
South Carolina would be given, as it had been in 1796,
to Jefferson and Pinckney. But Mr. Hamilton's finely
laid plan went astray, as that of 1793 had done to some
extent; and he only succeeded in defeating his party
wholly, in precipitating a constitutional crisis, and in
laying a broad foundation for a personal quarrel between
himself and Burr, which finally cost him his life.

The number of States which took part in the election
was sixteen, no State having been admitted during Mr.
Adams's administration. The only incident worthy of
notice, as regarding the election itself, was what happened
in the State of Pennsylvania, which shows that the fathers
were not above taking political advantages in a way that
smacks quite as strongly of sharp practice as anything
that is done at the present day.

At that period it was common for the legislatures of

the several States to pass a law providing for the appointment of electors every four years, the law expiring after each election. This had been the practice in Pennsylvania from the beginning, and the people had always enjoyed the privilege of choosing the electors by popular vote. In the year 1796, fourteen Jefferson electors had been chosen and only one Adams man. But in the time of Mr. Adams's popularity the Federalists had carried the State once or twice; and, as the senators were elected by classes, for four years, it happened that, in the year 1800, although the Governor and the House of Representatives were strongly Republican, the Senate was still Federalist by 13 to 11. As no law had been passed providing for a popular election in time to enable the people to make a choice, it became the duty of the legislature itself to choose the electors. The House passed a law providing for an election by joint ballot, the only way in which the legislature of that State ever elected officers. The Senate rejected the bill and proposed instead an election by concurrent vote. The House refused to adopt that method. At last the Senate proposed that each House should name eight electors, and that the two Houses should vote together for the combined list, or for fifteen of the sixteen. The House was forced to yield, and the result was that eight Jefferson and seven Adams electors were chosen. The Federal senators — "the Federal thirteen," as they were proudly termed by their admirers — were loudly praised for this act by the party organs. The editor of the United States "Gazette," of Philadelphia, wrote on Dec. 3, 1800, to his paper: —

The Federal thirteen deserve the praises and the blessings of all America. They have checked the mad enthusiasm of a deluded populace and the wicked speculation of designing demagogues. On reviewing the recent aspect of our political affairs, it may be figuratively said, *They have saved a falling world!*

At this election, for the first time, the people of Rhode Island chose electors by popular vote, thus taking the place of Pennsylvania, and leaving the number of States in which that system of appointment prevailed six, as before. The result of the election was as follows, by States : —

STATES.	Thomas Jefferson, Va.	Aaron Burr, N. Y.	John Adams, Mass.	C. C. Pinckney, S. C.	John Jay, N. Y.
New Hampshire	–	–	6	6	–
Vermont	–	–	4	4	–
Massachusetts	–	–	16	16	–
Rhode Island	–	–	4	3	1
Connecticut	–	–	9	9	–
New York	12	12	–	–	–
New Jersey	–	–	7	7	–
Pennsylvania	8	8	7	7	–
Delaware	–	–	3	3	–
Maryland *	5	5	5	5	–
Virginia	21	21	–	–	–
North Carolina	8	8	4	4	–
South Carolina	8	8	–	–	–
Georgia	4	4	–	–	–
Kentucky	4	4	–	–	–
Tennessee	3	3	–	–	–
	73	73	65	64	1

* One Maryland elector did not attend.

The proceedings preliminary to the count, and the count itself, were in all respects similar to those in former years, up to the declaration of the result, which was in these words : —

That the whole number of electors who had voted was one hundred and thirty-eight, of which number Thomas Jefferson and

Aaron Burr had a majority; but, the number of those voting for them being equal, no choice was made by the people; and that, consequently, the remaining duties devolve upon the House of Representatives.

Already a committee had been appointed to prepare a set of rules for the House, in case the count should show that it was the duty of the House to elect a President; and the rules, having been discussed in committee of the whole, were adopted as follows : —

First. In the event of its appearing, upon the counting and ascertaining of the votes given for President and Vice-President, according to the mode prescribed by the Constitution, that no person has a constitutional majority, and the same shall have been duly declared and entered on the Journals of this House, the Speaker, accompanied by the members of the House, shall return to their Chamber.

Second. Seats shall be provided in this House for the President and members of the Senate, and notification of the same shall be made to the Senate.

Third. The House, on their return from the Senate Chamber, it being ascertained that the constitutional number of States are present, shall immediately proceed to choose one of the persons from whom the choice is to be made for President; and in case upon the first ballot there shall not appear to be a majority of the States in favor of one of them, in such case the House shall continue to ballot for a President, without interruption by other business, until it shall appear that a President is duly chosen.

Fourth. After commencing the balloting for President, the House shall not adjourn until a choice is made.

Fifth. The doors of the House shall be closed during the balloting, except against the officers of the House.

Sixth. In balloting the following mode shall be observed, to wit: The representatives of the respective States shall be so seated that the delegation of each State shall be together. The representatives of each State, shall, in the first instance, ballot among themselves, in order to ascertain the vote of that State ; and it shall be allowed, where deemed necessary by the delegation, to name one or more persons of the representation to be tellers of the ballots. After the vote of each State is ascertained, duplicates thereof shall be made;

and in case the vote of the State be for one person, then the name of that person shall be written on each of the duplicates; and in case the ballots of, the State be equally divided, then the word "divided" shall be written on each duplicate, and the said duplicates shall be deposited, in manner hereafter prescribed, in boxes to be provided. That for the conveniently taking the ballots of the several representatives of the respective States, there be sixteen ballot-boxes provided; and that there be, additionally, two boxes provided for receiving the votes of the States; that after the delegation of each State shall have ascertained the vote of the State, the Sergeant-at-Arms shall carry to the respective delegations the two ballot-boxes, and the delegation of each State, in the presence and subject to the examination of all the members of the delegation, shall deposit a duplicate of the vote of the State in each ballot-box; and where there is more than one representative of a State, the duplicates shall not both be deposited by the same person. When the votes of the States are all thus taken in, the Sergeant-at-Arms shall carry one of the general ballot-boxes to one table, and the other to a second and separate table. Sixteen members shall then be appointed as tellers of the ballots, one of whom shall be taken from each State, and be nominated by the delegation of the State from which he was taken. The said tellers shall be divided into two equal sets, according to such agreements as shall be made among themselves, and one of the said sets of tellers shall proceed to count the votes in one of the said boxes, and the other set the votes in the other box; and in the event of no appointment of teller by any delegation, the Speaker shall in such case appoint. When the votes of the States are counted by the respective sets of tellers, the result shall be reported to the House; and if the reports agree, the same shall be accepted as the true votes of the States; but if the reports disagree, the States shall immediately proceed to a new ballot, in manner aforesaid.

Seventh. If either of the persons voted for shall have a majority of the votes of all the States, the Speaker shall declare the same; and official notice thereof shall be immediately given to the President of the United States, and to the Senate.

Eighth. All questions which shall arise after the balloting commences, and which shall be decided by the House voting *per capita* to be incidental to the power of choosing the President, and which shall require the decision of the House, shall be decided by States, and without debate; and in case of an equal division of the votes of States, the question shall be lost.

Immediately upon the retirement of the House from the Senate Chamber to its own hall, after the count had been made and the result declared, a ballot was taken. The Federalists had already taken the strange resolution to support Mr. Burr in opposition to Mr. Jefferson. It does not appear that there was any understanding between Burr and the Federalists, nor was it ever charged that there was such an understanding; but the alliance was immoral, nevertheless. On the part of Burr it showed a willingness to profit by an accident to gain the Presidency, for which, say what he and his friends might, he was not nominated or designedly voted for; while, so far as the Federalists were concerned, it was a trick to defeat the will of the people, to gratify their feelings of personal

STATES.	Jefferson.	Burr.	State voted for.
New Hampshire . . .	–	4	Burr.
Vermont	1	1	Divided — Blank.
Massachusetts. . . .	3	11	Burr.
Rhode Island	–	2	Burr.
Connecticut	–	7	Burr.
New York	6	4	Jefferson.
New Jersey	3	2	Jefferson.
Pennsylvania	9	4	Jefferson.
Delaware	–	1	Burr.
Maryland	4	4	Divided — Blank.
Virginia	16	3	Jefferson.
North Carolina . . .	9	1	Jefferson.
South Carolina . . .	–	5	Burr.
Georgia	1	–	Jefferson.
Kentucky	2	–	Jefferson.
Tennessee	1	–	Jefferson.
Total	55	49	

hostility to Jefferson. The first ballot and eighteen more on the first day, February 11, nine ballotings on the 12th, one on the 13th, four on the 14th, one on the 16th (Monday), and one on the 17th, making thirty-five trials in all, produced identically the same result. Eight States were for Mr. Jefferson, six for Mr. Burr, and two were divided. The vote of nine States being necessary, there was no choice. On all these ballots the votes of the members and of the States was as given on the preceding table (p. 43).

On the thirty-sixth ballot, taken also on the 17th of February, Mr. Jefferson was elected. He received the votes of ten States, and Burr of four States; and there were two blanks. One member from Vermont and four from Maryland declined to vote, giving Jefferson both of these States, and Delaware and South Carolina cast blank votes. Four New England States only continued to vote for Burr. No Federalist ever undertook to defend the course of his party at that election. Hamilton was very strongly against it, but his influence did not prevail. In a letter written by Mr. James A. Bayard,— the single member from Delaware, a Federalist, who had voted for Burr up to the last ballot, and then voted blank, — dated on the day the election was effected, but not made public until the year 1823, that gentleman said: —

> The New England gentlemen came out and declared they meant to go without a constitution and take the risk of a civil war. They agreed that those who would not agree to incur such an extremity ought to recede without loss of time. We pressed them to go with us and preserve unity in our measures. After great agitation and much heat, all agreed but one. But in consequence of his standing out the others refused to abandon their old ground.

Upon the election of Mr. Jefferson as President, Mr. Burr became Vice-President, in accordance with the Constitution, and a very grave peril to the young country was happily averted.

VI.

JEFFERSON RE-ELECTED.

THE danger that the will of the people might be frustrated by the selection of an inferior man as President, under the provisions of the Constitution as originally adopted, was fully revealed by the election of the year 1800. It might be done accidentally by a few scattering votes, or designedly, as might have been the case in 1801. Accordingly there was a determined movement in favor of an amendment of the Constitution to remedy this defect. Both New York and North Carolina adopted and sent to Congress, in February, 1802, a proposed amendment recommended by their respective legislatures, to the effect that, "in all future elections of President and Vice-President of the United States, the persons voted for shall be particularly designated, by declaring which is voted for as President and which as Vice-President."

The history of the adoption of the amendment which left the Constitution in its present form is not interesting or suggestive. An amendment in the above words was adopted by the House, May 1, 1802, by a vote of 47 to 17. The Senate refused to adopt it, 15 being in favor and 8 opposed, not two thirds. The proposition was brought forward substantially in its present form at the next session, but it did not pass. A third attempt was made at the October session of 1803; and, after careful consideration and long debate, it was adopted, having been passed by the Senate by a vote of 22 to 10, and by the House by the exact constitutional majority, 84 to 42. The vote of

Mr. Speaker Macon was necessary to make up the number of the majority to two thirds. The opposition came
chiefly from the Federalists, who complained that the
amendment was designed simply to gratify the wishes and
the ambition of a single person. Of the 42 votes in the
minority no less than 24 came from New England, while
only three members from that . section supported the
change. The amendment is in these words: —

The electors shall meet in their respective States and vote by
ballot for President and Vice-President, one of whom, at least, shall
not be an inhabitant of the same State with themselves; they shall
name in their ballots the persons voted for as President, and, in
distinct ballots, the persons voted for as Vice-President, and they
shall make distinct lists of all persons voted for as President, and
of all persons voted for as Vice-President, and of the number of
votes for each; which lists they shall sign and certify, and transmit
sealed to the seat of government of the United States, directed to the
President of the Senate. The President of the Senate shall, in the
presence of the Senate and House of Representatives, open all the
certificates, and the votes shall then be counted; the person having
the greatest number of votes for President shall be the President, if
such number be a majority of the whole number of electors appointed;
and if no person have such majority, then from the persons having the
highest numbers, not exceeding three on the list of those voted for as
President, the House of Representatives shall choose immediately, by
ballot, the President. But in choosing the President the vote shall
be taken by States, the representation from each State having one
vote. A quorum for this purpose shall consist of a member or members from two thirds of the States, and a majority of all the States
shall be necessary to a choice. And if the House of Representatives shall not choose a President, whenever the right of choice
shall devolve upon them, before the fourth day of March next following, then the Vice-President shall act as President, as in the case of
the death or other constitutional disability of the President.

The person having the greatest number of votes as Vice-President shall be Vice-President, if such number be a majority of the
whole number of electors appointed; and if no person have a majority, then from the two highest numbers on the list the Senate
shall choose the Vice-President; a quorum for the purpose shall

consist of two thirds of the whole number of senators, and a majority of the whole number shall be necessary to a choice. But no person constitutionally ineligible to the office of President shall be eligible to that of Vice-President of the United States.

At the same session Congress passed a law supplementary to the act of 1792, to take effect whenever the amendment should be ratified, directing that thereafter the electors —

Shall vote for President and Vice-President of the United States, respectively, in the manner directed by the above-mentioned amendment; and having made and signed three certificates of all the votes given by them, each of which certificates shall contain two distinct lists, one of the votes given for President and the other for Vice-President, they shall seal up the said certificates, certifying on each that lists of all the votes of such State given for President and of all votes given for Vice-President are contained therein, and shall cause the said certificates to be transmitted and disposed of, and in every other respect act in conformity with the provisions of the act to which this is a supplement. And every other provision of the act to which this is a supplement, and which is not virtually repealed by this act, shall extend and apply to every election of a President and Vice-President of the United States made in conformity to the above-mentioned amendment to the Constitution of the United States.

The above provisions are those which are now in force. It was further provided by the same act that until electors should receive a notice that the amendment had been duly ratified by a sufficient number of States, they should vote in both ways, the old and the new, make out six certificates, and send two sets of each kind to the President of the Senate; but only those which should be in conformity to the Constitution at the time of the election were to be opened. This provision, however, became inoperative by reason of the promptness of the States in ratifying the amendment, — which was declared adopted by the Secretary of State in a notification addressed to the several governors on the 25th of September, 1804. Thirteen of the sixteen States ratified the amendment. The dissenting States were Massachusetts, Connecticut, and Delaware.

The Republican victory in 1800 was, beyond a doubt, the triumph of a political school whose principles had been, both before and since the adoption of the Constitution, those of a large majority of the people. If there were nothing else to support this view it would be fully sustained by the facts that the opposition was so active and strong, even as against Washington, that it very nearly defeated Adams's first election, and that as soon as it attained power it held the reins of government, with scarcely a contest and without a single defeat — for the contest of 1824 was between candidates professing the same principles — for forty years. That Mr. Jefferson's policy and administration were very distasteful to those who had been intellectual, and not merely accidental, supporters of Washington and Adams is certainly true. But it was evident, after Jefferson had taken his seat, that he was upheld by a strong popular majority; and his party in Congress had no difficulty in carrying every measure upon which it resolved. The Federalists had no lack of reasons for opposing the President. His removals from office for political reasons; his hostility to the navy; the savage assault upon the independence of the judiciary, which he certainly did not discourage; his attempts to restrain within most narrow bounds the authority of the general government; his purchase of Louisiana, which was denounced as grossly unconstitutional and in violation of his own principles of "limited powers" and "strict construction;" the foreign policy of the President, which the Federalists deemed as unwisely lenient toward France as it was hostile to England, — these and other questions of public policy marked the differences between Mr. Jefferson and the Federalists. But the people were with the President.

The first regular caucus of members of Congress for the nomination of presidential candidates was held on the 25th of February, 1804. The report of it is very brief. The call was addressed to the Republican members of the two Houses. They met and unanimously nominated Mr. Jefferson for re-election; and, "by a very large majority," George Clinton of New York was nominated for Vice-President. Indeed, it was to nominate a Vice-President that the meeting was called. No one was in favor of the re-election of Burr. The Republicans particularly were opposed to him on account of his willingness to defeat the real desire of his party in 1801. There seems to have been no objection to the caucus at this time, and the candidates were cordially accepted. The Federalists agreed — it is not known where or by whom the agreement was made — to support Charles C. Pinckney for President and Rufus King for Vice-President.

Seventeen States took part in the election, Ohio having been admitted to the Union Nov. 29, 1802. A new apportionment, too, had been made, based upon the census of 1800, considerably enlarging the number of electoral votes. In most of the States there was no contest, and in Massachusetts alone was the battle fierce ; and, strange to say, that State chose the Republican electors by a majority of nearly 3,700 votes out of the — for that time — enormous number of more than 55,000 votes * cast. The Republican party swept the country.

The proceedings in connection with the electoral count were noticeable for one incident only. The Vice-President said, addressing the two Houses assembled in joint

* The vote was: Jefferson, 29,310; Pinckney, 25,777.

meeting: "You will now proceed, gentlemen, to count the votes, as the Constitution and laws direct." This was different from the practice of Mr. Adams, who counted himself. The electoral votes are shown by the following table : —

STATES.	PRESIDENT.		VICE PRESIDENT.	
	Thomas Jefferson.	Charles C. Pinckney.	George Clinton.	Rufus King.
New Hampshire	7	–	7	–
Vermont	6	–	6	–
Massachusetts	19	–	19	–
Rhode Island	4	–	4	–
Connecticut	–	9	–	9
New York	19	–	19	–
New Jersey	8	–	8	–
Pennsylvania	20	–	20	–
Delaware	–	3	–	3
Maryland	9	2	9	2
Virginia	24	–	24	–
North Carolina	14	–	14	–
South Carolina	10	–	10	–
Georgia	6	–	6	–
Kentucky	8	–	8	–
Tennessee	5	–	5	–
Ohio	3	–	3	–
Total	162	14	162	14

There were some irregularities in the certificates of the electors, and attention was called to them; but no objection was made to any votes, and the result was declared in accordance with the above list.

VII.

JAMES MADISON.

THE events of Mr. Jefferson's second term were almost entirely occurrences in our foreign relations. We had difficulties with Spain, with Great Britain, and with France. The President, to be sure, had his quarrel with the court which tried and did not convict Burr, but that was a mere incident. As the term drew toward its close, the relations with Great Britain became more unfriendly, and the accusation of undue partiality for France on the part of the administration was more loudly and persistently preferred. The administration party in Congress were clamorous at one time for a declaration of war against Spain. In 1807 Jefferson declined even to lay before the Senate a treaty with Great Britain, negotiated by the two envoys — James Monroe and William Pinkney, of Maryland — appointed by himself. The cavalier treatment of Mr. Monroe at this time by Mr. Jefferson, and by Mr. Madison, his Secretary of State, probably had something to do with the opposition, at one time threatening, but eventually ineffectual, to Mr. Madison, on the part of Mr. Monroe's friends. John Randolph at this time created great alarm in the administration ranks by his strong dissent from Jefferson's foreign policy, in which he was backed by some other Republican members of Congress. The Federalists had, of course, no difficulty in finding reasons for opposing him; but the last which he gave them was the greatest, the embargo, which was laid in December, 1807, and continued through the whole time of the presidential canvass. This measure was extremely unpopular in the Northern commercial States, which suffered most by it; and not even the attack upon the "Chesapeake," the avowed cause of the embargo, justified in the eyes of the Federalists a law which hurt England to some extent, but America more.

There was much preliminary intriguing for the support of the Republican party for the presidency. There was a strong movement in Virginia — representing, however, only a minority of the people — in favor of Mr. Monroe. On Jan. 21, 1808, there were two caucuses of members of the Virginia legislature, one of which recommended Mr. Madison, and the other, much the smaller gathering, nominated Mr. Monroe. This was almost simultaneous with the holding of the second congressional caucus for making nominations. On the 19th of January, Senator Stephen R. Bradley of Vermont issued a notice, "in pursuance of the powers vested in me, as president of the late Convention of the Republican members of both Houses of Congress," that is, of the caucus of 1804, summoning them to meet in the Senate Chamber, at 6 o'clock, on the 23d of the month.

It is possible that the form in which this notice was cast had something to do with the opposition which was immediately developed to the caucus system, and which eventually overthrew it. At all events it was then that the reasons afterward urged by the opponents of the caucus were first presented. Mr. Gray, a member from Virginia, published an answer to Mr. Bradley's summons, couched in the very vehement style of the political literature of that day: "I take the earliest moment to declare my abhorrence of the usurpation of power declared to be vested in you — of your mandatory style, and the object contemplated. . . . I cannot consent, either in an individual or representative capacity, to countenance, by my presence, the midnight intrigues of any set of men who may arrogate to themselves the right, which belongs only to the people, of selecting proper persons to fill the important offices of President and Vice-President. Nor do I suppose that the honest people of the United States can much longer suffer, in silence, so direct and palpable an invasion upon the most important and sacred right belonging exclusively to them."

Another member from New York published a burlesque upon Mr. Bradley's notification, in which, "in pursuance of a similar power vested in me," he deemed it expedient for the purpose of not nominating a President, not to call a Convention at the same time and place, and requested members not to attend it, "to aid and sanction an infringement of one of the most important features and principles of the Constitution of the United States." But the caucus was held. It is said to have been attended by 94 senators and representatives, although only 89 votes were cast. The latter number, however, was not only a large majority of the Republican strength in both Houses of Congress, but more than one half of the whole membership of both bodies. On a ballot Mr. Madison had 83 votes, Mr. George Clinton 3, and Mr. Monroe 3. The first ballot for a candidate for Vice-President resulted in 79 votes for Mr. Clinton, 5 for John Langdon of New Hampshire, 3 for Henry Dearborn of Massachusetts, the Secretary of War, and 1 for John Quincy Adams. Messrs. Madison and Clinton were then formally declared nominated, by resolution, to which announcement was appended a statement which, in a somewhat amended form, was employed by every subsequent caucus of the kind as long as the system was in vogue. It declared " that, in making the foregoing recommendation, the members of this meeting have acted only in their individual characters as citizens; that they have been induced to adopt this measure from the necessity of the case; from a deep conviction of the importance of union to the Republicans throughout all parts of the United States in the present crisis of both our external and internal affairs; and as being the most practicable mode of consulting and respecting the interests and wishes of all upon a subject so truly interesting to the whole people of the United States."

The Monroe movement caused not a little difficulty after the caucus. A gentleman in Richmond wrote to a friend in Washington, in March, 1808, that everything had been said by Mr. Monroe's real friends to induce him to withdraw, but it was treated as the deceitful counsel of enemies. At last, however, Mr. Jefferson's influence was exerted upon Monroe, and he yielded. If he had refused, he would probably have been treated as De Witt Clinton was for consenting to stand as a candidate in opposition to the regular nominee, four years later.

The Federalists do not seem to have taken any action for concentrating their votes. It was not necessary. They voted for their candidates of four years before, Messrs. Pinckney and King. The canvass was conducted without great excitement, and the result showed a considerable change of public sentiment, chiefly at the North, against the Republican party. New Hampshire, Massachusetts, and Rhode Island returned to their allegiance to the Federal party, and the votes of New York and North Carolina were divided. The number of States voting was seventeen, as it had been four years before, and there was no change, so far as is known in the method of appointment. An informality was charged, by memorial to the House of Representatives, in December, 1808, in the appointment of electors in Massachusetts. It was asserted that the legislature had not laid the appointment of the electors before the Governor, as the law required. A resolution was introduced for raising a joint committee " to examine the matter of said memorials and report their opinion thereon to both Houses," but it was not acted on. Some days later another resolution was introduced, directing the memorials to be sent to the Senate. After some debate, in which only one member expressed the opinion that Congress could take any action in the premises, the resolution was passed and sent to the Senate with the memorials, where it was ordered that all the papers be laid on the table ; and no action whatever was taken upon them.

On this occasion the count of electoral votes took place in the Hall of the Representatives, but by some oversight there was no provision, in the joint resolution directing how the count should proceed, that the President of the Senate should take the chair. Mr. Randolph, who could always be depended upon to create difficulties when there was opportunity, called attention to the fact, and objected to the chair being vacated by the speaker without a vote of the House. " He did not wish the privileges of this House any way diminished." The case was provided for by a formal vote, and the Senate was admitted. When the votes had all been opened and the returns tabulated, the President of the Senate was about to read the result, when one of the tellers remarked that one return was defective, not having a governor's certificate attached. Nothing further was said, however, and the President of the Senate, Mr. Milledge, Senator from Georgia, proceeded to declare the result, as follows : —

STATES.	PRESIDENT.			VICE-PRESIDENT.				
	James Madison, Va.	George Clinton, N.Y.	C. C. Pinckney, S.C.	George Clinton, N.Y.	James Madison, Va.	John Langdon, N.H.	James Monroe, Va.	Rufus King, N.Y.
New Hampshire	–	–	7	–	–	–	–	7
Vermont	6	–	–	–	–	6	–	–
Massachusetts.	–	–	19	–	–	–	–	19
Rhode Island	–	–	4	–	–	–	–	4
Connecticut	–	–	9	–	–	–	–	9
New York	13	6	–	13	3	–	3	–
New Jersey	8	–	–	8	–	–	–	–
Pennsylvania	20	–	–	20	–	–	–	–
Delaware	–	–	3	–	–	–	–	3
Maryland	9	–	2	9	–	–	–	2
Virginia.	24	–	–	24	–	–	–	–
North Carolina	11	–	3	11	–	–	–	3
South Carolina	10	–	–	10	–	–	–	–
Georgia	6	–	–	6	–	–	–	–
Kentucky *.	7	–	–	7	–	–	–	–
Tennessee	5	–	–	5	–	–	–	–
Ohio	3	–	–	–	–	3	–	–
	122	6	47	113	3	9	3	47

* One Kentucky elector did not attend. The State was entitled to eight votes.

VIII.

AN ELECTION IN WAR TIME.

The election of 1812 came on when this country was in the first months of the second war with Great Britain. Mr. Madison's administration had not been a strong one. Foreign questions engrossed the public attention, almost to the exclusion of domestic affairs. The matter of renewing the charter of the first United States Bank was almost the only one upon which there was a severe legislative conflict. It is probable that never before or since was there a question upon which there was so even a division of both Houses. A bill to renew the charter was postponed indefinitely by the House of Representatives in January, 1811, by one majority; and twelve days later a similar bill was rejected by the Senate, by the casting vote of the Vice-President.

The course pursued by the administration in foreign affairs was, no doubt, acceptable to the people as a whole. It was a policy on the lines of Jefferson's policy, and characterized by a somewhat inexplicable tenderness for France. The attitude of France toward this country was extremely insolent, and only because its power on the sea was inferior to that of Great Britain was its conduct less injurious to our interests. The weakness of the President's policy consisted in his well-nigh interminable diplomatic correspondence, backed up by retaliatory measures which were frequently modified, and always harmful to American as well as English commerce.

The advent of Mr. Clay from Kentucky, and of that great trio of promising young men — Lowndes, Calhoun, and Cheves — from South Carolina, into the House, and the energy of Mr. Crawford of Georgia in the Senate, served to inspire the administration with vigor. In fact, it is reported on good authority, that of Mr. James Fisk, then a Republican member of the House from Vermont, that a committee waited upon Mr. Madison, and informed him that war was resolved upon; that unless such a step was taken the Federalists might possibly carry the presidential election; and that if he was not ready to adopt that policy he would be abandoned, and another candidate chosen for the pending election. Mr. Madison yielded, and sent to Congress a message, which was taken into consideration in secret sessions by both branches of Congress, and war was declared in June, 1812.

Between the time of Mr. Madison's acquiescence in the war policy and his transmission of the confidential message to Congress, which resulted in war, he was nominated for re-election by a Republican caucus. The caucus was held on the 12th of May, and it does not appear to have been openly objected to in any quarter. The vote for Mr. Madison was unanimous, eighty-two members voting, and one being present who did not vote. On a ballot for a candidate for Vice-President, the venerable John Langdon of New Hampshire, who had been the first President *pro tempore* of the Senate, in 1789, received 64 votes, Elbridge Gerry of Massachusetts 16, and 2 were scattering. Vice-President George Clinton had died in office less than a month before. The caucus, after formally recommending the candidates selected, —

Resolved, That in making the foregoing recommendation, the members of this meeting have acted only in their individual characters as citizens; and that they have been induced to adopt the measure from a deep conviction of the importance of union to the Republicans throughout all parts of the United States in the present crisis of our public affairs.

Mr. Langdon declined the nomination on account of his age, he was then seventy-one; and a second caucus was held on the 8th of June, which nominated Mr. Elbridge Gerry by a vote of 74, to 3 scattering. Although there was apparent unanimity in all these proceedings, and although no public opposition was offered to the dictation of the caucus, yet it was a very partial caucus. There were at least one hundred and thirty-three Republican senators and members at the time, of whom fifty did not attend the caucus. Only one member was present from New York, and Virginia contributed to the meeting as many members as attended from the five New England States and New York.

The opposition had, in fact, already resolved upon a candidate, De Witt Clinton of New York. This gentleman had been for several years the idol of the New York Republicans, and those who were dissatisfied with the course of Mr. Madison had determined to put him forward for the succession. It is difficult to decide whether he was at first more the candidate of those who thought the administration not vigorous enough in its hostility to England, or of those who were opposed to war altogether. He had supporters among both classes, but ultimately he became the candidate chiefly of the peace party, with consequences which were most disastrous to himself. It was believed then, and long afterward, by those who were in a position to know, that if he had thrown in his fortunes with the administration at that time he, and not Mr. Monroe, would have been nominated and elected in 1816. But as it was, from that time forward he had no standing in national politics. His original nomination, however, was by Republicans solely. A caucus of the members of that party in the New York legislature was held on the 29th of May, 1812. Out of ninety-three Republicans in the legislature, ninety-one were present, and Mr. Clinton was presented as a candidate by a unanimous vote. A resolution of semi-apology for adopting that method of nomination terminated the proceedings.

The spring elections of 1812 were unfavorable to the Republicans. Two or three of the New England States, which had relapsed once more into the support of that party, were again carried by the Federalists. The South and West had united in declaring a war for the benefit of the North, while the North was opposed to the war. But the fact that it had been declared, and that hostilities had already begun, served to arouse both a sentiment of national pride and a wish that the party which, seemingly at all events, was upholding the honor of the country, should be sustained. The contest therefore resolved itself largely, as any far-seeing man might have foretold, into a struggle between the war and the peace parties. This became more clearly apparent when, in September, a convention of Federalists, in which eleven States were represented, met in New York, and nominated Mr. Clinton for President, and Mr. Jared Ingersoll of Pennsylvania for Vice-President.

Eighteen States took part in this election, Louisiana having been admitted to the Union on the 8th of April, 1812. At this election two States, which had previously appointed electors by popular vote, reverted, for that time only, to the method of choice by the legislature. These States were New Jersey and North Carolina. In the latter State, which was accustomed to a choice by districts, it was anticipated in 1811 that there would be an increase of electoral votes in consequence of a new apportionment, which would be made so late that the State could not be districted. Accordingly it was then enacted that the electors in 1812 should be chosen by the legislature. Such was the excuse given for the act, but it caused great excitement at the time; and, when the legislature met in 1812 to appoint the electors, there was much fear of popular outbreaks.

The proceedings in New Jersey were very extraordinary. There was a law passed in December, 1807, providing for the appointment of electors by the people. Owing to an irregularity in the time of the election of 1808 in that State, which the law required to be within thirty-four days of the time for the meeting of the electors, the legislature went through the form of appointing the electors already designated by popular vote, but the law of 1807 remained unrepealed. In the State election of 1812 the Republicans had a popular majority; but, owing to the peculiar apportionment of the State for the legislature, both branches were controlled by the Federalists. The annual meeting of the legislature was held in October; and on the 29th of that month, less than a week before the people were expecting to choose the electors, the legislature repealed the law of 1807, passed an act providing that electors should thereafter be chosen by the council and general assembly, and a few days afterward appointed eight federal electors.

The count of electoral votes, which took place on the 10th of February, 1813, in the Representatives' Hall, was marked by no incident worthy of notice. It was a proceeding in all respects similar to previous counts. The result was ascertained, and declared as follows: —

STATES.	PRESIDENT.		VICE-PRESIDENT.	
	James Madison, Va.	De Witt Clinton, N. Y.	Elbridge Gerry, Mass.	Jared Ingersoll, Penn.
New Hampshire	–	8	1	7
Vermont	8	–	8	–
Massachusetts	–	22	2	20
Rhode Island	–	4	–	4
Connecticut	–	9	–	9
New York	–	29	–	29
New Jersey.	–	8	–	8
Pennsylvania	25	–	25	–
Delaware	–	4	–	4
Maryland	6	5	6	5
Virginia	25	–	25	–
North Carolina	15	–	15	–
South Carolina	11	–	11	–
Georgia	8	–	8	–
Kentucky	12	–	12	–
Tennessee	8	–	8	–
Louisiana	3	–	3	–
Ohio	7	–	7	–
Total	128	89	131	86

It will be noticed that in the above table the vote of Maryland is divided, and that only one effective vote was given. On examining the votes of the State at former and subsequent elections, it will be seen that in 1796 Adams had seven votes and Jefferson four; that in 1800, owing to the absence of an elector, the votes were divided equally between the candidates; that Maryland gave only seven effective votes in 1804, and the same number in 1808; and that in 1824, 1828, and 1832, also, the vote of the State was divided. This was a very peculiar case. For while in several States the system of elections by districts prevailed a long time, — it was in vogue in 1824, in Maine, Massachusetts, Kentucky, Tennessee, and other States, — there was rarely a division of the votes. Yet Maryland, having by her district system given only eighteen effective votes altogether at the five elections 1796–1812, both inclusive, clung to it for twenty years longer.

IX.

THE THIRD VIRGINIA PRESIDENT.

The first election of Mr. Monroe possesses but little interest, and the second one still less. But his administration is noteworthy for a movement, at one time quite promising, to amend the Constitution in respect to the manner of choosing the President. The matter of rendering a President ineligible for a second term, sometimes coupled with a proposition to extend the term to six years, and sometimes independent of it, was also much urged at this time, as it has been frequently since. It is mentioned here as a matter of record only, for it does not come within the scope of this book.

The war of 1812, and the peace of 1814, which became known in the country in February, 1815, virtually destroyed the Federalist party. Not to enter upon any discussion of the Hartford Convention, it was certainly deemed unpatriotic by a very large majority of the people ; and, as the Federalist leaders in New England had been active agents in it, as well as bitter opponents of the war, the party fell into discredit, became a hopeless minority, and then was extinct, except in the Northern States. It still controlled Massachusetts, Connecticut, Delaware, and Maryland, and occasionally New Hampshire and Rhode Island, but in the South and West it had no organization whatever. The ascendancy of the Republican party was assured ; the prospect that the Federalists would exert any influence in national politics was gone forever.

At this distance of time, remembering only the almost

unopposed election and second election of Mr. Monroe, we are apt to think of him as the natural and easy choice of the people. As a matter of fact he was not a great favorite with Republican politicians. He was first nominated by a narrow majority. A meeting was called by an anonymous notice, dated March 10, 1816, inviting Republican senators and members of Congress to meet in the Representatives' Hall, on the 12th, "to take into consideration the propriety of nominating persons as candidates for President and Vice-President of the United States." Fifty-eight members attended this meeting, by which it was resolved to call a caucus for the 16th of the month, in the hope of a large attendance. Out of 141 Republican members, 118 attended the second caucus. The number was doubtless larger than it would have been, if there had not been a fear that the intrigues going on at the time in favor of Mr. Crawford might possibly succeed. The popular wish was for Mr. Monroe, beyond all question, but among the politicians the advocates of Crawford were numerous and active. Their exertions caused not a little anxiety; but the "National Intelligencer," while admitting by implication the chance that strategem might gain a preliminary victory, said, that, "If ever doubted, the public opinion has been recently so decidedly expressed as to leave little doubt that the prominent candidate will, in the end, unite the suffrage of the whole Republican party."

Notwithstanding the inducements to attend the caucus, there were twenty-four Republican absentees, of whom fifteen were known to be opposed to the caucus system of nomination. Immediately after an organization of the meeting was effected, Mr. Clay moved a resolution that it is inexpedient to present candidates. This motion was rejected — it is not recorded by what majority. But the fact that it was made by Mr. Clay in 1816, eight years before the grand revolt against the caucus, is enough to exonerate him from the charge of having opposed it in 1824 because he knew that he could not be nominated. The vote for a candidate for President was taken, and resulted in the selection of Mr. Monroe, by the narrow margin of eleven majority. Monroe had 65; Crawford, 54. The strength of the Crawford movement was chiefly in New York, New Jersey, North Carolina, Kentucky, and his own State of Georgia, which five States gave him forty of his fifty-four votes. A ballot for a candidate for Vice-President gave Governor Daniel D. Tompkins of New York 85 votes, and he was nominated.

These proceedings startled everybody, not so much because of what had been done, for that the people were ready to approve, but because the members who had assumed the right to make nominations had come near making recommendations which would not have been accepted. Numerous meetings were held in various parts of the country to protest against the caucus system, the most noteworthy of which, perhaps, was held in Baltimore, in which meeting Roger B. Taney, afterward Chief Justice, took a most prominent part.

The nomination being made, the presidential election was practically decided. There was no canvass, worthy of the name. In New England, the Federalists still had partial control, but it was already slipping away from them. It is a remarkable fact that all the electoral votes cast against Mr. Monroe were given by electors who owed their appointments to State legislatures; for on this occasion, Massachusetts, which had given the people the privilege of appointment from the first election of Washington, repealed the law, and the legislature appointed all the electors. In Connecticut and Delaware the legislatures had exercised the right of appointment from the first, and continued to do so on this occasion. The number of States whose votes were counted at this election was nineteen. Indiana, which had adopted a constitution in June, 1816, was admitted to the Union December 11, of that year. The question whether or not its electoral votes should be counted gave interest to the joint meeting of the two Houses of Congress in February, 1817. The table of electoral votes was as follows: —

STATES.	PRESIDENT.		VICE-PRESIDENT.				
	James Monroe, Va.	Rufus King, N.Y.	Daniel D. Tompkins, N.Y.	John E. Howard, Md.	James Ross, Penn.	John Marshall, Va.	Robert G. Harper, Md.
New Hampshire	8	–	8	–	–	–	–
Vermont	8	–	8	–	–	–	–
Massachusetts	–	22	–	22	–	–	–
Rhode Island	4	–	4	–	–	4	–
Connecticut	–	9	–	–	5	–	–
New York	29	–	20	–	–	–	–
New Jersey	8	–	8	–	–	–	–
Pennsylvania	25	–	25	–	–	–	–
Delaware	–	3	–	–	–	–	3
Maryland	8	–	8	–	–	–	–
Virginia	25	–	25	–	–	–	–
North Carolina	15	–	15	–	–	–	–
South Carolina	11	–	11	–	–	–	–
Georgia	8	–	8	–	–	–	–
Kentucky	12	–	12	–	–	–	–
Tennessee	8	–	8	–	–	–	–
Louisiana	3	–	3	–	–	–	–
Ohio	8	–	8	–	–	–	–
Indiana	3	–	3	–	–	–	–
Total	183	34	183	22	5	4	3

The preliminary arrangements in regard to the electoral count were made according to precedent. The two Houses met in the Representatives' Hall, and the certificates were duly opened. When all had been opened except the returns from Indiana, Mr. Taylor of New York — a member of the House of Representatives, and Speaker of the body some years later, when the Missouri compromise was passed — arose, and, addressing the Speaker, expressed his regret at being compelled to interrupt the proceedings, and to object to the vote from Indiana. He was proceeding to state his objections, when the Speaker (Mr. Clay) stopped him and said that the two Houses had met for the single specified purpose of performing the constitutional duty which they were then discharging; and that, while so acting in joint meeting, they could consider no proposition nor perform any business not prescribed by the Constitution.

At this point Mr. Varnum of Massachusetts, concurring in what the Speaker had said, suggested the propriety of the Senate retiring, that the House of Representatives might deliberate upon the question raised by one of its members. The President of the Senate put the question to the senators, and it was agreed to, and the Senate withdrew. Mr. Taylor immediately took the floor, and urged that, as Indiana was not a State in the Union at the time the election took place, its votes were no more entitled to be counted than if they had come from Missouri or any other Territory. He maintained that the question should be considered and decided now, when the result would not be affected by it, and suggested that a joint resolution be passed, declaring that the votes were illegal and ought not to be counted. A resolution was moved declaring the votes legal, and on this a long debate took place. The suggestion was made that the resolution should not be a joint one, as, by establishing a precedent, it might some time thereafter, when the House and Senate should be opposed to each other, " deprive this House of one of its powers, by permitting the Senate to participate in this question." The discussion turned wholly upon the point whether or not Indiana was a State in the Union after it adopted its Constitution, and before it was admitted by a formal act of Congress. The power of Congress to reject the votes, if Indiana were not a State for purposes of the election, was questioned by no one. Finally, by an almost unanimous vote, the whole matter was indefinitely postponed, and the House sent a message to the Senate that it was prepared to resume the count.

Meanwhile a somewhat similar debate was taking place in the Senate, but, before a decision was reached, the message of the House was received. Thereupon the resolution which had been under discussion, declaring the votes of Indiana legal, was withdrawn by its mover, Mr. Barbour of Virginia, and the Senate returned to the Representatives' Hall. After the two Houses had assembled, the Speaker informed them that the House of Representatives " had not seen it necessary to come to any resolution or to take any order on the subject which had produced the separation of the two Houses." Thereupon the count was completed, the result declared, and the proceedings were terminated.

X.

THE "ERA OF GOOD FEELINGS."

AT no time in the history of the country has party feeling been so nearly absent as it was during Mr. Monroe's administration. The time has passed into history as the "era of good feelings." The Federalist party was almost extinct, even in New England and Delaware, and there was hardly a public man in office in any of the States who cared longer to urge the doctrines which had once divided him from the Republican party, or, as it now began to be called, the Democratic party. The election of 1820 was not even a contest. In the early part of the year there was a secret movement to supersede Mr. Monroe; but it did not promise well at any time, and defeated itself without any effort on the part of Mr. Monroe or his friends. A caucus was called during the session of 1820; but only a few members attended it, and a resolution that it was not expedient to make any recommendation was adopted without opposition. The result of this election is well known. Mr. Monroe was elected by a vote which would have been absolutely unanimous had not one elector of New Hampshire, deeming it due to the memory of Washington that no President after him should share in the honor of a unanimous election, given his vote for John Quincy Adams. The result in detail was as follows: —

70

STATES.	PRESIDENT.		VICE-PRESIDENT.				
	James Monroe, Va.	John Quincy Adams, Mass.	Daniel D. Tompkins, N. Y.	Richard Stockton, N. J.	Robert G. Harper, Md.	Richard Rush, Penn.	Daniel Rodney, Del.
Maine	9	–	9	–	–	–	–
New Hampshire	7	1	7	–	–	1	–
Vermont	8	–	8	–	–	–	–
Massachusetts.	15	–	7	8	–	–	–
Rhode Island	4	–	4	–	–	–	–
Connecticut	9	–	9	–	–	–	–
New York	29	–	29	–	–	–	–
New Jersey	8	–	8	–	–	–	–
Pennsylvania *	24	–	24	–	–	–	–
Delaware	4	–	–	–	–	–	4
Maryland	11	–	10	–	1	–	–
Virginia.	25	–	25	–	–	–	–
North Carolina	15	–	15	–	–	–	–
South Carolina	11	–	11	–	–	–	–
Georgia	8	–	8	–	–	–	–
Alabama	3	–	3	–	–	–	–
Mississippi *	2	–	2	–	–	–	–
Louisiana	3	–	3	–	–	–	–
Kentucky	12	–	12	–	–	–	–
Tennessee *	7	–	7	–	–	–	–
Ohio	8	–	8	–	–	–	–
Indiana	3	–	3	–	–	–	–
Illinois	3	–	3	–	–	–	–
Missouri.	3	–	3	–	–	–	–
Total	231	1	218	8	1	1	4

* One elector in each of the States of Pennsylvania, Mississippi, and Tennessee died after appointment, and before the meetings of the electors.

Five new States participated in this election, namely : Mississippi, admitted Dec. 10, 1817; Illinois, admitted

Dec. 3, 1818; Alabama, admitted Dec. 14, 1819; Maine, separated from Massachusetts and admitted as a State March 15, 1820; and Missouri, which had adopted a Constitution in July, 1820, but which was not formally admitted by act of Congress until Aug. 10, 1821. The question, therefore, which had arisen in 1817 in reference to the right of Indiana to vote for President was raised again in a still more perplexing form than before; for, whereas Indiana had become a State at the time the votes were counted, conditions had been attached to the admission of Missouri which had not yet been met at the time of the count, and it was not certain that the legislature would accede to the demand of Congress. The inconvenience of a discussion upon this question, and the doubts of members as to the result of an attempt to decide it either in joint meeting or by the two Houses separately, led to the invention of a method of avoiding the point altogether. The joint committee of Congress which was, in accordance with custom, appointed to ascertain and report a mode of examining the votes, reported, in addition to the usual resolution, the following:—

Resolved, That if any objection be made to the votes of Missouri, and the counting, or omitting to count, which shall not essentially change the result of the election, in that case they shall be reported by the President of the Senate in the following manner: Were the votes of Missouri to be counted, the result would be, for A. B. for President of the United States, —— votes; if not counted, for A. B. for President of the United States, —— votes. But in either event A. B. is elected President of the United States. And in the same manner for Vice-President.

A long debate took place on this proposition in the Senate. The views advanced were various. But the Senate was persuaded to adopt the resolution upon the assurance of Mr. Barbour, who reported it, that it was his intention thereafter to bring up the matter of electoral votes objected to, to repair what he considered a *casus omissus* in the Constitution, either by an act of Congress, if that should appear sufficient, or by an amendment to the Constitution.

The discussion in the House was of a different character. Mr. John Randolph attacked the resolution providing for an alternative statement of the vote of Missouri, on constitutional grounds. He could not recognize in either House, or in both conjoined, the power to decide on the votes of any State. The Electoral Colleges were as independent of Congress as Congress was of them; and he would rather see an interregnum, or to see no votes at all counted, than that a principle should be adopted which went to the very foundation on which the presidential office rested. Several other gentlemen took similar views. The opposing argument was presented by Mr. Clay, then a private member, who said that Congress had been entrusted with the duty of enumerating the votes for President, and it was necessary for the two Houses to determine what were votes.

The resolution was adopted by a vote of 90 to 67, but the concurrence of the two Houses did not end the matter. When the votes of Missouri were announced by the President of the Senate and handed to the tellers, Mr. Livermore of New Hampshire, a member of the House, addressing the President and the Speaker, objected to them on the ground that Missouri was not a State in the Union. The Senate thereupon retired, a motion to that effect having been put by the President. The Senate does not appear to have taken any action upon the objection, but in the House a long debate took place on a resolution that the votes ought to be counted. Mr. Randolph made himself the most conspicuous person in this discussion, and spoke upon the question with characteristic violence of language. Mr. Clay came to the rescue with an argument intended to show that the President of the Senate had acted erroneously in putting the question on the retirement of the Senate, the objection having been already provided for by the joint resolution. On his motion the subject was laid on the table, and the Senate was invited to return. The count then proceeded, and the result was declared in accordance with the prescribed form. Thereupon Mr. Floyd, and after him Mr. Randolph, both of Virginia, rose and attempted to inquire what had been done with the votes of Missouri. Their voices were drowned by cries of "Order," and they were required to resume their seats. The Senate then retired, and Mr. Randolph made another violent speech, which he closed by proposing a series of resolutions, reciting that the votes of Missouri have been counted; but that the announcement of the whole number of electors appointed, and of the votes given by them, has not been declared " agreeably to the provisions of the Constitution of the United States, and that therefore the proceeding has been irregular and illegal." While Mr. Randolph was reducing these resolutions to writing, a motion was made and carried to adjourn, and nothing more was heard of them.

Questions concerning the presidential election system and the electoral count were much discussed during Mr. Monroe's administration, and at one time the prospect of submitting to the States for ratification an amendment of the Constitution, so that all elections might be uniform, seemed to be extremely good. This latter proposition had originated as long before as when it became necessary to guard against the recurrence of such a mishap as that of 1800–01. It was then urged, as a part of the new system of choosing one person as President, and another as Vice-President, that all electors should be chosen by popular vote, the States to be divided for that purpose into districts. Although the matter was somewhat discussed in the newspapers from time to time, it does not appear to have been heard of again in Congress until the close of 1813. On December 20 of that year, Mr. Pickens of North Carolina introduced in the House a proposition to amend the Constitution in this respect, and made a long speech in support of the measure. He referred to the popular excitement which had prevailed in his State in consequence of the act of the legislature of North Carolina depriving the people of the right to choose electors, in 1812, as the reason for bringing the matter to the attention of Congress. The resolution for submitting the amendment to the States was negatived after some debate, 57 voting in favor of, and 70 against it.

Mr. Pickens introduced the subject again on one or two occasions after this defeat, but he did not press the amendment further until 1816. In December of that year he once more presented his resolution, in a new form, embracing two propositions. It provided that the States should be divided into districts for the choice of representatives in Congress, and also into single districts for the choice of electors. After some debate in Committee of the Whole, the House adopted the principle of the district system for representatives, by a vote of 86 to 38. That part of the system which related to electors was approved by 87 votes against 51, but as this was not a two-thirds majority, the House never took the subject up.

At the next session two amendments, in almost identical words, were introduced, by Mr. Dickerson of New Jersey, and by Mr. Macon of North Carolina, in the Senate. Subsequently the proposition relating to electors

was changed so that one elector should be chosen from
each representative district, and that the two additional
electors for each State should be appointed "in such manner as the legislature thereof may direct," following the
words of the Constitution. This amendment was negatived by 20 in favor to 13 opposed, — not two thirds.
Again in 1818 Mr. Sanford of New York introduced the
amendment in the Senate, by instruction of the New
York legislature, — as on previous occasions it had been
introduced by others according to instructions from the
legislatures of New Jersey and North Carolina. This
time a great deal of attention was paid to the matter.
It was debated at much length, three times referred to
committees, and at last passed by a vote of 28 to 10.
In the House, it was laid on the table by 79 to 73. Introduced in the Senate again in 1819, by Mr. Dickerson, it
was again passed, — this time without debate, by 29 to 13.
Having been debated in the House, it was agreed to by
the Committee of the Whole; but when it was reported
to the House it was laid on the table, and never taken up.
Yet at the same session Mr. Smith of North Carolina
introduced this identical amendment, and, after debate,
it was passed to a third reading by a vote of 103 to 59;
but on the question of its passage it was lost, 92 voting in
favor and 54 against it, — not two thirds. The proposition never again came so near to success; but it was not
abandoned, and as late as March, 1822, the Senate again
passed the amendment by 29 to 11. The House did not
take the matter up for consideration.

Another effort was made during Mr. Monroe's administration to deal with the matter of the electoral count.
The Judiciary Committee of the Senate was instructed
to consider the subject, and Mr. Van Buren reported
a bill which, after amendment, was passed on April 19,

1824. It covered the whole ground of the election and the count. The electors were to make five lists of their votes instead of three. One of these was to be sent to the seat of government by a messenger, two were to be deposited in the post-office and forwarded by two successive mails to the President of the Senate, and the other two were to be delivered to the judge of the district in which the electoral meeting was held. This was the only change proposed in the method of electing the President. The important section was the fifth, as follows: —

SECTION 5. That at twelve o'clock of the day appointed for counting the votes that may be given at the next election for President and Vice-President, the Senate and House of Representatives shall meet in the hall of the House of Representatives, and on all future occasions in the centre-room of the Capitol, at which meeting the President of the Senate shall be the presiding officer, but no debate shall be had nor question taken. The packet containing the certificates from the electors of each State shall then be opened by the President of the Senate, beginning with the State of New Hampshire and going through to Georgia, in the order in which the thirteen original States are enumerated in the Constitution, and afterwards through the other States in the order in which they were respectively admitted into the Union; and if no exceptions are taken thereto, all the votes contained in such certificates shall be counted; but if any exceptions be taken, the person taking the same shall state it in writing directly, and not argumentatively, and sign his name thereto; and if the exception be seconded by one member from the Senate and one member from the House of Representatives, and each of whom shall sign the said exception as having seconded the same, the exception shall be read by the President of the Senate, and then each House shall immediately retire, without question or debate, to its own apartment, and shall take the question on the exception, without debate, by ayes and noes. So soon as the question shall be taken in either House, a message shall be sent to the other informing them of the decision of the question, and that the House sending the message is prepared to resume the count; and when such message shall have been received by both Houses, they shall meet again in the same room as before, and the

count shall be resumed.   And if the two Houses have concurred in
rejecting the vote or votes objected to, such vote or votes shall not
be counted.   The vote of one State being thus counted, another
shall, in like manner, be called, and the certificate of the votes of
the State thus called shall be proceeded on as is hereinbefore
directed; and so on, one after another, in the order above mentioned, until the count shall be completed.

The bill was sent to the House for concurrence, where it
was referred to the Committee on the Judiciary, and was
reported back by Mr. Webster on the 10th of May, without amendment.   It was then referred to the Committee
of the Whole, and was never taken up for consideration.

XI.

THE SECOND ADAMS.

THE election of 1824 was unlike any other before or since; and in certain respects it is the most interesting contest of the long series. The Federal party was practically extinct. Only in a few of the States did it make a pretence of existing still, and it was in power nowhere. There were great political contests during Mr. Monroe's presidency, notably that over the admission of Missouri in 1820, but they were not party struggles. Substantially all the statesmen and newspapers of the country professed the same constitutional principles. But the "era of good feelings," in the strict sense of the phrase, was of short duration. The succession to the presidency was to be the issue upon which the foundations of the new parties were to be laid.

The election was really pending almost three years. As early as April, 1822, Niles's "Register" remarked that there were already sixteen or seventeen candidates for the succession to Mr. Monroe; and very soon after that the discussion of "caucus or no caucus?" began in earnest. It was universally understood that Mr. W. H. Crawford of Georgia, the Secretary of the Treasury, was the candidate preferred by the President, who, however, did not obtrude his wishes upon the public in an unseemly manner. It was also known that the caucus, if one should be held, would be in the interest of Mr. Crawford.

Before the close of the year 1822, the minor candidates had been dropped, and there were six only before the

people, for four of whom there were electoral votes cast
two years later. They were, in alphabetical order, — John
Quincy Adams, Secretary of State; John C. Calhoun,
Secretary of War; Henry Clay, who had been Speaker of
the House, but was then a private citizen; De Witt
Clinton, Ex-Governor of New York, also in private life
at the time; William H. Crawford, Secretary of the
Treasury; and General Andrew Jackson, who had at that
time held no civil office at Washington. The first of these
candidates to be put in formal nomination was Mr. Clay,
who was "recommended as a suitable person to succeed
James Monroe as President," by the members of the Kentucky legislature on the 18th of November, 1822. In an
address which accompanied this resolution the members
of the meeting placed their preference upon "a warm
affection for and a strong confidence in their distinguished
fellow-citizen"; and their feeling that the time had come
"when the people of the West may, with some confidence,
appeal to the magnanimity of the whole Union for a favorable consideration of their equal and just claim to a fair
participation in the executive government of these States."
They nevertheless made the first consideration much the
more prominent and important. The members of the
Missouri legislature held a meeting about the same time,
and adopted a resolution recommending Mr. Clay. Similar action was taken in Illinois and Ohio in January, 1823,
and in Louisiana in March of the same year.

General Jackson seems first to have been nominated
formally — although it was well understood long before
that he was a candidate — by a mass convention of the
people of Blount County, Tennessee, in May or June,
1823, and afterwards by numerous conventions in all
parts of the country. Mr. Adams was nominated by the
legislatures of most of the New England States, early in

1824; Mr. Clinton by several counties in Ohio; Mr. Calhoun by the legislature of South Carolina; Mr. Crawford by the legislature of Virginia. Nominations, however, went for very little in those days. The people of one county might be all for a certain candidate, while those in the adjoining county would prefer another of the six quite as strongly.

It was a personal contest. In not one of the numerous series of resolutions in which the several candidates were presented was it alleged that there was any difference in their principles. The services, the ability, the integrity, and the eminent fitness of each gentleman were set forth in terms of high praise, but there was little or no disparagement of the others. On one point, however, there was strong feeling, — there was great opposition to the caucus. The friends of all the candidates except Mr. Crawford were angrily against that. Nor was this an afterthought. Much ill feeling had been excited throughout the country by the assumption, on the part of Congress, of the right to dictate who should be the regular candidate, at earlier elections. Now it was purely a question of persons, and there was a general expression of hostility to the system; but the very fact that it was a question of persons was one of the arguments used by the caucus party. They said that the result of a division of the electoral votes among several candidates would be deplorable, and that the members of Congress were in the best position to judge who, among half a dozen good men named, would make the best President.

The caucus party made an attempt to secure a meeting of members of Congress for the purpose of making a nomination as early as the session of 1822-23, but it met with little support. Some of those who were in favor of the practice believed that action at the time would be

premature. The discussion of the question whether or
not a caucus should be held, was very active during the
ensuing months. Although it must have been seen that
only a small minority of the members of the Senate and
House of Representatives would attend, and that none of
the advocates of either of the other candidates would
change their line of action and support Mr. Crawford, yet
the caucus party persisted, and carried out their plans.
On the 6th of February, 1824, a notice was printed, signed
by eleven persons, six senators and five representatives,
from as many States in the Union, calling a meeting of
the Democratic members of Congress to meet in the Representatives' Chamber on the evening of February 14, " to
recommend candidates to the people of the United States for
the offices of President and Vice-President of the United
States." At the same time appeared a card signed by twenty-
four senators and members, representing fifteen States, in
which it was asserted that they had satisfactory information
that of the two hundred and sixty-one senators and representatives, there were a hundred and eighty-one " who deem
it inexpedient, under existing circumstances, to meet in a
caucus " for the purpose named.

The event showed that their canvass was very nearly
correct. Only sixty-six members met. They represented
sixteen States of the Union, but a very large majority of
them were from four States. New York supplied sixteen,
its whole delegation numbering thirty-six; Virginia, fourteen out of a possible twenty-four; North Carolina ten,
out of a delegation of fifteen; while eight of the nine Georgia members were present. Thus four States supplied
forty-eight members, and the other twenty States only
eighteen members of the caucus. Eight States were not
represented at all, and five others by a single member
only. An attempt was made to carry an adjournment

for six weeks in order to have a fuller meeting, but it was opposed by Mr. Van Buren, and voted down. The caucus then proceeded to ballot for a candidate for President. The result was as follows: William H. Crawford had 64; John Quincy Adams, 2; Andrew Jackson, 1; Nathaniel Macon, 1. Two absent members, one each from Virginia and Georgia, voted by proxy.

The caucus then proceeded to ballot for a candidate for Vice-President. Albert Gallatin of Pennsylvania had 57 votes; Erastus Root of New York, 2; and the following-named, one each: John Q. Adams, William Eustis of Massachusetts, Samuel Smith of Maryland, William King of Maine, Richard Rush of Pennsylvania, John Tod of Pennsylvania, and Walter Lowrie of Pennsylvania. The caucus then adopted a resolution formally recommending Messrs. Crawford and Gallatin, and declaring that: —

In making the foregoing recommendation, the members of this meeting have acted in their individual characters as citizens; that they have been induced to this measure from a deep and settled conviction of the importance of union among Republicans throughout the United States, and as the best means of collecting and concentrating the feelings and wishes of the people of the Union upon this important subject.

The caucus did not help the cause of Mr. Crawford. On the contrary, it united the opponents of that gentleman to a certain extent. The hostility to the dictation of Congress, and more particularly to that of a small minority of the two Houses, was very strong. The nomination of Mr. Gallatin had been made with a view to securing the vote of Pennsylvania for the ticket, but it had no such effect. On the contrary, a war was at once opened upon him as "a foreigner," and, however unjust the assaults may have been, they had their effect. Pennsylvania was evidently for Mr. Calhoun for Vice-President, and public opinion gradually became fixed in his favor among the anti-caucus forces. The opposition to Mr. Gallatin was so strong that in October he withdrew from the canvass, " understanding that the withdrawal of my name may have a favorable effect on the result of the approaching election of President and Vice-President of the United States." The idea at the time seems to have been that a coalition might be made between the friends of Mr. Craw- ford and those of Mr. Clay, by which the latter should be supported for the second place. However that may have been, the withdrawal of Mr. Gallatin had no perceptible effect upon the canvass.

The campaign itself offers nothing of interest. All the arguments used, except upon the subject of the caucus, were purely personal, and added nothing to political his- tory. But it was foreseen that each of the four of the candidates would receive a good vote; that no one was likely to receive the support of a majority of the electors; and that, under the Constitution, only three of the four could go before the House of Representatives as candi- dates for election by that body. Consequently there was a determined effort on the part of the friends of each of the four to get as many electoral votes as possible, ineffec- tual though they were to be in deciding the result.

Twenty-four States took part in the election. Electors were chosen by the legislatures of Vermont, New York, Delaware, South Carolina, Georgia, and Louisiana. In all the other States they were elected by the people. In Maine, Massachusetts, Maryland, Illinois, and Kentucky, by districts; in most or all of the rest, by general ticket. The circumstances of the election in some of the States are worthy of notice.

The legislature of New York contained supporters of three

of the candidates. The law for all elections by the legislature prescribed separate balloting by the two branches until a choice had been made by each. If the two branches agreed in the election, they met in joint convention and declared the result. If different persons had been elected, the choice was determined by joint ballot. The election began on the 10th of November. On that day the Senate made choice of the Crawford electors. The senators were divided in their preferences thus: for Crawford, 17; for Adams, 7; for Clay, 7. In the Assembly there was no choice: the Crawford ticket had 43 votes, the Adams 50, the Clay 32. Combined, therefore, the strength of the three candidates was: Crawford, 60; Adams, 57; Clay, 39. The balloting in the Assembly continued on the 10th, 11th, and 12th of November with the change of only a single vote. On the last of the three days, some of the Crawford men announced their purpose of voting for the Adams ticket in order to transfer the contest to a joint convention and to defeat Mr. Clay. This threat produced an effect upon the Clay men, who on the following day voted for the Adams ticket themselves and secured a majority for it. The fact that an election had been effected by the Assembly was hurriedly communicated to some of the Crawford senators before the official notice could be sent, and the Senate hastily adjourned. On Monday, the 15th, the joint convention was held, and a ballot was taken. The whole number of ballots was 157, but three of them were blank votes. Seven friends of Mr. Clay, who had been placed upon the Crawford ticket in hope of attracting support for the whole ticket by the Clay men, had 95 votes. The rest of the Crawford ticket had 76 votes. Twenty-five of the names on the Adams ticket had 78 votes each. This number, 78, was exactly a majority of 154, the number of effective ballots, but one less than a majority of the whole number, including the blanks. A resolution was offered declaring the thirty-two electors who had 78 or more votes to be chosen. The Speaker of the Senate refused to put the question. A long debate and a scene of tumult and confusion such as has rarely taken place in a legislative body ensued; and in the end the presiding officer, followed by the sixteen Crawford senators, left the Assembly Chamber. But at last the resolution was separately adopted. The two branches met again, and completed the election by the choice of four Crawford men by a bare majority. At the meeting of the electors, however, three of the Clay electors deserted him and went, one each, to Adams, Crawford, and Jackson. But for this defection, Mr. Clay's name would have gone to the House of Representatives instead of Mr. Crawford's, and possibly Mr. John Quincy Adams would never have been President.

In Delaware there was another question of a somewhat similar character. The number of members present at the joint meeting of the two houses of the legislature was thirty. One elector (for Adams) received 21, and was no doubt elected. Two others, Crawford men, had 15 votes each, and seven other candidates had from 1 to 10 each. The law of Delaware provided that "if an equal division of ballots shall appear for two or more persons, not being elected by a majority of the votes, the Speaker of the Senate shall have an additional casting vote." This was clearly not a case of the kind contemplated by the statute, which intended that the Speaker should decide between two or more equal and opposing candidates. If only one of the two Crawford men had received 15 votes he could not have given a casting vote. As there were two equal candidates he gave an additional vote for each, and declared them elected. He followed the letter of the statute, beyond a doubt.

It has gone into history that General Jackson received a large plurality of the popular vote at this election. In Lanman's "Biographical Annals" the popular vote is set down as follows: —

For Jackson	152,899
" Adams	105,321
" Crawford	47,265
" Clay	47,087

This is a most misleading statement, even if it were accurate. It credits to Jackson a great many votes which, like the 20,000 in North Carolina, were cast for no candidate in particular, but in opposition to the caucus ticket generally, and of which it was estimated at the time that 5,000 were given by friends of Adams; and other votes which, in some Northern States, were cast against Adams generally, without being for any particular candidate. But its inaccuracy arises chiefly from two other causes. In the first place it does not include the votes of States where a choice was made by the legislature. These six States gave in the aggregate only 19 votes to Jackson, 36 to Adams, 6 to Crawford, and 4 to Clay. Jackson did not appear at all as a candidate in New York, except that on one day in the Assembly an attempt was made to create a diversion by a few Crawford men who voted a Jackson ticket. Again, there were real contests in very few of the States, so that the partisans of neither candidate were fully represented at the polls. Massachusetts cast more than 66,000 votes for governor in May, 1823, and only 37,000 for President in 1824. The whole vote of Virginia was less than 15,000. Other examples of an apparent lack of interest might be given; but they only show that the triumph of Mr. Adams in Massachusetts and other States, of Mr. Crawford in Virginia and other States, and so forth, was taken for granted, and that a full vote was not cast. The actual popular vote for the several candidates, as nearly as can be ascertained, — though, as has been said, any statistics of the election are misleading, unless all the circumstances are taken into account, — was as follows : —

STATES.	Jackson.	Adams.	Crawford.	Clay.
Maine	–	10,289	2,336*	–
New Hampshire . . .	643	4,107	–	–
Vermont §	–	–	–	–
Massachusetts . . .	–	30,687	6,616*	–
Rhode Island	–	2,145	200*	–
Connecticut	–	7,587	1,978*	–
New York §	–	–	–	–
New Jersey	10,985	9,110	1,196†	–
Pennsylvania	36,100	5,440	4,206	1,609
Delaware §	–	–	–	–
Maryland	14,523	14,632	3,646	695
Virginia	2,861	3,189	8,489	416
North Carolina . . .	20,415‡	–	15,621	–
South Carolina § . .	–	–	–	–
Georgia §	–	–	–	–
Alabama	9,443	2,416	1,680	67
Mississippi	3,234	1,694	119	–
Louisiana §	–	–	–	–
Kentucky	6,455	–	–	17,321
Tennessee	20,197	216	312	–
Missouri	987	311	–	1,401
Ohio	18,457	12.280	–	19,255
Indiana	7,343	3,095	–	5,315
Illinois	1,001	1,542	219	1,047
Totals	153,544	108,740	46,618	47,136

* "Opposition" ticket. † "Convention" ticket.
‡ "People's" ticket. § By legislature.

As had been anticipated before the election, there was no choice of a President, but Mr. Calhoun was elected Vice-President by more than two thirds of all the votes. Mr. Crawford, the caucus candidate, had barely succeeded in securing a place among the first three candidates. Congress met on the 6th of December, five days after the meeting of the electors. Although it was known that there had been no choice of a President, no notice was taken of the fact until the 13th of January, 1825, when Mr. Wright of Ohio offered a resolution for the appointment of a committee —

> To prepare and report such rules as, in their opinion, may be proper to be observed by this House in the choice of a President of the United States, for the period of four years, from the 4th day of March next, if, on counting the votes given in the several States, in the manner prescribed in the Constitution of the United States, it shall appear that no person has received a majority of all the electors of President and Vice-President appointed in the several States.

This resolution was adopted on the 18th of January, and the committee was appointed, which reported, on the 26th, a plan that was in some respects different from that adopted in 1801, but the changes were so unimportant that they need not be noted.

The Senate proposed, on the 1st of February, to raise a joint committee "to ascertain and report a mode of examining the votes," in the usual form. The committee was appointed, and reported a resolution similar to those adopted in former years, but containing a clause made necessary by the fact that there was no choice of a President. When this resolution came up in the Senate, Mr. Eaton of Tennessee moved to add a new paragraph to the effect that, if objection should be made to any vote, it should be filed in writing and entered on the Journals of the two Houses; that the two Houses should not separate until all the votes had been counted and reported; but that the report of the result should be "liable to be controlled and altered by the decision to be made by the two Houses after their separation, relative to any objections that may be made," provided that no objection should be considered valid unless so voted by both Houses.

Mr. Van Buren opposed this clause, and after debate it was rejected. No objections were made, it may be said here, to any votes, at the time of the count; but in May, after the election, Mr. Wilde of Georgia introduced in the House of Representatives a resolution that a message be sent to the Senate requesting copies of all the certificates of electoral votes. In a long speech he gave his reason for making this motion, which was that very few of the certificates were strictly correct and in due form. They either did not assert that the electors voted in distinct ballots for President and Vice-President, or they did not report a vote by ballot at all, — distinct ballots being required by the Constitution. The resolution was opposed on the ground that it was too late, and that "the elections in the States were not subject to revision by Congress," and, on motion, was laid on the table.

Before the day for counting the votes, February 9, there was a great scandal in the House of Representatives. The situation was one which invited intrigue, and no doubt there was much bargaining and attempted trading of votes. The excitement ran high. The votes of thirteen States were necessary to a choice. Mr. Adams was sure of the unanimous votes of the six New England States, and of a majority in New York, Maryland, and Ohio. Mr. Crawford would have Delaware, Virginia, North Carolina, and Georgia. The universal expectation was that Mr. Adams would be chosen; and a desire to avoid such a long and perilous contest as had taken place in 1801, as well as a desire to be on the winning side, helped his cause. In the midst of the excitement a letter was published in the "Columbian Observer" of Philadelphia, on January 28, dated at Washington, from which the following is extracted:—

> For some time past, the friends of Clay have hinted that they, like the Swiss, would fight for those who would pay best. Over-tures were said to have been made by the friends of Adams to the friends of Clay, offering him the appointment of Secretary of State, for his aid to elect Adams. And the friends of Clay gave this information to the friends of Jackson, and hinted that, if the friends of Jackson would offer the same price, they would close with them.

There was very much more of the same sort, but this contains the substance of the charge. Mr. Clay at once published a card in which he asserted that he believed the letter was a forgery, "but, if it be genuine, I pronounce the member, whoever he may be, a base and infamous calumniator, a dastard, and a liar." Mr. George Kremer of Pennsylvania avowed himself the author of the letter, and asserted his ability to prove his assertions. The mat-ter was brought to the attention of the House by Mr. Clay, who was speaker of the House at the time, and a com-mittee was raised to inquire into the matter. Mr. Kremer declined to appear before the committee in a long and labored but weak letter. The affair afterwards drifted into a newspaper fight. Mr. Kremer produced some of his so-called proofs, citing certain gentlemen as authority; but many of the latter printed cards in which they denied Mr. Kremer's assertions. The controversy was a very acrimonious one; but the general judgment, except among those who were sore over the defeat of General Jackson, was, that Mr. Clay had acted an honorable part. It was true that he had not been on very good terms with Mr. Adams, in consequence of a dispute over certain matters connected with the negotiations at Ghent ten years before; and the Legislature of Kentucky had asked the Kentucky members to vote for Jackson. But there were good and sufficient reasons, of a public as well as of a personal nature, why Mr. Clay should cast his influence in favor of Mr. Adams; and it is fair to believe that they controlled him. It was many years before the controversy over the alleged corrupt bargain died out wholly.

Mr. Clay was not the only member who brought down upon himself the wrath of Jackson's supporters for supporting Adams. Mr. Scott of Missouri, the sole member for that State, was an old friend and companion in politics of Senator Benton. The latter was even then, as in all his after life, a thick-and-thin partisan of the hero of New Orleans. When Mr. Scott announced his intention of supporting Adams, Senator Benton wrote a solemn letter to him, in which the act he was about to perform was denounced as a grave crime. "For nine years," he wrote, "we have been closely connected in our political course; at length the connection is dissolved, and dissolved under circumstances which denounce our everlasting separation. ... To-morrow is the day for your self-immolation. If you have an enemy he may go and feed his eyes upon the scene; your former friend will shun the afflicting spectacle." A great many members of Congress found it necessary to write letters to their constituents explaining their conduct.

The votes were counted on the 9th of February. The result of the voting by electors was declared as follows: —

STATES.	PRESIDENT.				VICE-PRESIDENT.					
	Andrew Jackson, Tenn.	J. Q. Adams, Mass.	W. H. Crawford, Ga.	H. Clay, Ky.	John C. Calhoun, S. C.	Nathan Sanford, N. Y.	Nathaniel Macon, N. C.	Andrew Jackson, Tenn.	M. Van Buren, N. Y.	H. Clay, Ky.
Maine	–	9	–	–	9	–	–	–	–	–
New Hampshire .	–	8	–	–	7	–	–	1	–	–
Vermont . . .	–	7	–	–	7	–	–	–	–	–
Massachusetts . .	–	15	–	–	15	–	–	–	–	–
Rhode Island . .	–	4	–	–	3	–	–	–	–	–
Connecticut . .	–	8	–	–	–	–	–	8	–	–
New York . . .	1	26	5	4	29	7	–	–	–	–
New Jersey . .	8	–	–	–	8	–	–	–	–	–
Pennsylvania . .	28	–	–	–	28	–	–	–	–	–
Delaware . . .	–	1	2	–	1	–	–	–	–	2
Maryland . . .	7	3	1	–	10	–	–	1	–	–
Virginia. . . .	–	–	24	–	–	–	24	–	–	–
North Carolina .	15	–	–	–	15	–	–	–	–	–
South Carolina .	11	–	–	–	11	–	–	–	–	–
Georgia	–	–	9	–	–	–	–	–	9	–
Alabama . . .	5	–	–	–	5	–	–	–	–	–
Mississippi . . .	3	–	–	–	3	–	–	–	–	–
Louisiana . . .	3	2	–	–	5	–	–	–	–	–
Kentucky . . .	–	–	–	14	7	7	–	–	–	–
Tennessee . . .	11	–	–	–	11	–	–	–	–	–
Missouri . . .	–	–	–	3	–	–	–	3	–	–
Ohio	–	–	–	16	–	16	–	–	–	–
Indiana	5	–	–	–	5	–	–	–	–	–
Illinois	2	1	–	–	3	–	–	–	–	–
Total . . .	99	84	41	37	182	30	24	13	9	2

The President of the Senate (Mr. Gaillard) then declared that no person had received a majority of the votes given for President of the United States; that Andrew Jackson, John Quincy Adams, and William H. Crawford, were the three persons who had received the highest number of votes, and that the remaining duties in the choice of a President now devolved upon the House of Representatives; and that John C. Calhoun was duly elected Vice-President.

The Senate having retired, the House immediately proceeded to elect a President. A roll-call showed that every member of the House except Mr. Garnett of Virginia, who was sick at his lodgings in Washington, was present. Mr. Webster of Massachusetts and Mr. Randolph of Virginia were appointed tellers. The House conducted the election according to the rules already adopted, and on the first ballot John Quincy Adams was chosen. The votes of thirteen States were given to him, those of seven to Jackson, and of four to Crawford. The Speaker declared Mr. Adams elected, and notice of the result was sent to the Senate. The votes of the States are shown by the following table, which indicates both the divisions within the delegations, and the person for whom the vote of each State was given.

STATES.	Adams.	Jackson.	Crawford.	VOTE FOR —
Maine	7	–	–	Adams.
New Hampshire . .	6	–	–	Adams.
Vermont	5	–	–	Adams.
Massachusetts . .	12	1	–	Adams.
Rhode Island . . .	2	–	–	Adams.
Connecticut . . .	6	–	–	Adams.
New York	18	2	14	Adams.
New Jersey . . .	1	5	–	Jackson.
Pennsylvania . . .	1	25	–	Jackson.
Delaware	–	–	1	Crawford.
Maryland	5	3	1	Adams.
Virginia	1	1	19	Crawford.
North Carolina . .	1	2	10	Crawford.
South Carolina . .	–	9	–	Jackson.
Georgia	–	–	7	Crawford.
Alabama	–	3	–	Jackson.
Mississippi	–	1	–	Jackson.
Louisiana	2	1	–	Adams.
Kentucky	8	4	–	Adams.
Tennessee	–	9	–	Jackson.
Missouri	1	–	–	Adams.
Ohio	10	2	2	Adams.
Indiana	–	3	–	Jackson.
Illinois	1	–	–	Adams.
	87	71	54	

The bitterness of this election did not cease when a choice had been effected; and the " Annals of Congress" show that the desirability of making another change in the Constitution, so as to prevent the calamity of an election by the House of Representatives, was urged by many members. But no action was taken, and fortunately there has been no need of such another election during the sixty years which have elapsed since Mr. Adams was chosen.

XII.

JACKSON'S TRIUMPH.

It was during the administration of the second Adams that parties took the form which they were destined to retain for the next quarter of a century. The partisans of Jackson were angry that he had not been chosen President instead of Mr. Adams, and the friends of Crawford were also greatly irritated. The choice of Mr. Clay as Secretary of State was especially a source of vexation to them. Although all politicians throughout the country professed the same constitutional principles, it was evident from the very beginning of Mr. Adams's term that he was to be strongly, bitterly opposed, and thwarted if possible. General Jackson was not to be outrun in the race of opposition by any one. In October, 1825, before the President had met Congress at all, and before he had indicated — except in his inaugural address, which was excellent in spirit, and well received by the country — what his policy was to be, the Tennessee legislature nominated Jackson for the succession. He accepted the nomination in an address which he delivered before the two Houses of the Legislature, and resigned his seat in the Senate.

Thus the presidential canvass was begun three years before the electors were to be appointed, and at a time when no other reason than a personal preference for one man rather than for another, by members of the House of Representatives, could be given for making a change; but when men are resolved to find reasons for opposing an administration they seldom fail. Especially was it easy to create an opposition party when a gentleman of so positive a character as Mr. Adams was at the head of affairs. His measures were such as gave room for wide difference of opinion. He had been the real author of the Monroe doctrine, and the proposition for a conference of American republics was one which was very dear to him; but his wishes were opposed and his plans thwarted. He was opposed in domestic politics, too, and his enemies could find nothing good in his propositions. They assailed his position on the tariff, although General Jackson had voted in the Senate for protection. They denounced the internal improvements policy as unconstitutional, although Jackson had voted for that also. They professed anger at the extravagance of the administration, because the expenditures had increased, — forgetting, or refusing to admit the validity of the argument, that the country was growing, — and preached economy, which was certainly not the distinguishing characteristic of Jackson's administration.

After the nomination of General Jackson by the Tennessee legislature, that gentleman received a great many similar nominations from conventions and meetings in all parts of the country; but in order to make his election certain it was necessary to combine the friends of Crawford with the "Jacksonians." This is supposed to have been effected in the course of a Southern tour made by Mr. Churchill C. Cambreleng, a great figure in New York politics at the time, and a member of Congress from the city of New York, from 1821 to 1839. Mr. Van Buren, a Crawford man in 1824, and a believer in the caucus system of nominating presidential candidates as long as he lived, was now a Jackson partisan and an advocate of the coalition. Mr. Calhoun, the Vice-President, had been one of the active spirits of the opposition from the very beginning.

On the other side were the friends of Mr. Adams, and those of the partisans of Clay whom the latter could carry to the support of the administration. But Mr. Adams did not, even for the highest offices, seek out his friends for appointment, and during his whole term he only made two removals from office, both for cause. More than one of the members of his cabinet had been opposed to his election, and only Mr. Clay could or did exercise any appreciable political influence in his favor. An administration which sought favor only upon its own merits, and relied upon the wisdom of its measures, — measures upon which public opinion was greatly and honestly divided, — was no match for the sharp politicians and the vigilant tacticians who were against it.

Yet the friends of the administration believed, or professed to believe, to the last moment, that Mr. Adams would be re-elected. They classed Pennsylvania among the doubtful States, counted confidently upon the new States of the northwest, — Ohio, Indiana, Illinois, — and were encouraged, by the success of the administration party in the State election of Kentucky, as late as August, 1828, to believe that the State of Clay would support them. And although Jackson's popular majority was large, a change from him to Adams of twelve thousand votes distributed in the States of New York, Ohio, Kentucky, Louisiana, and Indiana, would have re-elected Adams. The administration party, however, was grossly deceived; and in the result Mr. Adams received fewer electoral votes than he had in 1824; and not one of the votes given for Clay four years before was transferred to him.

The number of States participating in the election of

1828 was unchanged, — twenty-four. Since the preceding election, however, there had been a very general change on the part of those States which had previously chosen electors through the medium of the legislature, to the popular system. Of the six States wherein the legislature had exercised this privilege in 1824, four changed to a popular election before 1828, — Vermont, New York, Georgia, and Louisiana. The change in New York was not effected without a great agitation of the people. The legislature held to the powers it exercised as long as it dared. Governor De Witt Clinton recommended the change to the legislature at a special session called in 1820, on which occasion the Senate of New York refused to perform any legislative duty whatever, and treated the Governor with such open disrespect as has hardly ever been shown toward a State executive by any department of government. A bill was passed once, perhaps twice, by one branch of the legislature, some years later, to confer the right on the people, but the other branch rejected it. At last, affecting a doubt whether the people really cared for the privilege, the question was formally submitted to them. If there had been any real doubts the result of the popular vote speedily dispelled them, and the legislature reluctantly yielded to the urgent demand.

But there still existed differences in the systems of election, even among those where there was an appointment of electors by popular vote. In the following States the election of 1828 was by general ticket, — the system which is now universal: New Hampshire, Vermont, Massachusetts, Rhode Island, Connecticut, New Jersey, Pennsylvania, Virginia, North Carolina, Georgia, Alabama, Mississippi, Louisiana, Kentucky, Ohio, Indiana, Illinois, and Missouri, — eighteen. Some of these, like Massachusetts, New Jersey, and North Carolina, having tried for many years (see pp. 74 *et seq.*) to secure the district system by amendment of the Constitution, had despaired of success, and adopted the general ticket. Of the six States not named above, two, Delaware and South Carolina, clung to the old method of legislative appointment. In Maine and New York, an elector was chosen for each representative district, and the members so appointed chose the two additional electors. In Maryland and Tennessee, the States were specially divided into districts for the choice of all their electors. There was, however, a divided vote of the electors in only three of the States.

The following table shows the popular vote of the States, and the manner of choosing electors in each : —

STATES.	Jackson.	Adams.	Mode of Election.
Maine.	13,927	20,733	Districts.
New Hampshire . .	20,922	24,134	General ticket.
Vermont	8,350	25,363	General ticket.
Massachusetts . . .	6,016	29,876	General ticket.
Rhode Island . . .	821	2,754	General ticket.
Connecticut . . .	4,448	13,838	General ticket.
New York	140,763	135,413	Districts.
New Jersey	21,951	23,764	General ticket.
Pennsylvania . . .	101,652	50,848	General ticket.
Delaware	–	–	Legislature.
Maryland	24,565	25,527	Districts.
Virginia	26,752	12,101	General ticket.
North Carolina . .	37,857	13,918	General ticket.
South Carolina . .	–	–	Legislature.
Georgia	19,363	No opposition.	Legislature.
Alabama	17,138	1,938	Legislature.
Mississippi	6,772	1,581	Legislature.
Louisiana	4,603	4,076	Legislature.
Kentucky	39,397	31,460	Legislature.
Tennessee	44,293	2,240	Districts.
Missouri	8,272	3,400	General ticket.
Ohio	67,597	63,396	General ticket.
Indiana	22,257	17,052	General ticket.
Illinois	9,560	4,662	General ticket.
Totals	647,276	508,064	

The electoral count was quite devoid of incident. The result, which was ascertained and declared in the usual manner, was as follows: —

STATES.	PRESIDENT.		VICE-PRESIDENT.		
	Andrew Jackson, Tenn.	John Quincy Adams, Mass.	John C. Calhoun, S. C.	Richard Rush, Penn.	William Smith, S. C.
Maine.	1	8	1	8	–
New Hampshire . .	–	8	–	8	–
Vermont	–	7	–	7	–
Massachusetts . .	–	15	–	15	–
Rhode Island . . .	–	4	–	4	–
Connecticut . . .	–	8	–	8	–
New York	20	16	20	16	–
New Jersey . . .	–	8	–	8	–
Pennsylvania . . .	28	–	28	–	–
Delaware	–	3	–	3	–
Maryland	5	6	5	6	–
Virginia	24	–	24	–	–
North Carolina . .	15	–	15	–	–
South Carolina . .	11	–	11	–	–
Georgia	9	–	2	–	7
Alabama	5	–	5	–	–
Mississippi	3	–	3	–	–
Louisiana	5	–	5	–	–
Kentucky	14	–	14	–	–
Tennessee	11	–	11	–	–
Ohio	16	–	16	–	–
Indiana	5	–	5	–	–
Illinois	3	–	3	–	–
Missouri	3	–	3	–	–
Totals	178	83	171	83	7

XIII.

JACKSON'S SECOND ELECTION.

THE most bitter and violent period in American politics begins with the accession of Andrew Jackson to the presidency. The turmoil commenced with the President's wholesale, but not indiscriminate, removals from office, and his open practice of rewarding his friends and punishing his enemies. The six Presidents who had preceded him had made only seventy-four removals in the forty years over which their terms extended. Jackson removed more than twice as many in the first nine months of his term. The hot debates over the tariff, the nullification and land questions, and internal improvements, were enough of themselves to have rendered the politics of the time interesting; but the matters in which the President's own personality and his stubborn will were brought into prominence caused these public questions to sink into comparative insignificance. Among these were his quarrel with Mr. Calhoun, the Vice-President; his failure to consult with his cabinet, and the formation of what was known as the "Kitchen cabinet;" the grave complications which resulted from the refusal of some of the secretaries to associate with Mrs. Eaton, the wife of the Secretary of War; the nomination and rejection of Mr. Van Buren as minister to England; and, finally, the fierce and uncompromising war which was waged against the Bank of the United States.

All these events served, each in its way, to modify the character and the result of the presidential election which took place in 1832. Mr. Van Buren was, perhaps, the central figure in all the schemes and arrangements. He was credited with a large share in the break-up of the cabinet, in which he was Secretary of State; he fanned the flame of discord in the relations between Jackson and Calhoun; he persuaded the President, against his expressed intention, to become a candidate for a second term; he was an adept in the art of distributing office so as to promote political and personal ends; he knew how to make use of his own rejection by the Senate to make himself "Vice-President now, and President afterwards."

Jackson was a President unlike any of his predecessors; but he was the man of his time. He could not help alienating those who regarded government as a serious business, to be conducted from high motives and with decorum; but at the same time he attracted more than he repelled. Like all men of strong will and fixed purpose, he attached some politicians to him by gratitude and some by fear; and the people at large had for him an admiration which neither his quality as a statesman nor his skill as a politician justified. It is impossible not to see that he lowered the dignity of his office, demoralized the public service, degraded politics to the level of a game in which the sharpest and the strongest, rather than the best and wisest, were to come off victors, and yet that in all this he pleased the men of his own generation more than he offended them; and, when the appeal was to be made to the voters of the country to pass judgment upon his doings, a compact, enthusiastic body of supporters was behind him, while the Opposition was disorganized and discordant. It was united only in opposition to him; but, had all its elements been joined in one party, his defeat could not have been accomplished.

The canvass began early. The first party in the field was

that of the Anti-Masons, — an organization which had its birth in western New York, after the alleged abduction of William Morgan, in 1826, for having revealed the secrets of freemasonry. The party spread over a large part of the North, and had some successes in State elections. In September, 1830, a national convention of Anti-Masons was held in Philadelphia. Ten States, including four New England States, New York, Ohio, New Jersey, Pennsylvania, Delaware, and Maryland, and the Territory of Michigan, were represented by 96 delegates. It was voted to hold a second national convention in Baltimore on the 26th of September, 1831, to be composed of delegates equal in number to the representatives in both Houses of Congress from each State, and to be chosen by the people opposed to secret societies, for the purpose of making nominations for the offices of President and Vice-President.

The convention was held at the time and place designated. Delegates to the number of 112 were present, from all the States represented in the convention of 1830, and from Maine, New Hampshire, and Indiana beside. William Wirt of Maryland was nominated for President, and Amos Ellmaker of Pennsylvania for Vice-President. Mr. Wirt had been Attorney-General during the whole of the terms of Presidents Monroe and Adams, and it was believed that he could unite all the opposition to Jackson. He was nominated for that purpose. Indeed, it had been intended by the Anti-Masons, before the convention, to nominate Judge John M‘Lean of Ohio, formerly Postmaster-General, whom Jackson had transferred from that office to the Supreme Court, in order that a more subservient politician might work the post-office department for political purposes with greater effect; but as some of the "National Republicans," as the party of the Opposition had been called, gave notice that they could not support

Judge M'Lean, that gentleman withdrew his name. The Anti-Masonic convention did not adopt a platform, but issued a very long and diffuse address to the people of the country.

The next convention was that of the National Republicans. They met at Baltimore on Dec. 12, 1831. Seventeen States were represented by 157 delegates. All the Northern States of the East and West, except Illinois, sent delegates; but only Delaware, Maryland, Virginia, North Carolina, Kentucky, Tennessee, and Louisiana, of the Southern States, did so. Henry Clay of Kentucky was nominated by a unanimous vote for President, and John Sergeant of Pennsylvania by a similar vote for Vice-President. No resolutions were adopted, but the convention issued an address severely criticising the administration for its corruption, partisanship, and abuse of power; for the hostility it had manifested to internal improvement, for treachery on the tariff question, for the war on the bank, and for the humiliating surrender to Georgia in the matter of the Cherokee Indians. By recommendation of this convention a national assembly of young men met in Washington in May, 1832, which accepted the nominations made by the National Republicans and adopted the following series of resolutions, — the first platform ever adopted by a national convention : —

1. *Resolved*, That, in the opinion of this convention, although the fundamental principles adopted by our fathers, as a basis upon which to raise a superstructure of American independence, can never be annihilated, yet the time has come when nothing short of the united energies of all the friends of the American republic can be relied on to sustain and perpetuate that hallowed work.

2. *Resolved*, That an adequate protection to American industry is indispensable to the prosperity of the country; and that an abandonment of the policy at this period would be attended with consequences ruinous to the best interests of the nation.

3. *Resolved*, That a uniform system of internal improvements, sustained and supported by the general government, is calculated to secure, in the highest degree, harmony, the strength, and the permanency of the republic.

4. *Resolved*, That the Supreme Court of the United States is the only tribunal recognized by the Constitution for deciding in the last resort all questions arising under the Constitution and laws of the United States, and that upon the preservation of the authority and jurisdiction of that court inviolate depends the existence of the nation.

5. *Resolved*, That the Senate of the United States is pre-eminently a conservative branch of the federal government; that upon a fearless and independent exercise of its constitutional functions depends the existence of the nicely balanced powers of that government; and that all attempts to overawe its deliberations by the public press or by the national executive deserve the indignant reprobation of every American citizen.

6. *Resolved*, That the political course of the present executive has given us no pledge that he will defend and support these great principles of American policy and the Constitution; but, on the contrary, has convinced us that he will abandon them whenever the purposes of party require it.

7. *Resolved*, That the indiscriminate removal of public officers, for the mere difference of political opinion, is a gross abuse of power; and that the doctrine lately " boldly preached " in the Senate of the United States, that " to the victor belong the spoils of the enemy," is detrimental to the interests, corrupting to the morals, and dangerous to the liberties of this country.

8. *Resolved*, That we hold the disposition shown by the present national administration to accept the advice of the King of Holland, touching the northeastern boundary of the United States, and thus to transfer a portion of the territory and citizens of a State of this Union to a foreign power, to manifest a total destitution of patriotic American feeling, inasmuch as we consider the life, liberty, property, and citizenship of every inhabitant of every State as entitled to the national protection.

9. *Resolved*, That the arrangement between the United States and Great Britain relative to the colonial trade, made in pursuance of the instructions of the late Secretary of State, was procured in a manner derogatory to the national character, and is injurious to this country in its practical results.

10. *Resolved*, That it is the duty of every citizen of this republic, who regards the honor, the prosperity, and the preservation of our Union, to oppose by every honorable measure the re-election of Andrew Jackson, and to promote the election of Henry Clay of Kentucky, and John Sergeant of Pennsylvania, as President and Vice-President of the United States.

Thus was established the convention system of nominations, and the practice of adopting a platform of principles. The system was at once made use of by the Democrats, not for the nomination of a President, but in order to unite the party on a candidate for Vice-President, that is, on Mr. Van Buren. General Jackson had received the usual large number of State nominations, while similar compliments had likewise been bestowed upon Mr. Clay, Mr. Wirt, Judge M'Lean, and others. No opposition to Jackson was tolerated in the Democratic party, for the friends of Mr. Calhoun had ceased to profess allegiance to him or to the Democratic party, and South Carolina was going her own way all by herself; but acquiescence in the will of the President that Mr. Van Buren should be his associate on the ticket was not so general. In fact there was determined opposition to the arrangement. This was particularly the case in Pennsylvania, where, at a Jackson State Convention, held in March, 1832, Mr. Van Buren's name was not even mentioned, and a long contest between Mr. Dallas, Mr. Buchanan, and Mr. William Wilkins terminated in favor of the last-named gentleman. So strong was the determination not to accept Mr. Van Buren that the electors nominated were pledged to vote for Mr. Wilkins, and, if he should be induced to withdraw, or if, for any other reason he should not be a candidate, to vote for Mr. Dallas.

The call for a National Democratic Convention originated in New Hampshire, and the Convention met in Baltimore on the 21st of May, 1832. Delegates were present from every State except Missouri. General Robert Lucas was the temporary and also the permanent president. On the second day of the Convention the Committee on Rules reported the following : —

Resolved, That each State be entitled, in the nomination to be made of a candidate for the vice-presidency, to a number of votes equal to the number to which they will be entitled in the electoral colleges, under the new apportionment, in voting for President and Vice-President; and that two thirds of the whole number of the votes in the convention shall be necessary to constitute a choice.

This was the origin of the famous two-thirds rule, by which all subsequent Democratic conventions have governed themselves in making nominations. On the first ballot for a candidate for Vice-President, Martin Van Buren had 208 votes, Philip P. Barbour of Virginia, 49, and Richard M. Johnson of Kentucky, 26 votes. Mr. Van Buren, having received more than two thirds of all the votes, was declared the nominee. General Jackson was recommended in the following resolution : —

Resolved, That the Convention repose the highest confidence in the purity, patriotism, and talents of Andrew Jackson, and that we most cordially concur in the repeated nominations which he has received in various parts of the Union as a candidate for re-election to the office which he now fills with so much honor to himself and usefulness to his country.

The Convention accomplished the object for which it was held, although it did not wholly overcome the repugnance of Democrats in all the States to Mr. Van Buren, or suppress the movement in favor of the rival candidates. A Jackson-Barbour Convention was held in Charlottesville, Virginia, in June, by which Mr. P. P. Barbour was formally nominated as the candidate for the Vice-Presi-

dency in conjunction with General Jackson for President.
Later in the same month a similar convention was held in
North Carolina, in which delegates from eighteen counties
participated ; but the candidacy of Mr. Wilkins was purely
local in Pennsylvania, and that of Mr. Barbour came to
nothing.

The tone of political discussion during the canvass
which preceded and followed these nominations was unexampled for its violence and rancor. The veto by the
President of the bill rechartering the Bank of the United
States, which had been passed by both Houses of Congress in spite of executive opposition, although there was
a Democratic majority in each House, intensified the
bitterness of the conflict. It also showed the strength
of General Jackson's hold upon the people, that he could
still retain, not only the support of the people, who were
probably with him in his war on the bank, but that of
the politicians as well, — including that of men who had
even voted to pass the bank bill over the veto. Mr.
Dallas was one of his class. He had introduced the bill
for a new charter in the Senate, had supported it at
every stage, and voted for it after the veto; and yet,
within a month after the failure of the bill, he was found
addressing a meeting in Philadelphia which adopted a
series of resolutions referring to the bank veto and
expressing thanks to the President for his fearless discharge of duty. Nothing was too severe for the opponents of Jackson to say of him, and the violence of their
denunciations was equalled by the angry vituperation
which the Democrats poured out upon the National Republicans and all other advocates of the bank.

The early elections were not very clearly indicative of
the result in November. In the Kentucky election, which
took place in August, a " Jackson " governor and a " Clay "

lieutenant-governor were chosen, each by small majorities. Maine was carried for the Jackson ticket in September, but by a greatly reduced majority. The October elections also gave the Opposition hope, which the result in the ensuing month was not to justify; for Ohio, though giving a plurality to the Jackson ticket, seemed capable of being captured by the Opposition if it could be united, and Pennsylvania gave to Governor Wolf, the Democratic candidate, but a few thousand majority,—less, in fact, than a third of that two years before. New Jersey and Maryland gave anti-Jackson majorities. The chance of success in defeating the President led to fresh combinations and coalitions where there was not already union among the several elements of the Opposition. The National Republicans adopted the Anti-Masonic electoral ticket in New York, and there was a combination of the same kind in Ohio and elsewhere. But the Democrats professed a serene confidence in the result, and they were not mistaken. The doubtful States, with the exception of Kentucky, gave majorities — some of them small, but all sufficient — to the Jackson and Van Buren ticket. The Jackson party had, however, wisely determined not to put up a ticket in opposition to the Wilkins electors in Pennsylvania, and in South Carolina the contest for the legislature had been wholly between the Union men and the Nullifiers; and the latter carried the legislature which was to appoint the electors. On the whole it was a great victory for the Democrats.

As before, twenty-four States took part in this election, but the number of electors was enlarged by the new apportionment which had been made after the result of the census of 1830 was ascertained. Delaware joined the States which permitted the people to choose the electors, leaving only South Carolina to cling to the old system of appointment by the legislature; and she retained that method until and including the election of 1860. Maine, New York, and Tennessee also abandoned at this time the district system of election, leaving only Maryland to adhere to it. With the exception of South Carolina and Maryland, therefore, the method of choosing electors had now become uniform throughout the country, without the interposition of an amendment to the Constitution. The popular vote of the States in 1832 was as follows: —

STATES.	Jackson.	Clay.*
Maine.	33,201	27,204
New Hampshire	25,486	19,010
Vermont.	7,870	11,152
Massachusetts	14,545	33,003
Rhode Island	2,126	2,810
Connecticut	11,269	17,755
New York	168,497	154,896
New Jersey	23,856	23,393
Pennsylvania	90,983	56,716
Delaware	4,110	4,276
Maryland	19,156	19,160
Virginia	33,609	11,451
North Carolina	24,862	4,563
South Carolina †	–	–
Georgia	20,750	–
Alabama ‡	–	–
Mississippi	5,919	No opposition.
Louisiana	4,049	2,528
Kentucky	36,247	43,396
Tennessee	28,740	1,436
Missouri	5,192	–
Ohio	81,246	76,539
Indiana	31,552	15,472
Illinois	14,147	5,429
Totals	687,502	530,189

* The vote for Wirt is included in Clay's vote.   † By Legislature.
‡ No opposition to Jackson.

The count of electoral votes was conducted in strict accordance with precedent, without dispute or incident. The result was as follows : —

STATES.	PRESIDENT.				VICE-PRESIDENT.				
	Andrew Jackson, Tenn.	Henry Clay, Ky.	John Floyd, Va.	William Wirt, Md.	Martin Van Buren, N. Y.	John Sergeant, Penn.	William Wilkins, Penn.	Henry Lee, Mass.	Amos Ellmaker, Penn.
Maine	10	–	–	–	10	–	–	–	–
New Hampshire	7	–	–	–	7	–	–	–	–
Vermont . . .	–	–	–	7	–	–	–	–	7
Massachusetts .	–	14	–	–	–	14	–	–	–
Rhode Island .	–	4	–	–	–	4	–	–	–
Connecticut . .	–	8	–	–	–	8	–	–	–
New York . .	42	–	–	–	42	–	–	–	–
New Jersey . .	8	–	–	–	8	–	–	–	–
Pennsylvania .	30	–	–	–	–	–	30	–	–
Delaware . . .	–	3	–	–	–	3	–	–	–
Maryland . . .	3	5	–	–	3	5	–	–	–
Virginia . . .	23	–	–	–	23	–	–	–	–
North Carolina .	15	–	–	–	15	–	–	–	–
South Carolina .	–	–	11	–	–	–	–	11	–
Georgia . . .	11	–	–	–	11	–	–	–	–
Alabama . . .	7	–	–	–	7	–	–	–	–
Mississippi . .	4	–	–	–	4	–	–	–	–
Louisiana . .	5	–	–	–	5	–	–	–	–
Kentucky . .	–	15	–	–	–	15	–	–	–
Tennessee . .	15	–	–	–	15	–	–	–	–
Ohio	21	–	–	–	21	–	–	–	–
Indiana . . .	9	–	–	–	9	–	–	–	–
Illinois . . .	5	–	–	–	5	–	–	–	–
Missouri . . .	4	–	–	–	4	–	–	–	–
Totals . .	219	49	11	7	189	49	30	11	7

XIV.

VAN BUREN.

THE closing acts of General Jackson's first administration were his proclamation and message on the subject of nullification, which did him infinite credit, and his "pocket veto" of the land bill, — which had passed the House of Representatives by 96 to 40 and the Senate by 23 to 5 votes, — by which he assumed the right of an absolute veto for the first time in American political history. His first important act during his second term was the removal of the deposits from the Bank of the United States in direct violation of law. In order to effect this change, he was forced to make two changes in the Secretaryship of the Treasury before he could find an officer willing to aid him in his scheme. The personal influence of the President was constantly felt in Congress, where he was supported by a strong and trustworthy body of adherents composing a majority of the House of Representatives, but, owing to the hostility of State Rights senators, constituting only a minority of the upper branch. Among the people, too, he was regarded as a demi-god. Not only were his acts approved, but his sturdy obstinacy and fearless pugnacity gave him favor with the masses of the people such as no other President before him or since his time has enjoyed.

But the Opposition was earnest and active. The largest section of it was organized in 1834 as the Whig party. According to the "Whig Almanac" for 1838, the party as then constituted comprised: "(1) Most of those who, under the name of National Republicans, had previously
113

been known as supporters of Adams and Clay, and advocates of the American system; (2) Most of those who, acting in defence of what they deemed the assailed or threatened rights of the States, had been stigmatized as Nullifiers, or the less virulent State Rights' men, who were thrown into a position of armed neutrality towards the administration by the doctrines of the proclamation of 1832 against South Carolina; (3) A majority of those before known as Anti-Masons; (4) Many who had up to that time been known as Jackson men, but who united in condemning the high-handed conduct of the Executive, the immolation of Duane, and the subserviency of Taney; (5) Numbers who had not before taken any part in politics, but who were now awakened from their apathy by the palpable usurpations of the executive, and the imminent peril of our whole fabric of constitutional liberty and national prosperity."

It was not to be expected that a party composed of such various elements should be able to unite on one candidate with heartiness; and, as the event proved, it was necessary that some time should elapse before anything like homogeneity could be given to the organization. Nullification was not popular among the Whigs of the North, nor did the State Rights' people of South Carolina and other States care about the war on the bank and the removal of the deposits. But, leaving the Opposition for a time, let us see what steps were taken to unite the Democracy. It was no secret that the President desired that Mr. Van Buren should be his successor. It was rumored at one time, and quite generally believed, that he contemplated resigning and leaving the presidential office to the Vice-President, but that he abandoned this project in order the better to secure the succession to Van Buren. However this may have been, it is certain that an opposition to Van Buren, not unlike that which had existed in

1831 and 1832, threatened to make itself felt and to thwart the President's plans. It·manifested itself in the President's own State of Tennessee, where, in January, 1835, the legislature formally presented Judge Hugh L. White, then a senator from Tennessee, as a candidate to succeed Jackson. On the day when this action was expected to be taken, there was placed on the desk of every member of the Tennessee legislature a package containing three copies of the Washington "Globe," in which was a series of gross attacks upon Judge White. The peculiarity of this circumstance lay in the fact that these precious documents bore the frank of the President, and some of them were addressed in his own hand.

The convention system had been tried once and had served the purpose; and, as the White movement was making progress elsewhere, — for the legislature of Alabama also nominated him, and all the Tennessee delegation with two exceptions were in favor of him,— the President wrote to a friend in February, 1835, advocating the holding of a national convention for the nomination of candidates for President and Vice-President. The convention was called and held, in Baltimore, on the 20th of May in that year. Twenty-two States were represented, and upwards of six hundred delegates were in attendance, but the manner of choosing delegates was not what it is in our day. More than half of all those present were delegates from Maryland, and the convention was rather like what is now understood by the term "mass meeting" than like a convention of the present time. In the voting, however, each State was allowed only a number of votes equal to its delegation in Congress. On the first ballot Martin Van Buren received every vote as the candidate for President. Colonel Richard M. Johnson of Kentucky was nominated for the vice-presidency, also on the first ballot, by 178 votes to 87 cast for William C. Rives of Virginia. He thus had barely more than the two thirds which the rule of the convention required to effect a nomination. Previous to the voting a motion had been carried, but was afterwards reconsidered and rejected, that a majority should be sufficient to make a choice. Even after the nomination had been made, the delegates from Virginia refused to abide by the result, and declared that Virginia would not support Colonel Johnson. Although the business of the convention was small in amount, and although its sessions were brief, the meeting was a most exciting one, and did not promise much for the harmony of the party in the election that was to take place the next year. No platform was adopted.

The Opposition wisely determined not to attempt a concentration of their strength, but to take advantage of all elements of local hostility to the administration, in the hope of throwing the election into the House of Representatives. General William Henry Harrison was nominated by a meeting at Harrisburg, Penn.; Judge John M'Lean of Ohio by the legislature of that State; Daniel Webster by the Whigs in the Massachusetts legislature; South Carolina was safe to vote for some opponent of Jackson; and Tennessee, if no other State, would give its electoral vote to Judge White.

There were two Opposition candidates for the vice-presidency. One of them, Francis Granger of New York, was placed upon the ticket with Harrison in most of the States. He was an old Anti-Mason, and had been the candidate of the party for governor of New York. His nomination was a concession to that wing of the Whig party. It is a curious fact that one convention of Anti-Masons adopted Mr. Van Buren as a candidate, but its action excited only derision. In those States where Judge White was the Opposition candidate, John Tyler of Virginia was made the candidate for the second place on the ticket. In Massachusetts, where Mr. Webster was the choice of the Whigs for the presidency, Mr. Granger was supported.

The scheme was a promising one, and it came near success; but the margin of safety was on the side of the Democratic party once more, largely owing to the strictness of party discipline, and the determined use of the national patronage to perpetuate the Jackson dynasty under a new head. The battle between the contesting forces was a bitter one. Mr. Van Buren was the embodiment of all that was objected to on the part of the Whigs against General Jackson; and, on the other hand, the Democrats, honestly believing that the administration in power had acted for the best interests of the country, could find no words too severe to denounce those who would undo its work. They made it a special accusation against the Whigs that they were for the bank; and, while it was true of the most of them, — and, considering what the bank had done for the currency, and the great disasters which followed its overthrow, it was greatly to their credit that they were, — they had not quite courage enough to avow their principles in the face of the manifest, but strange, hostility of the people to "Biddle's bank."

As had happened in 1832, the early autumn elections did not promise a sweeping victory for the Democrats, and they even gave hope to the Opposition that the election would be thrown into the House of Representatives. Ohio and New Jersey, which had given their votes to Jackson four years before, were carried by the Whigs. The Democratic majority in Pennsylvania was uncomfortably small, and in Maine there was no choice of a congressman at the September election in any one of the eight districts. But the Democrats worked with extraordinary energy after these preliminary reverses and saved the day, although they came out of the contest with a largely reduced majority.

Twenty-six States took part in the election. Arkansas had been admitted on the 15th of June, 1836. Michigan, which had applied for admission as early as 1833, chose electors, and their votes were counted, as we shall see, in the same manner as were those of Missouri in 1821. The State was formally admitted on the 26th of January, 1837, so that she was a State at the time the electoral count took place. All the States except South Carolina, whose electors were appointed by the legislature, chose them by a popular vote and by general ticket. Since 1832 no State has chosen them by the separate vote of districts. The popular vote was as follows : —

STATES.	Van Buren.	Whig.	Whig Candidate.
Maine	22,990	15,239	Harrison.
New Hampshire	18,722	6,228	Harrison.
Vermont	14,039	20,996	Harrison.
Massachusetts	34,474	42,247	Webster.
Rhode Island	2,964	2,710	Harrison.
Connecticut	19,291	18,749	Harrison.
New York.	166,815	138,543	Harrison.
New Jersey	25,592	26,137	Harrison.
Pennsylvania	91,475	87,111	Harrison.
Delaware	4,153	4,733	Harrison.
Maryland	22,168	25,852	Harrison.
Virginia	30,261	23,468	White.
North Carolina	26,910	23,626	White.
South Carolina *	–	–	–
Georgia	22,104	24,876	White.
Alabama	20,506	15,612	White.
Mississippi	9,979	9,688	White.
Louisiana	3,653	3,383	White.
Arkansas	2,400	1,238	White.
Kentucky	33,025	36,687	Harrison.
Tennessee.	26,129	36,168	White.
Missouri	10,995	7,337	White.
Ohio	96,948	105,404	Harrison.
Indiana	32,478	41,281	Harrison.
Illinois	17,275	14,292	Harrison.
Michigan	7,332	4,045	Harrison.
Totals	762,678	735,651	

* Legislature.

The usual resolution for the appointment of a committee to report upon the manner of conducting the count of votes was introduced in the Senate on the 26th of January, 1837. An amendment offered by Mr. Clay, and adopted by the Senate, directed the committee also "to inquire into the expediency of ascertaining whether any votes were given at the recent election contrary to the prohibition contained in the second section of the second article of the Constitution ; and, if such votes were given, what ought to be done with them ; and whether any, and what, provision ought to be made for securing the faithful observance, in future, of that section of the Constitution." The House having assented to the resolution as thus amended, the committee reported to the Senate on the 4th of February. After remarking that the shortness of the time allowed had prevented a proper investigation of the matters referred to the committee, the report proceeds : —

The correspondence which has taken place between the chairman of the committee and the heads of the different departments of the executive branch of the government accompanies this report, from which it appears that Isaac Waldron, who was an elector in New Hampshire, was, at the time of his appointment as elector, president of a deposit bank at Portsmouth, and was appointed and acting as pension agent, without compensation, under the authority of the United States; that in two cases persons of the same names with the individuals who were appointed and voted as electors in the State of North Carolina held the offices of deputy-postmasters under the general government. It also appears that in New Hampshire there is one case, in Connecticut there is one case, in North Carolina there is one case, in which, from the report of the Postmaster-General, it is probable that, at the time of the appointment of electors in these States, respectively, the electors, or persons of the same name, were deputy-postmasters. The committee have not ascertained whether the electors are the same individuals who held, or are presumed to have held, the offices of deputy-postmasters at the time when the appointment of electors wa•

made; and this is the less to be regretted as it is confidently believed that no change in the result of the election of either the President or Vice-President would be affected by the ascertainment of the fact in either way, as five or six votes only would in any event be abstracted from the whole number; for the committee cannot adopt the opinion entertained by some that a single illegal vote would vitiate the whole electoral vote of the college of electors in which it was given, particularly in cases where the vote of the whole college has been given to the same persons.

The committee are of opinion that the second section of the second article of the Constitution, which declares that no senator or representative, or person holding an office of trust or profit under the United States, shall be appointed an elector, ought to be carried in its whole spirit into rigid execution in order to prevent officers of the general government from bringing their official power to influence the elections of President and Vice-President of the United States. This provision of the Constitution, it is believed, excludes and disqualifies deputy-postmasters from the appointment of electors; and the disqualification relates to the time of the appointment, and that a resignation of the office of deputy-postmaster after his appointment as elector would not entitle him to vote as elector under the Constitution.

Should a case occur in which it became necessary to ascertain and determine upon the qualification of electors of President and Vice-President of the United States, the important question would be presented, What tribunal would, under the Constitution, be competent to decide ? Whether the respective colleges of electors in the different States should decide upon the qualifications of their own members, or Congress should exercise the power, is a question which the committee are of opinion ought to be settled by a permanent provision upon the subject.

The committee reported no bill or resolution on the subject; but it appended to the usual resolution for counting the votes a second resolution, exactly like that which had been adopted in 1821 in regard to the votes of Missouri, to cover the new case of Michigan. This latter provoked some discussion, certain senators contending that Michigan was, and others that it was not, a State in the Union for the purposes of election, but the resolution was finally carried by a vote of 34 to 9. In the course of this debate a senator asked Mr. Grundy of Tennessee, who

STATES.	PRESIDENT.					VICE-PRESIDENT.			
	Martin Van Buren, N. Y.	William H. Harrison, O.	Hugh L. White, Tenn.	Daniel Webster, Mass.	Willie P. Mangum, N. C.	Richard M. Johnson, Ky.	Francis Granger, N. Y.	John Tyler, Va.	William Smith, Ala.
Maine	10	–	–	–	–	10	–	–	–
New Hampshire	7	–	–	–	–	7	–	–	–
Vermont . . .	–	7	–	–	–	–	7	–	–
Massachusetts .	–	–	–	14	–	–	14	–	–
Rhode Island .	4	–	–	–	–	4	–	–	–
Connecticut . .	8	–	–	–	–	8	–	–	–
New York . .	42	–	–	–	–	42	–	–	–
New Jersey . .	–	8	–	–	–	–	8	–	–
Pennsylvania .	30	–	–	–	–	30	–	–	–
Delaware . . .	–	3	–	–	–	–	3	–	–
Maryland . . .	–	10	–	–	–	–	–	10	–
Virginia . . .	23	–	–	–	–	–	–	–	23
North Carolina .	15	–	–	–	–	15	–	–	–
South Carolina .	–	–	–	–	11	–	–	11	–
Georgia . . .	–	–	11	–	–	–	–	11	.–
Alabama . . .	7	–	–	–	–	7	–	–	–
Mississippi . .	4	–	–	–	–	4	–	–	–
Louisiana . .	5	–	–	–	–	5	–	–	–
Arkansas . .	3	–	–	–	–	3	–	–	–
Kentucky . .	–	15	–	–	–	–	15	–	–
Tennessee . .	–	–	15	–	–	–	–	15	–
Missouri . . .	4	–	–	–	–	4	–	–	–
Ohio	–	21	–	–	–	–	21	–	–
Indiana . . .	–	9	–	–	–	–	9	–	–
Illinois . . .	5	–	–	–	–	5	–	–	–
Michigan . . .	3	–	–	–	–	3	–	–	–
Totals . .	170	73	26	14	11	147	77	47	23

had reported the resolutions, as chairman of the joint committee, what course would have been pursued if the vote of Michigan had varied the result? Mr. Grundy replied that the gentleman could not expect him "to answer a question which the wisest of their predecessors had purposely left undetermined. What might be done under the circumstances adverted to, should they ever occur, the wisdom of the day must decide."

The official count of the electoral votes is given on the preceding page.

The result was announced in the alternative form provided for by the joint resolution, concluding with the declaration that, whether the votes of Michigan were counted or not counted, Martin Van Buren was elected President, and that no person had a majority of votes for Vice-President; that an election to that office had not been effected; that Richard M. Johnson of Kentucky, and Francis Granger of New York, were the two highest on the lists of electoral votes, and that it devolved on the Senate to choose a Vice-President from these persons.

On returning to its own chamber, the Senate adopted a resolution prescribing the manner in which an election should be made. The names of the senators were to be called in alphabetical order, and they were to vote *viva voce*. On the first trial, Richard M. Johnson of Kentucky was chosen by a vote of 33 to 16 for Francis Granger. This was the only occasion in our political history that the choice of the Vice-President has devolved upon the Senate.

XV.

No other political canvass that has ever taken place in the United States bears even a near resemblance to the "log-cabin" and "hard-cider" campaign of 1840. It was marked by intense and extraordinary enthusiasm on the part of young men for a candidate who was close upon seventy years of age. The party which won the victory was a party only in name, for its only bond of union was opposition to the administration of the day. It announced no positive principles, it had no definite policy. Yet it triumphed over the closely-organized party which had governed the country since the beginning of the century, — unless the four years' term of the second Adams is to be excepted, — strongly intrenched in the offices, and using the public patronage without scruple to perpetuate its own power.

Mr. Van Buren's administration was a continuation of General Jackson's. The new President had far more political shrewdness than his predecessor, but far less personal force. His public life was characterized from beginning to end by *finesse*. He contrived to be on neither side of many of the most important questions of the day, — at least until it had become very evident which view was likely to be the more popular. But when he cast in his fortunes with Jackson, after the failure of the caucus in 1824, he supported his chief zealously and loyally, and he had his reward. The people had, however, begun to tire of Jackson before his second term expired, and Van

Buren was unequal to the task of bringing them back to their allegiance. The great panic of 1837 — the direct result of the reckless financing of Jackson, of the extinction of the Bank of the United States, which had given stability to the currency, of the treasury circular which required the payment of all dues of the United States in coin, and of the distribution of the surplus revenue — dealt a blow at the administration in the first year of its existence. Its weakness was shown by its repeated defeats in two successive Congresses, in each of which there was a Democratic majority, upon the President's favorite scheme of establishing that anomalous institution, the Independent Treasury, — the one great measure of Mr. Van Buren's administration.

Still, it would be a mistake to suppose either that Mr. Van Buren was abandoned by his party, or that his administration was an unpopular one among Democrats. On the contrary, a very large majority of them believed in him, approved his measures, and desired his re-election. They were in favor of completing the work which Jackson had begun, by divorcing the State altogether from private banking corporations. Mr. Van Buren was then, and to the end of his life, as his "Political History" shows, an enemy of *banks* as well as of the *The Bank*, the "monster" which Jackson crushed. It is extremely probable that if the issue in the canvass of 1840 had been made wholly upon the bank question, the result would have shown that the people were with Van Buren. The Whigs were too shrewd to avow friendliness to *the* bank, or to any bank. They took advantage of the opposition to, and the bad results of, the Jackson-Van Buren fiscal plans, without declaring themselves in favor of restoring what had been destroyed; and they also profited by the Southern hostility to the administration, without promising to reverse or to modify in any respect the policy of the general government on the subject of State Rights. In short, the Democrats had principles and a policy, right or wrong, as people may think ; the Whigs were united only in condemning, and, whatever they may have intended, whatever they may have done or attempted to do when they were in power, they did not venture to declare principles or policy beforehand.

The State elections in 1837 and 1838 resulted unfavorably to the Democrats. In the latter year the most of the elections of members of the twenty-sixth Congress took place; and they were so decidedly adverse to the Democrats that only by extraordinary exertions in the spring elections of 1839 did they succeed in saving any majority at all. So close was the contest that, when the House assembled in December, 1839, there were 119 Democrats, 118 Opposition, and five members from New Jersey whose seats were contested. The certificates were held by Whigs, who were not allowed to participate in the organization. On that occasion Mr. Adams, the ex-President, who had returned to the House of Representatives, prevented anarchy by calling the members to order and persuading them to choose a temporary chairman, — a position which was assigned to him.

Long before this, the plans of the Whigs had been forming; and, two days after the assembling of Congress, the National Whig convention met at Harrisburg, — on Dec. 4, 1839. The leaders were resolved on union, and the only question was as to the candidate who would command the largest support. Mr. Clay had the advantage of a very long public service, and of having been a leader in national affairs for almost thirty years ; but he also labored under the double disadvantage of being a Freemason, and therefore not acceptable to the faction which

still mustered many followers in the Eastern States, and
of having been a conspicuous advocate of the "American
system," or protective tariff, which was highly unpopular
in the South Atlantic States. General William Henry
Harrison was not a great leader; but he had been more or
less in the public service, military and civil, for nearly
half a century, and was well known throughout the country. Moreover, he had made a gallant run for the presidency in the Northern States in 1836, and was open to
neither of the objections urged against Mr. Clay. It was
evident that one of these two would be selected to lead
the Whig opposition. Each had his strong partisans;
but not only they, but the candidates as well, were anx-
ious chiefly that the Whig party should carry the election.
Mr. Clay's earnest and laudable ambition to be President
was not so great that he would put it before the cause.
Moreover, he was aware of the objections which some
Whigs entertained to him; and, when the autumn elections of 1839 indicated something of a reaction in favor
of the Democrats, and the necessity of a complete union
of the Opposition, he wrote, in a letter which was read
at the Harrisburg convention, that, "if the deliberations of the convention shall lead them to the choice of
another as the candidate of the Opposition, far from feeling any discontent, the nomination will have my best
wishes and receive my cordial support." He further
begged his friends to "discard all attachment or partiality to me, and be guided solely by the motive of res-
cuing our country from the dangers which now encom-
pass it." Already, during the preceding summer, he had
said in an address at Buffalo: "If my name creates any
obstacle to union and harmony, away with it, and concentrate upon some individual more acceptable to all branches
of the Opposition." The action of the great "union and

harmony" convention of Pennsylvania, held at Harrisburg on the 4th of September, probably did much to concentrate the Whig forces on Harrison, for, while that convention extolled Clay in extravagant phrases, it expressed the opinion that only General Harrison could unite the anti-Van Buren party.

Delegates appeared at the Whig convention from twenty-two States. South Carolina, Georgia, Tennessee, and Arkansas were not represented. On the second day of the convention, an organization was effected by the choice of Governor J. Barbour of Virginia as president. After a long debate, a plan of nomination was agreed upon. As this scheme was very peculiar, and is now quite obsolete, the order of the convention is given entire : —

That the delegates from each State be requested to assemble as a delegation, and appoint a committee, not exceeding three in number, to receive the views and opinions of such delegation, and communicate the same to the assembled committees of all the delegations, to be by them respectively reported to their principals. And that thereupon the delegates from each State be requested to assemble as a delegation, and ballot for candidates for the offices of President and Vice-President, and, having done so, to commit the ballot designating the votes of each candidate, and by whom given, to its committee. And thereupon all the committees shall assemble and compare the several ballots, and report the result of the same to their several delegations, together with such facts as may bear upon the nomination. And said delegations shall forthwith reassemble and ballot again for candidates for the above offices, and again commit the result to the above committees; and if it shall appear that a majority of the ballots are for any one man for candidate for President, said committee shall report the result to the convention for its consideration. If there shall be no such majority, then the delegations shall repeat the balloting until such a majority shall be obtained, and then report the same to the convention for its consideration. That the vote of a majority of each delegation shall be reported as the vote of that State.

And each State represented here shall vote its full electoral vote by such delegation in the committee."

It will be observed that this rule bears a resemblance to, although it was not precisely like, the "unit rule," which has caused so much trouble in Republican and Democratic conventions since that time. The action of the committees and of the delegations was not to be binding upon the convention until accepted by it. The scheme was adopted as a method of learning what candidate would be most acceptable to the States. An effort was made the next day, by Mr. Cassius M. Clay of Kentucky, to secure a reversal of the decision; but the convention adhered to its former resolution by a strong vote. The action of the committees and delegations is not a part of the official record; but it is known that on the first informal ballot, in which the wish of each delegate was expressed, without unifying the votes of the States, Mr. Clay had a small plurality. On the first ballot by States, Mr. Clay had 103, General Harrison 94, and General Winfield Scott 57. After repeated ballotings, late on Friday evening, the third day of the convention, a report was made by the committees that they had agreed upon a candidate. General Harrison had 148, Mr. Clay, 90, and General Scott, 16. On the next day a resolution was introduced declaring General Harrison the nominee of the convention, and it was supported in enthusiastic speeches by many of the friends of Clay. While the jubilee was still going on, the committees which had been considering the question of Vice-President, made a report that John Tyler had received the unanimous vote of the convention. His name was thereupon joined to that of General Harrison in the pending resolution, and the vote was carried amid a whirl of enthusiasm. The convention then adjourned, without having given expression to the principles of the party which it represented, in any form. Even in the many speeches made during the four days' session, there was hardly a positive assertion of a principle made by any delegate. It was all hatred and opposition to Van Buren and the "Loco-Focos."

The nomination was received with great enthusiasm by the Opposition. Meeting after meeting was held in many States, and the candidacy of the "Old Hero of Tippecanoe" was noisily ratified. The Whigs prepared to shout and sing their candidate into office. In February, 1840, the Whig Convention of Ohio at Columbus was made the occasion of a great "demonstration," a procession with banners, representations of log-cabins, coon-skins, pictures of the "old hero" drinking a mug of hard cider, and other equally logical appeals to the political sound sense of the voters of Ohio. A still more imposing affair was the great procession in Baltimore, on the 4th of May, in connection with the National Convention of young men, which was nicely timed to occur simultaneously with the Democratic Convention in the same city. An excellent illustration of the political eloquence of the time is afforded by the ostentatious failure of the Baltimore "Patriot" to express the emotions which this great procession excited; but the editor certainly tried to do his subject justice.

Monday was a proud day for Baltimore, for Maryland, for the Union. It was a day on which the Young Whigs of all the States were to meet in grand convention. Never before was seen such an assemblage of the people, in whose persons are concentrated the sovereignty of the government. In the language of the president of the day, — "*Every mountain sent its rill,* — EVERY VALLEY ITS STREAM, — and, Lo! THE AVALANCHE OF THE PEOPLE IS HERE!"

It is impossible to convey the slightest idea of the sublime spectacle presented by the procession as it moved through the city. All that pen could write, all that the mouth of man could speak, all that the imagination can conceive of beauty, grandeur, and sublimity, would fall short, far short of the reality. The excitement, the joy, the enthusiasm which everywhere prevailed, lighting up the countenance of every man in the procession; the shouts, the applause, the cheers, of those who filled the sidewalks and crowded the windows; the waving of handkerchiefs by the ladies; the responsive cries of the people; the flaunting banners; the martial music; the loud roar, at intervals, of the deep-mouthed cannon, — all these and more, much more, must be described, seen in the mind's eye, vibrate through the frame, fill the heart, before the reader can approach to any conception of the reality ; and when all these are done, if they were possible, he has still but a faint and meagre impression of the scene that was presented. In no country, in no time, never before in the history of man, was there a spectacle so full of "natural glory." The aged veteran, whose declining years forbade his joining the procession, looked on ; his feeble voice went to swell the general shout that penetrated even to the blue vault of heaven ; his hand waved above his head, whilst down his furrowed cheek ran tears, the overflowing of a heart full even to bursting with joy and happiness and gladness, of all that goes to make up life's best pleasures, and these crowded, as it were, into one moment. The father, who brought his children to see the patriots of the land ; the mother to look upon her son, one of the patriot crew ; the sister to behold the brother give vent to his youthful and extravagant joy, — were all there, and all went to make up the spectacle. Standing on an eminence commanding a view of the line of the procession in the whole extent of Baltimore Street, you beheld a moving mass of human beings. A thousand banners, burnished by the sun, floating in the breeze, ten thousand handkerchiefs waved by the fair daughters of the city, gave seeming life and motion to the very air. A hundred thousand faces were before you, — age, manhood, youth, and beauty filled every place where a foothold could be got, or any portion of the procession be seen ; and you gazed on the pageant with renewed and increasing delight, and words failed to express what your heart felt or your eyes beheld. Nothing was wanting, nothing left to be desired, — the cup of human joy was full. The free men of the land were there, — the fiery son of the South, the substantial citizen of the East, the hardy pioneer of the West, were all there. It was the epitome of a great nation, in itself realizing, filling up the imaginings, and may have been the very picture which the poet drew when he described our country, our institutions, and our people as a "land beyond the oceans of the West," where "freedom and truth are worshipped," by a "people mighty in their youth."

> That land is like an eagle, whose young gaze
> Feeds on the noontide beam ; whose golden plume
> Floats moveless on the storm, and in the blaze
> Of sunshine gleams when earth is wrapped in gloom.
> An epitaph of glory for the tomb
> Of murdered Europe, may thy fame be made,
> Great people ! as the sand shalt thou become !
> Thy growth is swift as morn, when night must fade;
> The multitudinous earth shall sleep beneath thy shade.

Thus much we may say in reference to what words can describe the procession to be, not what it was; for the reality we must give the dry details of the programme by which it was arranged. We can give nothing of the living spectacle, we can give nothing of the joy and gladness which, —

> Spread through the multitudinous streets fast flying
> Upon the wings of hope —
>   from house to house replying
> With loud acclaim; the living shook heaven's cope,
> And filled the earth with echoes !

We can give nothing of these, and here all fail; but we must essay to present the scene, as far as feeble words can do it.

The procession does really seem to have been a grand affair, and there were numerous emblems of the Whigs, — log-cabins, barrels of hard cider, brooms to sweep the Augean stables, and others which it would be tedious to enumerate. The poet was with the Whigs that year. Among the mottos on the banners was this : —

> Farewell, dear Van,
> You're not our man ;
> To guide the ship,
> We'll try old Tip.

But quite enough has been said to show the character of the canvass on the side of the Opposition, and we turn to the course of the Administration and its friends. The

party was not united on a candidate for the vice-presidency, and it was seen very early that any attempt to unite
it would result in failure. Colonel Johnson had not been
altogether popular with the Democrats, and it was certain
that if he were nominated he would not be able to command the strength of the party. On the other hand his
friends were by no means disposed to submit to his defeat.
Inasmuch as the party was united in the support of Van
Buren for the first place, there was a cry that there was
no need of a convention. The people, it was urged, have
already spontaneously nominated the President, and the
vice-presidency is safe in the hands of a Democratic
Senate, which had already once elected Colonel Johnson.
A list was made of ten States which already had declined,
or would decline, to send representatives to a national convention. By some of them Mr. Van Buren had even then
been nominated for the presidency in conjunction with
William R. King of Alabama for the second place, while
elsewhere Mr. Johnson was nominated for re-election.
James K. Polk of Tennessee and L. W. Tazewell of Virginia
also received nominations more or less important for the
position. But once more New Hampshire issued a call for
a national convention, to be held at Baltimore on the 5th
of May. Delegates from twenty-one States responded. The
States not represented were Connecticut, Delaware, Virginia, South Carolina, and Illinois. But some of the States
were represented by only one or two persons. Massachusetts sent but one delegate. Governor William Carroll of
Tennessee was chosen president of the convention, and,
pending the preparation of business, there was an abundance of speech-making. All who addressed the convention were sure that a great victory for the Democratic
party was impending, and each tried to outdo the rest in
jeering at the Whigs. The great procession of the day

before was referred to as an "animal show;" the Whigs were laughed at for shutting up their candidate and not allowing him the use of pen and ink; and one speaker said that he had tried to get an introduction to some of the log-cabin men in the procession "for the purpose of feeling their soft, delicate hands," but "as soon as he had done so he was pretty careful to put his hand on his purse."

On the second day of the convention the committee on resolutions reported the following platform of principles : —

1. *Resolved*, That the federal government is one of limited powers derived solely from the Constitution, and the grants of power shown therein ought to be strictly construed by all the departments and agents of the government, and that it is inexpedient and dangerous to exercise doubtful constitutional powers.

2. *Resolved*, That the Constitution does not confer upon the general government the power to commence and carry on a general system of internal improvement.

3. *Resolved*, That the Constitution does not confer authority upon the federal government, directly or indirectly, to assume the debts of the several States, contracted for local internal improvements, or other State purposes; nor would such assumption be just or expedient.

4. *Resolved*, That justice and sound policy forbid the federal government to foster one branch of industry to the detriment of another, or to cherish the interest of one portion to the injury of another portion of our common country; that every citizen and every section of the country has a right to demand and insist upon an equality of rights and privileges, and to complete and ample protection of person and property from domestic violence or foreign aggression.

5. *Resolved*, That it is the duty of every branch of the government to enforce and practise the most rigid economy in conducting our public affairs, and that no more revenue ought to be raised than is required to defray the necessary expenses of the government.

6. *Resolved*, That Congress has no power to charter a United States Bank; that we believe such an institution one of deadly

hostility to the best interests of the country, dangerous to our Republican institutions and the liberties of the people, and calculated to place the business of the country within the control of a concentrated money power, and above the laws and the will of the people.

7. *Resolved*, That Congress has no power, under the Constitution, to interfere with or control the domestic institutions of the several States, and that such States are the sole and proper judges of everything appertaining to their own affairs not prohibited by the Constitution; that all efforts of the Abolitionists or others, made to induce Congress to interfere with questions of slavery, or to take incipient steps in relation thereto, are calculated to lead to the most alarming and dangerous consequences, and that all such efforts have an inevitable tendency to diminish the happiness of the people, and endanger the stability and permanency of the Union, and ought not to be countenanced by any friend to our political institutions.

8. *Resolved*, That the separation of the moneys of the government from banking institutions is indispensable for the safety of the funds of the government and the rights of the people.

9. *Resolved*, That the liberal principles embodied by Jefferson in the Declaration of Independence, and sanctioned in the Constitution, which makes ours the land of liberty and the asylum of the oppressed of every nation, have ever been cardinal principles in the Democratic faith; and every attempt to abridge the present privilege of becoming citizens and the owners of soil among us ought to be resisted with the same spirit which swept the Alien and Sedition laws from our statute-book.

A committee, which had been appointed on the preceding day, to consider and report " upon the subject of the nominations of President and Vice-President," made a report, through Mr. C. M. Clay of Alabama, in the shape of two resolutions, to each of which a preamble was prefixed. The first, reciting that Mr. Van Buren had received numerous nominations, and that he was the unanimous choice of the party and the convention, *resolved*, that he should be presented as the Democratic candidate for the office of President. The second, reciting the fact that several gentlemen had been put in nomination for the vice-presidency; that some of the States presenting these candidates were not represented in the convention; and that all of them, by their discharge of public trusts, had shown themselves worthy to be elected to the office, —

Resolved, That the convention deem it expedient at the present time not to choose between the individuals in nomination, but to leave the decision to their Republican fellow-citizens in the several States, trusting that, before the election shall take place, their opinions shall become so concentrated as to secure the choice of a Vice-President by the electoral colleges.

The first resolution was adopted unanimously, without debate. The second was opposed, and debated at some length; but when it appeared that the differences among the delegates were really irreconcilable, opposition ceased, and the second resolution was also unanimously adopted. An address to the people was then accepted, on the report of a committee, and after more speech-making the convention came to an end.

There was another convention, small in numbers and local in character, which made a third nomination for the office of President. Although the party cast but few votes in 1840, it is mentioned here as the beginning of great things. It was the Abolition party, which held a convention at Warsaw, Genesee County, New York, at the beginning of December, 1839, and nominated James G. Birney of New York for President, and Francis J. Lemoyne of Pennsylvania for Vice-President. The question of slavery had been very much discussed in Congress and by the press for many years, but the issue was not yet a really important one in presidential elections. As will be seen from the platform of the Democrats, that party was ready to take its stand against any federal interference with slavery; but the Whigs were not, as long as

they constituted a party, willing to make an issue with
the Democrats on that subject.

What the canvass had been from the beginning it continued to be to the end. On the part of the Whigs it was
a season of great and enthusiastic meetings and stump-
speeches. So far was it from being true that General
Harrison was shut up by his political friends, that he even
appeared on the stump himself, at several places in Ohio,
and spoke at length. It is commonly supposed, at the
present day, and sometimes said, that no candidate of a
great party ever advocated his own election to the presidency in public addresses; but General Harrison did so
in September and October, 1840, at Urbana, Dayton, Chil-
licothe, Columbus, and other places. In an address at
Carthage, on August 20, he explicitly asserted the right
of the people to discuss any subject, and to petition Congress for the redress of any grievance, including that of
slavery; and for this he was roundly denounced as an
Abolitionist. The Democrats were unable to understand,
and still more unable to look with patience upon, the
shouting campaign of the Harrison men. They affected
to treat the party and its candidate with contempt, but
they were really very angry and very much alarmed. As
State after State upon whose electoral vote they had
counted gave the Whigs a majority, they became more
desperate. They could not and would not believe what
was going to happen, and predicted that "the bubble
would burst" before November. That was a time when
political slang was more current than it was ever before
or has been since. The phrases, "Crow, Chapman, crow,"
"The ball is rolling on," "Clear the kitchen," with numerous variations, and similar expressions, are still remembered by the men, now old, who took part in that famous

canvass. The Whig song to the tune of "The Little Pig's Tail" has become historical, with its chorus: —

"For Tippecanoe and Tyler too — Tippecanoe and Tyler too;
And with them we'll beat little Van, Van,
Van is a used up man;
And with them we'll beat little Van."

The shouts of the Whigs over their success in Vermont, Kentucky, Maine, Ohio, and other States had hardly ceased ringing when the presidential election began. The choice of all the electors was not then made on one day, as it is now, but in each State at a time fixed by the legislature. It was required, however, to be made within thirty-four days preceding the meeting of the electors. The election began in Pennsylvania and Ohio, on the 30th of October, and ended in North Carolina, on the 12th of November, so far as popular elections were concerned. South Carolina, whose legislature made the choice of the electors for that State, appointed them a fortnight later. But it was evident as soon as the returns of Pennsylvania were in, showing a large gain for the Whigs, even since the State election, four weeks before, that Harrison was to be President. The popular vote was as follows: —

STATES.	Harrison.	Van Buren.	Birney.
Maine	46,612	46,201	194
New Hampshire	26,163	32,761	126
Vermont	32,440	18,018	819
Massachusetts	72,874	51,944	1,621
Rhode Island	5,278	3,301	42
Connecticut	31,601	25,296	174
New York	225,817	212,527	2,808
New Jersey	33,351	31,034	69
Pennsylvania	144,021	143,672	343
Delaware	5,967	4,874	–
Maryland	33,528	28,752	–
Virginia	42,501	43,893	–
North Carolina	46,376	33,782	–
South Carolina *	–	–	–
Georgia	40,261	31,021	–
Alabama	28,471	33,991	–
Mississippi	19,518	16,995	–
Louisiana	11,296	7,616	–
Kentucky	58,489	32,616	–
Tennessee	60,391	48,289	–
Missouri	22,972	29,760	–
Arkansas	5,160	6,760	–
Ohio	148,157	124,782	903
Indiana	65,302	51,604	–
Illinois	45,537	47,476	149
Michigan	22,933	21,131	321
Totals	1,275,016	1,129,102	7,069

* By Legislature.

The electoral count was conducted in the usual manner, and there was no incident to mark the proceedings. The result was declared as follows : —

STATES.	PRESIDENT.		VICE-PRESIDENT.			
	W. H. Harrison, Ohio.	Martin Van Buren, N. Y.	John Tyler, Va.	R. M. Johnson, Ky.	L. W. Tazewell, Va.	James K. Polk, Tenn.
Maine	10	–	10	–	–	–
New Hampshire	–	7	–	7	–	–
Vermont	7	–	7	–	–	–
Massachusetts	14	–	14	–	–	–
Rhode Island	4	–	4	–	–	–
Connecticut	8	–	8	–	–	–
New York	42	–	42	–	–	–
New Jersey	8	–	8	–	–	–
Pennsylvania	30	–	30	–	–	–
Delaware	3	–	3	–	–	–
Maryland	10	–	10	–	–	–
Virginia	–	23	–	22	–	1
North Carolina	15	–	15	–	–	–
South Carolina	–	11	–	–	11	–
Georgia	11	–	11	–	–	–
Alabama	–	7	–	7	–	–
Mississippi	4	–	4	–	–	–
Louisiana	5	–	5	–	–	–
Kentucky	15	–	15	–	–	–
Tennessee	15	–	15	–	–	–
Missouri	–	4	–	4	–	–
Arkansas	–	3	–	3	–	–
Ohio	21	–	21	–	–	–
Indiana	9	–	9	–	–	–
Illinois	–	5	–	5	–	–
Michigan	3	–	3	–	–	–
Totals	234	60	234	48	11	1

XVI.

THE FIRST "DARK HORSE."

The canvass for the election of 1844 may be said to have begun before Harrison was inaugurated as President on the 4th of March, 1841. The Democrats, disgusted as well as angry at the success of the Whigs, ascribing it in one breath to fraud and in the next to the momentary madness of the people, were resolved to bring forward Mr. Van Buren again, and to elect him. The spirit of the party at that time is illustrated by an incident. A St. Louis paper placed Mr. Van Buren's name at the head of its columns as a candidate in 1844, and "nailed its colors to the mast," almost as soon as the result of the election of 1840 was known. Thereupon Senator Benton wrote a letter of commendation to the editor, saying that the Democratic party had won a victory twice before, after its only two national defeats, by adopting at once the candidate in whose person it had suffered a reverse. Mr. Benton, it is true, had been an ardent admirer and unwavering follower of Jackson, and had transferred his allegiance in all its fervor to Jackson's political heir; but, as subsequent events indicated, an overwhelming majority of the party took the same view of political policy and duty during the next three years.

The Whigs were doomed to a sad disappointment. One month after General Harrison took the oath of office he died, and John Tyler became President. Congress was summoned in extra session on the 31st of May, 1841. Among the first subjects to which the attention of Congress was called by the President was the question what should be substituted for the sub-treasury system,—a financial device which had certainly been condemned by the popular voice in the then recent elections. It would be profitless, if this were the place for such a discussion, to consider whether Mr. Tyler gave the Whigs to understand that he would sign *some* bill creating a bank, or not. What is certain is that the Whigs thought he gave them such an assurance; but when a bill which they supposed to have been drawn in accordance with his views was presented to him for approval he vetoed it, and the Whig majority was not strong enough to pass it over the veto. A second bill was prepared, after a conference with the President, submitted to him after it was drafted and approved, and then passed without the alteration of a word. The President, possibly in a fit of very natural anger at a letter written by John M. Botts, a leading Whig member from Virginia, which was published by a breach of confidence, in which Mr. Botts spoke of Mr. Tyler's " turns and twists " with contempt, vetoed that also.

It is needless to say that this act was received with uncontrollable indignation by the Whigs throughout the country. All the members of the cabinet except Mr. Webster, the Secretary of State, who retained office for reasons which were approved by the Whigs, resigned. A caucus of members of the Senate and House of Representatives adopted an address in which they announced that all political alliance between them and John Tyler was at an end, and that henceforth "those who brought the President into power can no longer, in any manner or degree, be justly held responsible or blamed for the administration of the executive branch of the government." It is matter of history that Mr. Tyler continued to the end of his term to be what his early acts as President had in-

dicated that he would be. It may be said that he was
what his whole political life had indicated that he would
be. The only inconsistency of which he was guilty was
in supposing, honestly no doubt, that he was "a firm and
decided Whig," when he was opposed to a bank, opposed
to a protective tariff, opposed to the distribution of the
proceeds of the public lands, opposed to internal improvements, and devoted to the principle of "strict construction" of the Constitution. The Whigs had not, to be sure,
formally professed different principles from his in resolutions adopted by a national convention; but they were
really unanimous, or substantially so, in holding all the
views from which he dissented.

Whatever part an ambition to be re-elected, not by the
Whigs, but by the Democrats, had in determining Mr.
Tyler's course, he did not gain new political friends when
he lost old ones. The Democrats were glad enough that
the fruits of victory were snatched away from the Whigs;
but, though they took advantage of the opportunity which
chance threw in their way, they made no pretence of taking the President up as their own man. They loved the
sin, but hated the sinner. There were some Democrats
and Democratic papers slightly tinctured with "Tyler-
ism," but they were few and uninfluential. By far the
largest number of the Democrats were zealous and unwavering in their adherence to the fortunes of Mr. Van Buren.
Yet it was not their unanimous sentiment. South Carolina was in favor of Mr. Calhoun, and so was Georgia; and
that gentleman carried his sense of propriety so far that,
in the autumn of 1843, he declined an invitation to visit
Ohio in a semi-public way, on the ground that he ought
not to do so while his name was before the country as a
candidate for its highest office. Colonel R. M. Johnson,
then lately Vice-President, was also advocated by the anti-

Benton men of Missouri, as well as by partisans in his own State of Kentucky. He had no such scruples as restrained Mr. Calhoun, and made a tour through the North, as far as Boston, in the course of which, if he was not belied, he assured the people that nothing could prevent the election of Mr. Clay in 1844 but his own candidacy. His belief in himself is shown by a letter written early in January, 1844, wherein he said that he had worn a certain " red vest " " when called upon to respond to my third unanimous nomination for the presidency by the annual convention of my native State." His friends always spoke of him as " the old hero " and " old Tecumseh." His willingness to be before the people was further exemplified in a letter, written in answer to an inquiry, in which he said plainly that he would accept the second place on the ticket if he did not get the first. The claims of General Lewis Cass were also urged by some of those who did not think the nomination of Mr. Van Buren advisable. Finally, in Pennsylvania, Mr. James Buchanan was brought forward as a " favorite son."

In point of fact, while a most decided preference was shown for Mr. Van Buren before any and all others, those who opposed him were bitter and violent. They declared that he could not be elected, and that it would be suicide for the party to nominate him. When the question of a convention was under discussion, South Carolina refused to send delegates, and a hot debate arose over the two questions, whether delegates should be chosen by districts or by general ticket, and whether Virginia (which was for Van Buren) should be allowed to enter the convention with her delegation numbering five times the votes she would be allowed to cast.

Such was the situation late in 1843. The Democrats seemed to be, and were, in hopeless discord ; and the Whigs

counted upon an easy victory, for they were absolutely
united in supporting Mr. Clay, while the alleged treachery
of Mr. Tyler had given them what was better, political
union. The next succeeding events seemed to work in
their favor, for they were as confident of their ability to
beat Mr. Van Buren as were that gentleman's enemies in
his own party that they would beat him. Mr. Buchanan
formally withdrew. his name in December, 1843; and in
the following month Mr. Calhoun published a letter which
was at first taken as a withdrawal, but which was afterwards
seen to be only a refusal to allow his name to go before
the convention. His friends were thus left free to give
him their independent support if they would. Meanwhile State after State convention instructed its delegates
to vote for Mr. Van Buren, and his nomination seemed to
be inevitable. A clear majority of all the delegates could
be counted for him beyond a question, and it was not
doubted that he would receive the necessary two thirds.

But the situation was changed as if by magic. The
question of the annexation of Texas loomed up suddenly.
An overture by Texas for absorption had been once rejected, years before; a suggestion from the government
of the United States that annexation might be acceptable,
some time later, had come to nothing; and now Mr. Tyler
thrust the matter again before the people, by submitting
to the Senate a treaty with Texas, providing for its annexation to the United States. "*Re*-annexation" was the
cry. Texas had been exchanged for Florida, in a negotiation with Spain; it had, in common with Mexico, of
which it formed a part, been separated from Spain; it
had been colonized by filibusters from the United States,
and declared and conquered its independence, in a war
with Mexico; and was now a republic by itself. But
Mexico had only suspended, not ceased, its efforts to

reconquer Texas, and had not acknowledged the independence of the republic. To annex it, therefore, was to assume the obligation of a war with Mexico, or to overawe her weakness by our own strength.

The sentiment of the South was very strong in favor of "immediate re-annexation," for obvious reasons, chief among them being the additional strength which would thereby be acquired for the slavery interest. The question suddenly became a political issue of the first magnitude. Mr. Tyler sent the treaty to the Senate on the 22d of April, 1844, but the fact that such a treaty was under consideration was made public some weeks earlier. At the beginning of May, letters were published from Henry Clay and Martin Van Buren, in which these two gentlemen, almost universally regarded as the two prospective rivals for the presidency, answered inquiries as to their views on the Texas question, at length. Singularly enough their views were similar in this: that they both foresaw that annexation meant war with Mexico; that they regarded annexation without the consent of Mexico as dishonorable; and that, consequently, both were opposed to the pending measure. Mr. Clay went further, and expressed grave doubts as to the wisdom of annexation at all, for reasons partly financial (Texas having a debt which must be assumed) and partly political (the strong opposition that existed throughout New England, and the North generally). Mr. Van Buren's letter, perhaps the most courageous act of a public life which was not characterized by great courage, and therefore one of the most creditable, cost him the nomination. It was dated April 20, 1844, and made public a week later; and the convention met at Baltimore on May 27. The time was short, but it was long enough to defeat him. The editor of the Richmond "Enquirer," who had been as firm and steadfast a Van Buren man as

Senator Benton himself, presided at a meeting intended to bring about a change in the instructions to the Virginia delegates, who had been directed to support Van Buren, and to instruct them to vote for a candidate in favor of immediate annexation. Some delegates from Southern States resigned rather than obey the instructions already given them to vote for Van Buren. Others declared that, although so instructed, they knew that the wishes of their constituents would be modified by the disclosure of Mr. Van Buren's opinions, and that they should support another candidate.

The story of the convention is interesting enough to be told at length, but its leading incidents are all that can be narrated here. Every State except South Carolina was represented. The number of delegates in attendance was 325, but they cast only 266 votes. Virginia sent 53 men to cast 17 votes; Kentucky, entitled to 12 votes, was represented by 29 delegates; and there were two or three other cases of over-representation. As soon as a temporary president and secretary had taken their places, a motion was made that the rules of the convention of 1832 be adopted for the government of this convention. This meant the two-thirds rule, and nothing else. The motion was opposed, as being premature, and laid aside; but Mr. Saunders of North Carolina, who was the author of the motion, brought it up after every fresh step in the organization, and at last secured its consideration. It was very warmly debated, the Van Buren men mostly opposing the rule, while all the opponents of that gentleman were in favor of it. At last the vote was taken, at about noon of the second day of the convention, and the rule was adopted by 148 votes against 118. The minority was made up of 104 votes from Northern States, 7 from Missouri, 5 from North Carolina, and 2 from Maryland; the

majority, of 58 from Northern and 90 from Southern
States. In the afternoon of the same day the "balloting," as it was called, — though the voting was *viva voce*,
— was begun. Of the 266 votes Mr. Van Buren had 146,
and all others 120, showing a clear majority of 26 for
him; but 178 — two thirds of all — were necessary to a
choice. Had all the delegates voted as they were instructed, Mr. Van Buren would have lacked less than ten
votes of a nomination on the first ballot. As it was, he
was defeated by the uncompromising opposition of the
Southern minority. He received but 12 of the 105 votes
to which the Southern States were entitled, while the
North gave him 134 votes out of its total of 151. Seven
trials took place, one after the other, resulting as follows : —

	1st.	2d.	3d.	4th.	5th.	6th.	7th.
M. Van Buren, N. Y . .	146	127	121	111	103	101	99
L. Cass, Mich.	83	94	92	105	107	116	123
R. M. Johnson, Ky. . .	24	33	38	32	29	23	21
J. Buchanan, Pa. . . .	4	9	11	17	26	25	22
L. Woodbury, N. H. . .	2	1	2	–	–	–	–
Com. Stewart, Pa. . . .	1	1	–	–	–	–	–
J. C. Calhoun, S. C. . .	6	1	2	–	–	–	–

At this point an Ohio delegate moved a resolution that
Martin Van Buren, having received a majority of votes on
the first ballot, be declared the candidate. It was ruled
that this would require a two-thirds vote, as rescinding an
order of the convention. An angry and confused debate
took place over the point of parliamentary law, but an
appeal from the decision of the chair was withdrawn, and
the eighth vote was taken. It resulted : For Van Buren,
104; for Cass, 114; for James K. Polk, 44. These latter
were all the votes of Tennessee, Alabama, and New

Hampshire, 7 from Massachusetts, and 7 scattering votes. The ninth ballot was taken amid a scene which has been repeated many times since that day in national conventions, — it was a " stampede." Delegation after delegation changed its vote, and, when the result was announced, James K. Polk of Tennessee had every vote, and was nominated. A scene of wild confusion ensued. A despatch was sent by telegraph to Washington, — the first line built in the country had not long before been opened between the two cities, — and a congratulatory reply was received from the Democratic members of Congress twenty minutes after the nomination.

At the afternoon session the convention voted for a candidate for Vice-President, and Silas Wright, then a senator from New York, was nominated, almost unanimously, by 256 votes. Eight members of the Georgia delegation alone did not vote for him, but supported Levi Woodbury of New Hampshire. Mr. Wright declined the nomination peremptorily; and, although requested to reconsider, and waited upon by a committee of the convention that night, he persisted in his determination. Accordingly the next morning the convention proceeded to vote again for a candidate. On the first trial Governor John Fairfield of Maine had 107 votes; Levi Woodbury of New Hampshire, 44; Lewis Cass of Michigan, 39; R. M. Johnson of Kentucky, 26; Commodore Stewart of Pennsylvania, 23; George M. Dallas of Pennsylvania, 13; William L. Marcy of New York, 5. An inquiry was made whether Governor Fairfield was in favor of annexation, but the question could not be answered authoritatively, and he was dropped. But Silas Wright, whom the convention had already nominated, held views similar to those of Mr. Van Buren, and it was probably partly for that reason that he would not accept the nomination. On the second vote George M. Dallas had 220 votes; Governor Fairfield, 30; Mr. Woodbury, 6; and Mr. Dallas was nominated. At the beginning of the morning session the following resolutions, the platform of the party, had been reported and adopted. In most of our political text-books the platform appears in a mutilated form, and does not contain the sarcastic allusion to the canvass of 1840 : —

Resolved, That the American Democracy place their trust, not in factitious symbols, not in displays and appeals insulting to the judgment and subversive of the intellect of the people, but in a clear reliance upon the intelligence, patriotism, and the discriminating justice of the American people.

Resolved, That we regard this as a distinctive feature of our political creed, which we are proud to maintain before the world, as the great moral element in a form of government springing from and upheld by the popular will; and we contrast it with the creed and practice of Federalism, under whatever name or form, which seeks to palsy the will of the constituent, and which conceives no imposture too monstrous for the popular credulity.

Resolved, Therefore, that, entertaining these views, the Democratic party of this Union, through the delegates assembled in general convention of the States, coming together in a spirit of concord, of devotion to the doctrines and faith of a free representative government, and appealing to their fellow-citizens for the rectitude of their intentions, renew and reassert before the American people the declaration of principles avowed by them on a former occasion, when, in general convention, they presented their candidates for the popular suffrage.

[Here follow all the resolutions adopted by the convention of 1840, see p. 133.]

Resolved, That the proceeds of the public lands ought to be sacredly applied to the national objects specified in the Constitution; and that we are opposed to the laws lately adopted, and to any law, for the distribution of such proceeds among the States, as alike inexpedient in policy and repugnant to the Constitution.

Resolved, That we are decidedly opposed to taking from the President the qualified veto power by which he is enabled, under restrictions and responsibilities amply sufficient to guard the public interest, to suspend the passage of a bill, whose merits cannot secure the approval of two thirds of the Senate and House of Representatives, until the judgment of the people can be obtained thereon, and which has thrice saved the American people from the corrupt and tyrannical domination of the Bank of the United States.

Resolved, That our title to the whole of the territory of Oregon is clear and unquestionable; that no portion of the same ought to be ceded to England or any other power; and that the re-occupation of Oregon and the re-annexation of Texas at the earliest practicable period are great American measures, which this convention recommends to the cordial support of the Democracy of the Union.

After a formal resolution naming Polk and Dallas as the party candidates, the platform concludes with the following resolution : —

Resolved, That this convention hold in the highest estimation and regard their illustrious fellow-citizen, Martin Van Buren of New York; that we cherish the most grateful and abiding sense of the ability, integrity, and firmness with which he discharged the duties of the high office of President of the United States, and especially of the inflexible fidelity with which he maintained the true doctrines of the Constitution and the measures of the Democratic party during his trying and nobly arduous administration; that in the memorable struggle of 1840 he fell a martyr to the great principles of which he was the worthy representative, and we revere him as such; and that we hereby tender to him, in honorable retirement, the assurance of the deeply seated confidence, affection, and respect of the American Democracy.

In order to present the events of the opening of the Democratic canvass without a break, chronological order has been somewhat disregarded. Two conventions had already been held when that of the Democrats met. The Abolitionists had assembled at Buffalo at the end of August, 1843, and had nominated James G. Birney of New York for President, and Thomas Morris of Ohio for

Vice-President. This action was to have a most important effect upon the ensuing canvass, unworthy of notice as the convention seemed. Only one hundred and forty-eight delegates were present, from twelve States. It adopted the following portentously long platform: —

Resolved, That human brotherhood is a cardinal principle of true democracy, as well as of pure Christianity, which spurns all inconsistent limitations; and neither the political party which repudiates it, nor the political system which is not based upon it, can be truly democratic or permanent.

Resolved, That the Liberty Party, placing itself upon this broad principle, will demand the absolute and unqualified divorce of the general government from slavery, and also the restoration of equality of rights among men, in every State where the party exists or may exist.

Resolved, That the Liberty Party has not been organized for any temporary purpose by interested politicians, but has arisen from among the people in consequence of a conviction, hourly gaining ground, that no other party in the country represents the true principles of American liberty, or the true spirit of the Constitution of the United States.

Resolved, That the Liberty Party has not been organized merely for the overthrow of slavery. Its first decided effort must indeed be directed against slaveholding as the grossest and most revolting manifestation of despotism, but it will also carry out the principle of equal rights into all its practical consequences and applications, and support every just measure conducive to individual and social freedom.

Resolved, That the Liberty Party is not a sectional party, but a national party; was not originated in a desire to accomplish a single object, but in a comprehensive regard to the great interests of the whole country; is not a new party nor a third party, but is the party of 1776, reviving the principles of that memorable era, and striving to carry them into practical application.

Resolved, That it was understood in the times of the Declaration and the Constitution that the existence of slavery in some of the States was in derogation of the principles of American liberty, and a deep stain upon the character of the country and the implied faith of the States; and the nation was pledged that slavery should never be extended beyond its then existing limits, but should be gradually, and yet at no distant day, wholly abolished by State authority.

Resolved, That the faith of the States and the nation - thus pledged was most nobly redeemed by the voluntary abolition of slavery in several of the States, and by the adoption of the ordinance of 1787 for the government of the Territory northwest of the River Ohio, then the only Territory in the United States, and consequently the only Territory subject in this respect to the control of Congress, by which ordinance slavery was forever excluded from the vast regions which now compose the States of Ohio, Indiana, Illinois, Michigan, and the Territory of Wisconsin, and an incapacity to bear up any other than free men was impressed on the soil itself.

Resolved, That the faith of the States and nation thus pledged has been shamefully violated by the omission on the part of many of the States to take any measures whatever for the abolition of slavery within their respective limits; by the continuance of slavery in the District of Columbia, and in the Territories of Louisiana and Florida; by the legislation of Congress; by the protection afforded by national legislation and negotiation to slaveholding in American vessels, on the high seas, employed in the coastwise slave traffic; and by the extension of slavery far beyond its original limits, by acts of Congress admitting new slave States into the Union.

Resolved, That the fundamental truth of the Declaration of Independence, that all men are endowed by their Creator with certain unalienable rights, among which are life, liberty, and the pursuit of happiness, was made the fundamental law of our national government, by that amendment of the Constitution which declares that no person shall be deprived of life, liberty, or property without due process of law.

Resolved, That we recognize as sound the doctrine maintained by slaveholding jurists, that slavery is against natural rights and strictly local, and that its existence and continuance rest on no other support than State legislation, and not on any authority of Congress.

Resolved, That the general government has, under the Constitution, no power to establish or continue slavery anywhere, and therefore that all treaties and acts of Congress establishing, continuing, or favoring slavery in the District of Columbia, in the Territory of

Florida, or on the high seas, are unconstitutional, and all attempts to hold men as property within the limits of exclusive national jurisdiction ought to be prohibited by law.

Resolved, That the provisions of the Constitution of the United States, which confers extraordinary political powers on the owners of slaves, and thereby constituting the two hundred and fifty thousand slaveholders in the slave States a privileged aristocracy; and the provision for the reclamation of fugitive slaves from service, are anti-republican in their character, dangerous to the liberties of the people, and ought to be abrogated.

Resolved, That the practical operation of the second of these provisions is seen in the enactment of the Act of Congress respecting persons escaping from their masters, which act, if the construction given to it by the Supreme Court of the United States in the case of Prigg *v.* Pennsylvania be correct, nullifies the *habeas corpus* acts of all the States, takes away the whole legal security of personal freedom, and ought therefore to be immediately repealed.

Resolved, That the peculiar patronage and support hitherto extended to slavery and slaveholding by the general government ought to be immediately withdrawn, and the example and influence of national authority ought to be arrayed on the side of liberty and free labor.

Resolved, That the practice of the general government, which prevails in the slave States, of employing slaves upon the public works, instead of free laborers, and paying aristocratic masters, with a view to secure or reward political services, is utterly indefensible and ought to be abandoned.

Resolved, That the freedom of speech and of the press, and the right of petition and the right of trial by jury, are sacred and inviolable; and that all rules, regulations, and laws in derogation of either are oppressive, unconstitutional, and not to be endured by free people.

Resolved, That we regard voting, in an eminent degree, as a moral and religious duty, which, when exercised, should be by voting for those who will do all in their power for immediate emancipation.

Resolved, That this convention recommend to the friends of liberty in all those free States where any inequality of rights and privileges exists on account of color, to employ their utmost energies to remove all such remnants and effects of the slave system.

Whereas, The Constitution of these United States is a series of agreements, covenants, or contracts between the people of the United States, each with all and all with each; and

Whereas, It is a principle of universal morality, that the moral laws of the Creator are paramount to all human laws; or, in the language of an Apostle, that "we ought to obey God rather than men;" and

Whereas, The principle of common law, that any contract, covenant, or agreement to do an act derogatory to natural rights is vitiated and annulled by its inherent immorality, has been recognized by one of the Justices of the Supreme Court of the United States, who in a recent case expressly holds that any "contract that rests upon such a basis is void;" and

Whereas, The third clause of the second section of the fourth article of the Constitution of the United States, when construed as providing for the surrender of a fugitive slave, does "rest upon such a basis," in that it is a contract to rob a man of a natural right, namely, his natural right to his own liberty, and is, therefore, absolutely void; therefore,

Resolved, That we hereby give it to be distinctly understood by this nation and the world, that, as abolitionists, considering that the strength of our cause lies in its righteousness, and our hope for it in our conformity to the laws of God and our respect for the rights of man, we owe it to the Sovereign Ruler of the universe, as a proof of our allegiance to him, in all our civil relations and offices, whether as private citizens or as public functionaries sworn to support the Constitution of the United States, to regard and to treat the third clause of the fourth article of that instrument, whenever applied to the case of a fugitive slave, as utterly null and void, and consequently as forming no part of the Constitution of the United States, whenever we are called upon or sworn to support it.

Resolved, That the power given to Congress by the Constitution, to provide for calling out the militia to suppress insurrection, does not make it the duty of the government to maintain slavery by military force, much less does it make it the duty of the citizens to form a part of such military force. When freemen unsheath the sword it should be to strike for liberty, not for despotism.

Resolved, That to preserve the peace of the citizens and secure the blessings of freedom, the legislature of each of the free States ought to keep in force suitable statutes rendering it penal for any of its inhabitants to transport, or aid in transporting from such State, any person sought to be thus transported merely because subject to the slave laws of any other State; this remnant of independence being accorded to the free States by the decision of the Supreme Court in the case of Prigg *v.* the State of Pennsylvania.

The Whigs, as has been said already, were enthusiastic and completely united in the support of Mr. Clay. No other candidate was mentioned or thought of in connection with the nomination. The convention was held in Baltimore on the 1st of May, 1844. Every State in the Union was fully represented. The whole business which occasioned the meeting was completed in a single sitting. Mr. Clay was nominated by acclamation, unanimously. Three ballots were taken for a candidate for Vice-President. On the first, Theodore Frelinghuysen of New Jersey had 101 : John Davis of Massachusetts, 83 ; Millard Fillmore of New York, 53, and John Sergeant of Pennsylvania, 38. Mr. Frelinghuysen gained on every ballot, and on the fourth received 155, against 116 for Fillmore and Davis combined. After numerous speeches had been made, in which the candidates were most highly commended, and the triumph of the party was confidently predicted, Mr. Reverdy Johnson of Maryland moved the following series of resolutions, which were adopted : —

Resolved, That, in presenting to the country the names of Henry Clay for President, and of Theodore Frelinghuysen for Vice-President of the United States, this convention is actuated by the conviction that all the great principles of the Whig party — principles inseparable from the public honor and prosperity — will be maintained and advanced by these candidates.

Resolved, That these principles may be summed as comprising : A well-regulated currency; a tariff for revenue to defray the necessary expenses of the government, and discriminating with special reference to the protection of the domestic labor of the country; the distribution of the proceeds from the sales of the public lands; a single term for the presidency; a reform of executive usurpations; and generally such an administration of the affairs of the country as shall impart to every branch of the public service the greatest practical efficiency, controlled by a well-regulated and wise economy.

Resolved, That the name of Henry Clay needs no eulogy. The history of the country since his first appearance in public life is his history. Its brightest pages of prosperity and success are identified with the principles which he has upheld, as its darkest and more disastrous pages are with every material departure in our public policy from those principles.

Resolved, That in Theodore Frelinghuysen we present a man pledged alike by his Revolutionary ancestry and his own public course to every measure calculated to sustain the honor and interest of the country. Inheriting the principles as well as the name of a father who, with Washington, on the fields of Trenton and of Monmouth, perilled life in the contest for liberty, and afterwards, as a senator of the United States, acted with Washington in establishing and perpetuating that liberty, Theodore Frelinghuysen, by his course as attorney-general of the State of New Jersey for twelve years, and subsequently as a senator of the United States for several years, was always strenuous on the side of law, order, and the Constitution, while, as a private man, his head, his hand, and his heart have been given without stint to the cause of morals, education, philanthropy, and religion.

The second only of these resolutions is printed in the political text-books, and always with a faulty punctuation, — the omission of a colon after the first phrase, — which makes nonsense of the whole resolution. The first resolution of the series is essential even to an understanding of the second, which stated the principles of the Whig party.

Although Mr. Tyler had not been mentioned as a candidate in the Democratic convention, he had his friends, — chiefly officeholders, it was said, by both Whigs and Democrats, — who held a convention, also in Baltimore, on the same day that the Democrats met there. It was a mass convention, rather than one of elected delegates. Mr. Tyler was unanimously nominated for the presidency, and accepted the nomination; but the movement fell dead, and Mr. Tyler withdrew his candidacy in a long, argumentative, and somewhat bitter letter, dated on the 20th of August.

The canvass which followed these nominations was to some extent a repetition of the campaign of 1840, with

the difference that there were shouting and enthusiasm on
both sides. Mr. Clay was undoubtedly the most popular
man in the United States at the time, but personal popularity did not decide the issue. The Democrats were
very much in earnest, both about the election and about
Texas. Mr. Polk was a comparatively unknown man,
although he had served as Speaker of the House of
Representatives. He therefore excited no antagonisms.
He was particularly acceptable to the South, and the
Northern Democrats had nothing against him. It was
believed and asserted that the movement in. his favor
in the convention had not been as spontaneous as its man-
agers wished people to suppose, but that the matter had
been carefully canvassed beforehand, and that the plan,
as carried out, was laid some time before at Nashville.
While, therefore, the Whigs carried on an enthusiastic
canvass, there were not wanting signs that a majority of
the people were still Democratic, and that the reverse of
1840 was really but a brief and half-thoughtless revulsion
against certain abuses which had crept in, which the people did not like at the time, but to which they have since
reconciled themselves most bravely. The early elections
gave indications here and there of a slight Whig gain
from the result in 1842, when the Democrats had been
again successful in carrying a majority of Congress; but
these were partially offset by Democratic gains, and were
nowhere great enough to give the Whigs good ground for
hope of success in November. Yet they continued to
hope and to fight to the last.

The number of States voting was twenty-six, as before;
but owing to the new apportionment, by which the number of representatives was cut down from 242 to 223, the
number of electors was reduced to 275. The popular
vote and the electoral vote are included in the same table,

inasmuch as all the electors who voted for Polk voted also for Dallas, and all who were for Clay also supported Frelinghuysen.

STATES.	POPULAR VOTE.			ELECTORS.	
	James K. Polk, Tenn.	Henry Clay, Ky.	James G. Birney, N. Y.	Polk.	Clay.
Maine	45,719	34,378	4,836	9	–
New Hampshire .	27,160	17,866	4,161	6	–
Vermont . . .	18,041	26,770	3,954	–	6
Massachusetts . .	52,846	67,418	10,860	–	12
Rhode Island . .	4,867	7,322	107	–	4
Connecticut . .	29,841	32,832	1,943	–	6
New York . . .	237,588	232,482	15,812	36	–
New Jersey . . .	37,495	38,318	131	–	7
Pennsylvania . .	167,535	161,203	3,138	26	–
Delaware . . .	5,996	6,278	–	–	3
Maryland . . .	32,676	35,984	–	–	8
Virginia	49,570	43,677	–	17	–
North Carolina .	39,287	43,232	–	–	11
South Carolina * .	–	–	–	9	–
Georgia	44,177	42,100	–	10	–
Alabama . . .	37,740	26,084	–	9	–
Mississippi . . .	25,126	19,206	–	6	–
Louisiana . . .	13,782	13,083	–	6	–
Kentucky . . .	51,988	61,255	–	–	12
Tennessee . . .	59,917	60,030	–	–	13
Missouri	41,369	31,251	–	7	–
Arkansas . . .	9,546	5,504	–	3	–
Ohio	149,117	155,057	8,050	–	23
Michigan . . .	27,759	24,337	3,632	5	–
Indiana	70,181	67,867	2,106	12	–
Illinois	57,920	45,528	3,570	9	–
Totals . . .	1,337,243	1,299,062	62,300	170	105

* By Legislature.

There were some very peculiar facts in connection with this election. The first was the magnitude of the electoral as compared with the popular majority. Polk had but 38,181 over Clay, and yet he received a majority of 65 in the votes of electors. Had the Abolitionists voted for Clay he would have had a popular majority of 24,119; he would have received the electoral votes of New York, 36, and Michigan, 5; and he would have been elected by 146 electoral votes against 129 for Mr. Polk. No doubt the Abolitionists acted with entire consistency in refusing to vote for Henry Clay, and no doubt it is as impossible to tell what might have happened if Clay had been elected, as it would be to guess what would have been the course of history if Van Buren had not written his Texas letter; but at all events the election of Clay would have postponed the annexation of Texas, and possibly it would have averted the Mexican war.

Another noteworthy incident of the election was what was known as the Plaquemines fraud. It will be noticed in the above table that the Polk majority in Louisiana is 699. The parish of Plaquemines, below New Orleans on the Mississippi, had voted in previous years, and was returned as voting in 1844, as follows: —

	Democrat.	Whig.
Election of 1840	250	40
Election of 1842	179	93
Election of 1843	310	36
Election of 1844	1,007	87

The Democratic gain over the best previous year was 697, almost exactly the whole Democratic majority in the State. The vote was suspicious in this: that the Democratic vote returned was greater in number than the entire white male population, of all ages, in the parish in 1840. The explanation that was given by the Whigs was that the steamboat "Agnes" went down from New Orleans with a load of passengers under the charge of a political magnate of Plaquemines, and that these passengers stopped at three different places and cast each time a unanimous vote for Polk and Dallas. The steamboat "Planter" took down one hundred and forty others, who also voted early and often for the same ticket. These assertions were not only made, but sworn to, by many witnesses, including some persons, one of them a minor, who voted several times each under the direction of the learned judge who managed the affair. The story bears all the marks of truth. If it is not true, it is at least singular that it was ten years after 1844 before Plaquemines parish could muster half as many Democratic votes as she gave that year to Polk.

Though the Whig newspapers rang with the charges of fraud, and though the accusation was supported by strong testimony, nothing was done about it. The election was lost, and a rectification of the fraud would not have changed the result. The Whigs quietly submitted, and when the electoral count took place in 1845, in the usual manner, no objection whatever was made, and Polk and Dallas were declared elected in due form.

XVII.

THE SECOND WHIG VICTORY.

THE administration of Mr. Polk was Democratic enough to please the most exacting of his partisans. Its leading events were the annexation of Texas in accordance with the joint resolution approved by Mr. Tyler three days before the close of his term; the Mexican war which that act naturally and, indeed, inevitably, provoked; the settlement of the Oregon question, — not on the line of 54° 40', which the Democrats had claimed as the true boundary; but on that of 49°; the re-establishment of the sub-treasury; and the tariff of 1846. On every one of these questions the Whigs were at issue with the dominant party. They knew that the annexation of Texas would lead to war, unless Mexico should feel too weak to resist the United States, and they opposed it on that account. They denounced Mr. Polk's instructions to General Taylor as calculated to goad Mexico to war, as indeed they did. They jeered at the President for having first transformed the claim of "the whole of Oregon" from a national into a party question, and then for having mildly accepted the proffered terms of Great Britain, which gave the United States only a part of what had been claimed. The sub-treasury and the tariff questions were old ones, and the Whigs were united in their opposition to the Democratic measures.

But meanwhile the question of slavery in the Territories was assuming large importance. The Abolitionists proper formed but a small body, but those who were hostile to the extension of slavery were very numerous. A vast majority of the Northern Whigs were against such extension, together with a very important body of Northern Democrats; but in neither party did the politicians have the courage to break with the pro-slavery section. Up to this time the Whigs had never mentioned the subject of slavery in their resolutions; and the opponents of extension, bravely as they might talk at home, did not venture to propose that it be made a party question. The Democrats had confined their declarations on the subject of slavery to an assertion of the right of States to regulate their domestic institutions.

It was partly due to accident that the question of slavery played so large a part as it did in the election of 1848. There had never been a time when there were not two factions of the New York Democrats. Silas Wright, at that time a senator from New York, was nominated for Vice-President on the ticket with Mr. Polk. As a friend of Mr. Van Buren, and as an opponent of annexation, he declined. But the reunion which took place after the convention brought him forward as a candidate for governor of New York the same year. He received a much larger majority than was given to Mr. Polk. The two factions fell apart again after the election; and when, in 1846, Mr. Wright was again a candidate for governor, he was defeated. His friends and followers believed that he was "slaughtered," and they ascribed his defeat not only to the secret opposition of the "Hunkers,"— so called because their opponents said they *hunkered* for office,— but to the machinations of the Administration. They gave as a reason for the hostility of Mr. Polk to him, an unreasonable jealousy, carefully fostered by the opponents of Mr. Wright, based upon the fact that the election of 1844 showed the governor to be more popular in New York than was the

President. Mr. Wright died suddenly in August, 1847; but his death, instead of ending the quarrel between the factions, served to aggravate it. Not all of Mr. Wright's followers were with him at the outset on the slavery question, but the most of them were; and the two factions finally divided on this issue. The anti-slavery wing were known as "Barn-burners," in allusion to the story of the Dutchman who burned his barn to clear it of the rats and mice.

The "Wilmot proviso," so called from its author, David Wilmot, a Democratic member of the House of Representatives from Pennsylvania, by which slavery was not to exist in any territory thereafter acquired by the United States, became the issue in numerous contests, and a question upon which the Democratic party was for the time hopelessly divided; and it was due to this division that the Democrats entered the canvass of 1848, which they were destined to lose, with so little spirit. Success was impossible without New York, and the split in that State was one which could not be healed.

Meanwhile all was not union and harmony in the Whig ranks. Henry Clay was still the most popular man in the party; but there was gradually springing up a feeling that, after his repeated defeats, and in the face of the uncompromising objections to him in anti-slavery quarters in the North, he could not be elected. At the same time there were those who thought that he should not have a permanent mortgage on the Whig party. Mr. Webster had strong friends and supporters to urge his pretensions. Judge M'Lean, General Scott, Mr. Clayton of Delaware, and Thomas Corwin of Ohio, were also put forward. But the movement in favor of General Taylor gradually overwhelmed all the other candidates. To make him a candidate would be to snatch the fruits of the Mexican victory from the Democrats without becoming responsible for the war. There was no assurance that General Taylor was a Whig when the movement began, nor did he say anything more definite, publicly at least, before his nomination, than that, although he had never voted, he should have supported Mr. Clay in 1844 if he had voted at all. The gallant general wrote many letters in 1847 and 1848 which proved him to be no politician, and even those who were most active in promoting his candidacy smiled inwardly at his extreme innocence. His nomination and election, as every one could see, would mean little or nothing. But the election of Mr. Clay would mean almost as little, for he was identified with the contests over questions which had been decided. Texas had been annexed; the sub-treasury was re-established; the tariff of 1846, though soon to develop its defects, was working well; the Oregon question was settled; and on the new issue then becoming prominent, Mr. Clay could not be acceptable to the "conscience Whigs." All these considerations, each in its own way, and others which have not been mentioned, worked in favor of the Taylor movement; and his nomination was certain before the Whig convention met.

The first convention preliminary to the canvass of 1848 was that of the Native Americans, — a party which had already been in existence locally, and which for some years past had elected a few representatives in Congress from New York and Pennsylvania. The national convention met in Philadelphia in September, 1847, and nominated General Henry A. S. Dearborn of Massachusetts for Vice-President. It recommended, but did not formally nominate, General Zachary Taylor for President.

In November of the same year the Liberty, or Abolition, party met at New York, and nominated for President John P. Hale of New Hampshire, and for Vice-President Leicester King of Ohio. After the Barn-burners' convention, hereafter to be noticed, Mr. Hale withdrew from the canvass. It was given out at the time that Mr. Van Buren was a good enough Abolitionist for this party, though he "could not be regarded as a perfect embodiment of their principles." The "Liberty League," another Abolition body, held a convention at Rochester, N. Y., on the 2d of June, 1848, and nominated Gerritt Smith of New York for President and the Rev. Charles E. Foote of Michigan for Vice-President. An "Industrial Congress" met at Philadelphia, June 13, 1848, and nominated Gerritt Smith for the first place and William S. Waitt of Illinois for the second place on the ticket. So far as is known, no votes were cast for either of these minor candidates, in any State.

The Democrats assembled in convention at Baltimore, on May 22, 1848. All the States were represented, most of them fully, some of them by two or three times as many delegates as they were entitled to votes. Virginia alone sent seventy delegates to cast seventeen votes. New York presented two full sets of delegates,— one of thirty-six "Hunkers," the other of as many "Barn-burners." It would require too much space to narrate the progress of the faction fight, although all the proceedings of the convention turned on the question of the New York delegation, and although that quarrel alone was enough to determine the result of the ensuing election. But any other course than that which was taken must have led to the same result, for each delegation claimed full recognition as the representatives of the New York Democrats, and would be satisfied with nothing less.

The wrangling began as soon as the opening prayer had been offered — over the constitution of the committee on

credentials. Nothing was done the first day beyond set-
tling the membership of the convention, except as it regarded the New York delegation, and effecting a permanent organization, with Mr. Andrew Stevenson of Virginia
as president. On the morning of the second day the two-
thirds rule was adopted, after long debate, by 175 votes
against 78. From that time until the evening of the 24th
of May the convention devoted itself wholly to New York.
On a resolution to admit the "Hunker" delegation, an
amendment was offered to admit both delegations, the two
combined to have only the vote to which New York was
entitled. This was carried by two majority,— 126 to 124.
Of the affirmative votes, 99 came from Northern States,
and the other 27 from Maryland, Delaware, Kentucky,
Tennessee, Missouri, and Texas. The North gave only
33 negative votes. Although this was, so far as it was a
victory for either side, a triumph for the "Barn-burners,"
they refused to take part in the proceedings, as did also
the "Hunkers." The former delegation afterward, at the
same sitting, withdrew from the convention.

As soon as the New York question was decided, balloting for a candidate for President began. Four trials were
necessary, the result of which was as follows:—

	1st.	2d.	3d.	4th.
Whole number	251	252	254	253
Necessary to a choice	168	168	169	169
Lewis Cass, Mich.	125	133	156	179
James Buchanan, Penn.	55	54	40	33
Levi Woodbury, N. H.	53	56	53	38
George M. Dallas, Penn.	3	3	–	–
W. J. Worth, Tenn.	6	6	5	1
John C. Calhoun, S. C.	9	–	–	–
W. O. Butler, Ky.	–	–	–	3

The vote for Mr. Cass at the beginning was almost exclusively from Western and Southern States, but there was little significance in this fact. All the candidates were against the Wilmot Proviso, — they were all classed as "Northern men with Southern principles," — and the preferences of delegates were personal rather than political. The nomination was made unanimous with enthusiasm. In the evening the convention proceeded to vote for a candidate for Vice-President. On the first trial General William O. Butler of Kentucky had 114; General John A. Quitman of Mississippi had 74; John Y. Mason of Virginia, 24; William R. King of Alabama, 25; James J. McKay of North Carolina, 13; Jefferson Davis of Mississippi, 1. As 169 were necessary to a choice, the convention proceeded to vote a second time. General W. O. Butler was nominated, receiving 169 votes, to 62 for Quitman and 22 for all others. This nomination was also made unanimous. On the fifth and last day of the convention, the platform was reported. It was for the most part a repetition of that of 1844. The first resolution was modified to read as follows : —

Resolved, That the American Democracy place their trust in the intelligence, the patriotism, and the discriminating justice of the American people.

Then followed the resolutions adopted in 1840 and 1844, as arranged in the platform of the latter year, except that to the fifth resolution (see p. 133) are appended the words : "And for the gradual, but certain, extinction of the debt created by the prosecution of a just and necessary war, after peaceful relations shall have been restored." The convention also added to this already ample platform the following new resolutions : —

Resolved. That the war with Mexico, provoked on her part by years of insult and injury, was commenced by her army crossing the Rio Grande, attacking the American troops, and invading our sister State of Texas; and that, upon all the principles of patriotism and the laws of nations, it is a just and necessary war upon our part, in which every American citizen should have shown himself on the side of his country, and neither morally nor physically, by word or deed, have given aid and comfort to the enemy.

Resolved, That we should be rejoiced at the assurance of a peace with Mexico, founded on the just principles of indemnity for the past and security for the future; but that, while the ratification of the liberal treaty offered to Mexico remains in doubt, it is the duty of the country to sustain the Administration in every measure necessary to provide for the vigorous prosecution of the war, should that treaty be rejected.

Resolved, That the officers and soldiers who have carried the arms of their country into Mexico have crowned it with imperishable glory. Their unconquerable courage, their daring enterprise, their unfaltering perseverance and fortitude when assailed on all sides by innumerable foes, — and that more formidable enemy, the diseases of the climate, — exalt their devoted patriotism into the highest heroism, and give them a right to the profound gratitude of their country and the admiration of the world.

Resolved, That the Democratic National Convention of thirty States, composing the American Republic, tender their fraternal congratulations to the National Convention of the Republic of France, now assembled as the free suffrage representatives of the sovereignty of thirty-five millions of republicans, to establish governments on those eternal principles of equal rights, for which their Lafayette and our Washington fought side by side in the struggle for our national independence; and we would especially convey to them and to the whole people of France our earnest wishes for the consolidation of their liberties, through the wisdom that shall guide their counsels, on the basis of a democratic constitution, not derived from the grants or concessions of kings or dynasties, but originating from the only true source of political power recognized in the States of this Union: the inherent and inalienable rights of the people, in their sovereign capacity, to make and to amend their forms of government in such a manner as the welfare of the community may require.

Resolved, That with the recent development of this grand political truth, — of the sovereignty of the people and their capacity and power for self-government, which is prostrating thrones and erect-

ing republics on the ruins of despotism in the Old World, — we feel
that a high and sacred duty is devolved, with increased responsibility, upon the Democratic party of this country, as the party of
the people, to sustain and advance among us constitutional liberty,
equality, and fraternity, by continuing to resist all monopolies and
exclusive legislation for the benefit of the few at the expense of
the many; and by a vigilant and constant adherence to those
principles and compromises of the Constitution, which are broad
enough and strong enough to embrace and uphold the Union as it
was, the Union as it is, and the Union as it shall be, in the full
expansion of the energies and capacity of this great and progressive people.

Resolved, That a copy of these resolutions be forwarded, through
the American Minister at Paris, to the National Convention of the
Republic of France.

Resolved, That the fruits of the great political triumph of 1844,
which elected James K. Polk and George M. Dallas President and
Vice-President of the United States, have fulfilled the hopes of the
Democracy of the Union in defeating the declared purposes of their
opponents to create a national bank; in preventing the corrupt
and unconstitutional distribution of the land proceeds, from the
common treasury of the Union, for local purposes; in protecting
the currency and labor of the country from ruinous fluctuations,
and guarding the money of the people for the use of the people;
by the establishment of the constitutional treasury; in the noble
impulse given to the cause of free trade, by the repeal of the tariff
of 1842, and the creation of the more equal, honest, and productive
tariff of 1846; and that, in our opinion, it would be a fatal error to
weaken the hands of a political organization by which these great
reforms have been achieved, and risk them in the hands of their
known adversaries, with whatever delusive appeals they may so-
licit our surrender of that vigilance which is the only safeguard of
liberty.

Resolved, That the confidence of the Democracy of the Union
in the principles, capacity, firmness, and integrity of James K.
Polk, manifested by his nomination and election in 1844, has been
signally justified by the strictness of his adherence to sound Democratic doctrines, by the purity of purpose, the energy and ability
which have characterized his administration in all our affairs at
home and abroad; that we tender to him our cordial congratulations upon the brilliant success which has hitherto crowned his

patriotic efforts, and assure him in advance that, at the expiration of his presidential term, he will carry with him to his retirement the esteem, respect, and admiration of a grateful country.

Resolved, That this convention hereby present to the people of the United States Lewis Cass of Michigan as the candidate of the Democratic party for the office of President, and William O. Butler of Kentucky as the candidate of the Democratic party for Vice-President of the United States.

Mr. Yancey of Alabama offered the following resolution in addition to the platform : —

Resolved, That the doctrine of non-interference with the rights of property of any portion of the people of this confederacy, be it in the States or Territories thereof, by any other than the parties interested in them, is the true republican doctrine, recognized by this body.

The resolution was rejected by a vote of yeas, 36; nays, 216. All the affirmative votes were given by delegates from the Slave States.

The Whig convention met at Philadelphia on the 7th of June, every State except Texas being represented. Ex-Governor John M. Morehead of North Carolina was the permanent president. Nothing beyond the organization was accomplished on the first day. A long and uninteresting contest took place on the following day on questions raised by the over-representation of some States and the under-representation of others; and it was not until evening that the convention reached a vote for a candidate for President. After two votes the convention adjourned until the next day, when two more votes were taken, and on the fourth General Taylor was nominated. The result of the four votes was as follows : —

	1st.	2d.	3d.	4th.
Zachary Taylor, La..	111	118	133	171
Henry Clay, Ky.	97	86	74	32
Winfield Scott, N. J. . . .	43	40	54	63
Daniel Webster, Mass.. . . .	22	22	17	14
John M'Lean, Ohio	2	–	–	–
John M. Clayton, Del.. . . .	4	4	1	–

The vote for General Taylor on the first ballot came
from all parts of the country. There were only eight of
the thirty States then in the Union from which he got
no votes. He received but six votes, however, from New
England, which supported Mr. Webster and Mr. Clay.
On the final vote every State gave him at least one vote.
The convention, after giving itself up for a time to enthusiasm, proceeded to vote for a candidate for Vice-
President. A large number of nominations was made.
On the first ballot, Millard Fillmore of New York had 115;
Abbott Lawrence of Massachusetts, 109; and 51 votes
were divided among ten other candidates. On the second
vote Fillmore had 173; Lawrence, 87; and all others, 6.
Mr. Fillmore's nomination was then declared, and, after a
season of speech-making, the convention adjourned. No
committee on resolutions was appointed, and the convention made no declaration of principles whatever. This
attitude of non-committalism was by no means approved
by a large section of the party; and it was late in the canvass, when some additional letters from General Taylor,
giving assurance that he really sympathized — mildly, at
least — with the purposes of the party, had been published, before some of the prominent Whig leaders came
cordially to his support.

Meanwhile the "Barn-burners," who had withdrawn
from the Baltimore convention, were not acquiescing in

the proceedings or supporting the candidates of that convention. They held a State convention at Utica, N. Y., on June 22 and 23, in which delegates from Massachusetts, Connecticut, Ohio, and Wisconsin participated, and nominated Martin Van Buren for President, and Henry Dodge of Wisconsin for Vice-President. Mr. Van Buren accepted the nomination, though with evident reluctance. Senator Dodge declined, and supported General Cass. Later in the year an Ohio State convention of persons dissatisfied with both the nominations recommended and called a national convention, which was held at Buffalo, August 9. Charles Francis Adams of Massachusetts was made permanent president of the convention, which contained representatives of seventeen States, and seems to have had a membership of about 300. On a ballot for a candidate for President, Martin Van Buren had 159 votes and John P. Hale of New Hampshire 129. Charles Francis Adams of Massachusetts was nominated by acclamation for Vice-President. The convention adopted the following resolutions : —

Whereas, We have assembled in convention, as a union of freemen, for the sake of freedom, forgetting all past political differences, in common resolve to maintain the rights of free labor against the aggressions of the slave power, and to secure free soil for a free. people; and

Whereas, The political conventions recently assembled at Baltimore and Philadelphia, the one stifling the voice of a great constituency, entitled to be heard in its deliberations, and the other abandoning its distinctive principles for mere availability, have dissolved the national party organizations heretofore existing, by nominating for the chief magistracy of the United States, under the slaveholding dictation, candidates, neither of whom can be supported by the opponents of slavery extension, without a sacrifice of consistency, duty, and self-respect; and

Whereas, These nominations so made furnish the occasion and demonstrate the necessity of the union of the people under the ✿

banner of free democracy, in a solemn and formal declaration of their independence of the slave power, and of their fixed determination to rescue the federal government from its control: —

Resolved, Therefore, that we, the people here assembled, remembering the example of our fathers in the days of the first Declaration of Independence, putting our trust in God for the triumph of our cause, and invoking his guidance in our endeavors to advance it, do now plant ourselves upon the national platform of freedom, in opposition to the sectional platform of slavery.

Resolved, That slavery in the several States of this Union which recognize its existence depends upon State laws alone, which cannot be repealed or modified by the federal government, and for which laws that government is not responsible. We therefore propose no interference by Congress with slavery within the limits of any State.

Resolved, That the proviso of Jefferson, to prohibit the existence of slavery after 1800 in all the Territories of the United States, southern and northern; the votes of six States and sixteen delegates, in the Congress of 1784 for the proviso, to three States and seven delegates against it; the actual exclusion of slavery from the Northwestern Territory by the ordinance of 1787, unanimously adopted by the States in Congress; and the entire history of that period, — clearly show that it was the settled policy of the nation not to extend, nationalize, or encourage, but to limit, localize, and discourage slavery; and to this policy, which should never have been departed from, the government ought to return.

Resolved, That our fathers ordained the Constitution of the United States in order, among other great national objects, to establish justice, promote the general welfare, and secure the blessings of liberty; but expressly denied to the federal government, which they created, all constitutional power to deprive any person of life, liberty, or property, without due legal process.

Resolved, That, in the judgment of this convention, Congress has no more power to make a slave than to make a king; no more power to institute or establish slavery than to institute or establish a monarchy. No such power can be found among those specifically conferred by the Constitution, or derived by any just implication from them.

Resolved, That it is the duty of the federal government to relieve itself from all responsibility for the existence or continuance of slavery wherever the government possesses constitutional authority to legislate on that subject, and is thus responsible for its existence.

Resolved, That the true and, in the judgment of this convention the only safe means of preventing the extension of slavery into territory now free is to prohibit its existence in all such territory by an act of Congress.

Resolved, That we accept the issue which the slave power has forced upon us; and to their demand for more slave States and more slave territory, our calm but final answer is, no more slave States and no more slave territory. Let the soil of our extensive domains be ever kept free for the hardy pioneers of our own land, and the oppressed and banished of other lands, seeking homes of comfort and fields of enterprise in the New World.

Resolved, That the bill lately reported by the committee of eight in the Senate of the United States was no compromise, but an absolute surrender of the rights of the non-slaveholders of all the States; and while we rejoice to know that a measure which, while opening the door for the introduction of slavery into territories now free, would also have opened the door to litigation and strife among the future inhabitants thereof, to the ruin of their peace and prosperity, was defeated in the House of Representatives, its passage, in hot haste, by a majority embracing several senators who voted in open violation of the known will of their constituents, should warn the people to see to it that their representatives be not suffered to betray them. There must be no more compromises with slavery; if made, they must be repealed.

Resolved, That we demand freedom and established institutions for our brethren in Oregon, now exposed to hardships, peril, and massacre by the reckless hostility of the slave power to the establishment of free government for free territory, and not only for them, but for our new brethren in New Mexico and California.

And whereas, It is due not only to this occasion, but to the whole people of the United States, that we should declare ourselves on certain other questions of national policy: therefore,

Resolved, That we demand cheap postage for the people; a retrenchment of the expenses and patronage of the federal government; the abolition of all unnecessary offices and salaries; and the election by the people of all civil officers in the service of the government, so far as the same may be practicable.

Resolved, That river and harbor improvements, whenever demanded by the safety and convenience of commerce with foreign nations, or among the several States, are objects of national concern; and that it is the duty of Congress, in the exercise of its constitutional powers, to provide therefor.

Resolved, That the free grant to actual settlers, in consideration of the expenses they incur in making settlements in the wilderness, which are usually fully equal to their actual cost, and of the public benefits resulting therefrom, of reasonable portions of the public lands, under suitable limitations, is a wise and just measure of public policy which will promote, in various ways, the interests of all the States of this Union; and we therefore recommend it to the favorable consideration of the American people.

Resolved, That the obligations of honor and patriotism require the earliest practicable payment of the national debt; and we are, therefore, in favor of such a tariff of duties as will raise revenue adequate to defray the necessary expenses of the federal government, and to pay annual instalments of our debt, and the interest thereon.

Resolved, That we inscribe on our banner, "Free Soil, Free Speech, Free Labor, and Free Men," and under it will fight on, and fight ever, until a triumphant victory shall reward our exertions.

The canvass was short. On the part of the Whigs it was spirited and confident, while on the Democratic side it was conducted with little hope of success. The early elections showed that the Whigs must carry the country. The number of States which took part in this election was thirty. Florida had been admitted as a State on March 3, 1845; Texas on Dec. 29, 1845; Iowa on Dec. 28, 1846; and Wisconsin on May 29, 1848. For the first time all the electors, except those from Massachusetts, were appointed on one day. This was in accordance with an act passed in 1845, which, by the way, was a party measure, and debated in an intensely partisan spirit, as follows: —

Be it enacted, etc., That the electors of President and Vice-President shall be appointed in each State on the Tuesday next after the first Monday in the month of November of the year in which they are to be appointed: —

Provided, That each State may by law provide for the filling of any vacancy or vacancies which may occur in its College of Electors when such college meets to give its electoral vote: —

And provided also, When any State shall have held an election for the purpose of choosing electors, and shall fail to make a choice on the day aforesaid, then the electors may be appointed on a subsequent day in such manner as the State shall by law provide.

The popular and the electoral votes in 1848 were as follows: —

	POPULAR VOTE.			ELECTORS.	
STATES.	Zachary Taylor, La.	Lewis Cass, Mich.	Martin Van Buren, N.Y.	Taylor.	Cass.
Maine	35,125	39,880	12,096	–	9
New Hampshire .	14,781	27,763	7,560	–	6
Vermont . . .	23,122	10,948	13,837	6	–
Massachusetts .	61,070	· 35,281	38,058	12	–
Rhode Island . .	6,779	3,646	730	4	–
Connecticut . .	30,314	27,046	5,005	6	–
New York . . .	218,603	114,318	120,510	36	–
New Jersey . .	40,015	36,901	829	7	–
Pennsylvania . .	185,513	171,176	11,263	26	–
Delaware . . .	6,421	5,898	80	3	–
Maryland . . .	37,702	34,528	125	8	–
Virginia. . . .	45,124·	46,586	9	–	17
North Carolina .	43,550	34,869	–	11	–
South Carolina*.	–	–	–	–	9
Georgia	47,544	44,802	–	10	–
Alabama . . .	30,482	31,363	–	–	9
Florida	3,116	1,847	–	3	–
Mississippi . . .	25,922	26,537	–	–	6
Louisiana . . .	18,217	15,370	–	6	–
Texas	4,509	10,668	–	–	4
Arkansas . . .	7,588	9,300	–	–	3
Missouri . . .	32,671	40,077	–	–	7
Tennessee . . .	64,705	58,419	–	13	–
Kentucky . . .	67,141	49,720	–	12	–
Ohio	138,360	154,775	35,354	–	23
Michigan . . .	23,940	30,687	10,389	–	5
Indiana	69,907	74,745	8,100	–	12
Illinois	53,047	56,300	15,774	–	9
Wisconsin . . .	13,747	15,001	10,418	–	4
Iowa	11,084	12,093	1,126	–	4
Totals . . .	1,360,099	1,220,544	291,263	163	127

* By Legislature.

In all the States except New Hampshire and Massachusetts, a plurality was sufficient to effect a choice. New Hampshire gave a majority to Cass over both the others. In Massachusetts there was no choice, and the legislature met and chose the Taylor electors. The aggregate vote at this election was 2,871,906, against 2,698,605, an increase of 173,301. But of these additional votes 83,609 were cast in the four new States, so that the increase in the old States was but 89,692, or barely three per cent in four years. This fact proves, not that slight interest was taken in the election, but that the result was foreseen, and that in many States less effort than usual to poll a full vote was put forth. The count of electoral votes proceeded in the usual manner, and was devoid of incident.

XVIII.

THE DEMOCRATS REUNITED.

QUESTIONS connected with slavery had been gradually but surely acquiring an overshadowing importance in national politics, until they split the Democratic party in the North almost in twain. In the election of 1848 more than one fourth of the Democrats of the North had voted for an independent candidate rather than support the party nominee, who had committed himself against the Wilmot proviso. The Whig party was also divided into two factions, and found safety only in silence. The power of slavery lay, however, rather in the weakness, the timidity, and the division of its opponents, than in its own inherent strength. It was to discover this fact later, but for the time being it was strongly intrenched. It governed the Democratic party ; and the Northern section of the Whig party, though stronger than the Southern, did not dare to try to govern it.

It became the business of the new Whig administration to organize the vast territory acquired from Mexico, and this not only made the subject of slavery in the Territories the leading issue in politics, but it reopened the whole question for agitation and contest. The result was the "compromise" measures of 1850, — all originally included in a single measure known as the "omnibus bill," but subsequently separated, when each matter was passed upon by itself. Slavery was not to be abolished in the District of Columbia; California was to be admitted as a State without restriction as to slavery ; a new and more stringent fugitive slave law was to be enacted; Texas was to receive ten million dollars for yielding her claim to New Mexico; Utah and New Mexico were to be organized as new Territories. To the passage of these measures Whigs and Democrats alike bent their energies, opposed on the one hand by the extremists among the Southern men, and on the other by the Anti-Slavery party of the North. General Taylor died while the measures were pending, but Mr. Fillmore, who succeeded him, was decidedly in favor of them, and promptly signed all the bills. Those who carried them through Congress, and those who supported them on the stump and in the press, deluded themselves with the idea that they were a finality; that they took away all matters of difference, or at least established the principles upon which all future questions arising out of them were to be decided; and that the people would regard a reopening of the agitation as unpatriotic and meddlesome.

Acquiescence in the settlement was really quite general in the Democratic party. The two wings of the party reunited, and carried most of the elections, as against the Whigs, who lost the unswerving Abolition and Anti-Slavery vote. It was evident that the Democrats would go into the election of 1852 a united party, provided a candidate unobjectionable to both wings could be found. It was equally evident that anything like a hearty union of Whigs was out of the question.

There was much preparation, and there was a great deal of discussion and intrigue, in either party, months before the time of nomination. The leading candidate on the Democratic side was General Cass, who had been defeated four years before. Mr. James Buchanan, however, was very strongly supported; and Stephen A. Douglas and William L. Marcy each had many friends. But it does

not seem to have been confidently anticipated that either
of these gentlemen would succeed in securing the necessary two thirds, and the experience of 1844 was frequently
in men's minds.

The Whigs were in a worse case. Mr. Webster was
the greatest of their statesmen, but after his 7th of March
speech he was impossible as a candidate to that wing of the
party which regarded the compromise measures of 1850 with
abhorrence. On the other hand, the Southern members of
the party were firmly resolved not to accept any candidate
who was not in favor of those measures. Mr. Fillmore,
although an accidental President, had stood by them, and
they were in favor of nominating him for re-election.
But as General Taylor had loomed up four years before
as a colorless and non-committal candidate, so now there
was a strong movement in favor of General Winfield
Scott. No one knew what was his position on the subject
of the "compromises," and there was a careful and successful effort to keep the Whig public in the dark. But,
as has happened before and since that time, the most ener-
getic movements in favor of the candidate who was eventually to be nominated came from States which could not
be expected to give him an electoral vote. Yet it is not
easy to see what course could have been taken to avert the
fate which awaited the Whigs in 1852. Had a candidate
been chosen who was identified with the compromise of
1850, like Mr. Webster or Mr. Fillmore, he would have
been slaughtered remorselessly in the North; had an opponent of these measures been selected, he would have failed
to secure an electoral vote in the South; and no other
non-committal candidate would have succeeded any better
than General Scott did.

The Democratic convention was held, first, on June 1,
1852, at Baltimore. It was a protracted convention, for it

did not adjourn until the 6th of the month, but it was not very interesting. John W. Davis of Indiana was the president. After a short contest, the two-thirds rule was adopted by an overwhelming majority. The struggle over the nomination was protracted. On the first ballot, General Cass had 116; James Buchanan, 93; William L. Marcy, 27; Stephen A. Douglas, 20; Joseph Lane, 13; Samuel Houston, 8; and there were 4 scattering. The number necessary to a choice was 188. In the succeeding ballots the vote for Mr. Cass fell off, while the number of delegates who voted for Mr. Douglas steadily increased, until, on the twenty-ninth trial, the votes were: for Cass, 27; for Buchanan, 93; for Douglas, 91; and no other candidate had more than 26. At this point Cass began to recover his strength, and reached his largest number on the thirty-fifth trial, namely, 131. On that same ballot, Virginia gave 15 votes to Franklin Pierce. Mr. Pierce gained 15 more votes on the thirty-sixth trial; but at that point his increase ceased, and was then slowly resumed, as the weary repetition of balloting without effect went ' on. The forty-eighth trial resulted as follows: For Cass, 73; for Buchanan, 28; for Douglas, 33; for Marcy, 90; for Pierce, 55; for all others, 8. The forty-ninth trial was the last. There was a " stampede " for Pierce, and he received 282 votes to 6 for all others.

Ten candidates were voted for as a candidate for the vice-presidency,— William R. King of Alabama had 126; S. U. Downs of Louisiana, 30; John B. Weller of California, 28; William O. Butler of Kentucky, 27; Gideon J. Pillow of Tennessee, 25; David R. Atchison of Missouri, 25; Robert Strange of North Carolina, 23; T. J. Rusk of Texas, 12; Jefferson Davis of Mississippi, 2; Howell Cobb of Georgia, 2. On the second ballot, William R. King of Alabama was unanimously nominated.

The platform adopted was made up of the previous
platforms of the party, with some additions. It was identical with that of 1848, up to and including the resolution
respecting slavery,— that numbered seven in the platform
of 1840 (p. 134), following which are these two resolutions : —

Resolved, That the foregoing proposition covers, and is intended
to embrace, the whole subject of slavery agitated in Congress; and
therefore the Democratic party of the Union, standing on this national platform, will abide by, and adhere to, a faithful execution
of the acts known as the "compromise" measures settled by the
last Congress, — the act for reclaiming fugitives from service or
labor included; which act, being designed to carry out an express
provision of the Constitution, cannot with fidelity thereto be repealed, nor so changed as to destroy or impair its efficiency.

Resolved, That the Democratic party will resist all attempts at
renewing in Congress, or out of it, the agitation of the slavery
question, under whatever shape or color the attempt may be made.

Then follow the resolutions in former platforms respecting the distribution of the proceeds of land sales, that
respecting the veto power, and these additions: —

Resolved, That the Democratic party will faithfully abide by and
uphold the principles laid down in the Kentucky and Virginia resolutions of 1792 and 1798, and in the report of Mr. Madison to the
Virginia legislature in 1799; that it adopts those principles as constituting one of the main foundations of its political creed, and is
resolved to carry them out in their obvious meaning and import.

Resolved, That the war with Mexico, upon all the principles of
patriotism and the law of nations, was a just and necessary war on
our part in which no American citizen should have shown himself
opposed to his country, and neither morally nor physically, by word
or deed, given aid and comfort to the enemy.

Resolved, That we rejoice at the restoration of friendly relations
with our sister republic of Mexico, and earnestly desire for her all
the blessings and prosperity which we enjoy under republican institutions, and we congratulate the American people on the results of
that war, which have so manifestly justified the policy and conduct

of the Democratic party, and insured to the United States indemnity for the past and security for the future.

Resolved, That, in view of the condition of popular institutions in the Old World, a high and sacred duty is devolved, with increased responsibility, upon the Democracy of this country, as the party of the people, to uphold and maintain the rights of every State, and thereby the union of States, and to sustain and advance among them constitutional liberty, by continuing to resist all monopolies and exclusive legislation for the benefit of the few at the expense of the many, and by a vigilant and constant adherence to those principles and compromises of the Constitution which are broad enough and strong enough to embrace and uphold the Union as it is, and the Union as it should be, in the full expansion of the energies and capacity of this great and progressive people.

The Whig convention met at Baltimore on the 16th of June. All the States were represented, and John G. Chapman of Maryland was the permanent presiding officer. The Southern delegates held a caucus on the first day of the convention, and agreed upon a platform, thus forestalling the action of the convention itself. It was afterwards charged that there was a secret understanding that if this platform should be accepted a sufficient number of the Southern delegates would, in due time, leave Mr. Fillmore and go over to the support of General Scott, whose strength was chiefly in the North. The platform was subsequently, it is said, submitted to Mr. Webster's friends, and agreed to. It was substantially the same as the platform adopted by the convention. The supporters of Scott had counted, before the day of meeting, upon 155 votes for him at the start. But the great strength of Mr. Fillmore was admitted; and the advocates of Mr. Webster's claims hoped that, when the two leading contestants had worn each other out, the Fillmore vote would be transferred to him.

On the first trial Mr. Fillmore had 133; General Scott, 131; and Mr. Webster, 29. The convention voted fifty times before any material change took place. At no time, in the first forty-nine votes, did General Scott fall below his original 131, or receive more than 139. Mr. Fillmore did not once receive more than 133 or fewer than 122. Mr. Webster's highest vote was 32, his lowest 28. But from the fiftieth vote on to the fifty-third General Scott drew ahead with 142, 142, 146, and 159, which last number was 12 more than were necessary to a choice. William A. Graham of North Carolina was easily nominated for Vice-President on the second ballot.

The platform, although reported by the committee on resolutions almost unanimously, was not adopted without a struggle. It was as follows : —

The Whigs of the United States, in convention assembled, adhering to the great conservative principles by which they are controlled and governed, and now, as ever, relying upon the intelligence of the American people, with an abiding confidence in their capacity for self-government, and their devotion to the Constitution and the Union, do proclaim the following as the political sentiments and determination for the establishment and maintenance of which their national organization as a party was effected : —

First. The government of the United States is of a limited character, and it is confined to the exercise of powers expressly granted by the Constitution, and such as may be necessary and proper for carrying the granted powers into full execution, and that powers not granted or necessarily implied are reserved to the States respectively and to the people.

Second. The State governments should be held secure to their reserved rights, and the general government sustained on its constitutional powers, and that the Union should be revered and watched over as the palladium of our liberties.

Third. That while struggling freedom everywhere enlists the warmest sympathy of the Whig Party, we still adhere to the doctrines of the Father of his Country, as announced in his Farewell Address, of keeping ourselves free from all entangling alliances with foreign countries, and of never quitting our own to stand upon foreign ground; that our mission as a republic is not to propagate our opinions, or impose on other countries our forms of government by artifice or force; but to teach by example, and show by our success, moderation and justice, the blessings of self-government, and the advantage of free institutions.

Fourth. That, as the people make and control the government, they should obey its Constitution, laws, and treaties, as they would retain their self-respect and the respect which they claim and will enforce from foreign powers.

Fifth. That the government should be conducted on principles of the strictest economy; and revenue sufficient for the expenses thereof, in time of peace, ought to be mainly derived from a duty on imports, and not from direct taxes; and in laying such duties sound policy requires a just discrimination, and protection from fraud by specific duties, when practicable, whereby suitable encouragement may be afforded to American industry, equally to all classes and to all portions of the country.

Sixth. The Constitution vests in Congress the power to open and repair harbors, and remove obstructions from navigable rivers, whenever such improvements are necessary for the common defence and for the protection and facility of commerce with foreign nations or among the States, — said improvements being in every instance national and general in their character.

Seventh. The Federal and State governments are parts of one system, alike necessary for the common prosperity, peace, and security, and ought to be regarded alike with a cordial, habitual, and immovable attachment. Respect for the authority of each, and acquiescence in the just constitutional measures of each, are duties required by the plainest considerations of national, State, and individual welfare.

Eighth. That the series of acts of the Thirty-second Congress, the act known as the Fugitive Slave Law included, are received and acquiesced in by the Whig party of the United States as a settlement in principle and substance of the dangerous and exciting questions which they embrace; and, so far as they are concerned, we will maintain them, and insist upon their strict enforcement, until time and experience shall demonstrate the necessity of further legislation to guard against the evasion of the laws on the one hand and the abuse of their powers on the other, not impairing their present efficiency; and we deprecate all further agitation of the question thus settled, as dangerous to our peace, and will discountenance all efforts to continue or renew such agitation, whenever, wherever, or however the attempt may be made; and we will maintain this system as essential to the nationality of the Whig party and the integrity of the Union.

The objection was, of course, to the last resolution of the series. It was warmly opposed, but was adopted by a vote of 212 to 70. The negative vote was given exclusively by Northern delegates, and by supporters of Scott as against Fillmore and Webster.

The nomination of Pierce was warmly received by the Democrats; that of Scott had a chilly reception in many parts of the North, and was nowhere welcomed in a spirit which gave promise of victory. The action of the Whig convention was coolly criticised by many of the party papers. The platform was distasteful to the Northern wing of the party, and the candidate excited no enthusiasm anywhere. He was esteemed as a gallant soldier, but he was not recognized as a statesman, and his views were too little known to inspire either section with confidence. On the other hand, Mr. Pierce, if not a very prominent man, was known to have opinions in accordance with the Democratic platform, upon which the party was substantially united.

The anti-slavery organization, the Free Soil Democrats, though a much less important political factor than they had been four years earlier, held their convention in Pittsburg on August 11. Henry Wilson of Massachusetts presided. John P. Hale of New Hampshire was nominated for President, and George W. Julian of Indiana for Vice-President, and the following platform was adopted : —

- Having assembled in national convention as the Democracy of the United States; united by a common resolve to maintain right against wrong and freedom against slavery; confiding in the intelligence, patriotism, and discriminating justice of the American people; putting our trust in God for the triumph of our cause, and invoking his guidance in our endeavors to advance it,— we now submit to the candid judgment of all men the following declaration of principles and measures: —

1. That governments deriving their just powers from the consent of the governed are instituted among men to secure to all those unalienable rights of life, liberty, and the pursuit of happiness with which they are endowed by their Creator, and of which none can be deprived by valid legislation, except for crime.

2. That the true mission of American Democracy is to maintain the liberties of the people, the sovereignty of the States, and the perpetuity of the Union, by the impartial application to public affairs, without sectional discriminations, of the fundamental principles of human rights, strict justice, and an economical administration.

3. That the federal government is one of limited powers, derived solely from the Constitution, and the grants of power therein ought to be strictly construed by all the departments and agents of the government, and it is inexpedient and dangerous to exercise doubtful constitutional powers.

4. That the Constitution of the United States, ordained to form a more perfect Union, to establish justice, and secure the blessings of liberty, expressly denies to the general government all power to deprive any person of life, liberty, or property without due process of law; and, therefore, the government, having no more power to make a slave than to make a king, and no more power to establish slavery than to establish a monarchy, should at once proceed to relieve itself from all responsibility for the existence of slavery wherever it possesses constitutional power to legislate for its extinction.

5. That, to the persevering and importunate demand of the slave power for more slave States, new slave Territories, and the nationalization of slavery, our distinct and final answer is: No more slave States, no slave Territory, no nationalized slavery, and no national legislation for the extradition of slaves.

6. That slavery is a sin against God, and a crime against man, which no human enactment or usage can make right; and that Christianity, humanity, and patriotism alike demand its abolition.

7. That the fugitive slave act of 1850 is repugnant to the Constitution, to the principles of the common law, to the spirit of Christianity, and to the sentiments of the civilized world. We therefore deny its binding force upon the American people, and demand its immediate and total repeal.

8. That the doctrine that any human law is a finality, and not subject to modification or repeal, is not in accordance with the creed of the founders of our government, and is dangerous to the liberties of the people.

9. That the acts of Congress known as the "compromise" measures of 1850, — by making the admission of a sovereign State contingent upon the adoption of other measures demanded by the special interest of slavery; by their omission to guarantee freedom in the free Territories; by their attempt to impose unconstitutional limitations on the power of Congress and the people to admit new States; by their provisions for the assumption of five millions of the State debt of Texas, and for the payment of five millions more, and the cession of a large territory to the same State under menace, as an inducement to the relinquishment of a groundless claim; and by their invasion of the sovereignty of the States and the liberties of the people, through the enactment of an unjust, oppressive, and unconstitutional fugitive slave law, — are proved to be inconsistent with all the principles and maxims of Democracy, and wholly inadequate to the settlement of the questions of which they are claimed to be an adjustment.

10. That no permanent settlement of the slavery question can be looked for except in the practical recognition of the truth that slavery is sectional and freedom national; by the total separation of the general government from slavery, and the exercise of its legitimate and constitutional influence on the side of freedom ; and by leaving to the States the whole subject of slavery and the extradition of fugitives from service.

11. That all men have a natural right to a portion of the soil ; and that, as the use of the soil is indispensable to life, the right of all men to the soil is as sacred as their right to life itself.

12. That the public lands of the United States belong to the people, and should not be sold to individuals nor granted to corporations, but should be held as a sacred trust for the benefit of the people, and should be granted in limited quantities, free of cost, to landless settlers.

13. That a due regard for the Federal Constitution and a sound administrative policy demands that the funds of the general government be kept separate from banking institutions; that inland and ocean postage should be reduced to the lowest possible point; that no more revenue should be raised than is required to defray the strictly necessary expenses of the public service, and to pay off

the public debt; and that the power and patronage of the government should be diminished, by the abolition of all unnecessary offices, salaries, and privileges, and by the election, by the people, of all civil officers in the service of the United States, so far as may be consistent with the prompt and efficient transaction of the public business.

14. That river and harbor improvements, when necessary to the safety and convenience of commerce with foreign nations or among the several States, are objects of national concern ; and it is the duty of Congress, in the exercise of its constitutional powers, to provide for the same.

15. That emigrants and exiles from the Old World should find a cordial welcome to homes of comfort and fields of enterprise in the New; and every attempt to abridge their privilege of becoming citizens and owners of soil among us ought to be resisted with inflexible determination.

16. That every nation has a clear right to alter or change its own government, and to administer its own concerns, in such a manner as may best secure the rights and promote the happiness of the people; and foreign interference with that right is a dangerous violation of the laws of nations, against which all independent governments should protest, and endeavor by all proper means to prevent; and especially is it the duty of the American government, representing the chief republic of the world, to protest against, and by all proper means to prevent, the intervention of kings and emperors against nations seeking to establish for themselves republican or constitutional governments.

17. That the independence of Hayti ought to be recognized by our government, and our commercial relations with it placed on a footing of the most favored nation.

18. That as, by the Constitution, the "citizens of each State shall be entitled to all the privileges and immunities of citizens in the several States," the practice of imprisoning colored seamen of other States, while the vessels to which they belong lie in port, and refusing the exercise of the right to bring such cases before the Supreme Court of the United States, to test the legality of such proceedings, is a flagrant violation of the Constitution, and an invasion of the rights of the citizens of other States, utterly inconsistent with the professions made by the slaveholders, that they wish the provisions of the Constitution faithfully observed by every State in the Union.

19. That we recommend the introduction into all treaties hereafter to be negotiated between the United States and foreign
nations, of some provision for the amicable settlement of difficulties by a resort to decisive arbitration.

20. That the Free Democratic party is not organized to aid
either the Whig or the Democratic wing of the great slave-com-
promise party of the nation, but to defeat them both; and that,
repudiating and renouncing both as hopelessly corrupt and
utterly unworthy of confidence, the purpose of the Free Democracy is to take possession of the Federal government, and administer it for the better protection of the rights and interests of
the whole people.

21. That we inscribe on our banner, "Free soil, free speech, free
labor, and free men!" and under it will fight on and fight ever
until a triumphant victory shall reward our exertions.

22. That upon this platform the convention presents to the
American people as a candidate for the office of President of the
United States, John P. Hale of New Hampshire, and as a candi-
date for the office of Vice-President of the United States, George
W. Julian of Indiana, and earnestly commends them to the sup-
port of all free men and all parties.

The canvass was not a very spirited one. All the early
autumn elections were favorable to the Democrats, and
the result in November was a crushing defeat of the
Whigs in the popular vote and one still more decisive in
the electoral vote. Thirty-one States took part in the
election, California having been admitted to the Union
Sept. 9, 1850. A new apportionment, based on the
census of 1850, changed the number of electoral votes of
many of the States. The popular and electoral votes
were as follows : —

| STATES. | POPULAR VOTE. | | | ELECTORS. | |
	Franklin Pierce, N.H.	Winfield Scott, N.Y.	John P. Hale, N.H.	Pierce.	Scott.
Maine.	41,609	32,543	8,030	8	–
New Hampshire .	29,997	16,147	6,695	5	–
Vermont . . .	13,044	22,173	8,621	–	5
Massachusetts . .	44,569	52,683	28,023	–	13
Rhode Island . .	8,735	7,626	644	4	–
Connecticut . .	33,249	30,357	3,160	6	–
New York . . .	262,083	234,882	25,329	35	–
New Jersey. . .	44,305	38,556	350	7	–
Pennsylvania . .	198,568	179,174	8,525	27	–
Delaware . . .	6,318	6,293	62	3	–
Maryland . . .	40,020	35,000	54	8	–
Virginia	73,858	58,572	–	15	–
North Carolina .	39,744	39,058	–	10	–
South Carolina* .	–	–	–	8	–
Georgia	34,705	16,660	–	10	–
Alabama . . .	26,881	15,038	–	9	–
Florida	4,318	2,875	–	3	–
Mississippi . . .	26,876	17,548	–	7	–
Louisiana . . .	18,647	17,255	–	6	–
Texas	13,552	4,995	–	4	–
Arkansas . . .	12,170	7,404	–	4	–
Missouri	38,353	29,984	–	9	–
Tennessee . . .	57,018	58,898	–	–	12
Kentucky . . .	53,806	57,068	–	–	12
Ohio	169,220	152,526	31,682	23	–
Michigan . . .	41,842	33,859	7,237	6	–
Indiana	95,340	80,901	6,929	13	–
Illinois	80,597	64,934	9,966	11	–
Wisconsin . . .	33,658	22,240	8,814	5	–
Iowa	17,763	15,856	1,604	4	–
California . . .	40,626	35,407	100	4	–
Totals . . .	1,601,274	1,386,580	155,825	254	42

*By Legislature.

There was no unusual incident connected with the electoral count.

XIX.

THE KANSAS-NEBRASKA CONTEST.

THE presidential election of 1852 was the death blow of the Whig party. That organization had outlived its usefulness. It attempted to delude itself and the country with the idea that the one question of the day, that of slavery in the Territories, was settled, and could thenceforth be disregarded. Organized as the Whig party was, it was impossible for it to antagonize the Democratic party, which, whatever comforting assurances it might put forth in platforms, was constantly acting in a way to make the introduction of slavery into the Territories easy, and to render its exclusion impossible. For it was held that any American citizen might settle in any Territory with all his property of any kind, including slaves; that there was no power in a territorial government to prohibit slavery; and that only when the people came together to form a State constitution could they decide whether the institution should or should not exist. There was no party organization which went the length of disputing this position of the Democratic party, without going so much further that moderate opponents of the extension of slavery were deterred from acting with it.

The Whig party became extinct because, from the very nature of its organization, it could not oppose the Democratic pretension. It failed in the South because it made the contest on an issue in which the people were not interested; in the North because it had not the courage to avow opinions which a large majority of the party held. But the Whig pretence, that the slavery question was settled by the compromise measures of 1850, was kept up for some years longer, until it became no longer possible to practise self-deception.

This delusion, however, very soon after the election of 1852, took a new phase. Native Americanism had been a favorite doctrine in certain parts of the North for many years, and of late it had been a growing sentiment. It was confined to no party, and the political method of those who believed in the principle that "Americans must rule America," and who were animated by hostility to the Roman Catholic Church, was to choose between candidates already nominated. Occasionally, however, in the cities of New York and Philadelphia, they nominated candidates of their own, and succeeded in electing them to local offices. The membership was carefully guarded; for the societies were secret, and the initiated were bound by oaths. The order which existed before 1850 was superseded, soon after the election of 1852, by a new one, the Order of United Americans, which became popularly known as the Know-Nothing Order, from the ignorance, even of the existence of such an association, which was professed by all its members. A very large proportion of the Whigs, hoping to transfer the political issue from slavery to Native Americanism, joined the order, and for some years it had extraordinary success in State elections; but, as Horace Greeley predicted at the time when it was at the height of its power, it was destined " to run its career rapidly, and vanish as suddenly as it appeared. It *may* last through the next presidential canvass; but hardly longer than that. . . . It would seem as devoid of the elements of persistence as an anti-cholera or an anti-potato-rot party would be." It was chiefly confined to the East at first, and later it extended to the South, even as far as Texas, where it became strong enough to carry one election; but it never had much success, or an organization, in the West.

It was impossible to keep the slavery question out of sight. Mr. Pierce congratulated the country, at the beginning of his administration, that the agitation had ceased, and both parties were pledged to treat a revival of the controversy as an unpatriotic act; but it was revived at once by the proposition to organize the Territories of Kansas and Nebraska, and by the repeal of the Missouri Compromise. The struggle between the pro-slavery and the anti-slavery factions over Kansas, both within and without the Territory, was one of unexampled bitterness; but during a large part of the administration of Mr. Pierce the opponents of the administration were fighting without any organization, or with only an imperfect one. The Republican party, composed largely of Whigs, but with a liberal contingent from the Democratic party, was formed in 1854. It first appeared in the elections of that year, and in 1855 carried the elections in Vermont and Ohio, barely failed in New York and Wisconsin, and gave promise of a great future in other States where it had been late in forming.

At the close of 1855 the situation was extremely complicated. In the Eastern States there were four parties,— the Democrats, the Whigs, the Know-Nothings, and the Republicans. The Democrats and Whigs were inclined to coalesce in order to withstand the common enemy, the Republicans, whose party was acquiring gigantic strength. The days of the Know-Nothing, or American, party were numbered, and most of the members had fallen away to the Republican party. In the West,—except in Ohio, where a remnant of the Whig party survived,— the parties were only two, the Democratic and the Republican.

In the South the American party was at the time of its greatest success, having absorbed most of the Whig strength. Although the Whig party had not formally acknowledged that it had ceased to exist, it was really only a memory, and the members merely accepted and voted for the candidates of the Know Nothings.

The first convention preliminary to the convention of 1856 was that of the Americans. It was held on Washington's birthday, Feb. 22, 1856. But already the "National Council" of the order had been in session three days, beginning on the 19th of the month, and had adopted the platform of the party. This platform was as follows : —

1. An humble acknowledgment of the Supreme Being, for His protecting care vouchsafed to our fathers in their successful revolutionary struggle, and hitherto manifested to us, their descendants, in the preservation of their liberties, the independence and the union of these States.

2. The perpetuation of the Federal Union and Constitution, as the palladium of our civil and religious liberties and the only sure bulwark of American independence.

3. Americans must rule America; and to this end native-born citizens should be selected for all State, Federal, and municipal offices of government employment, in preference to all others. Nevertheless,

4. Persons born of American parents residing temporarily abroad should be entitled to all the rights of native-born citizens.

5. No person should be selected for political station (whether of native or foreign birth) who recognizes any allegiance or obligation of any description to any foreign prince, potentate, or power, or who refuses to recognize the Federal and State Constitutions (each within its sphere) as paramount to all other laws as rules of political action.

6. The unqualified recognition and maintenance of the reserved rights of the several States, and the cultivation of harmony and fraternal good will between the citizens of the several States, and, to this end, non-interference by Congress with questions appertaining solely to the individual States, and non-intervention by each State with the affairs of any other State.

7. The recognition of the right of native-born and naturalized citizens of the United States, permanently residing in any Territory thereof, to frame their constitution and laws, and to regulate their domestic and social affairs in their own mode, subject only to the provisions of the Federal Constitution, with the privilege of admission into the Union whenever they have the requisite population for one representative in Congress; *provided, always,* that none but those who are citizens of the United States, under the Constitution and laws thereof, and who have a fixed residence in any such Territory, ought to participate in the formation of a constitution or in the enactment of laws for said Territory or State.

8. An enforcement of the principle that no State or Territory ought to admit others than citizens to the right of suffrage, or of holding political offices of the United States.

9. A change in the laws of naturalization, making a continued residence of twenty-one years, of all not heretofore provided for, an indispensable requisite for citizenship hereafter, and excluding all paupers and persons convicted of crime from landing upon our shores; but no interference with the vested rights of foreigners.

10. Opposition to any union between Church and State ; no interference with religious faith or worship, and no test oaths for office.

11. Free and thorough investigation into any and all alleged abuses of public functionaries, and a strict economy in public expenditures.

12. The maintenance and enforcement of all laws constitutionally enacted, until said laws shall be repealed or shall be declared null and void by competent judicial authority.

13. Opposition to the reckless and unwise policy of the present Administration in the general management of our national affairs, and more especially as shown in removing "Americans" (by designation) and conservatives in principle, from office, and placing foreigners and ultraists in their places; as shown in a truckling subserviency to the stronger, and an insolent and cowardly bravado toward the weaker powers; as shown in reopening sectional agitation, by the repeal of the Missouri Compromise; as shown in granting to unnaturalized foreigners the right of suffrage in Kansas and Nebraska; as shown in its vacillating course on the Kansas and Nebraska question; as shown in the corruptions which pervade some of the departments of the government; as shown in

disgracing meritorious naval officers through prejudice or caprice; and as shown in the blundering mismanagement of our foreign relations.

14. Therefore, to remedy existing evils, and to prevent the disastrous consequences otherwise resulting therefrom, we would build up the "American Party" upon the principles hereinbefore stated.

15. That each State Council shall have authority to amend their several constitutions, so as to abolish the several degrees, and substitute a pledge of honor, instead of other obligations, for fellowship and admission into the party.

16. A free and open discussion of all political principles embraced in our platform.

The convention, which met on the 22d, consisted of 227 delegates from 27 States of the Union, — all except Maine, Vermont, South Carolina, and Georgia. Having organized by the choice of Ephraim Marsh of New Jersey as President, and having decided cases of contested seats, the convention became involved in a long and angry debate over the right of the National Council to make the platform of the party. A resolution was presented : —

That the National Council has no authority to prescribe a platform of principles for this nominating convention, and that no candidates for President and Vice-President who are not in favor of interdicting slavery into territory north of 36° 30′, by congressional action, shall be nominated by this Convention.

A motion to lay this resolution on the table was accepted as a test of the strength of the two wings of the party. The motion was carried by a vote of 141 to 59. A motion to proceed to nominate a candidate for President was successful, 151 to 51. Thereupon nearly all the delegates from New England and Ohio, and a part of those from Pennsylvania, Illinois, and Iowa, withdrew from the convention. An informal ballot gave Millard Fillmore 71 votes, George Law of New York 27, Garrett Davis of

Kentucky 13, and 32 votes were given to seven other candidates, from one to eight each. On the formal vote Mr. Fillmore had 179, Mr. Law 24, Kenneth Raynor of North Carolina 14, Judge John M'Lean of Ohio 13, Garrett Davis 10, and Samuel Houston of Texas 3. Mr. Fillmore was therefore nominated. On the first ballot for a candidate for Vice-President, Andrew J. Donelson of Tennessee had 181, Henry J. Gardner of Massachusetts 12, Kenneth Raynor 8, and Percey Walker of Alabama 8. Mr. Donelson was declared nominated, and the convention adjourned. Soon after this the seceding delegates met and nominated for President Colonel John C. Fremont of California, and for Vice-President Ex-Governor William F. Johnston of Pennsylvania.

The meeting of the Democratic National Convention was looked forward to with much interest. A great many members still adhered to the party who were not disposed to yield to what the general drift of sentiment in the Northern States regarded as the arrogant and unreasonable demands of the slave interest. The division of the party was most serious in New York, where the two factions were now known as the "hards" and the "softs." Mr. Pierce was in high favor with the Southern delegates and with the Southern people; the Northern and more moderate wing of the party preferred Mr. Buchanan; while Mr. Douglas had a strong hold upon the popular heart, and was regarded as the most natural successor to Mr. Pierce's strength, should that gentleman's nomination become impossible. The excitement at Cincinnati, where the convention was to meet, ran very high on the days before the session began, and it was freely said that the Northern delegates would bolt if Mr. Buchanan should be defeated. The preliminary intriguing has probably never been greater in any national nominating convention than it was at that time.

The convention met on the 2d of June. All the States were fully represented, and two sets of delegates appeared from each of the States of New York and Missouri. The Anti-Bentonites were the "regulars" from the latter State. The contestants signalized their advent by knocking down the door-keeper, who endeavored to prevent them from entering the hall. The scene was an incipient riot. When order had been restored, the presiding officer administered to the intruders such a stinging rebuke for their lawless conduct that they retired, and, as the committee on credentials reported against their claim, they were seen no more. The "hards" and "softs" of New York were quite as bitter in their quarrel as the more turbulent Missourians; but they waited peaceably, and finally both delegations were admitted, each delegate to have half a vote. The permanent chairman was John E. Ward of Georgia. There was no opposition to the two-thirds rule. On the first vote for a candidate for President, James Buchanan had 135, Franklin Pierce 122, Stephen A. Douglas 33, and Lewis Cass 5. The Southern States gave on this vote 72 to Mr. Pierce, 29 to Mr. Buchanan, and 14 to Mr. Douglas. The North gave 106 to Buchanan, 50 to Pierce, 19 to Douglas, and five to Cass. On the second and succeeding votes Mr. Buchanan's strength increased very slowly but steadily; Mr. Pierce's fell off rapidly, and the most of this loss was Mr. Douglas's gain, so that on the sixteenth trial the result was, for Mr. Buchanan 168, for Mr. Pierce none, for Mr. Douglas 121, and for General Cass 6. Mr. Buchanan had had a majority on the tenth vote, and he now lacked but eighteen of two thirds. On the seventeenth vote the delegations began changing in his favor, and he received all the votes, 296, and was declared nominated. Ten candidates were voted for as candidates for Vice-President on the first trial. The leader was John A. Quitman of Mississippi, with 59 votes, closely followed by John C. Breckinridge of Kentucky with 55. Linn Boyd of Kentucky had 33, Herschell V. Johnson of Georgia 31, James A. Bayard of Delaware 31, Aaron V. Brown of Tennessee 29, James C. Dobbin of North Carolina 13, Benjamin Fitzpatrick of Alabama 11, Trusten Polk of Missouri 5, and Thomas J. Rusk of Texas 2. On the second vote the names of General Quitman and of most of the other leading candidates were withdrawn, and Mr. Breckinridge was unanimously nominated.

The platform, which was adopted without opposition, begins with the preamble first adopted in 1844, and repeated in subsequent platforms. Then follow ten of the resolutions which form a part of previous platforms, namely, the first five of 1840, in order, and those relating to the proceeds of the public lands; against a national bank; in favor of a separate treasury; regarding the veto power; and against abridgment of the privileges of aliens to become citizens. To these the following were added: —

And whereas, Since the foregoing declaration was uniformly adopted by our predecessors in national convention, an adverse political and religious test has been secretly organized by a party claiming to be exclusively American, and it is proper that the American Democracy should clearly define its relations thereto, and declare its determined opposition to all secret political societies, by whatever name they may be called,

Resolved, That the foundation of this Union of States having been laid in, and its prosperity, expansion, and pre-eminent example of free government built upon, entire freedom in matters of religious concernment, and no respect of persons in regard to rank or place, or birth, no party can be justly deemed national, constitutional, or in accordance with American principles which bases its exclusive organization upon religious opinions and accidental birthplace. And hence a political crusade in the nineteenth century, and in the United States of America, against Catholics and foreign-born, is neither justified by the past history nor future prospects of the country, nor in unison with the spirit of toleration and enlightened freedom which peculiarly distinguishes the American system of popular government.

Resolved, That we reiterate with renewed energy of purpose the well-considered declarations of former conventions upon the sectional issue of domestic slavery and concerning the reserved rights of the States, —

1. That Congress has no power under the Constitution to interfere with or control the domestic institutions of the several States, and that all such States are the sole and proper judges of everything appertaining to their own affairs not prohibited by the Constitution; that all efforts of the Abolitionists or others made to induce Congress to interfere with questions of slavery, or to take incipient steps in relation thereto, are calculated to lead to the most alarming and dangerous consequences, and that all such efforts have an inevitable tendency to diminish the happiness of the people and endanger the stability and permanency of the Union, and ought not to be countenanced by any friend of our political institutions.

2. That the foregoing covers, and was intended to embrace, the whole subject of slavery agitation in Congress, and therefore the Democratic party of the Union, standing on this national platform, will abide by and adhere to a faithful execution of the acts known as the "compromise" measures, settled by the Congress of 1850, the act for reclaiming fugitives from service or labor included; which act, being designed to carry out an express provision of the Constitution, cannot, with fidelity thereto, be repealed, or so changed as to destroy or impair its efficiency.

3. That the Democratic party will resist all attempts at renewing, in Congress or out of it, the agitation of the slavery question, under whatever shape or color the attempt may be made.

4. The Democratic party will faithfully abide by and uphold the principle laid down in the Kentucky and Virginia resolutions of 1797 and 1798, and in the report of Mr. Madison to the Virginia legislature in 1799; that it adopts these principles as constituting one of the main foundations of its political creed, and is resolved to carry them out in their obvious meaning and import.

And that we may more distinctly meet the issue on which a sectional party, subsisting exclusively on slavery agitation, now relies to test the fidelity of the people, North and South, to the Constitution and the Union,—

1. *Resolved*, That, claiming fellowship with and desiring the co-operation of all who regard the preservation of the Union under the Constitution as the paramount issue, and repudiating all sectional issues and platforms concerning domestic slavery which seek to embroil the States and incite to treason and armed resistance to law in the Territories, and whose avowed purpose, if consummated, must end in civil war and disunion, the American Democracy recognize and adopt the principles contained in the organic laws establishing the Territories of Nebraska and Kansas as embodying the only sound and safe solution of the slavery question, upon which the great national idea of the people of this whole country can repose in its determined conservation of the Union, and non-interference of Congress with slavery in the Territories or in the District of Columbia.

2. That this was the basis of the compromise of 1850, confirmed by both the Democratic and Whig parties in national conventions, ratified by the people in the election of 1852, and rightly applied to the organization of the Territories in 1854.

3. That by the uniform application of the Democratic principle to the organization of Territories, and the admission of new States with or without domestic slavery, as they may elect, the equal rights of all the States will be preserved intact, the original compacts of the Constitution maintained inviolate, and the perpetuity and expansion of the Union insured to its utmost capacity of embracing, in peace and harmony, every future American State that may be constituted or annexed with a republican form of government.

Resolved, That we recognize the right of the people of all the Territories, including Kansas and Nebraska, acting through the legally and fairly expressed will of the majority of the actual residents, and whenever the number of their inhabitants justifies it, to form a constitution, with or without domestic slavery, and be admitted into the Union upon terms of perfect equality with the other States.

Resolved, Finally, that in view of the condition of popular institutions in the Old World (and the dangerous tendencies of sectional agitation, combined with the attempt to enforce civil and religious disabilities against the rights of acquiring and enjoying citizenship in our own land), a high and sacred duty is devolved, with increased responsibility, upon the Democratic party of this country, as the party of the Union, to uphold and maintain the rights of every State, and thereby the Union of the States; and to

sustain and advance among us constitutional liberty, by continuing to resist all monopolies and exclusive legislation for the benefit
of the few at the expense of the many; and by a vigilant and constant adherence to those principles and compromises of the Constitution which are broad enough and strong enough to embrace and
uphold the Union as it was, the Union as it is, and the Union as it
shall be, in the full expansion of the energies and capacity of this
great and progressive people.

1. *Resolved*, That there are questions connected with the foreign policy of this country which are inferior to no domestic question whatever. The time has come for the people of the United
States to declare themselves in favor of free seas, and progressive
free trade throughout the world, and by solemn manifestations to
place their moral influence at the side of their successful example.

2. *Resolved*, That our geographical and political position with
reference to the other States of this continent, no less than the interest of our commerce and the development of our growing power,
requires that we should hold sacred the principles involved in the
Monroe doctrine. Their bearing and import admit of no miscon-
struction, and should be applied with unbending rigidity.

3. *Resolved*, That the great highway, which nature as well as
the assent of States most immediately interested in its maintenance
has marked out for free communication between the Atlantic and the
Pacific oceans, constitutes one of the most important achievements
realized by the spirit of modern times, in the unconquerable energy
of our people; and that result would be secured by a timely and
efficient exertion of the control which we have the right to claim
over it; and no power on earth should be suffered to impede or clog
its progress by any interference with relations that it may suit our
policy to establish between our government and the governments of
the States within whose dominions it lies. We can, under no circumstances, surrender our preponderance in the adjustment of all questions arising out of it.

4. *Resolved*, That, in view of so commanding an interest, the
people of the United States cannot but sympathize with the efforts
which are being made by the people of Central America to regen-
erate that portion of the continent which covers the passage across
the inter-oceanic isthmus.

5. *Resolved*, That the Democratic party will expect of the next
administration that every proper effort be made to insure our ascendancy in the Gulf of Mexico, and to maintain permanent pro-

tection to the great outlets through which are emptied into its waters the products raised out of the soil and the commodities created by the industry of the people of our Western valleys and of the Union at large.

Resolved, That the administration of Franklin Pierce has been true to Democratic principles, and therefore true to the great interests of the country. In the face of violent opposition he has maintained the laws at home, and vindicated the rights of American citizens abroad; and therefore we proclaim our unqualified admiration of his measures and policy.

The first Republican national convention was one of the most spontaneous conventions ever known in our political history. The delegates were not chosen by any settled rule, nor was there much, if any, regard paid to the number of votes to which a State should be entitled. New York cast 96 votes, Pennsylvania 81, and Ohio 69. All the Northern States were represented, as were also Delaware, Maryland, and Kentucky. Colonel Henry S. Lane of Indiana was made the president of the convention; and then, for lack of something better to do, the convention gave itself up to a season of speech-making of the most earnest and enthusiastic character. The delegates were meeting as members of the same party for the first time, and the exuberance of their satisfaction, in view of the extraordinary success the new party was having, and the constant accessions it was receiving from other organizations, was only natural. On an informal ballot for a candidate for President, John C. Fremont of California received 359, John M'Lean of Ohio 196, Charles Sumner of Massachusetts 2, and William H. Seward of New York 1. Colonel Fremont was thereupon unanimously nominated. An informal ballot was likewise taken for a candidate for Vice-President. William L. Dayton of New Jersey had 259, Abraham Lincoln of Illinois 110, Nathaniel P. Banks of Massachusetts 46, and twelve other candidates received some votes. Mr. Dayton was then unanimously nominated. The selection of Fremont was due in no small degree to the fact that he had already been nominated by the seceding Know-Nothings, and a communication from the officers of the convention which placed him in nomination was frequently referred to, but was not read. Governor Johnston, who was nominated by the seceding Americans for Vice-President, received only two votes in the Republican convention, however. The following platform was adopted by the Republicans : —

This convention of delegates, assembled in pursuance of a call addressed to the people of the United States, without regard to past political differences or divisions, who are opposed to the repeal of the Missouri Compromise, to the policy of the present administration, to the extension of slavery into free Territory; in favor of admitting Kansas as a free State, of restoring the action of the Federal government to the principles of Washington and Jefferson; and who purpose to unite in presenting candidates for the offices of President and Vice-President, do resolve as follows: —

Resolved, That the maintenance of the principles promulgated in the Declaration of Independence and embodied in the Federal Constitution is essential to the preservation of our Republican institutions, and that the Federal Constitution, the rights of the States, and the union of the States, shall be preserved.

Resolved, That with our Republican fathers we hold it to be a self-evident truth, that all men are endowed with the unalienable rights to life, liberty, and the pursuit of happiness, and that the primary object and ulterior designs of our Federal government were to secure these rights to all persons within its exclusive jurisdiction; that, as our republican fathers, when they had abolished slavery in all our national territory, ordained that no person should be deprived of life, liberty, or property without due process of law, it becomes our duty to maintain this provision of the Constitution against all attempts to violate it for the purpose of establishing slavery in any Territory of the United States, by positive legislation, prohibiting its existence or extension therein. That we deny the authority of Congress, of a Territorial legislature, of any individual or association of individuals, to give legal existence to slavery in any Territory of the United States, while the present Constitution shall be maintained.

Resolved, That the Constitution confers upon Congress sovereign power over the Territories of the United States, for their government, and that in the exercise of this power it is both the right and the duty of Congress to prohibit in the Territories those twin relics of barbarism, polygamy and slavery.

Resolved, That while the Constitution of the United States was ordained and established by the people in order to form a more perfect Union, establish justice, ensure domestic tranquillity, provide for the common defence, and secure the blessings of liberty, and contains ample provision for the protection of the life, liberty, and property of every citizen, the dearest constitutional rights of the people of Kansas have been fraudulently and violently taken from them; their territory has been invaded by an armed force; spurious and pretended legislative, judicial, and executive officers have been set over them, by whose usurped authority, sustained by the military power of the government, tyrannical and unconstitutional laws have been enacted and enforced; the rights of the people to keep and bear arms have been infringed; test oaths of an extraordinary and entangling nature have been imposed as a condition of exercising the right of suffrage and holding office; the right of an accused person to a speedy and public trial by an impartial jury has been denied; the right of the people to be secure in their persons, houses, papers, and effects against unreasonable searches and seizures has been violated; they have been deprived of life, liberty, and property without due process of law; that the freedom of speech and of the press has been abridged; the right to choose their representatives has been made of no effect; murders, robberies, and arsons have been instigated and encouraged, and the offenders have been allowed to go unpunished; — that all these things have been done with the knowledge, sanction, and procurement of the present administration; and that for this high crime against the Constitution, the Union, and humanity, we arraign the administration, the President, his advisers, agents, supporters, apologists, and accessories, either before or after the fact, before the country and before the world, and that it is our fixed purpose to bring the actual perpetrators of these atrocious outrages, and their accomplices, to a sure and condign punishment hereafter.

Resolved, That Kansas should be immediately admitted as a State of the Union, with her present free Constitution, as at once the most effectual way of securing to her citizens the enjoyment of the rights and privileges to which they are entitled, and of ending the civil strife now raging in her territory.

Resolved, That the highwayman's plea, that "might makes right," embodied in the Ostend circular, was in every respect unworthy of American diplomacy, and would bring shame and dishonor upon any government or people that gave it their sanction.

Resolved, That a railroad to the Pacific Ocean, by the most central and practicable route, is imperatively demanded by the interests of the whole country, and that the Federal government ought to render immediate and efficient aid in its construction; and, as an auxiliary thereto, the immediate construction of an emigrant route on the line of the railroad.

Resolved, That appropriations by Congress for the improvement of rivers and harbors, of a national character, required for the accommodation and security of our existing commerce, are authorized by the Constitution, and justified by the obligation of government to protect the lives and property of its citizens.

One other convention was held, that of the Whigs, at Baltimore, on the 17th of September, in which there was a more or less full representation of twenty-six States. No delegates were present from Michigan, Iowa, Wisconsin, Texas, or California. Edward Bates of Missouri was the President. The proceedings were brief and uninteresting. The nominations of Fillmore and Donelson were accepted by resolution, and the following platform was adopted: —

Resolved, That the Whigs of the United States, now here assembled, hereby declare their reverence for the Constitution of the United States, their unalterable attachment to the national Union, and a fixed determination to do all in their power to preserve them for themselves and their posterity. They have no new principles to announce, no new platform to establish, but are content to broadly rest — where their fathers rested — upon the Constitution of the United States, wishing no safer guide, no higher law.

Resolved, That we regard with the deepest interest and anxiety the present disordered condition of our national affairs, — a portion of the country ravaged by civil war, large sections of our population embittered by mutual recriminations; and we distinctly trace these calamities to the culpable neglect of duty by the present national administration.

Resolved, That the government of the United States was formed by the conjunction in political unity of widespread geographical sections, materially differing not only in climate and products, but in social and domestic institutions; and that any cause that shall permanently array the different sections of the Union in political hostility and organized parties, founded only on geographical distinctions, must inevitably prove fatal to a continuance of the national Union.

Resolved, That the Whigs of the United States declare, as a fundamental rule of political faith, an absolute necessity for avoiding geographical parties. The danger so clearly discerned by the Father of his Country has now become fearfully apparent in the agitation now convulsing the nation, and must be arrested at once if we would preserve our Constitution and our Union from dismemberment, and the name of America from being blotted out from the family of civilized nations.

Resolved, That all who revere the Constitution and the Union must look with alarm at the parties in the field in the present presidential campaign, — one claiming only to represent sixteen Northern States, and the other appealing mainly to the passions and prejudices of the Southern States; that the success of either faction must add fuel to the flame which now threatens to wrap our dearest interests in a common ruin.

Resolved, That the only remedy for an evil so appalling is to support a candidate pledged to neither of the geographical sections now arrayed in political antagonism, but holding both in a just and equal regard. We congratulate the friends of the Union that such a candidate exists in Millard Fillmore.

Resolved, That, without adopting or referring to the peculiar doctrines of the party which has already selected Mr. Fillmore as a candidate, we look to him as a well tried and faithful friend of the Constitution and the Union, eminent alike for his wisdom and firmness; for his justice and moderation in our foreign relations; for his calm and pacific temperament, so well becoming the head of a great nation; for his devotion to the Constitution in its true spirit; his inflexibility in executing the laws; but, beyond all these attributes, in possessing the one transcendent merit of being a representative of neither of the two sectional parties now struggling for political supremacy.

Resolved, That, in the present exigency of political affairs, we are not called upon to discuss the subordinate questions of administration in the exercising of the constitutional powers of the government. It is enough to know that civil war is raging, and that the Union is imperilled; and we proclaim the conviction that the restoration of Mr. Fillmore to the presidency will furnish the best if not the only means of restoring peace.

The canvass which followed was an extraordinary one. In the South it was sluggish enough, for the contest was only between Mr. Buchanan and Mr. Fillmore; and the former attracted to himself the support of the entire slaveholding interest and of all who were concerned for the maintenance of the political power of the slavery system. But in the North the Republicans conducted a canvass rivalling that of 1840 in enthusiasm, and having behind it what the "hard cider" campaign lacked, a definite moral purpose and a clearly understood policy. Great political clubs were organized, which marched from place to place visiting each other, uniformed and bearing torches. Immense public meetings were held, and the Northern heart was fired as it had never been before. But the Republican canvass was destined to end in defeat, although the earlier elections of the autumn indicated a Republican victory. In Vermont more than three fourths of the votes were Republican, and Maine, which had been carried in 1855 by a fusion party of Democrats and "Straight" Whigs, was now carried by the Republicans by almost 18,000 majority. But the October elections were unfavorable; for while Ohio gave a Republican majority, Indiana was lost, and Pennsylvania gave the Democratic candidates on the State ticket majorities over the united Republican and Whig vote. "The Quakers did not come out," it was said; but all who could read the signs of the time knew that the election was lost for the Republicans.

As before, thirty-one States participated in the election. The popular and electoral votes were as follows : —

STATES.	POPULAR VOTE.			ELECTORAL VOTE.		
	James Buchanan, Penn.	John C. Fremont, Cal.	Millard Fillmore, N.Y.	Buchanan.	Fremont.	Fillmore.
Maine	39,080	67,370	3,325	–	8	–
New Hampshire .	32,789	38,345	422	–	5	–
Vermont . . .	10,569	39,561	545	–	5	–
Massachusetts . .	39,240	108,190	19,626	–	13	–
Rhode Island . .	6,680	11,467	1,675	–	4	–
Connecticut . .	34,995	42,715	2,615	–	6	–
New York . . .	195,878	276,007	124,604	–	35	–
New Jersey. . .	46,943	28,338	24,115	7	–	–
Pennsylvania . .	230,710	147,510	82,175	27	–	–
Delaware . . .	8,004	308	6,175	3	–	–
Maryland . . .	39,115	281	47,460	–	–	8
Virginia	89,706	291	60,310	15	–	–
North Carolina .	48,246	–	36,886	10	–	–
South Carolina * .	–	–	–	8	–	–
Georgia	56,578	–	42,228	10	–	–
Alabama . . .	46,739	–	28,552	9	–	–
Florida	6,358	–	4,833	3	–	–
Mississippi . . .	35,446	–	24,195	7	–	–
Louisiana . . .	22,164	–	20,709	6	–	–
Texas.	31,169	–	15,639	4	–	–
Arkansas . . .	21,910	–	10,787	4	–	–
Missouri	58,164	–	48,524	9	–	–
Tennessee . . .	73,638	–	66,178	12	–	–
Kentucky . . .	74,642	314	67,416	12	–	–
Ohio	170,874	187,497	28,126	–	23	–
Michigan . . .	52,136	71,762	1,660	–	6	–
Indiana	118,670	94,375	22,386	13	–	–
Illinois	105,348	96,189	37,444	11	–	–
Wisconsin . . .	52,843	66,090	570	–	5	–
Iowa	36,170	43,954	9,180	–	4	–
California . . .	53,365	20,691	36,165	4	–	–
Totals . . .	1,838,169	1,341,264	874,534	174	114	8

* By Legislature.

The count of the electoral vote on this occasion was enlivened by a scene unlike any which had ever occurred. The usual resolution for counting the votes was adopted, and if the fact that there was anything unusual in the certificate of any State was known in advance, it does not appear from the record; but, in point of fact, the electors for Wisconsin had not met on the day fixed by law, which day, says the Constitution itself, "shall be the same throughout the United States," but on the next day after. A very severe snowstorm had prevented the electors from reaching the capital of the State in season to give their votes on the 3d of December, and they had met and voted on the 4th.

When the votes of Wisconsin were presented at the joint meeting of the two Houses, an objection was made to counting them. The president *pro tempore* of the Senate, the Hon. James M. Mason of Virginia, ruled that debate was not in order while the tellers were counting the votes. The count having been concluded, Mr. Letcher of Virginia, of the House of Representatives, inquired if it would then be in order to move that the votes of Wisconsin be excluded. The president ruled that it was not in order. Senator Crittenden of Kentucky wished to know if the chair decided "that Congress, in no form, has power to decide upon the validity or invalidity of a vote?" The president, having disclaimed the intention to make any such decision, proceeded to recapitulate the votes, giving Buchanan and Breckinridge 174 each, and Fremont and Dayton 114 each (which included the votes of Wisconsin), and to declare the election of the former. Protests were raised on all sides, from both parties and from both Houses. In spite of the declaration of the presiding officer that no debate was in order, there was a long and rambling debate, in which the most diverse views were advanced, and which was only cut short by the withdrawal of the Senate. The matter was immediately resumed in each House, and discussion was continued for two days. The debates on that occasion are the most valuable for the student of political history, as to this *casus omissus* of the Constitution, that have ever taken place, because the question was considered without a spirit of partizanship. The vote of Wisconsin would not affect the result, whether counted or rejected. There was very much ignorance of the Constitution displayed by many of the speakers, but, on the other hand, there was also much profound learning.

It is impossible here to give a sketch of this most interesting debate. Nothing more can be done than to summarize some of the views advanced. On the main question, Republicans generally thought the votes of Wisconsin ought to be counted; Democrats, for the most part, took the contrary view. Upon the question who, under the Constitution, should count, that is, who decide what were votes, the divergence of opinion was amazing. Some contented themselves with asserting that the power was in Congress to decide upon the validity of votes, leaving the method of exercising the power to be determined by law. But it was maintained in the Senate, by Mr. Thompson of Kentucky, that the "votes are to be returned to *us*, and counted by *us*, and the House of Representatives are admitted to be present at the count to prevent a combination, a clandestine operation, a secret session, a *coup d'état*. . . . The votes are to be returned to the Senate, and counted by the Senate." On the other hand, Mr. Humphrey Marshall of Kentucky maintained in the House that that body was the sole judge, and Mr. Henry Winter Davis of Maryland took the same view. The ground of this opinion was, that it was for the House to decide whether or not to go into an election of President.

There was still another point on which the difference of opinion was very decided. The president of the Senate stoutly affirmed that he had neither counted nor rejected the votes, although he had said : " The state of the votes as delivered by the tellers is . . . for John C. Fremont of California, 114 votes." Many senators sustained the assertion of Mr. Mason that he had not counted the votes, while others declared that he had counted them. Numerous resolutions were offered in each branch, but the debate produced nothing more than a resolution of formal notification to Messrs Buchanan and Breckinridge that they had been elected. The opinion that the whole subject ought to be taken up and considered, and the doubtful points determined by law, was very generally expressed; but, as soon as the matter in hand was disposed of, the subject was dropped. The Congress was then in the last month of its term, and it was too busy to take further notice of a danger past which might never return. So the disputed point was left for a Republican Congress to decide, according to the political exigency of the hour, in the midst of a civil war.

XX.

THE LAST STRUGGLE FOR SLAVERY.

DURING the whole of Mr. Buchanan's administration the country was on the verge of civil war. It was, considering the excited state of the public mind, an evidence of rare popular self-restraint that war did not break out. Parties were at last divided on the one great issue of slavery; but, while the line between the Republicans and the Democrats was a broad one, there was a great variety of opinion within the ranks of each party. The most conservative Republican, however, was firm and decided in the conviction that slavery could not exist in any Territory in opposition either to the will of Congress or to that of the people of the Territory. The Democratic party comprised two distinct wings. The radical wing held that all citizens of the United States had the right, without question, to carry any species of property, including slaves, into the Territories; that neither Congress nor the Territorial legislature had a right to forbid the introduction of slaves; and that only when the Territory was ready to apply for admission as a State did the right accrue to decide whether slavery should be allowed or prohibited. The other wing of the party, led by Senator Stephen A. Douglas, maintained the doctrine of popular, or "squatter," sovereignty. They held that the people of a Territory might decide, through their legislature, whether or not slavery should be permitted.

The struggle which had begun in the first year of Pierce's administration, over Kansas, was continued under his successor until early in 1861, after secession had begun,

214

when the State was admitted without slavery. The story of that contest forms one of the darkest pages of American political history. It is a record of perfidy and violence. The attempt to force the Lecompton Constitution upon the people, under the patronage of the executive department of the government, was matched by the baseness of the offer by Congress of a bribe to the people if they would accept it. The South, struggling as it was to maintain the political power of the section and of its social system, could not have claimed less than it did claim, and it had the support of the Supreme Court in its assertion of the national character of the slavery system. But, on the other hand, the moral sense of the Northern people was outraged by the effort to force slavery upon an unwilling people, and by the repeated violations of good faith which were resorted to in order to make the attempt successful. Kansas had seven governors in five years, one of whom was removed because he would not be the tool of the pro-slavery party, and another, a Mississippian, an ex-Senator, and Secretary of the Treasury during the whole of Polk's administration, resigned because the President would not keep the pledge, officially, which he had verbally made to the Governor, that the people of Kansas should be allowed to vote on the whole Lecompton Constitution.

The minor issues developed during this administration, in the contests over the homestead and pre-emption laws, in the revelations made by the Covode investigating committee, and by the state of the national finances, would have been enough to cause an exciting election in 1860, even if the Kansas struggle, the Dred Scott decision, and the John Brown raid at Harper's Ferry, had not kept the public attention unchangeably fixed on the question of slavery.

The state of parties at the beginning of 1860 has been indicated already, but it may be well to make the statement a little more precise. The Democratic party was in two factions, the first of which was led by the administration, and was supported by the Southern senators and members of the House of Representatives in almost unbroken phalanx. Its adherents filled the national offices, both North and South, and it had numerous representatives among the politicians of the North, some of whom were no doubt intellectually convinced that the constitutional position assumed in defence of slavery extension was correct; while others were with the administration because it was the administration, and favored the Southern view because the ascendancy of slavery, as a a political power, if secured by their assistance, would give them office and standing in the party.

On the other side was the faction whose shibboleth was "Popular Sovereignty," led by Senator Douglas, who was designated by the voice of this wing as the candidate for the presidency, long before he fell under the disapproval of the administration and of the Southern senators. This wing of the party was very powerful at the North. It constituted almost the whole of the Democratic party in New England and in the greater part of the West, more than half of the party in New York, and a strong minority of it in Pennsylvania.

The Republicans were of all shades of anti-slavery opinion, and while they were absolutely united in resisting the administration of Mr. Buchanan, it was by no means certain that the party could concentrate its force upon any one candidate. There was danger that the conservatives would be alienated if the person selected should be a man of too radical opinions; while, on the other hand, the Abolitionists had too often followed their principles, though it kept them in a petty minority, to be drawn into the support of a candidate of doubtful quality.

Besides these two parties, and their factions, there was a large surplus remnant. There were the old Whigs, whom time, in its rapid flight, had left behind the age; there were the Native Americans, who, in the South, hated the Democrats, and yet could not join with their great opponents the Republicans; and there were a great many well-meaning men, all over the country, who deprecated the prevailing strife, who really did not think the slavery question worth so much discussion, and who feared that unless something were done to calm down the angry disputants there would be war. These several elements became temporarily united in the Constitutional Union party, as patriotic a party as was ever organized, but one which could not succeed in its mission because the time had come when the self-preservation of the South, as a political power, and the moral sense of the North, demanded that the pending question be settled finally and forever.

The Democratic convention was the first to be held. It met at Charleston, S. C., on the 23d of April, 1860. There were full delegations from every State in the Union, and contesting delegations from New York and Illinois. In the former State the "hards," led by Fernando Wood, had been elected by districts, while the "softs," who were favorable to Senator Douglas, were chosen by a State convention, which met at Syracuse the autumn previous. The two Illinois delegations were respectively for and against Mr. Douglas. As soon as Mr. Francis B. Flournoy of Arkansas had taken the chair as temporary presiding officer of the convention, an angry debate began upon these contested seats, for the national committee had given tickets of admission, in each case, to the Douglas delegates, and had shut out their opponents.

On the first day of the convention nothing was done except to appoint committees. On the following day Mr. Caleb Cushing of Massachusetts was made the permanent presiding officer, a committee on resolutions was appointed, and it was voted not to vote for candidates of the party until a platform had been adopted. The third day was occupied in deciding the contests for seats, — in favor of the New York "softs," and the Douglas men from Illinois. It was only on the 27th of April, the fifth day of the convention, that the committee on resolutions reported to the assembly a majority and two or three minority sets of resolutions. Two days of fierce debate, and of numerous propositions to amend, followed; and, on the 28th, a motion was carried to recommit the whole subject to the committee on resolutions; a second part of the motion, to instruct the committee to report a platform which was offered by the mover, Senator William Bigler of Pennsylvania, was rejected. Later in the same day the committee reported back a series of resolutions, asserting, as the previous majority report had done, the extreme Southern view of the question of slavery in the Territories. These resolutions were subsequently adopted by the convention of seceders, some months later, and will be found on page 224. A minority report was made, after several long speeches had been made, which, although signed by less than one half of the members of the platform committee, represented more than one half the electoral votes of the whole country. General B. F. Butler, who, throughout the convention, occupied an attitude peculiar to himself, presented a second minority report, which consisted of the Cincinnati platform of 1856, without any change whatever. Much debate, and a determined effort to postpone the vote on the substitution of the minority reports followed; but on Monday, the 30th,

a vote was reached. General Butler's platform was rejected, by yeas 105, nays 198. The minority resolutions
presented by Mr. Samuels of Iowa were then substituted
for those of the majority, by 165 to 138. These resolutions
were in the following terms: —

1. *Resolved*, That we, the Democracy of the Union, in convention assembled, hereby declare our affirmance of the resolutions
unanimously adopted and declared as a platform of principles by
the Democratic convention at Cincinnati in the year 1856, believing that Democratic principles are unchangeable in their nature
when applied to the same subject-matters; and we recommend as
the only further resolutions the following: —
Inasmuch as differences of opinion exist in the Democratic party
as to the nature and extent of the powers of a Territorial legislature, and as to the powers and duties of Congress, under the Constitution of the United States, over the institution of slavery within
the Territories,—
2. *Resolved*, That the Democratic party will abide by the decisions of the Supreme Court of the United States on the questions
of constitutional law.
3. *Resolved*, That it is the duty of the United States to afford
ample and complete protection to all its citizens, whether at home
or abroad, and whether native or foreign.
4. *Resolved*, That one of the necessities of the age, in a military,
commercial, and postal point of view, is speedy communication between the Atlantic and Pacific States; and the Democratic party
pledge such constitutional government aid as will insure the construction of a railroad to the Pacific Coast at the earliest practicable period.
5. *Resolved*, That the Democratic party are in favor of the
acquisition of the island of Cuba, on such terms as shall be honorable to ourselves and just to Spain.
6. *Resolved*, That the enactments of State legislatures to defeat
the faithful execution of the fugitive slave law are hostile in character, subversive of the Constitution, and revolutionary in their
effects.

This series having been substituted for the majority
set, the several resolutions were then considered singly,

and, with the exception of that numbered two, which was rejected, they were adopted by an almost unanimous vote. This action was the signal for the withdrawal of a large number of the Southern delegates. Alabama led off with a formal protest. The delegation had been instructed not to waive the issue, and as the convention had decided against the Southern view, they had no alternative but to withdraw. Mississippi, Florida, and Texas followed, with their entire delegations, and all but two of those from Louisiana, all but three from South Carolina, three from Arkansas, two from Delaware, and one from North Carolina joined the seceders. On the next day, May 1st, 26 of the 33 delegates who cast the 10 votes of Georgia also withdrew. This made a loss of about 45 votes out of 303. The convention, after listening to some very remarkable speeches by Southern men who did not secede, voted that, in balloting for candidates, two thirds of a full convention, that is, 202 votes, should be necessary for a choice. The first vote was taken : —

Stephen A. Douglas of Illinois 145½
R. M. T. Hunter of Virginia 42
James Guthrie of Kentucky 35
Andrew Johnson of Tennessee 12
Daniel S. Dickinson of New York. 7
Joseph Lane of Oregon 6
Isaac Toucey of Connecticut 2¼
Jefferson Davis of Mississippi 1½
Franklin Pierce of New Hampshire 1

The convention took, on that and the two following days, 57 votes. Mr. Douglas's strength rose very slowly to 152½ on the 32d trial, then dropped to 151½, and remained at the same point from the 36th to the 57th vote. Mr. Hunter dropped slowly to 16 votes, which was his almost uniform number during the last twenty trials. Mr.

Guthrie, who gained most of the votes lost by Mr. Hunter, reached 66½ on the 39th trial, and had 65½ on the 57th. The strength of no other candidate reached 21 votes on any one of the 57 contests. The last vote of this series was: For Douglas, 151½; Guthrie, 65½; Hunter, 16; Lane, 14; Dickinson, 4; Davis, 1.

On the 3d of May, the tenth day of the convention, a resolution was adopted to adjourn to meet in Baltimore on the 18th of June, and that it be recommended to Democrats to fill the vacancies made by the withdrawal of delegates. This resolution was carried by 195 votes to 55. The only Southern votes given, on both sides of this question, were: Maryland, 8; Virginia, 15; North Carolina, 14; Kentucky, 2; Tennessee, 12; Missouri, 9; Arkansas, 1; total 61, of the 120 to which the South was entitled.

Meantime the seceders from the regular convention had met in another hall in Charleston, organized by the choice of Senator James A. Bayard of Delaware as president, and adopted as a platform the resolutions reported by the majority of the Committee on Resolutions of the National Convention (see page 224). After a session of four days they adjourned to meet in Richmond, Va., on the 11th of June. On reassembling at that time and place, Mr. John Erwin of Alabama was made president, and a resolution was adopted to adjourn again until the 21st of the month. At the adjourned session nothing was done, although the convention met every day, until the 28th of June, when what was left of the body adopted the nominations of Breckinridge and Lane, made by the seceders at Baltimore, and adjourned without day.

The regular convention reassembled at Baltimore on the 18th of June. The president, Caleb Cushing, on taking the chair, made a long address, in which he stated the condition of business, the significant part of which was an intimation that the adoption of the platform was subject to reconsideration. The first business in order was the admission of delegates from those States whose representatives had withdrawn at Charleston. Three whole days were occupied in the settlement of these questions; for in some cases the original delegates had presented themselves for readmission, and in other cases there were contesting delegations. The action of the convention was in most instances in favor of the delegates pledged to Mr. Douglas, and accordingly, as soon as the membership of the convention was fully decided, a portion of the Virginia delegation set the example of a second secession. They were followed by most of the remaining members from the Southern States, and by a few from the North; and Mr. Cushing, the president, also withdrew and resigned the chair, which was taken by Governor Tod of Ohio. The convention then proceeded to vote again for a candidate for President. On the first vote Douglas received 173½ votes, Guthrie 10, and John C. Breckinridge 5, and three votes were divided among four other candidates. All the Southern States combined cast but 35 votes, and 15 of these were given by the contesting delegates just before admitted by the convention. On the announcement of the result Mr. Sanford E. Church of New York moved a resolution that, as Mr. Douglas had received two thirds of the vote given in this convention, he be declared the regular nominee of the party. It was objected to that this was to rescind the rule that the candidate must receive the votes of two thirds of a full convention, but the resolution was declared in order, and a long debate took place upon it. Finally it was withdrawn to allow another vote to be taken, which resulted in Mr. Douglas receiving 181½, Mr. Breckinridge 7½, and

Mr. Guthrie 5½ votes. The resolution of Mr. Church was then taken up and passed. Benjamin Fitzpatrick of Alabama was nominated for Vice-President on the first vote, with almost complete unanimity. The following resolution, proposed from the floor, was adopted with only two dissenting votes, as an addition to the platform : —

> *Resolved*, That it is in accordance with the interpretation of the Cincinnati platform, that, during the existence of the Territorial governments, the measure of restriction, whatever it may be, imposed by the Federal Constitution on the power of the Territorial legislature over the subject of the domestic relations, as the same has been, or shall hereafter be, finally determined by the Supreme Court of the United States, should be respected by all good citizens, and enforced with promptness and fidelity by every branch of the general government.

This finished the proceedings of the convention. Mr. Fitzpatrick declined the nomination for Vice-President, and Herschel V. Johnson of Georgia was substituted in his place by the National Committee.

A few days later, on the 28th of June, the seceders from the Baltimore convention, joined by the delegates who had been refused admission to it in the contested cases already mentioned, and by some of the seceders from the Charleston convention, met in Baltimore. Twenty-one States were wholly or partially represented, but no delegates were present from the States of Maine, New Hampshire, Rhode Island, Connecticut, New Jersey, South Carolina, Ohio, Michigan, Indiana, Illinois, Iowa, and Wisconsin. The convention made short work. It adopted the platform reported by the majority of the Committee on Resolutions of the Charleston convention, nominated John C. Breckinridge of Kentucky for President, and Joseph Lane of Oregon for Vice-President, both by a unanimous vote, and adjourned. The platform adopted was as follows : —

Resolved, That the platform adopted by the Democratic party at Cincinnati be affirmed, with the following explanatory resolutions:—

1. That the government of a Territory organized by an act of Congress is provisional and temporary; and, during its existence, all citizens of the United States have an equal right to settle with their property in the Territory, without their rights, either of person or of property, being destroyed or impaired by Congressional legislation.

2. That it is the duty of the Federal government, in all its departments, to protect, when necessary, the rights of persons and property in the Territories, and wherever else its constitutional authority extends.

3. That when the settlers in a Territory, having an adequate population, form a State constitution, the right of sovereignty commences, and, being consummated by admission into the Union, they stand on an equal footing with the people of other States; and the State thus organized ought to be admitted into the Federal Union, whether its constitution prohibits or recognizes the institution of slavery.

4. That the Democratic party are in favor of the acquisition of the island of Cuba, on such terms as shall be honorable to ourselves and just to Spain, at the earliest practicable moment.

5. That the enactments of State legislatures to defeat the faithful execution of the fugitive slave law are hostile in character, subversive of the Constitution, and revolutionary in their effect.

6. That the Democracy of the United States recognize it as the imperative duty of this government to protect the naturalized citizen in all his rights, whether at home or in foreign lands, to the same extent as its native-born citizens.

Whereas, One of the greatest necessities of the age, in a political, commercial, postal, and military point of view, is a speedy communication between the Pacific and Atlantic coasts,—

Therefore be it Resolved, That the Democratic party do hereby pledge themselves to use every means in their power to secure the passage of some bill, to the extent of the constitutional authority of Congress, for the construction of a Pacific railroad from the Mississippi River to the Pacific Ocean, at the earliest practicable moment.

Meantime another convention had been held, and had

put its candidates before the people. The Constitutional Union party held its first and only general convention at Baltimore on the 9th of May. Most of the States were represented, though not in all cases by delegates duly elected in primary meetings and conventions. Young as it was, the party was divided into two wings. The Southerners, mostly representatives of the still surviving Native American sentiment, desired to nominate General Sam Houston of Texas, while the old Whigs of the North did not relish such a candidacy. The latter were adjured not to pay so much attention to gentility, but to take a candidate who, rough as he might be, would carry many of the Southern States. Although the party was, by its very name, one of union, it had no sooner organized, by the choice of Washington Hunt of New York as president, than it fell into a very bitter debate as to the manner of voting, and as to the number of votes which delegations might cast. The Houston party was present in great force, and it was feared that, unless a strict rule were adopted, that candidate might be thrust upon the convention. When this difficulty had been surmounted, the Committee on Resolutions made a report, which was unanimously adopted, and the following platform was accepted : —

Whereas, Experience has demonstrated that platforms adopted by the partisan conventions of the country have had the effect to mislead and deceive the people, and at the same time to widen the political divisions of the country by the creation and encouragement of geographical and sectional parties, therefore,—

Resolved, That it is both the part of patriotism and of duty to recognize no political principle other than the Constitution of the country, the union of the States, and the enforcement of the laws, and that, as representatives of the constitutional Union men of the country in national convention assembled, we hereby pledge ourselves to maintain, protect, and defend, separately and unitedly, these great principles of public liberty and national safety, against all enemies at home and abroad, believing that thereby peace may once more be restored to the country, the rights of the people and of the States re-established, and the government again placed in that condition of justice, fraternity, and equality which, under the example and Constitution of our fathers, has solemnly bound every citizen of the United States to maintain a more perfect union, establish justice, ensure domestic tranquillity, provide for the common defence, promote the general welfare, and secure the blessings of liberty to ourselves and our posterity.

Two votes only were necessary to effect a nomination of a candidate for President. They resulted as follows:—

	First.	Second.
John Bell of Tennessee	68½	138½
Samuel Houston of Texas	57	69
John J. Crittenden of Kentucky	28	9½
Edward Everett of Massachusetts	25	9½
John M'Lean of Ohio	22	—
William A. Graham of North Carolina	22	18½
William C. Rives of Virginia	13	—
John M. Botts of Virginia	9½	5½
William L. Sharkey of Mississippi	6	5
William L. Goggin of Virginia	3	—

The number necessary to a choice on the second vote was 127, and Mr. Bell was accordingly nominated. Edward Everett of Massachusetts was the only person proposed as a candidate for Vice-President, and he was unanimously nominated. Not a little enthusiasm was manifested over the two nominations which, if they did not ensure a vigorous treatment of the questions of the day, did certainly represent the desire of the convention that the country should have union and peace.

All the political interest of the country was now concentrated upon the Republican convention, called to meet at Chicago on the 16th of May. While the Democrats were divided and discordant, and were evidently unable to unite upon a platform or a candidate, the

Republicans were confident. They had carried every Northern State in which an election was held, in 1859, except California; Oregon, where the adverse majority was only 59; New York, where the combined vote of the Democrats and third party men was less than 2,000 more than that of the Republicans; and Rhode Island, where they were defeated by a fusion of all the opposition. Mr. Seward was beyond a doubt the leading candidate, but there were several others who were strongly supported; and there was a very large section of the party which, though not unfriendly to Mr. Seward, and though grateful for his services, questioned the wisdom of putting in the field a candidate whose views were so pronounced, and whose attitude might alienate some elements which needed to be conciliated. Mr. Seward also encountered the bitter hostility of Horace Greeley, whose "Tribune" was the most powerful organ of opinion in the party. Nevertheless a large, influential, and well-organized body of delegates went to Chicago with a determination to effect the nomination of Mr. Seward.

The convention opened with delegates present from all the free States, also from Delaware, Maryland, Virginia, Kentucky, Missouri, and Texas, and from the Territories of Kansas, Nebraska, and the District of Columbia. David Wilmot of Pennsylvania was the temporary chairman, but the convention organized on the first day of its session by the choice of George Ashmun of Massachusetts as permanent president. There was a contest over the standing of the delegates from some of the Southern States, owing to a strong suspicion that they represented nobody but themselves, and were Republicans of the States which they claimed as their own, only for convention purposes. The convention, however, took a liberal view and allowed the delegates to retain their seats with a somewhat diminished voting strength in some cases.

On the second day there was a debate over the question whether a majority of the whole number of delegates, were all the States of the Union fully represented, or only a majority of the delegates voting, should be necessary to nominate. The first proposition, which would have been almost equivalent to the two-thirds rule of the Democrats, was rejected by 331 votes to 130.

The platform was reported, amended, and adopted as follows : —

Resolved, That we, the delegated representatives of the Republican electors of the United States, in convention assembled, in discharge of the duty we owe to our constituents and our country, unite in the following declarations: —

1. That the history of the nation, during the last four years, has fully established the propriety and necessity of the organization and perpetuation of the Republican party, and that the causes which called it into existence are permanent in their nature, and now, more than ever before, demand its peaceful and constitutional triumph.

2. That the maintenance of the principles promulgated in the Declaration of Independence and embodied in the Federal Constitution, — "that all men are created equal; that they are endowed by their Creator with certain unalienable rights; that among these are life, liberty, and the pursuit of happiness; that, to secure these rights, governments are instituted among men, deriving their just powers from the consent of the governed,"— is essential to the preservation of our republican institutions; and that the Federal Constitution, the rights of the States, and the union of the States, must and shall be preserved.

3. That to the union of the States this nation owes its unprecedented increase in population, its surprising development of material resources, its rapid augmentation of wealth, its happiness at home, and its honor abroad; and we hold in abhorrence all schemes for disunion, come from whatever source they may; and we congratulate the country that no Republican member of Congress has uttered or countenanced the threats of disunion so

often made by Democratic members, without rebuke and with applause from their political associates; and we denounce those threats of disunion, in case of a popular overthrow of their ascendancy, as denying the vital principles of a free government, and as an avowal of contemplated treason, which it is the imperative duty of an indignant people sternly to rebuke and forever silence.

4. That the maintenance inviolate of the rights of the States, and especially the right of each State to order and control its own domestic institutions according to its own judgment exclusively, is essential to that balance of power on which the perfection and endurance of our political fabric depends; and we denounce the lawless invasion by armed force of the soil of any State or Territory, no matter under what pretext, as among the gravest of crimes.

5. That the present Democratic administration has far exceeded our worst apprehensions, in its measureless subserviency to the exactions of a sectional interest, as especially evinced in its desperate exertions to force the infamous Lecompton Constitution upon the protesting people of Kansas; in construing the personal relation between master and servant to involve an unqualified property in person; in its attempted enforcement, everywhere, on land and sea, through the intervention of Congress and of the Federal courts, of the extreme pretensions of a purely local interest; and in its general and unvarying abuse of the power entrusted to it by a confiding people.

6. That the people justly view with alarm the reckless extravagance which pervades every department of the Federal Government; that a return to rigid economy and accountability is indispensable to arrest the systematic plunder of the public treasury by favored partisans; while the recent startling developments of frauds and corruptions at the Federal metropolis show that an entire change of administration is imperatively demanded.

7. That the new dogma that the Constitution, of its own force, carries slavery into any or all of the Territories of the United States, is a dangerous political heresy, at variance with the explicit provisions of that instrument itself, with contemporaneous exposition, and with legislative and judicial precedent; is revolutionary in its tendency, and subversive of the peace and harmony of the country.

8. That the normal condition of all the territory of the United States is that of freedom; that as our Republican fathers, when they had abolished slavery in all our national territory, ordained

that no person should be deprived of life, liberty, or property without due process of law, it becomes our duty, by legislation, whenever such legislation is necessary, to maintain this provision of the Constitution against all attempts to violate it; and we deny the authority of Congress, of a territorial legislature, or of any individual, to give legal existence to slavery in any Territory of the United States.

9. That we brand the recent reopening of the African slave-trade, under the cover of our national flag, aided by perversions of judicial power, as a crime against humanity, and a burning shame to our country and age; and we call upon Congress to take prompt and efficient measures for the total and final suppression of that execrable traffic.

10. That in the recent vetoes, by their Federal governors, of the acts of the legislatures of Kansas and Nebraska, prohibiting slavery in those Territories, we find a practical illustration of the boasted Democratic principle of non-intervention and popular sovereignty, embodied in the Kansas-Nebraska Bill, and a demonstration of the deception and fraud involved therein.

11. That Kansas should of right be immediately admitted as a State under the Constitution recently formed and adopted by her people and accepted by the House of Representatives.

12. That, while providing revenue for the support of the general government by duties upon imports, sound policy requires such an adjustment of these imposts as to encourage the development of the industrial interests of the whole country; and we commend that policy of national exchanges which secures to the workingmen liberal wages, to agriculture remunerating prices, to mechanics and manufacturers an adequate reward for their skill, labor, and enterprise, and to the nation commercial prosperity and independence.

13. That we protest against any sale or alienation to others of the public lands held by actual settlers, and against any view of the free-homestead policy which regards the settlers as paupers or suppliants for public bounty; and we demand the passage by Congress of the complete and satisfactory homestead measure which has already passed the House.

14. That the Republican party is opposed to any change in our naturalization laws, or any State legislation by which the rights of citizenship hitherto accorded to immigrants from foreign lands shall be abridged or impaired; and in favor of giving a full and efficient protection to the rights of all classes of citizens, whether native or naturalized, both at home and abroad.

15. That appropriations by Congress for river and harbor improvements of a national character, required for the accommodation and security of our existing commerce, are authorized by the Constitution, and justified by the obligations of government to protect the lives and property of its citizens.

16. That a railroad to the Pacific Ocean is imperatively demanded by the interests of the whole country; that the Federal Government ought to render immediate and efficient aid in its construction; and that, as preliminary thereto, a daily overland mail should be promptly established.

17. Finally, having thus set forth our distinctive principles and views, we invite the co-operation of all citizens, however differing on other questions, who substantially agree with us in their affirmance and support.

As originally reported, the second resolution did not contain the passage from the Declaration of Independence. It was proposed by Mr. Joshua R. Giddings of Ohio to insert it in the form of a separate resolution, "that we solemnly reassert the self-evident truth that all men," etc., but was rejected. Mr. George William Curtis of New York afterward moved to insert the passage in its present place, and the motion prevailed. On the third day of the convention the names of candidates for President were formally presented, but no speeches were allowed to be made by those who nominated the candidates. Three votes were taken amid increasing excitement, with the following result : —

	1st.	2d.	3d.
Whole number of votes	465	465	465
Necessary to a choice	233	233	233
William H. Seward of New York . .	173½	184½	180
Abraham Lincoln of Illinois	102	181	231½
Simon Cameron of Pennsylvania . .	50½	2	–
Salmon P. Chase of Ohio	49	42½	24½
Edward Bates of Missouri	48	35	22
William L. Dayton of New Jersey . .	14	10	1
John M'Lean of Ohio	12	8	5
Jacob Collamer of Vermont	10	–	–
Scattering	6	2	1

Mr. Lincoln was within one and a half votes of a nomination when the roll call was completed. His majority was secured by a transfer of four votes from Ohio, and then delegation after delegation changed in his favor until he had 354 in all. On motion of Mr. W. M. Evarts of New York, seconded by Mr. John A. Andrew of Massachusetts, the nomination was made unanimous with the greatest enthusiasm. At a later session on the same day the convention voted twice for a candidate for Vice-President, with this result: —

	First.	Second.
Hannibal Hamlin of Maine	194	367
Cassius M. Clay of Kentucky	101½	86
John Hickman of Pennsylvania	58	13
Andrew H. Reeder of Pennsylvania	51	–
Nathaniel P. Banks of Massachusetts	38½	–
Scattering	15	–

The nomination of Mr. Hamlin having been made unanimous, the convention adopted the following resolution, on motion of Mr. Giddings of Ohio, and then adjourned: —

Resolved, That we deeply sympathize with those men who have been driven, some from their native States and others from the States of their adoption, and are now exiled from their homes on account of their opinions; and we hold the Democratic party responsible for the gross violation of that clause of the Constitution which declares that citizens of each State shall be entitled to all the privileges and immunities of citizens of the several States.

The canvass which ensued after these several nominations had been made was fierce and exciting. On the part of the Republicans there was a well-grounded confidence that they were to be victorious. The nomination of Mr. Lincoln was one which appealed peculiarly to the young men of the country, or rather to those of the Northern half of the country. The tactics which had been so efficacious in the successful Whig campaigns were again resorted to, and the Northern States were alive with processions, torch-light parades, and mass-meetings. In the South there was a grim determination to win the victory if possible, but not to submit to defeat. The mutterings of secession and war, in case Mr. Lincoln were elected, were frequently heard, but the supporters of the Republican party refused to believe that the South would be guilty of that madness. In the Northern section of the Democratic party there was an earnest effort to fuse all the elements in support of a union ticket of electors, with the implied, and in some cases the expressed, agreement that the electoral votes should be given to that candidate who should come the nearest to an election. This course was pursued only in the close States. Where there was no hope of a Democratic majority in any event, the two wings of the party had each its own electoral ticket. But it was all without avail. The early elections in Maine, Ohio, Indiana, and Pennsylvania, to say nothing of other States where the contest was not so close, foreshadowed the certain election of Mr. Lincoln, and the result in November more than justified the deductions from the September and October elections. Every Northern State except New Jersey was carried by the Republicans. The decision was hardly made by the people of the country before the South began to carry out the threats which had been only muttered before the election, and the new President succeeded to the administration of a government which was to fight for its very existence.

Thirty-three States took part in this election. Minnesota had been admitted to the Union on the 11th of May, 1858, and Oregon on the 12th of February, 1859. The popular and electoral vote was as follows: —

STATES.	POPULAR VOTE.				ELECTORAL VOTE.			
	Abraham Lincoln, Ill.	Stephen A. Douglas, Ill.	John C. Breckinridge, Ky.	John Bell, Tenn.	Lincoln.	Douglas.	Breckinridge.	Bell.
Maine	62,811	26,693	6,368	2,046	8	-	-	-
New Hampshire	37,519	25,881	2,112	441	5	-	-	-
Vermont	33,808	6,849	218	1,969	5	-	-	-
Massachusetts	106,533	34,372	5,939	22,331	13	-	-	-
Rhode Island	12,244	7,707†	-	-	4	-	-	-
Connecticut	43,792	15,522	14,641	3,291	6	-	-	-
New York	362,646	312,510†	-	-	35	-	-	-
New Jersey	58,324	62,801†	-	-	4	3	-	-
Pennsylvania	268,030	16,765	178,871†	12,776	27	-	-	-
Delaware	3,815	1,023	7,337	3,864	-	-	3	-
Maryland	2,294	5,966	42,482	41,760	-	-	8	-
Virginia	1,929	16,290	74,323	74,681	-	-	-	15
North Carolina	-	2,701	48,539	44,990	-	-	10	-
South Carolina *	-	-	-	-	-	-	8	-
Georgia	-	11,590	51,889	42,886	-	-	10	-
Florida	-	367	8,543	5,437	-	-	3	-
Alabama	-	13,651	48,831	27,875	-	-	9	-
Mississippi	-	3,283	40,797	25,040	-	-	7	-
Louisiana	-	7,625	22,681	20,204	-	-	6	-
Texas	-	-	47,548	15,438†	-	-	4	-
Arkansas	-	5,227	28,732	20,094	-	-	4	-
Missouri	17,028	58,801	31,317	58,372	-	9	-	-
Tennessee	-	11,350	64,709	69,274	-	-	-	12
Kentucky	1,364	25,651	53,143	66,058	-	-	-	12
Ohio	231,610	187,232	11,405	12,194	23	-	-	-
Michigan	88,480	65,057	805	405	6	-	-	-
Indiana	139,033	115,509	12,295	5,306	13	-	-	-
Illinois	172,161	160,215	2,404	4,913	11	-	-	-
Wisconsin	86,110	65,021	888	161	5	-	-	-
Minnesota	22,069	11,920	748	62	4	-	-	-
Iowa	70,409	55,111	1,048	1,763	4	-	-	-
California	39,173	38,516	34,334	6,817	4	-	-	-
Oregon	5,270	3,951	5,006	183	3	-	-	-
Totals	1,866,452	1,375,157	847,953	590,631	180	12	72	39

* By Legislature. † Fusion electoral tickets.

The vote of New Jersey was divided because of the "scratching" of the fusion ticket, so that three of the Lincoln electors were chosen.

The official record of the electoral count contains nothing of interest. The proceedings were in strict accordance with precedent. But a single remark made by a member of the House of Representatives after the count was over suggests the condition of affairs at the time. Some trouble had been feared on the occasion of the count of votes, and no doubt precautions were taken against violence at any time, and particularly at that time. At any rate, the Southerners scented hostile preparations; and Mr. Hindman of Arkansas suggested that the committee to wait on the President elect "be directed to inform General Scott that there is no further need for his janizaries about the capitol, the votes being counted and the result proclaimed." The only attention paid to the sneer was in a retort from Mr. Grow of Pennsylvania, that "gentlemen seem to trouble themselves a good deal about General Scott on all occasions." The proceedings then terminated.

XXI.

THE WAR ELECTION.

The election of 1864 took place while the country was still rent by civil strife. The war had been prosecuted by the Union armies with partial success; but, when the first mutterings of the coming political contest made themselves heard, the prospect of a speedy termination of the war was not cheering. President Lincoln was beset on the one hand by the Democrats, who maintained that the war had not been carried on according to the Constitution, and on the other by a small but active minority of the Republican party, who complained of his conservatism and his unwillingness to adopt the radical measures which they deemed essential to national success. With the great majority of his own party, however, he was strong. The people had learned to trust his calmness and good sense. They had seen him refuse to proclaim emancipation when it had been clamorously demanded by those who called themselves radicals; but when his own cool judgment told him that the time had come for that great measure, he had adopted it. His wisdom and strength commended him to thoughtful men, and his quaint shrewdness in word and act brought him very near to the common people.

Mr. Lincoln neither obtrusively urged himself as a candidate for re-election, nor made any coy professions of unwillingness to be chosen again. He was simply and frankly a candidate. He believed that it was best for the country, under the circumstances, that he should be con-

236

tinued in office. It was not good policy, he said,— and the
phrase made the one argument which in any case would
have turned the scale in his favor,—" to swap horses while
crossing a stream."

The certainty that the Republican convention, — which
was called on Feb. 22, 1864, to meet in Baltimore on
the 7th of June, — would nominate Mr. Lincoln, led the
radical opponents of his administration in various parts
of the country to attempt to forestall its action by calling
a convention to meet on an earlier day at Cleveland.
Several calls were published, all of them inviting the
people to meet in mass convention in that city on the 31st
of May. Among the signers of these calls were the Rev.
Dr. Cheever of New York, B. Gratz Brown of Missouri,
Lucius Robinson of New York, and other gentlemen then
or since prominent in public affairs. Wendell Phillips,
Frederick Douglass, and others sent letters approving the
objects of the convention.

In answer to these calls, about three hundred and fifty
persons met in Cleveland on the appointed day. General
John Cochrane of New York was made president. A
platform was adopted as follows : —

First. That the Federal Union shall be preserved.

Second. That the Constitution and laws of the United States
must be observed and obeyed.

Third. That the rebellion must be suppressed by force of arms,
and without compromise.

Fourth. That the rights of free speech, free press, and the
habeas corpus be held inviolate, save in districts where martial
law has been proclaimed.

Fifth. That the rebellion has destroyed slavery, and the Federal
Constitution should be amended to prohibit its re-establishment,
and to secure to all men absolute equality before the law.

Sixth. That integrity and economy are demanded at all times
in the administration of the government, and that in time of war
the want of them is criminal.

Seventh. That the right of asylum, except for crime and subject to law, is a recognized principle of American liberty; that any violation of it cannot be overlooked, and must not go unrebuked.

Eighth. That the national policy known as the "Monroe Doctrine" has become a recognized principle, and that the establishment of an anti-republican government on this continent by any foreign power cannot be tolerated.

Ninth. That the gratitude and support of the nation are due to the faithful soldiers and the earnest leaders of the Union army and navy for their heroic achievements of deathless valor in defence of our imperilled country and civil liberty.

Tenth. That the one-term policy for the presidency adopted by the people is strengthened by the force of the existing crisis, and should be maintained by constitutional amendments.

Eleventh. That the Constitution should be so amended that the President and Vice-President shall be elected by a direct vote of the people.

Twelfth. That the question of the reconstruction of the rebellious States belongs to the people, through their representatives in Congress, and not to the Executive.

Thirteenth. That the confiscation of the lands of the rebels, and their distribution among the soldiers and actual settlers, is a measure of justice.

General John C. Fremont was nominated by acclamation for President, and General John Cochrane, a few dissenting, for Vice-President. In letters dated at New York, June 4, both gentlemen accepted these nominations. As a manifestation of one phase of the opposition to Mr. Lincoln, these proceedings and those which followed are interesting; but the candidacy of General Fremont came to nothing. In August (20th) a letter was addressed to him by citizens of Boston, asking him if, "in case Mr. Lincoln will withdraw, you will do so," and "unite the thorough and earnest friends of a vigorous prosecution of the war in a new convention?" The ultimate result of this movement, although Mr. Lincoln did not join in it, was the withdrawal of both General Fremont and General Cochrane on the 21st of September, and the union of the Republican party in support of its regular candidates.

The call for the Republican National Convention was addressed to those "who desire the unconditional main-tenance of the Union, the supremacy of the Constitution, and the complete suppression of the existing rebellion, with the cause thereof, by vigorous war, and all apt and efficient means." It met at Baltimore, June 7, 1864, and was presided over, temporarily, by the Rev. Dr. Robert J. Breckinridge of Kentucky, and, as permanent president, by ex-Governor William Dennison of Ohio. The platform was reported by Mr. Henry J. Raymond of New York, and was adopted unanimously, as fol-lows: —

1. *Resolved*, That it is the highest duty of every American citizen to maintain against all their enemies the integrity of the Union, and the permanent authority of the Constitution and laws of the United States; and that, laying aside all differences of political opinion, we pledge ourselves as Union men, animated by a common sentiment, and aiming at a common object, to do every-thing in our power to aid the government in quelling by force of arms the rebellion now raging against its authority, and in bring-ing to the punishment due to their crimes the rebels and traitors arrayed against it.

2. *Resolved*, That we approve the determination of the govern-ment of the United States not to compromise with rebels, or to offer them any terms of peace, except such as may be based upon an unconditional surrender of their hostility and a return to their just allegiance to the Constitution and laws of the United States; and that we call upon the government to maintain this position, and to prosecute the war with the utmost possible vigor to the complete suppression of the rebellion, in full reliance upon the

self-sacrificing patriotism, the heroic valor, and the undying devotion of the American people to their country and its free institutions.

3. *Resolved*, That as slavery was the cause, and now constitutes the strength of this rebellion, and as it must be, always and everywhere, hostile to the principles of republican government, justice and the national safety demand its utter and complete extirpation from the soil of the Republic; and that, while we uphold and maintain the acts and proclamations by which the government, in its own defence, has aimed a deathblow at this gigantic evil, we are in favor, furthermore, of such amendment to the Constitution, to be made by the people in conformity with its provisions, as shall terminate and forever prohibit the existence of slavery within the limits or the jurisdiction of the United States.

4. *Resolved*, That the thanks of the American people are due to the soldiers and sailors of the army and navy who have perilled their lives in defence of their country and in vindication of the honor of its flag; that the nation owes to them some permanent recognition of their patriotism and their valor, and ample and permanent provision for those of their survivors who have received disabling and honorable wounds in the service of the country; and that the memories of those who have fallen in its defence shall be held in grateful and everlasting remembrance.

5. *Resolved*, That we approve and applaud the practical wisdom, the unselfish patriotism, and the unswerving fidelity with which Abraham Lincoln has discharged, under circumstances of unparalleled difficulty, the great duties and responsibilities of the presidential office; that we approve and indorse, as demanded by the emergency and essential to the preservation of the nation and as within the provisions of the Constitution, the measures and acts which he has adopted to defend the nation against its open and secret foes; that we approve, especially, the proclamation of emancipation and the employment as Union soldiers of men heretofore held in slavery; and that we have full confidence in his determination to carry these and all other constitutional measures essential to the salvation of the country into full and complete effect.

6. *Resolved*, That we deem it essential to the general welfare that harmony should prevail in the national councils, and we regard as worthy of public confidence and official trust those only who cordially indorse the principles proclaimed in these resolutions,

and which should characterize the administration of the government.

7. *Resolved*, That the government owes to all men employed in its armies, without regard to distinction of color, the full protection of the laws of war; and that any violation of these laws, or of the usages of civilized nations in time of war, by the rebels now in arms, should be made the subject of prompt and full redress.

8. *Resolved*, That foreign immigration, which in the past has added so much to the wealth, development of resources, and increase of power to this nation, — the asylum of the oppressed of all nations, — should be fostered and encouraged by a liberal and just policy.

9. *Resolved*, That we are in favor of a speedy construction of the railroad to the Pacific coast.

10. *Resolved*, That the national faith, pledged for the redemption of the public debt, must be kept inviolate, and that for this purpose we recommend economy and rigid responsibility in the public expenditures, and a vigorous and just system of taxation; and that it is the duty of every loyal State to sustain the credit and promote the use of the national currency.

11. *Resolved*, That we approve the position taken by the government, that the people of the United States can never regard with indifference the attempt of any European power to overthrow by force, or to supplant by fraud, the institutions of any republican government on the western continent; and that they will view with extreme jealousy, as menacing to the peace and independence of their own country, the efforts of any such power to obtain new footholds for monarchical governments, sustained by foreign military force, in near proximity to the United States.

On a formal vote for a candidate for President, Mr. Lincoln received all the votes of every State, except those of Missouri, which were cast, in accordance with instructions, for General U. S. Grant. The nomination was then made unanimous. On the first ballot for a candidate for Vice-President, Andrew Johnson received 200; Hannibal Hamlin, 150; Daniel S. Dickinson, 108, and seven other candidates an aggregate of 61. Before the vote was declared

a great many changes took place, and the final result was:
For Johnson, 494 votes, for Dickinson 17, for Hamlin 9.
Mr. Johnson was declared the candidate for Vice-President.

The Democratic convention met on August 29 at Chicago. Ex-Governor William Bigler of Pennsylvania was
the temporary president, and Governor Horatio Seymour
of New York the permanent president. The platform
was reported by Mr. James Guthrie of Kentucky, as follows : —

Resolved, That in the future, as in the past, we will adhere with
unswerving fidelity to the Union under the Constitution as the only
solid foundation of our strength, security, and happiness as a people,
and as a framework of government equally conducive to the welfare and prosperity of all the States, both Northern and Southern.

Resolved, That this convention does explicitly declare, as the
sense of the American people, that after four years of failure to
restore the Union by the experiment of war, during which, under the
pretence of a military necessity, or war power higher than the Constitution, the Constitution itself has been disregarded in every part, and
public liberty and private right alike trodden down, and the material prosperity of the country essentially impaired, — justice, humanity, liberty, and the public welfare demand that immediate
efforts be made for a cessation of hostilities, with a view to an ultimate convention of the States, or other peaceable means, to the
end that, at the earliest practicable moment, peace may be restored
on the basis of the Federal union of the States.

Resolved, That the direct interference of the military authorities of the United States in the recent elections held in Kentucky,
Maryland, Missouri, and Delaware was a shameful violation of the
Constitution; and a repetition of such acts in the approaching election will be held as revolutionary, and resisted with all the means
and power under our control.

Resolved, That the aim and object of the Democratic party is to
preserve the Federal Union and the rights of the States unimpaired;
and they hereby declare that they consider that the administrative
usurpation of extraordinary and dangerous powers not granted by

the Constitution; the subversion of the civil by military law in States not in insurrection; the arbitrary military arrest, imprisonment, trial, and sentence of American citizens in States where civil law exists in full force; the suppression of freedom of speech and of the press; the denial of the right of asylum; the open and avowed disregard of State rights; the employment of unusual test oaths; and the interference with and denial of the right of the people to bear arms in their defence; are calculated to prevent a restoration of the Union and the perpetuation of a government deriving its just powers from the consent of the governed.

Resolved, That the shameful disregard of the administration to its duty in respect to our fellow-citizens who are now, and long have been, prisoners of war and in a suffering condition, deserves the severest reprobation, on the score alike of public policy and common humanity.

Resolved, That the sympathy of the Democratic party is heartily and earnestly extended to the soldiery of our army and the sailors of our navy, who are and have been in the field and on the sea, under the flag of our country; and, in the event of its attaining power, they will receive all the care, protection, and regard that the brave soldiers and sailors of the Republic have so nobly earned.

On the first ballot for a candidate for President, General George B. McClellan was nominated. He had been repeatedly mentioned in connection with the nomination for many months, and the sentiments of the Democratic party were concentrated in his favor long before the convention met. The vote as first taken resulted in 174 votes for McClellan; 38 for Thomas H. Seymour of Connecticut; 12 for Horatio Seymour of New York; ½ vote for Charles O'Conor of New York, and 1½ votes blank. But before the result was announced several changes were made, and the announcement was: For McClellan, 202½ votes; for Thomas H. Seymour, 28½, — the whole of the latter votes having been given by delegates from Ohio, Indiana, and the "border States." The nomination of General

McClellan was made unanimous, on motion of Mr. Vallandigham of Ohio.

The first vote for a candidate for Vice-President resulted as follows: James Guthrie of Kentucky, 65½; George H. Pendleton of Ohio, 55½; Lazarus W. Powell of Kentucky, 32½; George W. Cass, 26; Daniel W. Voorhees of Indiana, 13; J. H. Caton, 16; Augustus C. Dodge of Iowa, 9; John S. Phelps of Missouri, 8; blank, ½ vote. On the second trial, Mr. Guthrie's name having been withdrawn, the friends of all the other candidates, except those of Mr. Pendleton, withdrew their names also, and Mr. Pendleton was unanimously nominated.

The canvass that followed was one of great spirit. The attention of the country was, it is true, earnestly fixed upon the progress of the war, and it could not be greatly or for a long time diverted to a political contest; but the latter was regarded and treated by the Republicans as one of the important campaigns of the war, and those who were not with them were against the Union. They denounced the Democratic platform as a base and cowardly surrender to the enemy, and as an encouragement to those in arms against the old flag to persevere in their hostilities until the peace party should be in a position to make terms with them on the basis of a peaceable secession. The Republicans had called their convention as one of Union men. War Democrats took a prominent part in the proceedings of that assembly, and one of them was the candidate for the Vice-Presidency on the ticket with Mr. Lincoln. They called upon all Union men to support the armies in the field by voting down the party which would make a disgraceful peace.

The Democratic platform was unpopular from its first promulgation, and grew more so as the canvass proceeded.

General McClellan repudiated its obvious meaning in his letter of acceptance. Where the convention had demanded " a cessation of hostilities with a view to an ultimate convention of the States," the candidate expressed the belief that " so soon as it is clear, or even probable, that our present adversaries are ready for peace on the basis of the Union, we should exhaust all the resources of statesmanship . . . to secure such peace." The convention had proclaimed " four years of failure to restore the Union by the experiment of war; " General McClellan wrote : " I could not look in the face of my gallant comrades of the army and navy, who have survived so many bloody battles, and tell them that their labors and the sacrifice of so many of our slain and wounded brethren had been in vain ; that we had abandoned that Union for which we have so often perilled our lives." The convention said : peace first, and Union afterward, if it can be had. General McClellan said : The Union first, and then peace ; " no peace can be permanent without union." The convention said that the war had been a failure ; General McClellan could not look his old comrades in the face and say that.

This open repudiation of the expressed sentiments of the party saved many of the votes to General McClellan which would otherwise have been given to Mr. Lincoln. But although the party held its forces together much more generally than might have been expected, the plain common sense of the people taught them that Mr. Lincoln was the candidate whose election meant earnest and uncompromising war until the power of the rebellion was destroyed and the Union was restored, and they supported him. The general result was in doubt at no time.

The following table shows the electoral and popular vote in each of the States which participated in the election : —

STATES.	POPULAR VOTE.		ELECTORAL VOTE.	
	Lincoln.	McClellan.	Lincoln.	McClellan.
Maine	72,278	47,736	7	-
New Hampshire . . .	36,595	33,034	5	-
Vermont	42,422	13,325	5	-
Massachusetts . . .	126,742	48,745	12	-
Rhode Island	14,343	8,718	4	-
Connecticut	44,603	42,288	6	-
New York	368,726	361,986	33	-
New Jersey	60,723	68,014	-	7
Pennsylvania	296,389	276,308	26	-
Delaware	8,155	8,767	-	3
Maryland	40,153	32,739	7	-
Kentucky	27,786	64,301	-	11
West Virginia . . .	23,223	10,457	5	-
Ohio	265,154	205,568	21	-
Indiana	150,422	130,233	13	-
Illinois	189,487	158,349	16	-
Michigan	85,352	67,370	8	-
Iowa	87,331	49,260	8	-
Wisconsin	79,564	63,875	8	-
Minnesota	25,060	17,375	4	-
Kansas	14,228	3,871	3	-
Missouri	72,991	31,026	11	-
Nevada *	9,826	6,594	2	-
California	62,134	43,841	5	-
Oregon	9,888	8,457	3	-
Totals	2,213,665	1,802,237	212	21

* Nevada chose three electors, one of whom died before election.

In some of the States provision had been made, before the war broke out, for taking the votes of soldiers absent from their respective States with the army. Other States adopted similar provisions during the war of the rebellion. The army votes for President in 1864, which were counted in canvassing the returns for electors, were as follows : —

STATES.	Lincoln.	McClellan.
Maine	4,174	741
New Hampshire	2,066	690
Vermont	243	49
Pennsylvania	26,712	12,349
Maryland	2,800	321
Kentucky	1,194	2,823
Ohio	41,146	9,757
Michigan	9,402	2,959
Iowa	15,178	1,364
Wisconsin	11,372	2,458
California	2,600	237
Totals	116,887	33,748

The total vote *counted*, including both the home and the army votes, was 4,166,537, and Mr. Lincoln's plurality was 494,567. The army votes of Vermont, Kansas, and Minnesota, which arrived too late to be counted, and certain votes rejected for informality in Wisconsin, would have brought up the total to about 4,175,000, and Mr. Lincoln's majority to a number in excess of half a million.

This was the first election since the adoption of the Constitution in which any State had deliberately neglected to appoint electors. In 1864 the authority of the United States was denied in, and complete sovereignty was claimed by the regular governments of, eleven States. But in some of these latter there had been set up rival governments, asserting their own loyalty to the Union, and claiming the recognition of Congress as the true government of those States. In one case at least the question presented was a puzzling one. The consent of the State of Virginia to the erection of the State of West Virginia within its territory, — consent which was required by the terms of the Constitution, — was given by one of these mushroom governments. After the creation of that new State, however, the territory and the population which admitted the authority of this government of Virginia were so small that Congress refused to recognize the claims of those who presented themselves as senators and representatives.

Nevertheless, pretended elections had been held in Louisiana and Tennessee, and the question was evidently to be pressed upon Congress whether or not the electoral votes cast in those States by a handful of men, many of them mere adventurers, were to be received. No such question had ever arisen before. Never had there been offered, at the joint meeting of the two Houses of Congress, a certificate of electoral votes which it was clearly the duty of Congress to reject, if Congress had any power to reject. In most such cases a decision of the question whether or not the disputed votes should be counted had been evaded; but in all these instances a determination either way could not affect the result. Nor would the admission or the rejection of the Southern votes in 1864 change the result. But if these votes were allowed, the act would be equivalent to a declaration that the governments by whose authority they were given were valid and regular, and such a declaration might make trouble when the time for reconstruction should come.

Under these circumstances, and in order to fix the status of the seceded States until their governments had been duly reconstructed by Congress, a joint resolution was passed by both Houses in January, 1865. It was in the following words: —

Whereas, The inhabitants and local authorities of the States of Virginia, North Carolina, South Carolina, Georgia, Florida, Alabama, Mississippi, Louisiana, Texas, Arkansas, and Tennessee, rebelled against the government of the United States, and were in such condition on the 8th day of November, 1864, that no valid election of electors for President and Vice-President of the United States, according to the Constitution and laws thereof, was held therein on said day: therefore, —

Be it resolved, By the Senate and House of Representatives of the United States of America in Congress assembled, that the States mentioned in the preamble to this joint resolution are not entitled to representation in the Electoral College for the choice of President and Vice-President of the United States for the term commencing on the 4th day of March, 1865, and no electoral votes shall be received or counted from said States concerning the choice of President and Vice-President for said term of office.

President Lincoln was committed to the validity and regularity of the governments of Louisiana and Tennessee. A State government was in full operation in the former State with Governor Hahn at the head of it, and the election in Tennessee had been ordered by Governor Andrew Johnson, Mr. Lincoln's associate on the ticket. Accordingly, the President was earnestly opposed to the resolution just recited, which virtually declared the invalidity of governments which he recognized if Congress did not. But the Republicans in Congress were resolved that the votes should not be counted, and they determined that if they could not exclude Louisiana and Tennessee by law, they would do it by joint action of the two Houses in counting the vote. Owing to a fear that the President would not sign the joint resolution, the "twenty-second joint rule," which played an important part during the sixteen years it was in force, was hastily drawn and as hastily adopted by both branches. At the same time great pressure was brought to bear upon the President to sign the joint resolution. He finally yielded on the very day of the count, February 8, but not in time to notify Congress officially that he had done so. But the joint rule, which would have been unnecessary if he had signed the resolution promptly, and which was to make so much mischief in after years, had been adopted. It was as follows: —

The two Houses shall assemble in the hall of the House of Representatives at the hour of one o'clock P. M., on the second Wednesday in February next succeeding the meeting of the electors of President and Vice-President of the United States, and the President of the Senate shall be their presiding officer. One teller shall be appointed on the part of the Senate, and two on the part of the House of Representatives, to whom shall be handed, as they are opened by the President of the Senate, the certificates of the electoral votes; and said tellers, having read the same in the presence and hearing of the two Houses then assembled, shall make a list of the votes as they shall appear from the said certificates; and the votes having been counted, the result of the same shall be delivered to the President of the Senate, who shall thereupon announce the state of the vote and the names of the persons, if any, elected; which announcement shall be deemed a sufficient declaration of the persons elected President and Vice-President of the United States, and, together with a list of the votes, be entered on the journals of the two Houses.

If, upon the reading of any such certificate by the tellers, any question shall arise in regard to counting the votes therein certified, the same having been stated by the presiding officer, the Senate shall thereupon withdraw, and said question shall be submitted to that body for its decision; and the Speaker of the House of Representatives shall, in like manner, submit said question to the House of Representatives for its decision; and no question shall be decided affirmatively, and no vote objected to shall be counted, except by the concurrent votes of the two Houses, which being obtained, the two Houses shall immediately reassemble, and the presiding officer shall then announce the decision of the question submitted, and upon any such question there shall be no debate in either House; and any other question pertinent to the object for which the two Houses are assembled may be submitted and determined in like manner.

At such joint meeting of the two Houses, seats shall be provided as follows: For the President of the Senate, the Speaker's chair; for the Speaker, a chair immediately upon his left; for the senators in the body of the hall, upon the right of the presiding officer; for the

Representatives, in the body of the hall not occupied by the senators; for the tellers, Secretary of the Senate, and Clerk of the House of Representatives, at the Clerk's desk; for the other officers of the two Houses, in front of the Clerk's desk, and upon either side of the Speaker's platform.

Such joint meeting shall not be dissolved until the electoral votes are all counted and the result declared; and no recess shall be taken unless a question shall have arisen in regard to counting any of such votes, in which case it shall be competent for either House, acting separately, in the manner hereinbefore provided, to direct a recess, not beyond the next day at the hour of one o'clock P. M.

The power assumed by Congress in the adoption of this joint resolution has frequently been assailed as an invention of the Republican party, and as a power never before asserted. But by reference to the proceedings in Congress in the year 1800 (p. 31 *et seq.*), it will be seen that a bill making permanent provision for counting the electoral vote failed only because the Senate then insisted that either branch of Congress might reject a vote, while the House of Representatives maintained that it should be rejected only by a concurrent vote.

On the 8th of February the joint meeting was held. The Vice-President, Mr. Hamlin, presided. The votes were opened by him and read by the tellers. Having completed this ceremony, as the result was about to be declared, Senator Cowan of Pennsylvania inquired if there were any more returns to be counted, and if so, "why they are not submitted to this body in joint convention, which alone is capable of determining whether they should be counted or not." The Vice-President replied: —

The chair has in his possession returns from the States of Louisiana and Tennessee, but, in obedience to the law of the land, the chair holds it to be his duty not to present them to the convention.

Senator Cowan thereupon asked if the joint resolution had become a law by the signature of the President, to which the Vice-President responded that it had been signed, but there had been no official notification of the act. A debate ensued upon the question whether the proceedings should have been had under the joint resolution or under the joint rule. The Vice-President ultimately acted under the resolution, and did not present the doubtful votes. The election of Abraham Lincoln of Illinois as President, and of Andrew Johnson of Tennessee as Vice-President, for the term commencing March 4, 1865, was then proclaimed, and the joint convention was dissolved.

XXII.

GENERAL GRANT.

Mr. Lincoln was assassinated six weeks after taking the oath of office for a second term, and Andrew Johnson became President. The civil war was virtually at an end, and already the general plan of reconstruction of the States in rebellion was much discussed. That Mr. Lincoln's own views were much more liberal than those of most of the Northern statesmen who had supported his re-election, was known before his death. But a combination of circumstances was to make of the new President a more strenuous opponent of conditions to the readmission of the Southern States than Mr. Lincoln could ever have been.

The four years of Mr. Johnson's administration form the most agitated period in American political history. A bare list of some of the political events of the time is enough to show that the civil war between the two sections, North and South, was succeeded by war, bloodless but severe, between the executive and legislative departments of the government. Mr. Johnson's training had been that of a Southern State-rights Democrat, and although his patriotism was strong enough to keep him loyal when Tennessee voted herself out of the Union, no sooner was the military conquest of the Southern Confederacy accomplished, than his former principles reasserted themselves. The more radical Republicans of the North, remembering the experience of the Whigs with Mr. Tyler, were only too ready to see in all that Mr.

Johnson did an evidence that he was to be treacherous to those who had elected him. He was continually under suspicion, and subjected to adverse criticism, from his earliest proclamations and his appointment of provisional governors for the seceded States, until, led by his life-long principles, adhered to with all the more obstinacy because of the persistent and violent opposition he encountered, he was in full sympathy with the Democratic party. Congress carried through its measures of reconstruction only by overcoming a succession of vetoes. The President expressed his constitutional views, which were shared by few Republicans, in returning the bills to establish the Freedmen's Bureau, to secure civil rights, to admit Colorado to the Union, and many others. He tried to remove from office Republicans, and to fill their places with Democrats; and Congress retorted upon him with the Tenure-of-Office Bill, which Mr. Johnson returned without his signature, and which Congress promptly passed in spite of the veto. The savage contest with Secretary Stanton, and the correspondence with General Grant, the disrespectful manner in which the President spoke of Congress, in "swinging round the circle," all these events aggravated a contest which culminated in the impeachment of the President by the House of Representatives and his trial by the Senate. In all this time the Republicans in Congress were strongly supported in the North, which then, constitutionally or not, governed the country without assistance from the South. The resolution that the long struggle against rebellion should not be fruitless was firm and unchangeable, and the Republicans had the satisfaction of seeing all their measures adopted, ineffectual as some of them have since proved to be.

During this period another set of questions began to be discussed, and some of these were to be the basis of a new

party and a new school of politicians, and to form the
issue on which future elections were to be decided. In
the prosecution of the war a great debt had been created,
and a part of this debt consisted of treasury notes, made
a legal tender for all public and private debts, except
duties on imports and the interest of the public debt. An
attempt in the early part of Mr. Johnson's term to reduce
the amount of legal-tender notes, or greenbacks, outstand-
ing, had resulted in a temporary stringency in the money
market, and had led to action by Congress which forbade
a further reduction of the volume of the currency. The
heavy taxation caused by the war, the high premium on
gold, and the rapidly increasing value of government
bonds which were drawing gold interest, induced some
politicians to propose a variety of schemes which would
lighten the burden of the taxpayer at the cost of a virtual
breach of faith on the part of the government. One of
these was the taxation of bonds, which were by their terms
expressly exempted from State and municipal taxation.
Taxation of them by national authority would have been
the same thing as reducing the rate of interest which had
been promised upon them. The most popular form of
attack upon the bondholders was a proposition to pay the
principal of the bonds in greenbacks. The letter of the
law did not forbid this, but the Republicans maintained
that the spirit of the law was against any such step, and
that it would be virtual repudiation. A very large number of Democrats, particularly in the West, took up this
proposition with great enthusiasm, among whom Mr.
Pendleton of Ohio, who had been General McClellan's
associate on the National Ticket in 1864, and was now
regarded as the leading candidate for the first place in
1868, was one of the most prominent. While this view
of public policy was most prevalent among Democrats,

there were many Republicans also who shared it; Thaddeus Stevens being the most conspicuous example of dissent from the general opinion of the party, although even he finally voted in favor of a bill to strengthen the public credit, which President Johnson defeated by a "pocket veto." It was in the canvass preliminary to the election of 1868 that the Democrats first manifested that preference for the greenback currency which has ever since been a principle of the controlling wing of the party.

A great many circumstances united to make General Ulysses S. Grant the natural and inevitable choice of the Republicans for a candidate for President. The chief of these reasons were his military success and the conspicuous position into which he was thrust by the controversy with Mr. Johnson. But added to these recommendations was the confidence reposed in his judgment in the choice of men; and the fact that he was no politician increased not a little his popularity with the people who were tired of the wrangles of the past few years. General Grant, it was well known, had never voted for Republican candidates in his life, and there were many persons who feared that the risk of taking for the leader of the party, at such a time, a man whose political principles were thought not to be well defined, was too great, and that the Republicans might be about to repeat their own mistake of 1864. But nothing could stay the tide of public sentiment in General Grant's favor, and the warnings of the dissentients were drowned in the nearly universal demand that he should be selected. The wisest and most cautious men of the party convinced themselves by General Grant's letters and private conversation that he was fully to be trusted, and their confidence was not misplaced.

The question of the candidacy for the first place being fully decided by the action of the State and District Con-

ventions, as well as by popular sentiment, all the interest
in the Republican Convention was concentrated upon the
vice-presidency and the platform. The vote of the Senate upon the impeachment of the President had been
taken the week before the convention met, and as several
Republican senators had voted for acquittal on the
eleventh article, which had been taken for a test, some of
the more radical and impulsive delegates were in favor of
expressing decided condemnation of the act which had
rendered the removal of the President impossible. But
in spite of the vehemence of the more hot-headed members of the party, the proposed action was defeated, and
the convention contented itself with expressing the opinion that those who voted for conviction were in the right.
There was a long list of candidates for the nomination for
Vice-President. There was Mr. Hamlin, who had been
left off the ticket four years before in order to give a
representation to the loyalty of the South; Mr. B. F.
Wade, senator from Ohio, who was President of the Senate
during a part of the time that the war between the President and Congress was waging; Mr. Colfax, the speaker
of the House of Representatives; Senators Fenton of
New York, and Wilson of Massachusetts, Governor Cur-
tin of Pennsylvania, and other candidates of less prominence.

Prior to the meeting of the National Convention of the
Republicans, a convention of soldiers and sailors was held
at Chicago. It was presided over by General John A.
Logan, and was full of enthusiasm for General Grant. The
Republican Convention met on May 20, at Chicago, and
completed its work in two days. General Carl Schurz was
the temporary presiding officer, and General Joseph R.
Hawley of Connecticut was made permanent president.
The first day was occupied with preliminaries. On the

morning of the second day the Committee on Resolutions reported a platform, which was adopted. Two additional resolutions were afterwards appended to the platform, having been moved from the floor by Mr. Schurz, and unanimously approved. The platform in full was as follows: —

The National Republican party of the United States, assembled in national convention in the city of Chicago, on the twenty-first day of May, 1868, make the following declaration of principles: —

1. We congratulate the country on the assured success of the reconstruction policy of Congress, as evinced by the adoption, in the majority of the States lately in rebellion, of constitutions securing equal civil and political rights to all; and it is the duty of the government to sustain those institutions and to prevent the people of such States from being remitted to a state of anarchy.

2. The guarantee by Congress of equal suffrage to all loyal men at the South was demanded by every consideration of public safety, of gratitude, and of justice, and must be maintained; while the question of suffrage in all the loyal States properly belongs to the people of those States.

3. We denounce all forms of repudiation as a national crime; and the national honor requires the payment of the public indebtedness in the uttermost good faith to all creditors at home and abroad, not only according to the letter, but the spirit of the laws under which it was contracted.

4. It is due to the labor of the nation that taxation should be equalized, and reduced as rapidly as the national faith will permit.

5. The National debt, contracted as it has been for the preservation of the Union for all time to come, should be extended over a fair period for redemption; and it is the duty of Congress to reduce the rate of interest thereon, whenever it can be honestly done.

6. That the best policy to diminish our burden of debt is so to improve our credit that capitalists will seek to loan us money at lower rates of interest than we now pay, and must continue to pay, so long as repudiation, partial or total, open or covert, is threatened or suspected.

7. The government of the United States should be administered

with the strictest economy; and the corruptions which have been so shamefully nursed and fostered by Andrew Johnson call loudly for radical reform.

8. We profoundly deplore the untimely and tragic death of Abraham Lincoln, and regret the accession to the presidency of Andrew Johnson, who has acted treacherously to the people who elected him and the cause he was pledged to support; who has usurped high legislative and judicial functions; who has refused to execute the laws; who has used his high office to induce other officers to ignore and violate the laws; who has employed his executive powers to render insecure the property, the peace, the liberty and life of the citizen; who has abused the pardoning power; who has denounced the national legislature as unconstitutional; who has persistently and corruptly resisted, by every means in his power, every proper attempt at the reconstruction of the States lately in rebellion; who has perverted the public patronage into an engine of wholesale corruption; and who has been justly impeached for high crimes and misdemeanors, and properly pronounced guilty thereof by the vote of thirty-five Senators.

9. The doctrine of Great Britain and other European powers, that because a man is once a subject he is always so, must be resisted at every hazard by the United States as a relic of feudal times, not authorized by the laws of nations, and at war with our national honor and independence. Naturalized citizens are entitled to protection in all their rights of citizenship, as though they were native born; and no citizen of the United States, native or naturalized, must be liable to arrest and imprisonment by any foreign power for acts done or words spoken in this country; and, if so arrested and imprisoned, it is the duty of the government to interfere in his behalf.

10. Of all who were faithful in the trials of the late war, there were none entitled to more special honor than the brave soldiers and seamen who endured the hardships of campaign and cruise, and imperilled their lives in the service of the country; the bounties and pensions provided by the laws for these brave defenders of the nation are obligations never to be forgotten; the widows and orphans of the gallant dead are the wards of the people, — a sacred legacy bequeathed to the nation's protecting care.

11. Foreign immigration, which in the past has added so much to the wealth, development, and resources, and increase of power to this Republic, — the asylum of the oppressed of all nations, — should be fostered and encouraged by a liberal and just policy.

12. This convention declares itself in sympathy with all oppressed peoples struggling for their rights.

13. We highly commend the spirit of magnanimity and forbearance with which men who have served in the rebellion, but who now frankly and honestly co-operate with us in restoring the peace of the country and reconstructing the Southern State governments upon the basis of impartial justice and equal rights, are received back into the communion of the loyal people; and we favor the removal of the disqualifications and restrictions imposed upon the late rebels in the same measure as the spirit of disloyalty will die out, and as may be consistent with the safety of the loyal people.

14. We recognize the great principles laid down in the immortal Declaration of Independence as the true foundation of Democratic government; and we hail with gladness every effort toward making these principles a living reality on every inch of American soil.

When the convention was ready to proceed with its nominations, General Logan presented the name of General Grant in a brief but stirring speech, and the roll of the States being called, every vote — 650 in all — was given to him. While the enthusiasm of the convention was at its height, a large portrait of General Grant was uncovered behind the President's chair, and the delegates again went wild with cheering. Five votes were necessary to effect a nomination for the second place on the ticket. The several votes were as follows : —

	1st.	2d.	3d.	4th.	5th.
Benjamin F. Wade of Ohio . .	147	170	178	206	38
Reuben E. Fenton of N. York .	126	144	139	144	69
Henry Wilson of Mass. . . .	119	114	101	87	–
Schuyler Colfax of Indiana .	115	145	165	186	541
Andrew G. Curtin of Penn. . .	51	45	40	–	–
Hannibal Hamlin of Maine . .	28	30	25	25	–
James Speed of Kentucky . .	22	–	–	–	–
James Harlan of Iowa . . .	16	–	–	–	–
John A. J. Creswell of Md. . .	14	–	–	–	–
Samuel C. Pomeroy of Kansas,	6	–	–	–	–
William D. Kelley of Penn. .	4	–	–	–	–

The nomination of Mr. Colfax, the youngest candidate of all, was made unanimous, and the convention adjourned.

The Democrats were summoned to meet at Tammany Hall, New York, on the fourth of July; and Democratic soldiers and sailors were summoned to meet on the same day, also in New York. The interest centred wholly in the nomination of a candidate for the presidency, and it was from the first a contest of "the field" against Mr. Pendleton. Other candidates had strong supporters. The sentiment in the soldiers' convention was all in favor of General W. S. Hancock, who commended himself to those who had favored the war by his own gallant services, and to Democrats by his action as military commander at New Orleans during Mr. Johnson's administration. The Southern delegations were for Mr. Johnson himself, at least outwardly. There was an undercurrent in favor of Chief Justice Chase, who was openly charged by Republicans with having bid for the nomination. But most of the delegates from the Eastern States were chosen without instructions, and were prepared to support any candidate, except perhaps Mr. Pendleton, who seemed to have a chance of success.

Meantime, the Northwest was strong for Mr. Pendleton, though, as the event proved, the feeling was not very deep. A day or two before the convention a body of three hundred men — the "Pendleton Escort" — arrived from Ohio and marched through New York, each man wearing, pinned to his breast, a flag on which was a representation of a five-dollar greenback, and an inscription demanding the payment of the five-twenty bonds in that currency.

The fourth of July was Saturday. The convention organized by the choice of ex-Governor John M. Palmer of Illinois as temporary chairman, and afterward Horatio Seymour of New York was made permanent president. The convention was from the first extremely suspicious of the Pendleton men. A motion that the rules of the National House of Representatives be the rules of the convention was offered, and voted down because it was proposed by an Ohio man, and because of a fear that it might mean an abrogation of the two-thirds rule. This latter rule was, however, adopted without opposition. On the first day the supporters of Mr. Pendleton were in favor of prompt work, that a ballot might be taken before their opponents could have an opportunity to concentrate; but they were defeated, and the convention adjourned until Monday. Afterward the Pendleton men were in favor of all possible delay, and on Monday they "filibustered" to retard the progress of business. It was not until Tuesday that the committee on resolutions was ready to report. The platform was unanimously reported and unanimously adopted, as follows: —

The Democratic party, in National Convention assembled, reposing its trust in the intelligence, patriotism, and discriminating justice of the people, standing upon the Constitution, as the foundation and limitation of the powers of the government, and the guarantee of the liberties of the citizen, and recognizing the questions of slavery and secession as having been settled, for all time to come, by the war, or the voluntary action of the Southern States in constitutional conventions assembled, and never to be renewed or re-agitated, do, with the return of peace, demand: —

1. Immediate restoration of all the States to their rights in the Union under the Constitution, and of civil government to the American people.

2. Amnesty for all past political offences, and the regulation of the elective franchise in the States by their citizens.

3. Payment of the public debt of the United States as rapidly as practicable; all moneys drawn from the people by taxation, except

so much as is requisite for the necessities of the government, economically administered, being honestly applied to such payment, and where the obligations of the government do not expressly state upon their face, or the law under which they were issued does not provide that they shall be paid in coin, they ought, in right and in justice, to be paid in the lawful money of the United States.

4. Equal taxation of every species of property according to its real value, including government bonds and other public securities.

5. One currency for the government and the people, the laborer and the officeholder, the pensioner and the soldier, the producer and the bondholder.

6. Economy in the administration of the government; the reduction of the standing army and navy; the abolition of the freedmen's bureau, and all political instrumentalities designed to secure negro supremacy; simplification of the system, and discontinuance of inquisitorial modes of assessing and collecting internal revenue, so that the burden of taxation may be equalized and lessened; the credit of the government and the currency made good; the repeal of all enactments for enrolling the State militia into national forces in time of peace; and a tariff for revenue upon foreign imports, and such equal taxation under the internal revenue laws as will afford incidental protection to domestic manufacturers, and as will, without impairing the revenue, impose the least burden upon, and best promote and encourage the great industrial interests of the country.

7. Reform of abuses in the administration, the expulsion of corrupt men from office, the abrogation of useless offices, the restoration of rightful authority to, and the independence of, the executive and judicial departments of the government, the subordination of the military to the civil power, to the end that the usurpations of Congress and the despotism of the sword, may cease.

8. Equal rights and protection for naturalized and native-born citizens, at home and abroad; the assertion of American nationality which shall command the respect of foreign powers, and furnish an example and encouragement to peoples struggling for national integrity, constitutional liberty, and individual rights, and the maintenance of the rights of naturalized citizens against the absolute doctrine of immutable allegiance, and the claims of foreign powers to punish them for alleged crime committed beyond their jurisdiction.

In demanding these measures and reforms, we arraign the Radical party for its disregard of right, and the unparalleled oppression and tyranny which have marked its career.

After the most solemn and unanimous pledge of both Houses of Congress to prosecute the war exclusively for the maintenance of the government and the preservation of the Union under the Constitution. it has repeatedly violated that most sacred pledge under which alone was rallied that noble volunteer army which carried our flag to victory. Instead of restoring the Union it has, so far as in its power. dissolved it. and subjected ten States, in the time of profound peace, to military despotism and negro supremacy. It has nullified there the right of trial by jury; it has abolished the *habeas corpus*. that most sacred writ of liberty; it has overthrown the freedom of speech and the press; it has substituted arbitrary seizures and arrests, and military trials and secret star-chamber inquisitions for the constitutional tribunals; it has disregarded. in time of peace. the right of the people to be free from searches and seizures: it has entered the post and telegraph offices, and even the private rooms of individuals. and seized their private papers and letters without any specific charge or notice or affidavit, as required by the organic law; it has converted the American capitol into a bastile; it has established a system of spies and official espionage to which no constitutional monarchy of Europe would now dare to resort; it has abolished the right of appeal. on important constitutional questions. to the supreme judicial tribunals, and threatened to curtail or destroy its original jurisdiction, which is irrevocably vested by the Constitution. while the learned chief justice has been subjected to the most atrocious calumnies, merely because he would not prostitute his high office to the support of the false and partisan charges preferred against the President. Its corruption and extravagance have exceeded anything known in history. and. by its frauds and monopolies. it has nearly doubled the burden of the debt created by the war. It has stripped the President of his Constitutional power of appointment, even of his own Cabinet. Under its repeated assaults the pillars of the government are rocking on their base. and should it succeed in November next, and inaugurate its President, we will meet, as a subjected and conquered people. amid the ruins of liberty, and the scattered fragments of the Constitution.

And we do declare and resolve that ever since the people of the United States threw off all subjection to the British crown the privilege and trust of suffrage have belonged to the several States, and have been granted, regulated, and controlled exclusively by the political power of each State respectively, and that any attempt by Congress, on any pretext whatever, to deprive any State of this right, or interfere with its exercise, is a flagrant usurpation of power, which can find no warrant in the Constitution, and, if sanctioned by the people, will subvert our form of government, and can only end in a single centralized and consolidated government, in which the separate existence of the States will be entirely absorbed, and unqualified despotism be established in place of a federal union of coequal States. And that we regard the Reconstruction Acts (so-called) of Congress, as such, as usurpations, and unconstitutional, revolutionary, and void.

That our soldiers and sailors, who carried the flag of our country to victory against a most gallant and determined foe, must ever be gratefully remembered, and all the guarantees given in their favor must be faithfully carried into execution.

That the public lands should be distributed as widely as possible among the people, and should be disposed of either under the pre-emption or homestead lands, or sold in reasonable quantities, and to none but actual occupants, at the minimum price established by the government. When grants of the public lands may be allowed, necessary for the encouragement of important public improvements, the proceeds of the sale of such lands, and not the lands themselves, should be so applied.

That the President of the United States, Andrew Johnson, in exercising the powers of his high office in resisting the aggressions of Congress upon the constitutional rights of the States and the people, is entitled to the gratitude of the whole American people, and in behalf of the Democratic party we tender him our thanks for his patriotic efforts in that regard.

Upon this platform the Democratic party appeal to every patriot, including all the conservative element and all who desire to support the Constitution and restore the Union, forgetting all past differences of opinion, to unite with us in the present great struggle for the liberties of the people; and that to all such, to whatever party they may have heretofore belonged, we extend the right hand of fellowship, and hail all such co-operating with us as friends and brethren.

To this platform two additional resolutions were subsequently appended, on motion, as follows: —

Resolved, That this convention sympathize cordially with the workingmen of the United States in their efforts to protect the rights and interests of the laboring classes of the country.

Resolved, That the thanks of the convention are tendered to Chief Justice Salmon P. Chase, for the justice, dignity, and impartiality with which he presided over the court of impeachment on the trial of President Andrew Johnson.

Voting for a candidate then began, and continued until Thursday. The whole number of votes — each delegate having one half a vote — was 317, and 212, two thirds of the whole, were necessary to a choice. A few only of the twenty-two separate trials are necessary to show the increase and decrease of strength of the respective candidates.

	1st.	8th.	16th.	18th.	19th.	21st.
George H. Pendleton of Ohio	105	156½	107½	56½	–	–
Andrew Johnson of Tennessee . . .	65	6	5½	10	–	5
Winfield S. Hancock of Pennsylvania,	33½	28	113½	144½	135½	135½
Sanford E. Church of New York . .	33	–	–	–	–	–
Asa Packer of Pennsylvania	26	26	–	–	22	–
Joel Parker of New Jersey	13	7	7	3½	–	–
James E. English of Connecticut . .	16	6	–	–	6	19
James R. Doolittle of Wisconsin . .	13	12	12	12	12	12
Thomas A. Hendricks of Indiana . .	2½	75	70½	87	107½	132
Salmon P. Chase of Ohio	–	–	–	½	½	½
All others	9	½	–	3½	33	12¼

Great excitement had prevailed during the voting. On several occasions, delegates from States which had instructed their members to vote "as a unit," insisted upon their right to a record of their individual votes, but it was uniformly decided that the delegations had a right to decide how their votes should be cast, and that only one spokesman from a State could be heard. A great deal of intriguing went on during the three days of voting, — the New York and Pennsylvania delegations, with a combined vote of 59, assisted by the delegations from other Eastern States, blocking the way to a nomination by abandoning growing candidates when they became too dangerous. On the twenty-first vote the contest was apparently narrowed down to Hancock and Hendricks, neither of whom was acceptable to New York. At this point a sensation was created, when the twenty-second vote had progressed through a few States, by a member giving some votes to Horatio Seymour, the president of the convention. Mr. Seymour promptly refused to be a candidate, but there was a hurried consultation, and the vote was persisted in. More votes were given to Seymour, and a "stampede" began. Mr. Seymour withdrew from the chair, and the changes of votes went on, amid the greatest excitement and enthusiasm, until he was made the nominee of the convention by 317 votes, — all the convention was capable of casting. It was asserted then, as it has been on every other occasion of a nomination suddenly made, after a long contest, from that of Mr. Polk in 1844 to that of General Garfield in 1880, that the whole affair was carefully planned and rehearsed beforehand. But if it was so in 1868, and not a line of evidence was ever adduced to prove it, only a few persons could have been in the secret, and the enthusiasm of the delegates was genuine and sincere.

General Francis P. Blair, Jr., of Missouri, was nominated unanimously for Vice President at the first trial. Mr. Blair had just brought himself into prominence by a violent, not to say a revolutionary letter, addressed to Col. J. O. Brodhead, dated a few days before the Convention met, and the nomination seemed to be, and probably was, a result of that letter.

The canvass was shorter than usual, and, although one-sided, was decidedly interesting. The fame of General Grant, and the high regard in which he was held, did not allow the result to be doubtful, but there were already some noteworthy defections from the Republican party at the North, on account of the radical character of its Southern legislation, and a new element of discord in politics appeared, in the shape of the movement already referred to, to pay the five-twenty bonds in greenbacks. Although it was never seriously believed that Governor Seymour was in favor of that measure, he "stood upon the platform," and declared, in accepting the nomination, that the resolutions "are in accord with my views." The Republicans made much of the virtual repudiation which such a financial policy as the resolutions demanded would effect, and, while they lost some votes of a certain class, they gained many others which were better worth having, even if they did not count any more. Toward the end of the canvass there was a very strong movement by business men to defeat the Democrats, and it contributed not a little to the overwhelming success of General Grant.

The South was secure for the Republicans. Reconstruction with negro suffrage, protected by the general government, and with extensive disfranchisement of those who had joined in the rebellion, made the triumph of the Republican electoral ticket a certainty. Only Delaware, Maryland, Kentucky, and Louisiana, of all the Southern States, gave Governor Seymour a majority; but some of the States were not, under the act of Congress, entitled to representation in Congress, and consequently not to electoral votes. The votes of thirty-three States were counted, while that of Georgia was treated as the vote of Missouri had been in 1820. Nebraska having been admitted to the Union, — the proclamation declaring its admission was dated March 1, 1867, — raised the number of States to thirty-seven. All the Southern States, except Virginia, Mississippi, and Texas, had been readmitted to representation in Congress, and to the right to choose electors. The position of Georgia was in doubt. In the reorganization of South Carolina the practice of a choice of electors by the legislature was abandoned; but Florida adopted the discarded system, and accordingly there was still not complete uniformity. The electoral and popular votes of the States, including Georgia, were as follows:—

STATES.	POPULAR VOTE.		ELECTORAL VOTE.	
	Grant.	Seymour.	Grant.	Seymour.
Maine	70,426	42,396	7	–
New Hampshire . . .	38,191	31,224	5	–
Vermont	44,167	12,045	5	–
Massachusetts	136,477	59,408	12	–
Rhode Island	12,993	6,548	4	–
Connecticut	50,641	47,600	6	–
New York	419,883	429,883	–	33
New Jersey	80,121	83,001	–	7
Pennsylvania	342,280	313,382	26	–
Delaware	7,623	10,980	–	3
Maryland	30,438	62,357	–	7
Virginia *	–	–	–	–
West Virginia	29,025	20,306	5	–
North Carolina	96,226	84,090	9	–
South Carolina	62,301	45,237	6	–
Georgia	57,134	102,822	–	9
Florida †	–	–	3	–
Alabama	76,366	72,086	8	–
Mississippi *	–	–	–	–
Louisiana	33,263	80,225	–	7
Texas *	–	–	–	–
Arkansas	22,152	19,078	5	–
Missouri	85,671	59,788	11	–
Tennessee	56,757	26,311	10	–
Kentucky	39,566	115,889	–	11
Ohio	280,128	238,700	21	–
Michigan	128,550	97,069	8	–
Indiana	176,552	166,980	13	–
Illinois	250,293	199,143	16	–
Wisconsin	108,857	84,710	8	–
Minnesota	43,542	28,072	4	–
Iowa	120,399	74,040	8	–
Nebraska	9,729	5,439	3	–
Kansas	31,049	14,019	3	–
Nevada	6,480	5,218	3	–
California	54,592	54,078	5	–
Oregon	10,961	11,125	–	3
Totals	3,012,833	2,703,249	214	80

* No vote.   † By Legislature.

There were many charges of gross frauds in the election. Aside from those alleged in the Southern States, the most famous case was that of New York. At the time the election took place, the "Tweed Ring" was in full power; and some telegrams which the Republicans regarded as highly suspicious passed between members of the Democratic State Central Committee and certain prominent politicians. It will be observed that the vote as canvassed gave a majority of exactly ten thousand to Mr. Seymour. This result, it was believed by many persons, was brought about intentionally, with a view to certain large wagers upon the Democratic majority in New York.

Reference has already been made to the fact that some of the Southern States were, while others according to the legislation of Congress were not, entitled to vote for electors of President and Vice-President. Congress had passed a joint resolution declaring that none of the States lately in rebellion should be entitled to electoral votes unless, at the time prescribed for the election, such State had adopted a constitution since the 4th of March, 1867, under which a State government had been organized; unless the election was held under the authority of that government; and unless the State had become entitled to representation in Congress under the reconstruction laws. President Johnson vetoed this resolution on July 20, 1868, and both Houses of Congress passed it over his veto, the Senate by 45 to 8, and the House of Representatives by 134 to 36, and it was proclaimed a law. Under this resolution, Virginia, Mississippi, and Texas were excluded absolutely from the election. All the other seceded States, except Georgia, had been admitted to representation in Congress and were entitled to vote for President. The question whether or not Georgia had complied with the terms of the act authorizing a representation of that State in Congress was in dispute. Accordingly, on the 6th of February, 1869, two days before the count of electoral votes was to take place, Mr. Edmunds of Vermont introduced in the Senate a concurrent resolution, which does not require the approval of the President, in the following terms: —

Whereas, The question whether the State of Georgia has become and is entitled to representation in the two Houses of Congress is now pending and undetermined; and whereas by the joint resolution of Congress, passed July 20, 1868, entitled "resolution excluding from the Electoral College votes of States lately in rebellion which shall not have been reorganized," it was provided that no electoral votes from any of the States lately in rebellion should be received or counted for President or Vice-President of the United States until, among other things, such State should have become entitled to representation in Congress pursuant to acts of Congress in that behalf; therefore

Resolved, etc., That, on the assembling of the two Houses on the second Wednesday of February, 1869, for the counting of the electoral votes for President and Vice-President, as provided by law and the joint rules, if the counting or omitting to count the electoral votes, if any, which may be presented as of the State of Georgia, shall not essentially change the result, in that case they shall be reported by the President of the Senate in the following manner: Were the votes presented as of the State of Georgia to be counted, the result would be, for —— for President of the United States —— votes; if not counted, for —— for President of the United States —— votes; but, in either case, —— is elected President of the United States; and in the same manner for Vice-President.

Mr. Hendricks of Indiana was the only senator who took an active part in the debate against this resolution, although Mr. Trumbull of Illinois expressed the opinion that it would be best to count the vote of Georgia and say nothing about it, and finally voted (alone among the Republicans) against the resolution. It was passed by the House of Representatives on the same day under a suspension of the rules. It is worth noting that three of the candidates on presidential tickets in 1884 — Messrs. Blaine, Logan, and Butler — voted in the affirmative in the House on the passage of this resolution, while a fourth — Mr. Hendricks — voted against it in the Senate.

The count of the electoral votes took place on the 10th of February. It proceeded regularly until the votes of Louisiana were presented, when a member from Tennessee objected to them, under the twenty-second joint rule (see page 250), and the two Houses separated to consider the matter. Although no debate was in order, a great deal of time was consumed by the Senate in agreeing upon a form in which the decision of the question should be put. In the end the Senate voted to admit the votes by 51 to 7. The House promptly decided the question the same way by 137 to 63. The count was then resumed, and all the votes were opened and recorded, · except those of Georgia. On the presentation of the votes of that State, General Butler of Massachusetts arose and objected in writing to them on four distinct grounds: first, that the votes were not given on the day fixed by law, — the electoral college of Georgia had met on the 9th instead of the 2d of December, 1868; secondly, because at the date of the election Georgia had not been admitted to representation in Congress; thirdly, because Georgia had not complied with the reconstruction acts; and, fourthly, because the election had not been fair and free. The question arose at once whether the concurrent resolution of the Senate and House, directing how the vote of Georgia should be treated, or the joint rule, was to govern. The presiding officer, Senator Wade of Ohio, was at first inclined to hold the two Houses to the former; but, as the situation became complicated, he led the Senate back to its chamber.

The House of Representatives quickly decided, without debate, — 150 to 41, — that the vote of Georgia should not be counted. In the Senate there was a long and somewhat ungoverned discussion. Mr. Wade explained that the reason why he had yielded his first position in the joint meeting was that two of Mr. Butler's objections were not of the kind contemplated by the concurrent resolution directing how the votes of Georgia should be declared. A great many propositions were made, and at last the Senate voted, by 28 votes against 25, "that, under the special order of the two Houses respecting the electoral vote from the State of Georgia, the objections made to the counting of the vote of the electors for the State of Georgia are not in order." The action of each House having been communicated to the other, the Senate returned to the Representatives' Hall. Then ensued one of the most remarkable and disgraceful scenes ever enacted in Congress. Mr. Wade, on taking the chair, remarked that the objections of the gentleman from Massachusetts had been overruled by the Senate, and that the vote would be announced according to the terms of the concurrent resolution. General Butler said that the House had sustained the objections, and proposed to offer a resolution, remarking, "I do not understand that we are to be overruled by the Senate in that way." The President of the Senate refused to entertain the resolution, and General Butler appealed from the decision of the chair. The President declined to entertain the appeal. A scene of indescribable disorder and confusion followed, several members speaking at once, Mr. Butler distinguishing himself by the violence of his language, and, as General Garfield said, in the debate which followed the joint meeting, by "a manner and bearing of unparalleled insolence." Some of his remarks

were omitted in the revision of them, which appears in
the "Congressional Globe;" but they were referred to in
the debate just mentioned. The last remark he made, as
revised, is thus reported: —

Mr. BUTLER of Massachusetts: I move that this convention
now be dissolved, and that the Senate have leave to retire. [Con-
tinued cries of "Order!" "Order!"] And on that motion I
demand a vote. [Cries of "Order!" "Order!" from various
parts of the hall.] We certainly have the right to clear the hall of
interlopers.

The presiding officer, not noticing these interruptions,
proceeded to sum up the result, as directed by the concurrent resolution, and declared Grant and Colfax elected.
The Senate then retired.

As soon as the House was by itself, Mr. Butler rose to
a question of privilege, and offered a resolution that "the
House protest that the counting of the vote of Georgia
by the order of the Vice-President *pro tempore* was a
gross act of oppression and an invasion of the rights and
privileges of the House." Upon this resolution a long
and most acrimonious debate took place, which lasted
three days. It contributed little or nothing to the settlement of the constitutional questions that have arisen in
regard to the count of votes. The position of affairs was
quite novel, and the gentlemen who took part in the
debate seemed, without exception, to give their hasty
impressions, rather than the result of careful study. The
only point which was made clear was that the constitution
and the action of Congress left room for a variety of
views, and that no member need be at a loss for pre-
cedents to sustain his own opinion. General Butler
changed his resolution several times before a vote was
taken. In one of its forms it proposed to abrogate the
twenty-second joint rule, — a proposition which was re-

ceived with derision by many Republican members, who all declared that it was not possible for one House to rescind a joint rule. But eight years later the Senate rescinded the same rule, and refused to be bound by it, although the House was then in favor of acting under it. General Butler's resolution, greatly toned down, and providing for the reference of the subject to a select committee, was at last brought to a vote, on a motion to lay it on the table, which was carried by 130 to 55, and the matter was dropped.

XXIII.

THE "GREELEY CAMPAIGN."

THE reconstruction of the Southern States had been substantially completed before the term of General Grant as President began. It only remained for three of the States to comply with the conditions already established. This they did soon afterward, and the legislation of the Forty-first Congress was accomplished, with every State in the Union fully represented. But the Southern question was not yet settled. The constitutions of the re-admitted States contained guaranties of the right of the people to vote without reference to their race, color, or previous condition of servitude; but, in effect, both the political and social rights of the colored people were much restricted. A state of terrorism existed in some parts of the South, where a secret organization known as the Ku-Klux-Klan committed outrages upon the colored people, intended to intimidate them and to prevent them from voting. To defeat the schemes of those who endeavored by lawless acts to render the legislation of Congress nugatory, the act for the enforcement of the Fourteenth Amendment to the Constitution, commonly known as the Ku-Klux Act, was passed. This measure, although it seemed necessary at the time, gave the Democrats an opportunity, which they were not slow to improve, to sneer at the clumsiness of a party which, with unlimited power, had not been able in five years since the war closed to finish its work with the South. Military force was constantly necessary to uphold the Southern

State governments, and the internal condition of some districts was sadly disturbed.

Beside the Southern question there were others which now began to assume political importance. The first act signed by President Grant pledged the faith of the government to the payment of the interest-bearing bonds of the United States in coin, and to an early resumption of specie payments. For the time being, the Opposition confined their attacks upon the financial system to the national banks. The annexation of San Domingo to the United States was a favorite scheme with the President, and he did all that was in his power, both publicly and privately, to accomplish it. In the course of his negotiations to that end, and by other measures, he alienated the support of Mr. Sumner and of Horace Greeley, whose standing as Republicans and as public men was almost unique, and whose adhesion to the Opposition in the ensuing canvass was deemed at the time to be most disastrous to the Republicans. There was another issue, which had its origin at this time, which has since played an important part in congressional and presidential elections. The principle tersely expressed by Mr. Marcy to justify the wholesale removals from office practised by General Jackson, that "to the victors belong the spoils of the enemy," had been adopted by every Democratic and Opposition administration which followed that of Jackson. On the accession of Mr. Lincoln, the Democratic officers were driven out and Republicans took their places, in every department of the government, from the foreign minister to the country postmaster. Mr. Johnson had been restrained from substituting Democrats for them all only by the tenure-of-office act. General Grant found few Democrats to expel from public positions; but an evil, which had grown up with that of a partisan civil service, now took on portentous proportions. Certain gentlemen, usually one for each State, became practically recognized as dispensers of patronage within those States, and, by the exercise of the power which the virtual right to dismiss and appoint to office gave them, made themselves "bosses" and dictators of Republican politics in their respective States. The heads of the custom-houses, the post-offices, and other government offices, were in many cases the servants of these bosses, and were forced to work in the interest of the personal fortunes of their protectors, and to employ the subordinates under them to promote the same object, — all under the penalty of removal. This manipulation of the offices for private purposes developed a demand for a reform of the civil service, and emphasized the objections of many who had been sturdy Republicans to the administration of General Grant.

The supporters of the administration were, however, neither few nor inactive. In addition to those who cordially approved the public acts of Grant, there were many others who were not prepared to abandon it on account of its mistakes. They set down some of the President's errors to his inexperience in public life; and while other errors could not be so explained, the Republicans generally held that for certain tasks which they thought remained to be done before the South could be safely left to itself, General Grant was the best executive the country could have. While, therefore, the elements existed for an unusually powerful opposition to the Republican party, the leaders of that party had no doubt of their ability to carry the election of 1872.

The beginning of a united opposition was made in Missouri in 1870, when a part of the Republicans united with the Democrats in a "liberal" movement, and carried

the State election. It was further developed the next
year. Meetings were held in St. Louis and Cincinnati in
the spring, in which opposition to the re-election of
General Grant was freely expressed, for even then it was
assumed that he would expect to be nominated for re-
election. About the same time Mr. Vallandigham of
Ohio, who had been identified with the most extreme
form of Democratic opposition to the war for the Union,
and had been equally radical in his condemnation of
Republican reconstruction and treatment of the South,
presented and supported in a local caucus in Ohio a series
of resolutions looking to a union of all elements of opposition on the basis of a full acceptance of the results of
the war, the legislation already enacted, and the three
amendments made to the constitution. Finally, at a mass
meeting of Liberal Republicans of Missouri, held at
Jefferson City in January, 1872, in which nearly all the
counties of the State were represented, it was voted to
call a national convention of Liberal Republicans, to be
held at Cincinnati on the first of May.

The first conventions for making nominations for the
Presidency were held at Columbus, Ohio, in February.
The Labor Reformers met on the twenty-first of that month,
with representatives present from seventeen States.
Edwin M. Chamberlin of Massachusetts was the permanent presiding officer. The convention was in session
two days, and adopted the following platform : —

We hold that all political power is inherent in the people, and
free government is founded on their authority and established for
their benefit ; that all citizens are equal in political rights, entitled
to the largest religious and political liberty compatible with the
good order of society, as also to the use and enjoyment of the fruits
of their labor and talents; and no man or set of men is entitled to
exclusive separable endowments and privileges, or immunities from
the government, but in consideration of public services; and any

laws destructive of these fundamental principles are without moral binding force, and should be repealed. And believing that all the evils resulting from unjust legislation now affecting the industrial classes can be removed by the adoption of the principles contained in the following declaration, therefore,

Resolved, That it is the duty of the government to establish a just standard of distribution of capital and labor by providing a purely national circulating medium, based on the faith and resources of the nation, issued directly to the people without the intervention of any system of banking corporations; which money shall be legal tender in the payment of all debts, public and private, and interchangeable at the option of the holder for government bonds bearing a rate of interest not to exceed 3.65 per cent, subject to future legislation by Congress.

2. That the national debt should be paid in good faith, according to the original contract, at the earliest option of the government, without mortgaging the property of the people or the future earnings of labor, to enrich a few capitalists at home and abroad.

3. That justice demands that the burdens of government should be so adjusted as to bear equally on all classes, and that the exemption from taxation of government bonds bearing extortionate rates of interest is a violation of all just principles of revenue laws.

4. That the public lands of the United States belong to the people and should not be sold to individuals nor granted to corporations, but should be held as a sacred trust for the benefit of the people, and should be granted to landless settlers only, in amounts not exceeding one hundred and sixty acres of land.

5. That Congress should modify the tariff so as to admit free such articles of common use as we can neither produce nor grow, and lay duties for revenue mainly upon articles of luxury and upon such articles of manufacture as will, we having the raw materials in abundance, assist in further developing the resources of the country.

6. That the presence in our country of Chinese laborers, imported by capitalists in large numbers for servile use, is an evil, entailing want and its attendant train of misery and crime on all classes of the American people, and should be prohibited by legislation.

7. That we ask for the enactment of a law by which all mechanics and day-laborers employed by or on behalf of the government, whether directly or indirectly, through persons, firms, or

corporations, contracting with the State, shall conform to the reduced standard of eight hours a day, recently adopted by Congress
for national employés, and also for an amendment to the acts of
incorporation for cities and towns, by which all laborers and
mechanics employed at their expense shall conform to the same
number of hours.

8. That the enlightened spirit of the age demands the abolition
of the system of contract labor in our prisons and other reformatory
institutions.

9. That the protection of life, liberty, and property are the three
cardinal principles of government, and the first two are more
sacred than the latter; therefore money needed for prosecuting
wars should, as it is required, be assessed and collected from the
wealth of the country, and not entailed as a burden upon posterity.

10. That it is the duty of the government to exercise its power
over railroads and telegraph corporations, that they shall not in any
case be privileged to exact such rates of freight, transportation, or
charges, by whatever name, as may bear unduly or unequally upon
the producer or consumer.

11. That there should be such a reform in the civil service of the
national government as will remove it beyond all partisan influence, and place it in the charge and under the direction of intelligent and competent business men.

12. That as both history and experience teach us that power
ever seeks to perpetuate itself by every and all means, and that its
prolonged possession in the hands of one person is always dangerous to the interests of a free people, and believing that the
spirit of our organic laws and the stability and safety of our free
institutions are best obeyed on the one hand, and secured on the
other, by a regular constitutional change in the chief of the
country at each election; therefore, we are in favor of limiting
the occupancy of the presidential chair to one term.

13. That we are in favor of granting general amnesty and restoring the Union at once on the basis of equality of rights and privileges to all, the impartial administration of justice being the only
true bond of union to bind the States together and restore the
government of the people.

14. That we demand the subjection of the military to the civil
authorities, and the confinement of its operations to national
purposes alone.

15. That we deem it expedient for Congress to supervise the

patent laws. so as to give labor more fully the benefit of its own ideas and inventions.

16. That fitness, and not political or personal considerations, should be the only recommendation to public office, either appointive or elective, and any and all laws looking to the establishment of this principle are heartily approved.

One informal and three formal ballots were required to effect the nomination of a candidate for President. These several votes were as follows: —

	Informal.	1st.	2d.	3d.
John W. Geary of Penn. . .	60	–	–	–
Horace H. Day of New York .	59	21	59	3
David Davis of Illinois . . .	47	88	93	201
Wendell Phillips of Mass. . .	13	76	12	–
J. M. Palmer of Illinois. . .	8	–	–	–
Joel Parker of New Jersey. .	7	7	7	7
George W. Julian of Indiana .	6	1	5	–
B. Gratz Brown of Missouri .	–	–	14	–
Horace Greeley of New York .	–	–	11	–

On the first vote for a candidate for Vice-President, E. M. Chamberlin of Massachusetts had 72, Joel Parker of New Jersey 70, Alanson M. West of Mississippi 18, Thomas Ewing of Ohio 31, and W. G. Bryan of Tennessee 10. On the second trial, Parker had 112; Chamberlin 57, and Ewing 22.

The candidates nominated were entitled to much more respect than was the convention, which, although including some able men, was for the most part made up of trade union bosses and political adventurers. While the convention went mad in its platform, it was evidently directed by skilful tacticians in making its nominations. Judge Davis was popularly credited with having political aspirations, and was known to be no longer in full sympathy with the Republican party. It seems to have been hoped that the united Opposition would take up with this ticket. Judge Davis sent a non-committal despatch to the convention, thanking it for the honor without accepting the nomination. In June both he and Judge Parker formally declined. The convention was called together again, but only a small number of delegates attended. Charles O'Conor of New York was nominated for President, and no nomination was made for the second place on the ticket.

The Prohibitionists met at Columbus on February 22, with 194 delegates present, from nine States; Samuel Chase of Ohio was the President. A very long platform was reported and adopted by the convention, of which the newspapers of the day give but a brief abstract. In addition to a declaration in favor of the main principle of the party, — the legislative prohibition of the sale of intoxicating liquor, — the resolutions declare that sobriety is one of the main qualifications for a public officer; that officers should not be removed for political reasons; that public servants should be paid fixed salaries, and not by fees; that all possible measures should be adopted to prevent corruption in the government; that Congress should pass laws which will secure a sound national currency convertible at the will of the holder into gold and silver coin; that the rates of inland and ocean postage, and the charges for transportation by railway and water conveyances, and for communication by telegraph, should be as low as possible; that there should be no discrimination in favor of capital against labor; that monopoly and class legislation are evils; that the right of suffrage should be conferred without regard to sex; that the common-school system should be fostered : and that all judicious means should be employed to promote immigration.

The names of James Black of Pennsylvania, as a candidate for President, and of John Russell of Michigan for Vice-President, were presented by a committee on nominations, and accepted by acclamation by the convention.

The Liberal Republican convention attracted a great deal of attention, and caused not a little uneasiness in advance among the friends of the administration. It was evident that the Democrats were ready to take up with any good candidates whom the dissatisfied Republicans might nominate. Suggestions were numerous, but unity of purpose there was not. Some of the most influential politicians and newspapers which supported the movement were strongly in favor of a free-trade policy; Mr. Greeley and his "Tribune" being almost the only conspicuous exceptions. Of candidates there was a full supply. Illinois furnished no less than three, — Judge David Davis, Governor John M. Palmer, and Senator Lyman Trumbull. Missouri brought forward her favorite son, B. Gratz Brown. Ohio suggested ex-Secretary Jacob D. Cox, and Chief Justice Chase was not forgotten. The candidate most spoken of at the east was Mr. Charles Francis Adams of Massachusetts. The aspirations of Mr. Greeley were well known, but, even when the convention met, the idea of nominating him was treated almost as a joke.

Just before sailing for Europe, as arbitrator at Geneva on the Alabama Claims, Mr. Adams addressed a letter to Mr. David A. Wells, which was made public a day or two before the convention. The writer expressed his indifference in regard to the nomination, and declared his unwillingness to authorize anyone to speak for him, except that if he was expected to give any pledges or assurances of his own honesty, " you will please to draw me out of that crowd." In spite of the cautious way in which Mr. Adams refused to commit himself to the movement, which alienated many who might have supported him, his nomination was urgently pressed by his friends upon the assembling members of the convention. But on the other hand some of the most influential Democrats in Congress and elsewhere sent word that, should Mr. Adams be nominated, they would oppose the acceptance of the Cincinnati ticket by the Democratic convention. As the Liberal Republicans felt confident that, with the assistance of the Democrats, victory was assured, the several cliques made great exertions to secure the nominations for their respective favorites.

The convention was a mass meeting. Except in a few places the Liberal Republicans had no organization, and the members were all volunteers. Mr. Stanley Matthews of Ohio was made temporary chairman. The question of membership was a puzzling one, certain States having but a small, and others a very large, number of representatives, while in the case of New York there were two distinct and opposing factions. It was finally determined that the membership should be on the basis of two delegates for each senator and representative to which a State was entitled; that if a smaller number of members were present from any State, they should be allowed to cast the full vote of the State; and that delegations too numerous should meet and designate the delegates; and the New York quarrel was composed. The organization was completed by the choice of Carl Schurz of Missouri as permanent president. Although the free-traders were a majority of the convention, the importance of uniting all who were opposed to General Grant was recognized, and greatly to the chagrin of the very earnest advocates of free trade, a resolution on the subject of the tariff, which had been sent on by Mr. Greeley, was adopted. The convention issued an address to the people of the country and a platform of principles, which are given in full: —

The administration now in power has rendered itself guilty of wanton disregard of the laws of the land, and of usurping powers not granted by the Constitution; it has acted as if the laws had binding force only for those who were governed, and not for those who govern. It has thus struck a blow at the fundamental principles of constitutional government and the liberties of the citizen.

The President of the United States has openly used the powers and opportunities of his high office for the promotion of personal ends.

He has kept notoriously corrupt and unworthy men in places of power and responsibility, to the detriment of the public interest.

He has used the public service of the government as a machinery of corruption and personal influence, and has interfered with tyrannical arrogance in the political affairs of States and municipalities.

He has rewarded with influential and lucrative offices men who had acquired his favor by valuable presents, thus stimulating the demoralization of our political life by his conspicuous example.

He has shown himself deplorably unequal to the task imposed upon him by the necessities of the country, and culpably careless of the responsibilities of his high office.

The partisans of the administration, assuming to be the Republican party and controlling its organization, have attempted to justify such wrongs and palliate such abuses to the end of maintaining partisan ascendancy.

They have stood in the way of necessary investigations and indispensable reforms, pretending that no serious fault could be found with the present administration of public affairs, thus seeking to blind the eyes of the people.

They have kept alive the passions and resentments of the late civil war, to use them for their own advantage; they have resorted to arbitrary measures in direct conflict with the organic law, instead of appealing to the better instincts and latent patriotism of the Southern people by restoring to them those rights the enjoyment of which is indispensable to a successful administration of their local affairs, and would tend to revive a patriotic and hopeful national feeling.

They have degraded themselves and the name of their party, once justly entitled to the confidence of the nation, by a base sycophancy to the dispenser of executive power and patronage, unworthy of republican freemen; they have sought to silence the voice of just criticism, and stifle the moral sense of the people, and to subjugate public opinion by tyrannical party discipline.

They are striving to maintain themselves in authority for selfish ends by an unscrupulous use of the power which rightfully belongs to the people, and should be employed only in the service of the country.

Believing that an organization thus led and controlled can no longer be of service to the best interests of the Republic, we have resolved to make an independent appeal to the sober judgment, conscience, and patriotism of the American people.

We, the Liberal Republicans of the United States, in national convention assembled at Cincinnati, proclaim the following principles as essential to just government: —

1. We recognize the equality of all men before the law, and hold that it is the duty of government, in its dealings with the people, to mete out equal and exact justice to all, of whatever nativity, race, color, or persuasion, religious or political.

2. We pledge ourselves to maintain the union of these States, emancipation, and enfranchisement, and to oppose any reopening of the questions settled by the Thirteenth, Fourteenth, and Fifteenth Amendments of the Constitution.

3. We demand the immediate and absolute removal of all disabilities imposed on account of the rebellion, which was finally subdued seven years ago, believing that universal amnesty will result in complete pacification in all sections of the country.

4. Local self-government, with impartial suffrage, will guard the rights of all citizens more securely than any centralized power. The public welfare requires the supremacy of the civil over the military authority, and the freedom of the person under the protection of the *habeas corpus*. We demand for the individual the largest liberty consistent with public order, for the State self-government, and for the nation a return to the methods of peace and the constitutional limitations of power.

5. The civil service of the government has become a mere instrument of partisan tyranny and personal ambition, and an object of selfish greed. It is a scandal and reproach upon free institutions, and breeds a demoralization dangerous to the perpetuity of republican government. We therefore regard a thorough reform of the civil service as one of the most pressing necessities of the hour; that honesty, capacity and fidelity constitute the only valid claims to public employment; that the offices of the government cease to be a matter of arbitrary favoritism and patronage, and that public station shall become again a post of honor. To this end it is imperatively required that no President shall be a candidate for re-election.

6. We demand a system of Federal taxation which shall not unnecessarily interfere with the industry of the people, and which shall provide the means necessary to pay the expenses of the government, economically administered, the pensions, the interest on the public debt, and a moderate reduction annually of the principal thereof; and recognizing that there are in our midst honest but irreconcilable differences of opinion with regard to the respective systems of protection and free trade, we remit the discussion of the subject to the people in their congressional districts and the decision of Congress thereon, wholly free from executive interference or dictation.

7. The public credit must be sacredly maintained, and we denounce repudiation in every form and guise.

8. A speedy return to specie payments is demanded alike by the highest considerations of commercial morality and honest government.

9. We remember with gratitude the heroism and sacrifices of the soldiers and sailors of the Republic, and no act of ours shall ever detract from their justly earned fame or the full rewards of their patriotism.

10. We are opposed to all further grants of lands to railroads or other corporations. The public domain should be held sacred to actual settlers.

11. We hold that it is the duty of the government in its intercourse with foreign nations to cultivate the friendships of peace by treating with all on fair and equal terms, regarding it alike dishonorable to demand what is not right or submit to what is wrong.

12. For the promotion and success of these vital principles, and the support of the candidates nominated by this convention, we invite and cordially welcome the co-operation of all patriotic citizens, without regard to previous political affiliations.

Mr. Greeley was nominated for President on the sixth vote. The several votes were as follows: —

	1st.	2d.	3d.	4th.	5th.	6th.
Charles Francis Adams, Mass. . . .	203	243	264	279	258	324
Horace Greeley, New York	147	245	258	251	309	332
Lyman Trumbull, Illinois	110	148	156	141	81	19
B. Gratz Brown, Missouri	95	2	2	2	2	–
David Davis, Illinois	92½	75	41	51	30	6
Andrew G. Curtin, Pennsylvania . .	62	–	–	–	–	–
Salmon P. Chase, Ohio	2½	1	–	–	24	32

Before the result of the sixth trial was announced, members began to change their votes, and when these changes had been made the result stood, for Greeley 482, for Adams 187. On a motion that the nomination of Mr. Greeley be made unanimous, the negative votes were numerous. Two votes only were required to effect a nomination of a candidate for Vice-President. They were as follows:—

	1st.	2d.
B. Gratz Brown, Missouri	237	435
Lyman Trumbull, Illinois	158	175
George W. Julian, Indiana	134½	–
Gilbert C. Walker, Virginia	84½	75
Cassius M. Clay, Kentucky	34	–
Jacob D. Cox, Ohio	25	–
John M. Scoville, New Jersey	12	–
Thomas W. Tipton, Nebraska	8	3
John M. Palmer, Illinois	–	8

The nomination of Mr. Brown was then made unanimous, and the convention adjourned. Its work was received by Republicans throughout the country with a shout of derision. Greatly as Mr. Greeley was esteemed for his sincerity and respected for his ability, he had always been regarded as an erratic man, and there were few persons who credited him with the cool judgment and tact needed in a President. But the cry of " anybody to beat Grant" had been raised, and it very soon became evident that, although many members of the Cincinnati convention were chagrined at the failure, as they regarded it, to present acceptable candidates, and although a great many Democrats hardly concealed their disappointment, the Democratic convention would adopt both the platform and the candidates of that convention. The Tennessee Democratic convention, held the week after Greeley and Brown had been nominated, instructed its delegates to the Baltimore convention to support that ticket. The New York Democrats did the same thing a week or two later, and sixteen other Democratic State conventions held in June followed the example. Accordingly it was not doubtful, when the Democratic convention met, what its action would be.

The interest in the Republican convention was confined to the question of the vice-presidency. The renomination of General Grant by a unanimous vote was a foregone conclusion. There was no dissatisfaction with Mr. Colfax as Vice-President at that time. He had been most assiduous in his attention to the few duties of his office, and had given general satisfaction as presiding officer of the Senate. The scandal which involved him and others at a later date had not then been whispered. But Mr. Colfax had given offence to certain of the fraternity of Washington correspondents, and they determined to use all their power to prevent his nomination. They were assisted in their work by the presentation of the name of Mr. Henry Wilson, by the Republicans of Massachusetts, as a candidate. Considering the closeness of the vote in the convention it is not too much to say that Mr. Wilson owed his nomination to these correspondents.

The convention met at Philadelphia on June 5, and did its work with promptness and harmony. Mr. Morton McMichael of Pennsylvania was the temporary chairman, and Judge Thomas Settle of North Carolina the permanent president of the convention. The committee on resolutions reported the following platform, which was unanimously adopted: —

The Republican party of the United States, assembled in national convention in the city of Philadelphia on the fifth and sixth days of June, 1872, again declares its faith, appeals to its history, and announces its position upon the questions before the country.

During eleven years of supremacy it has accepted with grand courage the solemn duties of the time. It suppressed a gigantic rebellion, emancipated four millions of slaves, decreed the equal citizenship of all, and established universal suffrage. Exhibiting unparalleled magnanimity, it criminally punished no man for political offences, and warmly welcomed all who proved loyalty by obeying the laws and dealing justly with their neighbors. It has steadily decreased with firm hand the resultant disorders of a great war, and initiated a wise and humane policy toward the Indians. The Pacific Railroad and similar vast enterprises have been generously aided and successfully conducted, the public lands freely given to actual settlers, immigration protected and encouraged, and a full acknowledgment of the naturalized citizens' rights secured from European powers. A uniform national currency has been provided, repudiation frowned down, the national credit sustained under the most extraordinary burdens, and new bonds negotiated at lower rates. The revenues have been carefully collected and honestly applied. Despite annual large reductions of the rates of taxation, the public debt has been reduced during General Grant's presidency at the rate of a hundred millions a year. Great financial crises have been avoided, and peace and plenty prevail throughout the land. Menacing foreign difficulties have been peacefully and honorably composed, and the honor and power of the nation kept in high respect throughout the world. This glorious record of the past is the party's best pledge for the future. We believe the people will not entrust the government to any party or combination of men composed chiefly of those who have resisted every step of this beneficent progress.

2. The recent amendments to the National Constitution should be cordially sustained because they are right, not merely tolerated because they are law, and should be carried out according to their spirit by appropriate legislation, the enforcement of which can safely be entrusted only to the party that secured these amendments.

3. Complete liberty and exact equality in the enjoyment of all civil, political, and public rights should be established and effectually maintained throughout the Union by efficient and appropriate State and Federal legislation. Neither the law nor its administration should admit any discrimination in respect of citizens by reason of race, creed, color, or previous condition of servitude.

4. The national government should seek to maintain honorable peace with all nations, protecting its citizens everywhere, and sympathizing with all peoples who strive for greater liberty.

5. Any system of the civil service under which the subordinate positions of the government are considered rewards for mere party

zeal is fatally demoralizing, and we therefore favor a reform of the system by laws which shall abolish the evils of patronage and make honesty, efficiency, and fidelity the essential qualifications for public positions, without practically creating a life-tenure of office.

6. We are opposed to further grants of the public lands to corporations and monopolies, and demand that the national domain be set apart for free homes for the people.

7. The annual revenue, after paying current expenditures, pensions, and the interest on the public debt, should furnish a moderate balance for the reduction of the principal, and that revenue, except so much as may be derived from a tax upon tobacco and liquors, should be raised by duties upon importations, the details of which should be so adjusted as to aid in securing remunerative wages to labor, and promote the industries, prosperity, and growth of the whole country.

8. We hold in undying honor the soldiers and sailors whose valor saved the Union. Their pensions are a sacred debt of the nation, and the widows and orphans of those who died for their country are entitled to the care of a generous and grateful people. We favor such additional legislation as will extend the bounty of the government to all soldiers and sailors who were honorably discharged, and who, in the line of duty, became disabled, without regard to the length of service or cause of such discharge.

9. The doctrine of Great Britain and other European powers concerning allegiance — "Once a subject always a subject" — having at last, through the efforts of the Republican party, been abandoned, and the American idea of the individual right to transfer allegiance having been accepted by European nations, it is the duty of our government to guard with jealous care the rights of adopted citizens against the assumption of unauthorized claims by their former governments, and we urge continued careful encouragement and protection of voluntary immigration.

10. The franking privilege ought to be abolished, and the way prepared for a speedy reduction in the rates of postage.

11. Among the questions which press for attention is that which concerns the relations of capital and labor, and the Republican party recognizes the duty of so shaping legislation as to secure full protection and the amplest field for capital, and for labor, the creator of capital, the largest opportunities and a just share of the mutual profits of these two great servants of civilization.

12. We hold that Congress and the President have only fulfilled

an imperative duty in their measures for the suppression of violent and treasonable organizations in certain lately rebellious regions, and for the protection of the ballot-box; and therefore they are entitled to the thanks of the nation.

13. We denounce repudiation of the public debt, in any form or disguise, as a national crime. We witness with pride the reduction of the principal of the debt, and of the rates of interest upon the balance, and confidently expect that our excellent national currency will be perfected by a speedy resumption of specie payment.

14. The Republican party is mindful of its obligations to the loyal women of America for their noble devotion to the cause of freedom. Their admission to wider spheres of usefulness is viewed with satisfaction; and the honest demand of any class of citizens for additional rights should be treated with respectful consideration.

15. We heartily approve the action of Congress in extending amnesty to those lately in rebellion, and rejoice in the growth of peace and fraternal feeling throughout the land.

16. The Republican party proposes to respect the rights reserved by the people to themselves as carefully as the powers delegated by them to the States and to the Federal government. It disapproves of the resort to unconstitutional laws for the purpose of removing evils by interference with the rights not surrendered by the people to either the State or the National government.

17. It is the duty of the General government to adopt such measures as may tend to encourage and restore American commerce and ship-building.

18. We believe that the modest patriotism, the earnest purpose, the sound judgment, the practical wisdom, the incorruptible integrity, and the illustrious services of Ulysses S. Grant have commended him to the heart of the American people, and with him at our head we start to-day upon a new march to victory.

19. Henry Wilson, nominated for the Vice-Presidency, known to the whole land from the early days of the great struggle for liberty as an indefatigable laborer in all campaigns, an incorruptible legislator, and representative man of American institutions, is worthy to associate with our great leader and share the honors which we pledge our best efforts to bestow upon them.

General Grant was nominated by the unanimous vote of all the delegates, amid great enthusiasm. A single trial was sufficient to give the nomination as Vice-President to Mr. Wilson, who received 364½ votes, to 321½ for Mr. Colfax.

In spite of their apparent unanimity the Democrats were not really united in the movement for Greeley and Brown. But most of the leaders believed that nothing better remained to be done than to adopt the principles and the candidates of the Liberal Republicans, and they had gone too far to recede. The convention met at Baltimore July 9. Mr. Thomas Jefferson Randolph of Virginia was the temporary, and Mr. James R. Doolittle of Wisconsin the permanent, president. The committee on resolutions reported the Cincinnati platform without change. Its acceptance was strongly opposed by Senator Thomas F. Bayard of Delaware, but the platform was adopted by a vote of 670 to 62. It was decided not to nominate candidates by acclamation, but to take the vote as usual. Mr. Greeley received 686 votes, Jeremiah S. Black of Pennsylvania 21, Thomas F. Bayard of Delaware 16, William S. Groesbeck of Ohio 2, and 7 votes were cast blank. Mr. Greeley was thus nominated by much more than the necessary two thirds. On a vote for a candidate for Vice-President, Mr. Brown received 713, John W. Stevenson of Kentucky 6, and 13 votes were blank.

Although this result of the convention had been universally expected, there was great dissatisfaction with it in many Democratic circles. Some members of the party were outspoken in their objection to what they regarded as a cowardly surrender of principle for the sake of a possible victory. Others said little, but it was easy to see that they had not much heart in the "new departure," and would not cordially support Mr. Greeley, even if they should so far overcome their repugnance as to vote the ticket. The open opposition to the Greeley

movement found expression in a call for a straight Democratic convention which was held at Louisville, Kentucky,
on September 3, and was quite well attended. Mr. James
Lyon of Virginia was the President. The following
resolutions were adopted : —

Whereas, A frequent recurrence to first principles, and eternal
vigilance against abuses, are the wisest provisions for liberty,
which is the source of progress, and fidelity to our constitutional
system is the only protection for either; therefore,

Resolved, That the original basis of our whole political struc-
ture is a consent in every part thereof. The people of each State
voluntarily created their State, and the States voluntarily formed
the Union; and each State has provided, by its written Constitution, for everything a State should do for the protection of life, liberty, and property within it; and each State, jointly with the others,
provided a Federal Union for foreign and inter-State relations.

Resolved, That all government powers, whether State or Federal, are trust powers coming from the people of each State; and
that they are limited to the written letter of the Constitution and
the laws passed in pursuance of it, which powers must be exercised
in the utmost good faith, the Constitution itself providing in what
manner they may be altered and amended.

Resolved, That the interests of labor and capital should not be
permitted to conflict, but should be harmonized by judicious legislation. While such a conflict continues, labor, which is the parent
of wealth, is entitled to paramount consideration.

Resolved, That we proclaim to the world that principle is to be
preferred to power; that the Democratic party is held together by
the cohesion of time-honored principles which they will never surrender in exchange for all the offices which presidents can confer.
The pangs of the minorities are doubtless excruciating; but we
welcome an eternal minority under the banner inscribed with our
principles, rather than an almighty and everlasting majority purchased by their abandonment.

Resolved, That, having been betrayed at Baltimore into a false
creed and a false leadership by the convention, we repudiate both,
and appeal to the people to approve our platform and to rally to
the polls and support the true platform, and the candidates who
embody it.

Resolved, That we are opposed to giving public lands to corporations, and favor their disposal to actual settlers only.

Resolved, That we favor a judicious tariff for revenue purposes only, and that we are unalterably opposed to class legislation which enriches a few at the expense of the many under the plea of protection.

The convention nominated Mr. Charles O'Conor for President, and John Quincy Adams of Massachusetts for Vice-President. Mr. Adams had written a letter, in which he had said that while he did not wish for the nomination, he would not refuse it if Mr. O'Conor should head the ticket. Mr. O'Conor, on being notified by telegraph of his nomination, declined peremptorily. The convention then hastily passed a vote nominating Mr. Lyon, the president of the convention, in his place; but Mr. Lyon wisely declined. Mr. Adams also refused to take any but the second place, and not even that, unless Mr. O'Conor were to stand at the head of the ticket. Under these circumstances, the convention returned to Mr. O'Conor, and left the ticket as it had been originally arranged, whether its candidates would accept or decline.

The result of the canvass was at no time in doubt. Some of the Democrats deluded themselves with the idea that there was a chance for Mr. Greeley, and that gentleman departed from the usual custom of candidates by going on the stump. But the result of the early elections made the result certain; and General Grant was elected by a larger majority than he had received at his first election. As before, thirty-seven States formed the Union; and on this occasion, for the first time in the history of the government, all the States of the Union chose electors by a popular vote. The apportionment which followed the census of 1870 enlarged the number of electors. Mr. Greeley died a few days after the choice of electors had been made, and the Democratic electors cast their votes without any serious attempt at concentration. The popular vote was as follows: —

STATES.	Grant.	Greeley.	O'Conor.	Black.
Maine	61,422	29,087	–	–
New Hampshire. . . .	37,168	31,424	100	200
Vermont	41,481	10,927	593	–
Massachusetts	133,472	59,260	–	–
Rhode Island.	13,665	5,329	–	–
Connecticut	50,638	45,880	204	206
New York.	440,736	387,281	1,454	201
New Jersey	91,656	76,456	630	–
Pennsylvania.	349,589	212,041	–	1,630
Delaware	11,115	10,206	487	–
Maryland	66,760	67,087	19	–
Virginia	93,468	91,654	42	–
West Virginia	32,315	29,451	600	–
North Carolina	94,769	70,094	–	–
South Carolina	72,290	22,703	187	–
Georgia	62,550	76,356	4,000	–
Florida	17,763	15,427	–	–
Alabama	90,272	79,444	–	–
Mississippi	82,175	47,288	–	–
Louisiana *	71,663	57,029	–	–
Louisiana †	59,975	66,467	–	–
Texas	47,468	66,540	2,580	–
Arkansas	41,373	37,027	–	–
Missouri	119,196	151,434	2,439	–
Tennessee	85,655	94,391	–	–
Kentucky	88,766	99,995	2,374	–
Ohio.	281,852	244,321	1,163	2,100
Michigan	138,455	78,355	2,861	1,271
Indiana	186,147	163,632	1,417	–
Illinois	241,944	184,938	3,058	–
Wisconsin	104,997	86,477	834	–
Minnesota.	55,117	34,423	–	–
Iowa	131,566	71,196	2,221	–
Nebraska	18,329	7,812	–	–
Kansas	67,048	32,970	596	–
Nevada.	8,413	6,236	–	–
California	54,020	40,718	1,068	–
Oregon	11,819	7,730	572	–
Totals	3,597,132	2,834,125	29,489	5,608

* "Custom house" count. The total vote of the country, as given above, includes these returns.

† Count by the Warmoth returning board. If these returns should be substituted for the others, the total vote of the country would be: for Grant, 3,585,444; Greeley, 2,843,563.

It will be observed that the popular vote of Louisiana is given in two forms. Political affairs in that State were in a chaotic condition both then and subsequently. The Governor, Henry C. Warmoth, had been elected as a Republican, but had joined the Greeley movement, and was disposed to do all that lay in his power to give the vote of the State to the Democratic candidates. The votes of the State were at that time canvassed by a "returning board," consisting of the Governor, Lieutenant-Governor, Secretary of State, and two others. The Lieutenant-Governor and one of the unofficial members became disqualified by being candidates for office. The Governor then removed the Secretary of State and appointed another man in his place; and he, with this new Secretary, proceeded to fill up the vacancies in the returning board. But the old Secretary of State, before his removal, and the remaining unofficial member of the board, had previously filled the vacancies. Accordingly there were two returning boards. The official returns were canvassed only by that board of which the Governor was the head; the other board made up returns from the best sources of information it could command. Each board seems to have manipulated the figures so as to bring about a desired result. This is a very brief account of a long and complicated controversy, full particulars of which may be found in the newspapers and in official documents of the time. Two sets of electors met, voted, and forwarded their returns to Washington; but the vote of the State was excluded, as will be noticed in the report of the electoral count. The votes of the electoral colleges as actually cast, including both the votes of Louisiana, are given below. For convenience, those which were rejected by Congress are marked with an asterisk: —

STATES.	PRESIDENT.						VICE-PRESIDENT.								
	Ulysses S. Grant, Ill.	Thomas A. Hendricks, Ind.	B. Gratz Brown, Mo.	Horace Greeley, N.Y.	Charles J. Jenkins, Ga.	David Davis, Ill.	Henry Wilson, Mass.	B. Gratz Brown, Mo.	George W. Julian, Ind.	Alfred H. Colquitt, Ga.	John M. Palmer, Ill.	Thomas E. Bramlette, Ky.	Nathaniel P. Banks, Mass.	William S. Groesbeck, O.	Willis B. Machen, Ky.
Maine	7	–	–	–	–	–	7	–	–	–	–	–	–	–	–
New Hampshire	5	–	–	–	–	–	5	–	–	–	–	–	–	–	–
Vermont	5	–	–	–	–	–	5	–	–	–	–	–	–	–	–
Massachusetts	13	–	–	–	–	–	13	–	–	–	–	–	–	–	–
Rhode Island	4	–	–	–	–	–	4	–	–	–	–	–	–	–	–
Connecticut	6	–	–	–	–	–	6	–	–	–	–	–	–	–	–
New York	35	–	–	–	–	–	35	–	–	–	–	–	–	–	–
New Jersey	9	–	–	–	–	–	9	–	–	–	–	–	–	–	–
Pennsylvania	29	–	–	–	–	–	29	–	–	–	–	–	–	–	–
Delaware	3	–	–	–	–	–	3	–	–	–	–	–	–	–	–
Maryland	–	8	–	–	–	–	–	8	–	–	–	–	–	–	–
Virginia	11	–	–	–	–	–	11	–	–	–	–	–	–	–	–
West Virginia	5	–	–	–	–	–	5	–	–	–	–	–	–	–	–
North Carolina	10	–	–	–	–	–	10	–	–	–	–	–	–	–	–
South Carolina	7	–	–	–	–	–	7	–	–	–	–	–	–	–	–
Georgia	–	–	6	3*	2	–	–	5	–	5	–	–	1	–	–
Florida	4	–	–	–	–	–	4	–	–	–	–	–	–	–	–
Alabama	10	–	–	–	–	–	10	–	–	–	–	–	–	–	–
Mississippi	8	–	–	–	–	–	8	–	–	–	–	–	–	–	–
Louisiana	8*	–	–	–	–	–	–	–	–	–	–	–	–	–	–
Louisiana	–	–	–	–	–	–	8*	–	–	–	–	–	–	–	–
Texas	–	8	–	–	–	–	–	8	–	–	–	–	–	–	–
Arkansas	6*	–	–	–	–	–	6*	–	–	–	–	–	–	–	–
Missouri	–	6	8	–	–	1	–	6	5	–	3	–	–	1	–
Tennessee	–	12	–	–	–	–	–	12	–	–	–	–	–	–	–
Kentucky	–	8	4	–	–	–	–	8	–	–	–	3	–	–	1
Ohio	22	–	–	–	–	–	22	–	–	–	–	–	–	–	–
Michigan	11	–	–	–	–	–	11	–	–	–	–	–	–	–	–
Indiana	15	–	–	–	–	–	15	–	–	–	–	–	–	–	–
Illinois	21	–	–	–	–	–	21	–	–	–	–	–	–	–	–
Wisconsin	10	–	–	–	–	–	10	–	–	–	–	–	–	–	–
Minnesota	5	–	–	–	–	–	5	–	–	–	–	–	–	–	–
Iowa	11	–	–	–	–	–	11	–	–	–	–	–	–	–	–
Nebraska	3	–	–	–	–	–	3	–	–	–	–	–	–	–	–
Kansas	5	–	–	–	–	–	5	–	–	–	–	–	–	–	–
Nevada	3	–	–	–	–	–	3	–	–	–	–	–	–	–	–
California	6	–	–	–	–	–	6	–	–	–	–	–	–	–	–
Oregon	3	–	–	–	–	–	3	–	–	–	–	–	–	–	–
Total (as declared)	286	42	18	–	2	1	286	47	5	5	3	3	1	1	1

Many questions arose during the count of electoral votes, which took place on Feb. 12, 1873, was conducted in accordance with the twenty-second joint rule, and occupied seven hours. The first objection was made by Mr. Hoar of Massachusetts to counting the three votes cast in Georgia for Horace Greeley, on the ground that Mr. Greeley was dead at the time the votes were given. This raised the question whether Congress might take cognizance of the ineligibility of a candidate for the presidential office. The next objection was raised by Senator Trumbull of Illinois to the vote of Mississippi, on the ground that the certificates did not state that the electors voted by ballot. Mr. Potter of New York also objected especially to one vote of Mississippi, cast by an elector chosen to fill a vacancy, the choice of whom was certified only by the Secretary of State of Mississippi, and by him only upon information and not of his own knowledge. Upon these three objections the two Houses separated. The House of Representatives voted to reject the Greeley votes in Georgia; the Senate voted to accept them; under the joint rule they were cast out and not counted. Each House overruled both objections to the vote of Mississippi, and it was counted. Upon the resumption of the count, when the State of Missouri was reached, attention was called to the fact that votes were cast for Mr. Brown both as President and as Vice-President, but the objection that this was contrary to the provision of the Constitution that electors shall vote for two persons, "one of whom, at least, shall not be an inhabitant of the same State with themselves," was obviated by reading the concluding part of the certificate, that no person who voted for Mr. Brown as President also voted for him as Vice-President. The vote of Texas was next objected to, on the ground that the choice of the electors was certified to only by the acting Secretary of State, and not, as the law required, by the Governor. A second objection was made on the ground that only four of the eight electors (not a majority) had met and filled vacancies. Both objections were overruled by each House, and the vote of Texas was counted.

The count then proceeded until the only votes remaining were those of Arkansas and Louisiana. The votes of both States were objected to. The returns for Arkansas were certified to only by the Secretary of State, and his office seal was the only one which the papers bore. Both sets of electors for Louisiana were objected to. The two Houses having separated, the Senate passed a resolution that the votes of Arkansas should not be counted; the House of Representatives agreed to admit them. The vote in the Senate was a consequence of the bad rule that no debate should be allowed. In fact the only seal in use in the State was that of the Secretary of State; and the rejection of the vote was a hasty act upon the most frivolous of pretexts. Each House voted not to count any votes from Louisiana. The result of this action, under the twenty-second joint rule, was that the votes of Arkansas and Louisiana were excluded. The joint session of Congress was then resumed and the result of the election was declared according to the totals in the table given above.

XXIV.

THE DISPUTED ELECTION.

THE events of General Grant's second term which had an influence upon the election of 1876 were, in addition to the Southern question, the financial panic of 1873, which caused great distress and led to the formation of a strong party in various sections of the country, but particularly in the West, favoring an increase of the greenback currency, and its permanence as a standard of value; and the condition of the public service, which, in the popular view of the matter, if not as a matter of fact, was brought into startling prominence by the revelation of official complicity in the frauds of the "Whiskey Ring," and by the discovery of the transactions of General Belknap, Secretary of War, who was impeached for his offences, but escaped punishment by having resigned his office before the House of Representatives could act. The people began to be somewhat weary of the Southern question, and as the States in that part of the country had become almost "solid" already in the support of the Democratic party, it required but a slight change in the North to give a majority to the Opposition. The effect of hard times in inducing people to vote against the government of the day is well known, and this effect was felt strongly in the congressional elections of 1874. It was almost universally believed, when those elections had resulted in the choice of a Democratic House of Representatives for the first time in eighteen years, that the Democrats would carry the election of 1876. Subsequent events did not dissipate that impression altogether, though the presence and the acts of the "Confederate Brigadiers" in the House served to consolidate Republican strength to a certain extent.

At the beginning of the session of 1874–5, Senator Oliver P. Morton called up, and endeavored to secure action upon, several propositions which had for their object to remedy the constitutional defects which ninety years of experience had developed. The first of these was a proposition to amend the Constitution, the origin of which was this: Under a resolution offered by Mr. Morton in March, 1873, the Committee on Privileges and Elections, of which he was chairman, was directed to examine and report at the next session upon the best and most practicable mode of electing the President and Vice-President, and providing a tribunal to adjust and decide all contested questions connected therewith. The committee reported, May 28, 1874, a proposition to amend the Constitution by the adoption of the following new article: —

1. The President and Vice-President shall be elected by the direct vote of the people in the manner following: Each State shall be divided into districts, equal in number to the number of Representatives to which the State may be entitled in the Congress, to be composed of contiguous territory, and to be as nearly equal in population as may be; and the person having the highest number of votes in each district for President shall receive the vote of that district, which shall count one presidential vote.

2. The person having the highest number of votes for President in a State shall receive two presidential votes from the State at large.

3. The person having the highest number of presidential votes in the United States shall be President.

4. If two persons have the same number of votes in any State, it being the highest number, they shall receive each one presidential vote from the State at large; and if more than two persons shall

have each the same number of votes in any State, it being the highest number, no presidential vote shall be counted from the State at large. If more persons than one shall have the same number of votes, it being the highest number in any district, no presidential vote shall be counted from that district.

5. The foregoing provisions shall apply to the election of Vice-President.

6. The Congress shall have the power to provide for holding and conducting the elections of President and Vice-President, and to establish tribunals for the decision of such elections as may be contested.

7. The State shall be divided into districts by the legislatures thereof, but the Congress may at any time by law make or alter the same.

The report which accompanied this proposition was one of great ability and thoroughness. It was the work of Senator Morton himself, who probably devoted more time and thought to this part of the Constitution than have been given to it by any other statesman of any period in our history. The resolution of amendment was called up in the Senate on the 20th of January, 1875, and Mr. Morton made a long speech in favor of it, pointing out once more in forcible language the evils and dangers of the existing system. He maintained that the twenty-second joint rule was grossly unconstitutional. Senators Thurman, Conkling, and Anthony followed. They all agreed that some change was absolutely necessary, but the general judgment was that the greatest danger lay in the matter of the electoral count. Mr. Anthony went so far as to say that "all the machinery of the existing system is absurd." But notwithstanding the concurrence of the leaders of the Senate in the opinion that some measure should be passed, the resolution was laid aside and debate upon it was never resumed.

A few days later, however, the Senate began a discussion of a resolution, also submitted by Mr. Morton, that the twenty-second joint rule be repealed. But he modified this resolution so that it would amend instead of repealing the rule, making an affirmative vote of both Houses necessary for the rejection of an electoral vote. A long debate took place upon this proposition, and the resolution was finally referred to the Committee on Privileges and Elections. The committee reported speedily a bill, which, if enacted, would take the place of the joint rule. For the most part it followed the language of that rule, but with these exceptions: no vote could be rejected except by the concurrent vote of the two Houses; if more than one return should be presented from a State, that one was to be accepted which the two Houses acting separately should determine to be the true return; and when the Houses separated to decide upon any objection, debate was to be allowed, each member being permitted to speak for ten minutes, once only, and when the debate had lasted two hours the House was to have the right, by a majority vote, to order the main question to be put. This bill was very fully debated, and numerous amendments were offered. None of these latter were adopted, except for the purpose of perfecting the language. The only important suggestion of amendment was made by Mr. Edmunds of Vermont, who proposed to substitute for the whole bill a plan for a joint committee, resembling the grand committee provided for in the bill of the year 1800 (see p. 17 *et seq.*). The bill was passed by a vote of 28 to 20. All the affirmative votes were given by Republicans, but six members of that party, including Senators Carpenter, Conkling, Edmunds, and Windom, voted against the bill. It was never taken up in the House of Representatives.

Mr. Morton was very much in earnest in regard to this matter. Immediately on the reassembling of Congress —

it was a new Congress, and the House of Representatives was Democratic — he introduced the bill again. It was referred and reported back, and a debate was begun upon it on the 13th of March, 1876, which occupied a large part of nearly every daily session until the 24th of the month, when it was passed — 32 to 26. Although this was nearly a party vote, Mr. Thurman supported the bill. But he had an objection to one feature of it, and therefore moved that the vote passing it be reconsidered for the purpose of amendment. The motion was agreed to late in April, and the bill was then laid aside. It was again taken up, just at the close of the session, in August, but no action was had upon the bill, and of course it failed.

It began to be rumored in 1875 that General Grant would be a candidate for a third term. Since the time of Washington it had been an unwritten law that eight years should be the limit of any man's service at the head of the government. The idea that the rule established by the Father of his Country was to be broken was highly displeasing to a large body of Republicans, and of course to all Democrats. There was much public and private discussion on the subject. The President himself allowed it to be understood that he was not disposed to refuse a third term if it should be offered him. In a letter addressed to General Harry White of Pennsylvania he expressed himself in terms that could not be misunderstood. The Republican State convention, over which General White presided, had passed a resolution of unalterable " opposition to the election to the presidency of any person for a third term." This drew from General Grant the letter referred to, in which he said : " Now for the third term. I do not want it any more than I did the first ; " but he also remarked that the people were not restricted to two terms by the Constitution ; that the time

might come when it would be unfortunate to make a
change at the end of eight years; and that he "would not
accept a nomination if it were tendered, unless it should
come under such circumstances as to make it an imperative duty — circumstances not likely to arise." The universal interpretation of these phrases was that General
Grant's friends were at liberty to make it appear to be the
imperative duty of the Republicans to nominate him
again, and of the President to accept the nomination.
But the idea made but little headway except among the
officials of the government and the most devoted adherents of the President. There was, however, much appre-
hension that the close organization of the official class
would make it possible to manipulate the primary meetings and secure his nomination. A death-blow to the
movement was dealt soon after the opening of Congress,
in December, 1875. A Democratic member from Illinois
offered a resolution, "that, in the opinion of this House,
the precedent established by Washington and other Presidents of the United States, in retiring from the presidential office after their second term, has become, by universal
concurrence, a part of our republican system of government, and that any departure from this time-honored custom would be unwise, unpatriotic, and fraught with peril
to our free institutions." This resolution was passed by
the immense majority of 234 to 18. Not only did all the
Democrats present support it, but 70 out of the 88 Republicans voting were also found in the affirmative.

Nothing more was heard that year of the third term, and
the Republicans who had been willing to entertain the idea
turned their attention to other candidates, while the Republican leaders who had been special friends of the administration felt themselves at liberty to become candidates
for the Republican nomination. There were many candi-

dates. The favor of the administration was believed to have gone chiefly to Senator Conkling of New York; but there was no hostility to Senator Morton of Indiana, who ultimately secured most of the Southern delegations. Both of these gentlemen had been ardent defenders of the President whenever he had been attacked, and trustworthy supporters of all administration measures.

But the strongest movement, outside of the official circles, was in favor of Mr. James G. Blaine of Maine. Mr. Blaine had been six years Speaker of the House of Representatives, and had gained extraordinary popularity among members of Congress. At the beginning of the Forty-fourth Congress, in 1875, the control of the House having passed into the hands of the Democrats, he had become the natural leader of the minority on the floor, and had drawn the attention of the country by some brilliant parliamentary victories. Many Republicans, however, regretted that in so doing he had revived memories of the war which they were entirely willing should be forgotten. When he began to be talked of for the Republican nomination these latter felt constrained to oppose him. Soon afterward some whispers were heard that his public career was not free from acts which, if not corrupt, involved corrupt motives and desires; and these insinuations soon took form which led to the investigation into Mr. Blaine's connection with the Little Rock and Fort Smith Railroad Company and the Union Pacific Railroad Company. Inasmuch as the alleged revelations at that time are now regarded by many persons as having an important bearing upon the pending election of 1884, it is improper to express an opinion upon the subject; but there can be no doubt that the charges and the evidence had a serious effect upon the prospects of Mr. Blaine for the nomination in 1876.

There was also a strong party in favor of Mr. Benjamin H. Bristow, the Secretary of the Treasury. Mr. Bristow had won the high opinion of the country by his vigorous operations against the Western "whiskey rings." The heavy tax upon distilled spirits was a great temptation to fraud in its manufacture. Evidence was obtained that many Western distilleries were enabled by collusion with government officers to manufacture vast amounts of whiskey upon which no tax was paid. They secured a great profit, and this profit was divided between those who committed the frauds and those who permitted them. Certain persons very near the administration were implicated, or at least open to serious suspicion. The President directed that the prosecutions should be pressed with all vigor; but it was surmised, unjustly no doubt, that he was not so earnest in the work as his words implied that he was; and Mr. Bristow received most of the credit for the unrelenting vigor with which the prosecutions were carried to a successful issue. Accordingly he became the favorite candidate of those who were most opposed to what it was the fashion to call "Cæsarism" and "Grantism."

Ohio presented her governor, Rutherford B. Hayes, a general in the Union army during the war, formerly a member of Congress, and in 1876, for the third time, governor of Ohio. Governor John F. Hartranft of Pennsylvania and Mr. Marshall Jewell, who had been Governor of Connecticut, Minister to Russia, and Postmaster-General, were also candidates.

The leading candidate on the Democratic side was Governor Samuel J. Tilden of New York, but his supremacy was not undisputed. Mr. Hendricks of Indiana, who had received most of the votes of Democratic electors in 1872, after the death of Mr. Greeley, had very strong Western support. General Hancock was a favorite with the soldiers, as he had been in 1868. Ohio was in the field with Ex-Governor William Allen, who had carried the State in 1873. But as the State and district conventions made Mr. Blaine the leading candidate on the Republican side, so those of the Democrats placed Mr. Tilden far in advance of all competitors. Mr. Tilden had gained a high reputation by his warfare against the "Tweed ring" in New York some years before, and had added to it by his career as governor of New York. But he was opposed most warmly by the Tammany organization in his own city, and this was deemed by many a sufficient reason why he should not be nominated. Such was the situation when the season of national conventions began, in May, 1876.

The first convention of the series was that of the Prohibitionists, which was held in Cleveland, Ohio, on the 17th of May. This convention nominated for President, Green Clay Smith of Kentucky, and for Vice-President, G. T. Stewart of Ohio; and adopted the following platform : —

The Prohibition Reform party of the United States, organized in the name of the people to revive, enforce, and perpetuate in the government the doctrines of the Declaration of Independence, submit in this centennial year of the Republic, for the suffrages of all good citizens, the following platform of national reforms and measures: —

1. The legal prohibition in the District of Columbia, the Territories, and in every other place subject to the laws of Congress, of the importation, exportation, manufacture, and traffic of all alcoholic beverages as high crimes against society; an amendment of the national Constitution to render these prohibitory measures universal and permanent; and the adoption of treaty stipulations with foreign powers to prevent the importation and exportation of all alcoholic beverages.

2. The abolition of class legislation and of special privileges in the government, and of the adoption of equal suffrage and eligibility to office without distinction of race, religious creed, property, or sex.

3. The appropriation of the public lands in limited quantities to actual settlers only; the reduction of the rates of inland and ocean postage; of telegraphic communication; of railroad and water transportation and travel to the lowest practicable point by force of law, wisely and justly framed, with reference not only to the interests of capital employed, but to the higher claims of the general good.

4. The suppression by law of lottery and gambling in gold, stocks, produce, and every form of money and property, and the penal inhibition of the use of the public mails for advertising schemes of gambling and lotteries.

5. The abolition of those foul enormities, polygamy and the social evil, and the protection of purity, peace, and happiness of homes by ample and efficient legislation.

6. The national observance of the Christian Sabbath, established by laws prohibiting ordinary labor and business in all departments of public service and private employment (works of necessity, charity, and religion excepted) on that day.

7. The establishment by mandatory provisions in national and State constitutions, and by all necessary legislation, of a system of free public schools for the universal and forced education of all the youth of the land.

8. The free use of the Bible, not as a ground of religious creeds, but as a text-book of the purest morality, the best liberty, and the noblest literature, in our public schools, that our children may grow up in its light, and that its spirit and principles may pervade the nation.

9. The separation of the government in all departments and institutions, including the public schools and all funds for their maintenance, from the control of every religious sect or other association, and the protection alike of all sects by equal laws, with entire freedom of religious faith and worship.

10. The introduction into all treaties hereafter negotiated with foreign governments of a provision for the amicable settlement of international difficulties by arbitration.

11. The abolition of all barbarous modes and instruments of punishment; the recognition of the laws of God and the claims of humanity in the discipline of jails and prisons, and of that higher and wiser civilization worthy of our age and nation, which regards the reform of criminals as a means for the prevention of crime.

12. The abolition of executive and legislative patronage, and

the election of President, Vice-President, United States senators, and of all civil officers, so far as practicable, by the direct vote of the people.

13. The practice of a friendly and liberal policy to immigrants from all nations, the guarantee to them of ample protection, and of equal rights and privileges.

14. The separation of the money of government from all banking institutions. The national government only should exercise the high prerogative of issuing paper money, and that should be subject to prompt redemption on demand in gold and silver, the only equal standards of value recognized by the civilized world.

15. The reduction of the salaries of public officers in a just ratio with the decline of wages and market prices, the abolition of sinecures, unnecessary offices, and official fees and perquisites; the practice of strict economy in government expenses, and a free and thorough investigation into any and all alleged abuses of public trusts.

On the 18th of May the Greenback, or Independent National party, held its convention at Indianapolis. Ignatius Donnelly of Minnesota was the temporary, and Thomas J. Durant of Washington, D. C., the permanent president. Peter Cooper of New York was nominated on the first ballot for President, and Senator Newton Booth of California for Vice-President. The latter gentleman afterward declined the nomination, and General Samuel F. Cary of Ohio was substituted. This convention, in which nineteen States were represented by 239 delegates, adopted the following platform : —

The Independent party is called into existence by the necessities of the people, whose industries are prostrated, whose labor is deprived of its just reward, by a ruinous policy which the Republican and Democratic parties refuse to change, and in view of the failure of these parties to furnish relief to the depressed industries of the country, thereby disappointing the just hopes and expectations of the suffering people, we declare our principles, and invite all independent and patriotic men to join our ranks in this movement for financial reform and industrial emancipation.

1. We demand the immediate and unconditional repeal of the specie-resumption act of January 14, 1875, and the rescue of our industries from ruin and disaster resulting from its enforcement; and we call upon all patriotic men to organize, in every congressional district of the country, with a view of electing representatives to Congress who will carry out the wishes of the people in this regard, and stop the present suicidal and destructive policy of contraction.

2. We believe that a United States note, issued directly by the government, and convertible on demand into United States obligations, bearing a rate of interest not exceeding one cent a day on each one hundred dollars, and exchangeable for United States notes at par, will afford the best circulating medium ever devised. Such United States notes should be full legal tender for all purposes except for the payment of such obligations as are, by existing contracts, especially made payable in coin, and we hold that it is the duty of the government to provide such circulating medium, and insist, in the language of Thomas Jefferson, that bank paper must be suppressed, and the circulation restored to the nation, to whom it belongs.

3. It is the paramount duty of the government, in all its legislation, to keep in view the full development of all legitimate business, agricultural, mining, manufacturing, and commercial.

4. We most earnestly protest against any further issue of gold bonds, for sale in foreign markets, by which we would be made, for a long period, hewers of wood and drawers of water for foreigners, especially as the American people would gladly and promptly take, at par, all bonds the government may need to sell, provided they are made payable at the option of the holder, and bearing interest at 3.65 per cent per annum, or even a lower rate.

5. We further protest against the sale of government bonds for the purpose of purchasing silver, to be used as a substitute for our more convenient and less fluctuating fractional currency, which, although well calculated to enrich owners of silver mines, yet in operation it will still further oppress, in taxation, an already overburdened people.

The Republican convention was called to meet at Cincinnati on June 14. As the day approached, the public interest in the meeting became very great. The delegates

elected in most of the States were pledged to one or
another of the candidates. Each of the three largest
States had a candidate of its own. New York, with 70
delegates, was substantially unanimous for Mr. Conkling;
Pennsylvania, with 58 delegates, was instructed to vote
for General Hartranft; Ohio, whose delegates numbered
44, was united in support of Governor Hayes. These
three candidates thus held 172 votes out of the 756 to
which all the States and Territories were entitled. Mr.
Morton had, in addition to the 30 votes of his own Indiana delegation, nearly 100 more pledged to him, every
one of which was from the Southern States. The Bristow
strength was unknown, but was believed to be about 100
votes. It was evident from ·the beginning that if the
votes for these five candidates could be united, the defeat
of Mr. Blaine, whose delegates were more than twice as
numerous as those of any other candidate, was assured.
The party was roughly divided into two wings, one of
which was warmly in favor of the Grant administration,
while the other desired " reform within the party." The
prevailing sentiment was decidedly hostile to a perpetuation of the Grant administration under a new head.
The administration strength was represented, accurately
enough, by the Conkling and Morton contingents. The
rest of the delegates were, for the most part, opposed to
any one who might seem to be the political heir of the
President. A large part of the adherents of Mr. Bristow
were as strongly opposed to Mr. Blaine as they were to
what they called " the Grant dynasty." The charges
brought against Mr. Blaine were in process of investigation almost up to the very day that the convention met.
Many delegates believed the charges to be true; and
although a large majority of the delegates probably dis-
believed them, some of these latter feared that it would

be dangerous to nominate a man who was so seriously assailed. On the Sunday morning before the convention, Mr. Blaine received a sunstroke, and was, for a day or two, believed to be dangerously sick. This also was unfortunate for him, and probably cost him some votes.

Theodore M. Pomeroy of New York was temporary chairman of the convention, and Edward McPherson of Pennsylvania was the permanent president. On the second day the adoption of the rules drafted by the committee on rules introduced some important reforms in national convention work. It was decided that the report of the committee on credentials should be disposed of first, the platform next, and only then should the nomination of candidates be in order. Another rule put an end to the practice of "stampeding," by providing that the roll-call should in no case be dispensed with; and that after the vote of a State for candidates was announced it should not be changed on that ballot.

There were several contested elections, but the only important case was that of Alabama, where one delegation, headed by Senator Spencer, was in favor of Mr. Morton, the other, headed by Mr. Haralson, a colored member of Congress, was divided between Mr. Blaine and Mr. Bristow. The Spencer delegation was refused admittance by a vote of 375 to 354, and the Haralson delegation was admitted. The following platform was then reported by General Joseph R. Hawley of Connecticut: —

When, in the economy of Providence, this land was to be purged of human slavery, and when the strength of government of the people, by the people, and for the people, was to be demonstrated, the Republican party came into power. Its deeds have passed into history, and we look back to them with pride. Incited by their memories to high aims for the good of our country and mankind, and looking to the future with unfaltering courage, hope, and purpose, we, the representatives of the party in national convention assembled, make the following declaration of principles: —

1. The United States of America is a nation, not a league. By the combined workings of the national and State governments, under their respective Constitutions, the rights of every citizen are secured, at home and abroad, and the common welfare promoted.

2. The Republican party has preserved these governments to the hundredth anniversary of the nation's birth, and they are now embodiments of the great truths spoken at its cradle, "That all men are created equal; that they are endowed by their Creator with certain unalienable rights, among which are life, liberty, and the pursuit of happiness; that for the attainment of these ends governments have been instituted among men, deriving their just powers from the consent of the governed." Until these truths are cheerfully obeyed, or, if need be, vigorously enforced, the work of the Republican party is unfinished.

3. The permanent pacification of the Southern section of the Union, and the complete protection of all its citizens in the free enjoyment of all their rights, is a duty to which the Republican party stands sacredly pledged. The power to provide for the enforcement of the principles embodied by the recent constitutional amendments is vested by those amendments in the Congress of the United States, and we declare it to be the solemn obligation of the legislative and executive departments of the government to put into immediate and vigorous exercise all their constitutional powers for removing any just causes of discontent on the part of any class, and for securing to every American citizen complete liberty and exact equality in the exercise of all civil, political, and public rights. To this end we imperatively demand a Congress and a Chief Executive whose courage and fidelity to these duties shall not falter until these results are placed beyond dispute or recall.

4. In the first act of Congress signed by President Grant, the national government assumed to remove any doubts of its purpose to discharge all just obligations to the public creditors, and "solemnly pledged its faith to make provision, at the earliest practicable period, for the redemption of the United States notes in coin." Commercial prosperity, public morals, and national credit demand that this promise be fulfilled by a continuous and steady progress to specie payment.

5. Under the Constitution the President and heads of departments are to make nominations for office; the Senate is to advise

and consent to appointments, and the House of Representatives is to accuse and prosecute faithless officers. The best interest of the public service demands that these distinctions be respected; that Senators and Representatives, who may be judges and accusers, should not dictate appointments to office. The invariable rule in appointments should have reference to the honesty, fidelity, and capacity of the appointees, giving to the party in power those places where harmony and vigor of administration require its policy to be represented, but permitting all others to be filled by persons selected with sole reference to the efficiency of the public service, and the right of all citizens to share in the honor of rendering faithful service to the country.

6. We rejoice in the quickened conscience of the people concerning political affairs, and will hold all public officers to a rigid responsibility, and engage that the prosecution and punishment of all who betray official trusts shall be swift, thorough, and unsparing.

7. The public-school system of the several States is a bulwark of the American Republic, and, with a view to its security and permanence, we recommend an amendment to the Constitution of the United States forbidding the application of any public funds or property for the benefit of any schools or institutions under sectarian control.

8. The revenue necessary for current expenditures and the obligations of the public debt must be largely derived from duties upon importations, which, so far as possible, should be adjusted to promote the interests of American labor and advance the prosperity of the whole country.

9. We reaffirm our opposition to further grants of the public land to corporations and monopolies, and demand that the national domain be devoted to free homes for the people.

10. It is the imperative duty of the government so to modify existing treaties with European governments, that the same protection shall be afforded to the adopted American citizen that is given to the native-born; and that all necessary laws should be passed to protect emigrants, in the absence of power in the States for that purpose.

11. It is the immediate duty of Congress fully to investigate the effect of immigration and importation of Mongolians upon the moral and material interests of the country.

12. The Republican party recognizes with its approval the substantial advances recently made toward the establishment of equal

rights for women by the many important amendments effected by Republican legislatures in the laws which concern the personal and property relations of wives, mothers, and widows, and by the appointment and election of women to the superintendence of education, charities, and other public trusts. The honest demands of this class of citizens for additional rights, privileges, and immunities should be treated with respectful consideration.

13. The Constitution confers upon Congress sovereign power over the Territories of the United States for their government, and in the exercise of this power it is the right and duty of Congress to prohibit and extirpate, in the Territories, that relic of barbarism — polygamy; and we demand such legislation as shall secure this end and the supremacy of American institutions in all the Territories.

14. The pledges which the nation has given to her soldiers and sailors must be fulfilled, and a grateful people will always hold those who imperilled their lives for the country's preservation in the kindest remembrance.

15. We sincerely deprecate all sectional feeling and tendencies. We therefore note with deep solicitude that the Democratic party counts, as its chief hope of success, upon the electoral vote of a united South, secured through the efforts of those who were recently arrayed against the nation; and we invoke the earnest attention of the country to the grave truth that a success thus achieved would reopen sectional strife and imperil national honor and human rights.

16. We charge the Democratic party with being the same in character and spirit as when it sympathized with treason; with making its control of the House of Representatives the triumph and opportunity of the nation's recent foes; with reasserting and applauding in the national capitol the sentiments of unrepentant rebellion; with sending Union soldiers to the rear, and promoting Confederate soldiers to the front; with deliberately proposing to repudiate the plighted faith of the government; with being equally false and imbecile upon the overshadowing financial questions; with thwarting the ends of justice by its partisan mismanagement and obstruction of investigation; with proving itself, through the period of its ascendancy in the lower house of Congress, utterly incompetent to administer the government; and we warn the country against trusting a party thus alike unworthy, recreant, and incapable.

17. The national administration merits commendation for its

honorable work in the management of domestic and foreign affairs, and President Grant deserves the continued hearty gratitude of the American people for his patriotism and his eminent services, in war and in peace.

18. We present as our candidates for President and Vice-President of the United States two distinguished statesmen, of eminent ability and character, and conspicuously fitted for those high offices, and we confidently appeal to the American people to entrust the administration of their public affairs to Rutherford B. Hayes and William A. Wheeler.

The last resolution, of course, was only added to the series after the nominations had been made. When the resolutions had been read, Mr. E. L. Pierce of Massachusetts moved to strike out the eleventh resolution, relating to the Chinese. After a brief debate the motion was rejected, yeas 215, nays 532. Mr. E. J. Davis of Texas moved to strike out the fourth resolution, and to substitute the following : —

That it is the duty of Congress to provide for carrying out the act known as the Resumption Act of Congress, to the end that the resumption of specie payments may not be longer delayed.

A debate took place upon this proposition also, but the motion was rejected without a count, and the platform was then adopted. The proceedings of the second day closed with the formal nomination of candidates. Some of the speeches were remarkable efforts, and excited the partisans of the several candidates to the highest pitch of enthusiasm.

On the third day the nominations were made. On the first vote Mr. Blaine received 285, Mr. Morton 125, Mr. Bristow 113, Mr. Conkling 99, Mr. Hayes 61, Mr. Hartranft 58, Mr. Jewell 11, and Mr. William A. Wheeler of New York 3. Mr. Blaine's strength was made up of 77 votes from the South, and of 208 from

Northern States, the latter including some votes from
almost every State except those which presented candidates of their own. Mr. Morton had 30 votes from Indiana, and 95 from Southern States. Mr. Bristow's votes
were given by seventeen States and one Territory, and
were strictly scattering, except the votes of Kentucky, his
own State, and 17 from Massachusetts, and 10 from Tennessee. Mr. Conkling's 99 were made up of 69 from New
York and a few scattering votes from nine other States;
the South contributing 25 of the 30. Mr. Hayes had 17
votes from other States than Ohio. The other candidates
received no votes except from their respective States.
Seven ballots were necessary to effect a choice. They resulted as follows : —

	1st.	2d.	3d.	4th.	5th.	6th.	7th.
Blaine	285	296	293	292	286	308	351
Morton	125	120	113	108	95	85	–
Bristow	113	114	121	126	114	111	21
Conkling	99	93	90	84	82	81	–
Hayes	61	64	67	68	104	113	384
Hartranft	58	63	68	71	69	50	–
Jewell	11	–	–	–	–	–	–
Scattering	3	4	3	5	5	5	–
Whole number	754	754	755	754	755	755	756
Necessary	378	378	378	378	378	378	379

The nomination of Mr. Hayes was made unanimous.
It seemed to be inevitable as soon as the fifth ballot was
announced. Mr. Hayes was the only candidate who had
made a gain on every vote; and as he was, if not very
well known, entirely unobjectionable to the friends of all
other candidates, it was less difficult to concentrate votes
upon him than upon any other person in the list. Mr.
Blaine, who was informed by telegraph at his house in

Washington of the progress of the voting, wrote a despatch congratulating Mr. Hayes immediately on receiving the result of the fifth vote. During the progress of the voting a stormy scene took place upon the demand of four Pennsylvania delegates to have their votes separately recorded. The delegation had been instructed to vote "as a unit," and these delegates claimed the right to vote for themselves. Mr. McPherson, the president of the convention, sustained their demand, and, on an appeal, his decision was affirmed, 395 to 354. Thus was broken the famous "unit rule," which, after one more contest at Chicago, four years later, was abandoned by the Republicans, probably forever.

Several candidates were presented for the nomination for Vice-President, but, as the voting proceeded, nearly all the votes were for William A. Wheeler of New York. The other candidates were thereupon withdrawn, and Mr. Wheeler was unanimously nominated. The convention soon afterward adjourned, with cheers for the ticket.

The Democrats met at St. Louis two weeks later. The convention was deprived of much of its interest by the fact that Mr. Tilden's lead for the nomination was so very great. He was known to have more than four hundred delegates out of the whole convention of 744, and while his candidacy was opposed, the opposition came from States which nevertheless chose unanimous delegations in his favor. The delegates chosen in the interest of other candidates were for the latter, but not against Tilden. His nomination was therefore universally expected, except by the more sanguine friends of other candidates.

Mr. Henry Watterson of Kentucky was the temporary chairman, but at the close of the first day of the convention he yielded the chair to General John A. McClernand of Illinois, the permanent president. On the next day

the platform was reported by Mr. Dorsheimer of New
York, as follows : —

We, the delegates of the Democratic party of the United States,
in national convention assembled, do hereby declare the administration of the Federal government to be in urgent need of immediate reform; do hereby enjoin upon the nominees of this
convention, and of the Democratic party in each State, a zealous
effort and co-operation to this end; and do hereby appeal to our
fellow-citizens of every former political connection to undertake
with us this first and most pressing patriotic duty.

For the Democracy of the whole country, we do here reaffirm
our faith in the permanence of the Federal Union, our devotion to
the Constitution of the United States, with its amendments universally accepted as a final settlement of the controversies that
engendered civil war, and do here record our steadfast confidence
in the perpetuity of Republican self-government.

In absolute acquiescence in the will of the majority, — the vital
principle of republics; in the supremacy of the civil over the military authority; in the total separation of Church and State, for the
sake alike of civil and religious freedom: in the equality of all
citizens before just laws of their own enactment; in the liberty of
individual conduct, unvexed by sumptuary laws; in the faithful
education of the rising generation, that they may preserve, enjoy,
and transmit these best conditions of human happiness and hope,
— we behold the noblest products of a hundred years of changeful
history; but, while upholding the bond of our Union and great
charter of these our rights, it behoves a free people to practise also
that eternal vigilance which is the price of liberty.

Reform is necessary to rebuild and establish in the hearts of the
whole people the Union, eleven years ago happily rescued from the
danger of a secession of States, but now to be saved from a corrupt
centralism which, after inflicting upon ten States the rapacity of
carpet-bag tyrannies, has honeycombed the offices of the Federal
government itself with incapacity, waste, and fraud; infected
States and municipalities with the contagion of misrule, and locked
fast the prosperity of an industrious people in the paralysis of hard
times.

Reform is necessary to establish a sound currency, restore the
public credit, and maintain the national honor.

We denounce the failure, for all these eleven years of peace, to make good the promise of the legal tender notes, which are a changing standard of value in the hands of the people, and the non-payment of which is a disregard of the plighted faith of the nation.

We denounce the improvidence which, in eleven years of peace, has taken from the people in Federal taxes thirteen times the whole amount of the legal tender notes, and squandered four times their sum in useless expense without accumulating any reserve for their redemption.

We denounce the financial imbecility and immorality of that party which, during eleven years of peace, has made no advance toward resumption, no preparation for resumption, but instead has obstructed resumption, by wasting our resources and exhausting all our surplus income; and, while annually professing to intend a speedy return to specie payments, has annually enacted fresh hindrances thereto. As such hindrance, we denounce the resumption clause of the act of 1875, and we here demand its repeal.

We demand a judicious system of preparation by public economy, by official retrenchment, and by wise finance, which shall enable the nation soon to assure the whole world of its perfect ability and its perfect readiness to meet any of its promises at the call of the creditor entitled to payment.

We believe such a system, well devised, and, above all, entrusted to competent hands for its execution, creating at no time an artificial scarcity of currency, and at no time alarming the public mind into a withdrawal of that vaster machinery of credit by which ninety-five per cent of all business transactions are performed, — a system open, public, and inspiring general confidence, — would, from the day of its adoption, bring healing on its wings to all our harassed industries, set in motion the wheels of commerce, manufactures, and the mechanic arts, restore employment to labor, and renew in all its natural resources the prosperity of the people.

Reform is necessary in the sum and modes of Federal taxation, to the end that capital may be set free from distrust, and labor lightly burdened.

We denounce the present tariff, levied upon nearly four thousand articles, as a masterpiece of injustice, inequality, and false pretense. It yields a dwindling, not a yearly rising revenue. It has impoverished many industries to subsidize a few. It prohibits imports that might purchase the products of American labor. It has degraded American commerce from the first to an inferior rank on the high seas. It has cut down the sales of American manufactures at home and abroad and depleted the returns of American agriculture, — an industry followed by half our people. It costs the people five times more than it produces to the treasury, obstructs the processes of production, and wastes the fruits of labor. It promotes fraud, fosters smuggling, enriches dishonest officials, and bankrupts honest merchants. We demand that all custom-house taxation shall be only for revenue.

Reform is necessary in the scale of public expense, — Federal, State, and municipal. Our Federal taxation has swollen from sixty millions gold, in 1860, to four hundred and fifty millions currency, in 1870; our aggregate taxation from one hundred and fifty-four millions gold, in 1860, to seven hundred and thirty millions currency, in 1870; or in one decade from less than five dollars per head to more than eighteen dollars per head. Since the peace, the people have paid to their tax gatherers more than thrice the sum of the national debt, and more than twice that sum for the Federal government alone. We demand a rigorous frugality in every department, and from every officer of the government.

Reform is necessary to put a stop to the profligate waste of the public lands and their diversion from actual settlers by the party in power, which has squandered two hundred million acres upon railroads alone, and out of more than thrice that aggregate has disposed of less than a sixth directly to tillers of the soil.

Reform is necessary to correct the omissions of a Republican Congress, and the errors of our treaties and diplomacy, which have stripped our fellow-citizens of foreign birth and kindred race recrossing the Atlantic, of the shield of American citizenship, and have exposed our brethren of the Pacific Coast to the incursions of a race not sprung from the same great parent stock, and, in fact, now by law denied citizenship through naturalization as being neither accustomed to the traditions of a progressive civilization nor exercised in liberty under equal laws. We denounce the policy which thus discards the liberty-loving German and tolerates a revival of the Cooly trade in Mongolian women imported for immoral purposes, and Mongolian men held to perform servile labor-contracts, and demand such modification of the treaty with the Chinese empire or such legislation within constitutional limitations as shall prevent further importation or immigration of the Mongolian race.

Reform is necessary, and can never be effected but by making it the controlling issue of the elections, and lifting it above the two false issues with which the office-holding class and the party in power seek to smother it:—

1. The false issue with which they would enkindle sectarian strife in respect to the public schools, of which the establishment and support belong exclusively to the several States, and which the Democratic party has cherished from their foundation, and is resolved to maintain without prejudice or preference for any class, sect, or creed, and without largesses from the treasury to any.

2. The false issue by which they seek to light anew the dying embers of sectional hate between kindred peoples once estranged, but now reunited in one indivisible republic and a common destiny.

Reform is necessary in the civil service. Experience proves that efficient, economical conduct of the governmental business is not possible if its civil service be subject to change at every election; be a prize fought for at the ballot-box; be a brief reward of party zeal, instead of posts of honor assigned for proved competency, and held for fidelity in the public employ; that the dispensing of patronage should neither be a tax upon the time of all our public men, nor the instrument of their ambition. Here, again, promises falsified in the performance attest that the party in power can work out no practical or salutary reform.

Reform is necessary even more in the higher grades of the public service. President, Vice-President, judges, senators, representatives, cabinet officers, — these and all others in authority are the people's servants. Their offices are not a private perquisite; they are a public trust.

When the annals of this Republic show the disgrace and censure of a Vice-President; a late Speaker of the House of Representatives marketing his rulings as a presiding officer; three senators profiting secretly by their votes as law-makers; five chairmen of the leading committees of the House of Representatives exposed in jobbery; a late Secretary of the Treasury forcing balances in the public accounts; a late Attorney-General misappropriating public funds; a Secretary of the Navy enriched or enriching friends by percentages levied off the profits of contractors with his department; an ambassador to England censured in a dishonorable speculation; the President's private secretary barely escaping conviction upon trial for guilty complicity in frauds upon the revenue; a Secretary of War impeached for high crimes and misdemeanors,

—the demonstration is complete that the first step in reform must be the people's choice of honest men from another party, lest the disease of one political organization infect the body politic, and lest, by making no change of men or parties, we get no change of measures and no real reform.

All these abuses, wrongs, and crimes, the product of sixteen years ascendency of the Republican party, create a necessity for reform confessed by Republicans themselves; but their reformers are voted down in convention and displaced from the cabinet. The party's mass of honest voters is powerless to resist the eighty thousand office-holders, its leaders and guides.

Reform can only be had by a peaceful civic revolution. We demand a change of system, a change of administration, a change of parties, that we may have change of measures and of men.

Resolved, That this convention, representing the Democratic party of the United States, do cordially indorse the action of the present House of Representatives in reducing and curtailing the expenses of the Federal government, in cutting down salaries, extravagant appropriations, and in abolishing useless offices and places not required by the public necessities: and we shall trust to the firmness of the Democratic members of the House that no committee of conference, and no misinterpretation of the rules shall be allowed to defeat these wholesome measures of economy demanded by the country.

Resolved, That the soldiers and sailors of the Republic, and the widows and orphans of those who have fallen in battle, have a just claim upon the care, protection, and gratitude of their fellow-citizens.

When the report was read, General Thomas Ewing of Ohio moved to strike out from the platform, in the eighth paragraph, the words: "As such hindrance we denounce the resumption clause of the act of 1875, and we here demand its repeal," in order to insert the words: "The law for the resumption of specie payments on the 1st of January, 1879, having been enacted by the Republican party without deliberation in Congress or discussion before the people, and being both ineffective to secure its objects and highly injurious to the business of the country, ought

to be forthwith repealed." This was in accordance with
a minority report signed by eight members of the Committee on Resolutions, among whom was Mr. Voorhees
of Indiana. The amendment was rejected, ayes 219, noes
550 ; and the platform as reported was then adopted, ayes
651, noes 83.

The convention then proceeded to the work of nominating a candidate for President. After the formal presentation of names, two votes were taken amid great excitement, with the following result : —

	First.	Second.
Samuel J. Tilden, N. Y.	417	535
Thomas A. Hendricks, Ind.	140	60
Winfield S. Hancock, Penn.	75	59
William Allen, Ohio	56	54
Thomas F. Bayard, Del.	33	11
Joel Parker, N. J.	18	18
Allen G. Thurman, Ohio	—	7

The whole number of votes on the second ballot being
744, the number necessary to a choice was 496, — the two-
thirds rule having been adopted. Mr. Tilden was accordingly nominated, and the choice was enthusiastically made
unanimous. On the next day Thomas A. Hendricks was
nominated for Vice-President by a unanimous vote, though
the Indiana delegation protested that they did not know
if he would accept the second place on the ticket, and the
convention shortly afterward adjourned.

The canvass which followed was comparatively spirit-
less. Mr. Hayes was not sufficiently well known to arouse
enthusiasm, and Mr. Tilden, though commanding respect
for his ability, was not a candidate to draw to himself
strong personal supporters. The Republicans were on
the defensive ; but this fact served to make the political
discussion of the time more strictly a debate about

measures and policies than it had been for many years. The Democrats denounced the alleged bad record of the Republicans; the latter derided the reform professions of their opponents. Great efforts were made by the Republicans to cast discredit upon Mr. Tilden for his connection with certain railroad enterprises; and a suit was brought against him for income tax alleged to be due by him to the government. The Democrats sneered at Mr. Hayes as an unknown man, and they roundly denounced the political assessments which were mercilessly levied upon the office-holders for funds to carry the elections. The Republicans made much of the opposition of the Democrats to the resumption policy, though it was well known that Mr. Tilden was a "hard money man." But on the whole there was less than the usual amount of excitement during the canvass, and less of the fireworks of presidential campaigns. Not many Republicans were confident of success, and the result of the early elections, particularly that of Indiana in October, indicated that the Democrats would have enough Northern votes, together with the "solid South," to give them a victory.

Thirty-eight States participated in the election. Colorado had been admitted to the Union in August, 1876, and, in order to save an additional election, the choice of electors for that occasion was conferred upon the legislature. All the other States appointed them by popular vote. The polls had hardly closed on the day of election, the 7th of November, when the Democrats began to claim the presidency. The returns came in so unfavorably for the Republicans that there was hardly a newspaper organ of the party which did not, on the following morning, concede the election of Mr. Tilden. He was believed to have carried every Southern State, as well as New York,

Indiana, New Jersey, and Connecticut. The whole number of electoral votes was 369. If the above estimate were correct, the Democratic candidates would have 203 votes, and the Republican candidates 166 votes. But word was sent out on the same day from Republican headquarters at Washington that Hayes and Wheeler were elected by one majority; that the States of South Carolina, Florida, and Louisiana had chosen Republican electors.

Then began the most extraordinary contest that ever took place in the country. The only hope of the Republicans was in the perfect defence of their position. The loss of a single vote would be fatal. An adequate history of the four months between the popular election and the inauguration of Mr. Hayes, would fill volumes. Space can be given here for only a bare reference to some of the most important events. Neither party was over-scrupulous, and no doubt the acts of some members of each party were grossly illegal and corrupt. Certain transactions preceding the meetings of electors were not known until long afterward, when the key to the famous "cipher despatches" was accidentally revealed.

In four States, South Carolina, Florida, Louisiana, and Oregon, there were double returns. In South Carolina there were loud complaints that detachments of the army, stationed near the polls, had prevented a fair and free election. Although the board of State canvassers certified to the choice of the Hayes electors, who were chosen on the face of the returns, the Democratic candidates for electors met on the day fixed for the meeting of electors and cast ballots for Tilden and Hendricks. In Florida there were allegations of fraud on both sides. The canvassing board and the governor certified to the election of the Hayes electors, but, fortified by a court decision in their favor, the Democratic electors also met and voted. In Louisiana there was anarchy. There were two governors, two returning boards, two sets of returns showing different results, and two electoral colleges. In Oregon the Democratic governor adjudged one of the Republican electors ineligible, and gave a certificate to the highest candidate on the Democratic list. The Republican electors, having no certificate from the governor, met and voted for Hayes and Wheeler. The Democratic elector, whose appointment was certified to by the governor, appointed two others to fill the vacancies, when the two Republican electors would not meet with him, and the three voted for Tilden and Hendricks. All of these cases were very complicated in their incidents, and a brief account which should convey an intelligible idea of what occurred is impossible. Pending the meetings of the electoral colleges, efforts were made on the part of one or more Democrats — but the final responsibility for them was never absolutely fixed upon any one — to procure one or more electoral votes by bribery. Thus, for the first and only time in the history of the country, the election ended in such a way as to leave the result in actual doubt, and in two States the number of legal votes given for the electors was in dispute. In these States the returns were also open to the suspicion of having been manipulated by each party to bring about a desired result. The following table of the popular vote shows both returns in the disputed States: —

STATES.	Samuel J. Tilden, N. Y.	Rutherford B. Hayes, Ohio.	Peter Cooper, N. Y.	Green Clay Smith, Ky.
Maine	49,917	66,300	663	–
New Hampshire	38,509	41,539	76	–
Vermont	20,350	44,428	–	–
Massachusetts	108,777	150,063	779	84
Rhode Island	10,712	15,787	68	60
Connecticut	61,931	59,034	774	378
New York	521,949	489,207	1,987	2,359
New Jersey	115,962	103,517	712	43
Pennsylvania	366,204	384,164	7,187	1,319
Delaware	13,381	10,752	–	–
Maryland	91,780	71,981	33	10
Virginia	139,670	95,558	–	–
West Virginia	56,495	42,046	1,373	–
North Carolina	125,427	108,417	–	–
South Carolina	90,896	91,870	–	–
Georgia	130,088	50,446	–	–
Florida *	22,927	23,849	–	–
Florida †	24,434	24,340	–	–
Alabama	102,989	68,708	–	–
Mississippi	112,173	52,605	–	–
Louisiana *	70,508	75,315	–	–
Louisiana †	83,723	77,174	–	–
Texas	104,803	44,803	–	–
Arkansas	58,071	38,669	289	–
Missouri	203,077	145,029	3,498	64
Tennessee	133,166	89,566	–	–
Kentucky	159,696	97,156	1,944	818
Ohio	323,182	330,698	3,057	1,636
Michigan	141,095	166,534	9,060	766
Indiana	213,526	208,011	17,233	141
Illinois	258,601	278,232	9,533	–
Wisconsin	123,926	130,070	1,509	27
Minnesota	48,799	72,962	2,311	72
Iowa	112,121	171,326	9,001	36
Nebraska	17,554	31,916	2,820	1,599
Kansas	37,902	78,322	7,776	110
Colorado ‡	–	–	–	–
Nevada	9,308	10,383	–	–
California	76,468	78,322	44	–
Oregon	14,149	15,206	510	–
Total, Republican count	4,285,992	4,033,768	81,737	9,522
Total, Democratic count	4,300,590	4,036,298	81,737	9,522

* Republican count.   † Democratic count.   ‡ By Legislature.

As soon as the electoral votes were cast it became a question of the very first importance how they were to be counted. It was evident that the Senate would refuse to be governed by the twenty-second joint rule — in fact the Senate voted to rescind the rule, — and it was further evident that if the count were to take place in accordance with that rule it would result in throwing out electoral votes on both sides on the most frivolous pretexts. It was asserted by the Republicans that, under the Constitution, the President of the Senate alone had the right to count, in spite of the fact that the joint rule, the work of their party, had assumed the power for the two Houses of Congress. On the other hand, the Democrats, who had always denounced that rule as unconstitutional, now maintained that the right to count was conferred upon Congress. A compromise became necessary, and the moderate men on both sides determined to effect the establishment of a tribunal, as evenly divided politically as might be, which should decide all disputed questions so far as the Constitution gave authority to Congress to decide them. The outcome of their efforts was the Electoral Commission law of 1877, which was passed as originally reported, as follows : —

An act to provide for and regulate the counting of votes for President and Vice-President, and the decision of questions arising thereon, for the term commencing March 4, A. D. 1877.

Be it enacted, etc., That the Senate and House of Representatives shall meet in the hall of the House of Representatives at the hour of one o'clock, post meridian, on the first Thursday in February, A. D. 1877, and the President of the Senate shall be their presiding officer. Two tellers shall be previously appointed on the part of the Senate, and two on the part of the House of Representatives, to whom shall be handed, as they are opened by the President of the Senate, all the certificates and papers purporting to be certificates of electoral votes, which certificates and papers shall be opened, presented, and acted upon in the alphabetical order of

the States, beginning with the letter A; and said tellers having
then read the same in the presence and hearing of the two Houses,
shall make a list of the votes as they shall appear from the said
certificates; and the votes having been ascertained and counted as
in this act provided, the result of the same shall be delivered to
the President of the Senate, who shall thereupon announce the
state of the vote and the names of the persons, if any, elected,
which announcement shall be deemed a sufficient declaration of
the persons elected President and Vice-President of the United
States, and, together with a list of the votes, shall be entered upon
the Journals of the two Houses. Upon such reading of any such
certificate or paper, when there shall be only one return from a
State, the President of the Senate shall call for objections, if any.
Every objection shall be made in writing, and shall state clearly
and concisely, and without argument, the ground thereof, and
shall be signed by at least one senator and one member of the
House of Representatives, before the same shall be received.
When all objections so made to any vote or paper from a State
shall have been received and read, the Senate shall thereupon withdraw, and such objections shall be submitted to the Senate for its
decision, and the Speaker of the House of Representatives shall in
like manner submit such objections to the House of Representatives for its decision, and no electoral vote or votes from any State
from which but one return has been received shall be rejected
except by the affirmative vote of the two Houses. When the two
Houses have voted they shall immediately again meet, and the
presiding officer shall then announce the decision of the question
submitted.

SEC. 2. That if more than one return or paper, purporting to be
a return from a State, shall have been received by the President
of the Senate, purporting to be the certificates of the electoral
votes given at the last preceding election for President and Vice-
President in such State, unless they shall be duplicates of the
same return, all such returns and papers shall be opened by him in
the presence of the two Houses, when met as aforesaid, and read
by the tellers; and all such returns and papers shall thereupon be
submitted to the judgment and decision, as to which is the true
and lawful electoral vote of such State, of a commission constituted
as follows, namely: —

During the session of each House on the Tuesday next preceding
the first Thursday in February, A. D. 1877, each House shall by

viva voce vote appoint five of its members, who, with the five associate Justices of the Supreme Court of the United States, to be ascertained as hereinafter provided, shall constitute a commission for the decision of all questions upon or in respect of such double returns named in this section. On the Tuesday next preceding the first Thursday in February, A. D. 1877, or as soon thereafter as may be, the Associate Justices of the Supreme Court of the United States, now assigned to the first, third, eighth, and ninth circuits, shall select, in such manner as a majority of them shall deem fit, another of the associate justices of said court, which five persons shall be members of the said commission; and the person longest in commission of said five justices shall be the president of said commission. Members of said commission shall respectively take and subscribe the following oath: —

"I, ——, do solemnly swear (or affirm, as the case may be) that I will impartially examine and consider all questions submitted to the commission of which I am a member, and a true judgment give thereon, agreeably to the Constitution and the laws, so help me God."

Which oath shall be filed with the Secretary of the Senate. When the commission shall have been thus organized it shall not be in the power of either House to dissolve the same, or to withdraw any of its members; but if any such senator or member shall die or become physically unable to perform the duties required by this act, the fact of such death or physical inability shall be by said commission, before it shall proceed further, communicated to the Senate or House of Representatives, as the case may be, which body shall immediately and without debate proceed by *viva voce* vote to fill the place so vacated, and the person so appointed shall take and subscribe the oath hereinbefore prescribed, and become a member of said commission; and, in like manner, if any of said justices of the Supreme Court shall die or become physically incapable of performing the duties required by this act, the other of said justices, members of the said commission, shall immediately appoint another justice of said court a member of said commission (and in such appointments regard shall be had to the impartiality and freedom from bias sought by the original appointments to said commission), who shall thereupon immediately take and subscribe to the oath hereinbefore prescribed, and become a member of said commission to fill the vacancy so occasioned.

All the certificates and papers purporting to be certificates of the electoral votes of each State shall be opened in the alphabetical order of the States as provided in section 1 of this act; and when there shall be more than one such certificate or paper, as the certificates or papers from such State shall so be opened (excepting duplicates of the same return), they shall be read by the tellers, and thereupon the President of the Senate shall call for objections, if any. Every objection shall be made in writing, and shall state clearly and concisely, and without argument, the ground thereof, and shall be signed by at least one senator and one member of the House of Representatives before the same shall be received. When all such objections so made to any certificates, vote, or paper from a State shall have been received and read, all such certificates, votes, and papers so objected to, and all papers accompanying the same, together with such objections, shall be forthwith submitted to said commission, which shall proceed to consider the same, with the same powers, if any, now possessed for that purpose by the two Houses, acting separately or together, and, by a majority of votes, decide whether any and what votes from such State are the votes provided for by the Constitution of the United States, and how many and what persons were duly appointed electors in such State; and may therein take into view such petitions, depositions, and other papers, if any, as shall, by the Constitution and now existing law, be competent and pertinent in such consideration, which decision shall be made in writing, stating briefly the ground thereof, and signed by the members of said commission agreeing therein; whereupon the two Houses shall again meet, and such decision shall be read and entered in the Journal of each House, and the counting of the votes shall proceed in conformity therewith, unless, upon objection made thereto in writing by at least five senators and five members of the House of Representatives, the two Houses shall separately concur in ordering otherwise, in which case such concurrent order shall govern. No votes or papers from any other State shall be acted upon until the objections previously made to the votes or papers from any State shall have been finally disposed of.

SEC. 3. That while the two Houses shall be in meeting, as provided in this act, no debate shall be allowed, and no question shall be put by the presiding officer, except to either House on a motion to withdraw, and he shall have power to preserve order.

SEC. 4. That when the two Houses separate to decide upon an objection that may have been made to the counting of any electoral vote or votes from any State, or upon objection to a report of said commission, or other question arising under this act, each senator or representative may speak to such objection or question ten minutes, and not oftener than once; but, after such debate shall have lasted two hours, it shall be the duty of each House to put the main question without further debate.

Sec. 5. That at such joint meeting of the two Houses, seats shall be provided as follows: For the President of the Senate, the Speaker's chair; for the Speaker, immediately upon his left; the senators in the body of the hall, upon the right of the presiding officer; for the representatives, in the body of the hall not provided for the senators; for the tellers, Secretary of the Senate, and Clerk of the House of Representatives, at the clerk's desk; for the other officers of the two Houses, in front of the clerk's desk, and upon each side of the Speaker's platform. Such joint meeting shall not be dissolved until the count of the electoral votes shall be completed and the result declared; and no recess shall be taken unless a question shall have arisen in regard to counting any such votes or otherwise under this act, in which case it shall be competent for either House, acting separately in the manner hereinbefore provided, to direct a recess of such House, not beyond the next day, Sunday excepted, at the hour of ten o'clock in the forenoon; and while any question is being considered by said commission, either House may proceed with its legislative or other business.

Sec. 6. That nothing in this act shall be held to impair or affect any right now existing under the Constitution and laws to question by proceeding in the judicial courts of the United States the right or title of the person who shall be declared elected, or who shall claim to be President or Vice-President of the United States, if any such right exists.

Sec. 7. That said commission shall make its own rules, keep a record of its proceedings, and shall have power to employ such persons as may be necessary for the transaction of its business and the execution of its powers.

This bill was supported and opposed on both sides of each House. In the House of Representatives 191 members voted in favor of it, of whom there were 158 Democrats and 33 Republicans; while 86 members — 68 Republicans and 18 Democrats — voted in the negative. In the

Senate an attempt was made to forbid the commission to
" go behind the returns," but the amendment was rejected,
yeas 18, all Republicans; nays 47, of whom 27 were Democrats, and 20 Republicans. The bill was passed by the Senate, yeas 47,— 26 Democrats and 21 Republicans ; nays 17,
— 16 Republicans and 1 Democrat. The bill became a law,
by the approval of the President, on the 29th of January.
On the next day each House proceeded to choose the five
members who were to be members of the commission.
The Senate made choice of senators George F. Edmunds,
Oliver P. Morton, and Frederick T. Frelinghuysen, Republicans, and Allen G. Thurman and Thomas F. Bayard,
Democrats. The House of Representatives chose Messrs.
Henry B. Payne, Eppa Hunton, and Josiah G. Abbott,
Democrats, and James A. Garfield and George F. Hoar,
Republicans. The four justices of the Supreme Court
designated by the act were Justices Nathan Clifford,
William Strong, Samuel F. Miller, and Stephen J. Field,
of whom Messrs. Clifford and Field were Democrats in
national politics; and they selected Justice Joseph P.
Bradley as the fifth member of the commission on the
part of the Supreme Court. Mr. Bradley was a Republican. The natural choice of the justices would have
been their associate, David Davis; but he had been
elected only five days before as senator from Illinois, and
it was regarded by him and by others as improper that he
should serve. Thus the commission consisted of eight
Republicans and seven Democrats. If Judge Davis had
been selected, there would have been only seven Republicans, and the result of the operation of the law might
have been different.

At the time the count began, on the 1st of February,
1877, each party was confident of victory. The Democrats relied upon a great variety of objections which had

been prepared, the sustaining of any one of which would be sufficient to give the election to Mr. Tilden. The Republican hope was in a refusal of the commission to "go behind the returns." Senator Thomas W. Ferry of Michigan, President *pro tempore* of the Senate, was the presiding officer. The count proceeded, under the law, in the alphabetical order of the States. When the vote of Florida was reached, the certificates of the Hayes and also of the Tilden electors were read. Objections were made to each. The Democrats asserted that the Hayes electors were not duly chosen; that the certificate of the governor to their election was the result of a conspiracy; that its validity, if any, had been annulled by a subsequent certificate by the governor, to the effect that the Tilden electors were chosen; that a court decision made certain the election of the Democratic electors; and that one of the Republican electors was a shipping commissioner under appointment from the government of the United States at the time of his election, and was therefore disqualified. The Republican objection to the Tilden votes was that the returns were not duly authenticated by any person holding at the time an office under the State of Florida. It was only on the 7th of February that the commission, after very long arguments by eminent counsel selected to appear for the two parties, decided the case of Florida. The decision was that it was not competent for the commission "to go into evidence *aliunde* the papers opened by the President of the Senate, to prove that other persons than those regularly certified to by the governor" were appointed. With reference to the case of the elector alleged to have been disqualified, it was decided that the evidence did not show that he held an office on the day of his appointment. The several votes were passed by eight to seven,

— all the Republicans being on one side, and all the Democrats on the other. The formal decision, which was submitted to the two Houses, was that the four Hayes electors, naming them, were duly appointed electors, and that their votes are the constitutional votes. The Houses met on February 10, and received this decision. Formal objection was then made to the decision of the Electoral Commission, and the Houses separated to consider it. The Senate, by a strict party vote, decided that the votes should be counted. The House of Representatives, by a vote which was on party lines, except that one Democrat voted with the Republicans, voted that the electoral votes given by the Tilden electors should be counted. The two Houses not having agreed in rejecting the decision of the commission, it stood, and the joint session was resumed. The votes of Florida having been recorded, the count proceeded until Louisiana was reached.

The Republican objections to the Tilden votes from Louisiana were, like those to the votes of Florida, brief and formal. The government, of which W. P. Kellogg was the head, had been recognized by every department of the government of the United States as the true government of Louisiana, and the certificates of the Hayes electors certified by him were in due form. The Democrats made a great variety of objections to the Hayes votes. They asserted that John McEnery was the lawful Governor of the State; that the certificates asserting the appointment of the Hayes electors were false; and that the canvass of votes by the returning board was without jurisdiction and void. Special objection was made to three of the electors: to two of them as being disqualified, under the Constitution; and to the third, Governor Kellogg, because he certified to his own elec-

tion. Several days were consumed in argument before
the commission. On the 16th of February the commission voted, once more by eight to seven, that the evidence
offered to prove that the Tilden electors were chosen
be not received, and that the certificates of the Hayes
electors are the true votes of Louisiana. The decision
having been communicated to the two Houses, the count
was resumed on the 19th. Objection was made to the
decision of the commission, and the two Houses separated
again to act upon them. The Senate voted, by 41 to 28,
that the decision of the commission should stand. The
House voted that the electoral votes cast by the Hayes
electors for Louisiana ought not to be counted, — 173 to
99. In each case this was a party vote, except that two
Republicans in the House voted with the Democrats.

The Houses then met again on the 20th, and resumed
the count, which proceeded without dispute as far as
the State of Michigan, when objection was made from the
Democratic side to one vote from that State, on the
ground that one of the persons chosen by the people held
a Federal office at the time of his appointment, and that
the act of the other electors in filling the alleged vacancy
caused by his failure to act was not justified. This not
being a case of double returns, the two Houses separated
to decide it for themselves. The objection was overruled
by each House. A somewhat similar case of an elector
for Nevada was the next stumbling-block in the count,
and it too was decided in favor of the elector objected to.
Oregon was reached in the count on the 21st. An out-
line sketch of the extremely complicated situation of
affairs in Oregon has been given already. There were
objections from both sides to the votes, and the papers
were referred to the Electoral Commission, by whom
further argument was heard. The commission unani-

mously rejected the made-up vote of the Tilden board of electors, but decided, eight to seven, that the full board of Hayes electors were the legal electors for the State. The decision was objected to when communicated to the two Houses, and once more they separated, and each decided, substantially by a party vote, as before, — the Senate for accepting the decision, and the House of Representatives for rejecting it. They then met again, and resumed the count until Pennsylvania was reached. This was another case of an elector alleged to have been ineligible on account of his being a centennial commissioner. The other electors treated the place as vacant, and chose another person to act in it. The Senate agreed, without a division, to a resolution that the vote be counted. The House rejected it, 135 to 119, the affirmative consisting entirely of Democrats, and the negative containing only 15 of that party. The full vote of Pennsylvania was accordingly counted under the law, the two Houses not having agreed to reject. Rhode Island furnished a case not very different, but the two Houses this time concurred unanimously in deciding that the disputed vote should be counted.

To the Hayes votes in South Carolina the Democrats next objected that there was no legal election in the State, that there was not, in South Carolina, during the year 1876, a Republican form of government, and that the army and the deputy United States marshals stationed at and near the polls prevented the free exercise of the right of suffrage. The Republicans asserted that the Tilden board was not duly appointed, and that the certificates were wholly defective in form and lacking the necessary official certification. The papers having been referred to the Electoral Commission, that body met again on the 26th. Senator Thurman was obliged to retire from service upon the commission, on account of illness, and Senator Francis Kernan was substituted for him. After a day devoted to arguments, the commission voted unanimously that the Tilden electors were not the true electors of South Carolina, and, by the old majority of eight to seven, that the Hayes electors were the constitutional electors duly appointed. The two Houses separated upon renewed objections to the decision of the commission, and as before the Senate sustained the finding, while the House voted to reject it.

There were two further objections, the first to a vote cast by an elector for Vermont, substituted for an ineligible person who had been chosen by the people, on which the result was the same as in the other similar cases; and finally, a case of the same kind in Wisconsin, which was decided in like manner. The Vermont case was complicated by the presentation, by Mr. Hewitt of New York, of a packet purporting to contain a return of electoral votes given in Vermont. The President of the Senate having received no such vote, nor any vote different from that of the regularly chosen Hayes electors, refused to receive it.

The count had begun on the first day of February, and the final vote upon Wisconsin was not reached until the early morning of March 2. As question after question was decided uniformly in favor of the Republicans, it became evident to the Democrats that their case was lost. They charged gross partisanship upon the Republican members of the Electoral Commission, in determining every point involved in the dual returns for their own party, though as a matter of fact there does not seem to have been much room for choice between the two parties on the score of partisanship. Each member of the commission favored by his vote that view which would result in adding to the electoral vote of his own party. But as the result of the count became more and more certainly a Republican triumph, the anger of the Democrats rose. Some of them were for discontinuing the count; and the symptoms of a disposition to filibuster so that there should be no declaration of the result gave reason for public disquietude. But the conservative members of the party were too patriotic to allow the failure of a law which they had been instrumental in passing to lead to anarchy or revolution, and they sternly discountenanced all attempts to defeat the conclusion of the count. The summing up of the votes was read by Mr. Allison of Iowa, one of the tellers on the part of the Senate, at a little after four o'clock, on the morning of the 2d of March, amid great excitement. That result, as declared, was as follows: —

STATES.	Hayes.	Tilden.	STATES.	Hayes.	Tilden.
Maine	7	–	Texas	–	8
New Hampshire .	5	–	Arkansas . . .	–	6
Vermont . . .	5	–	Missouri . . .	–	15
Massachusetts .	13	–	Tennessee . . .	–	12
Rhode Island . .	4	–	Kentucky . . .	–	12
Connecticut . .	–	6	Ohio	22	–
New York . . .	–	35	Michigan . . .	11	–
New Jersey . .	–	9	Indiana	–	15
Pennsylvania . .	29	–	Illinois	21	–
Delaware . . .	–	3	Wisconsin . . .	10	–
Maryland . . .	–	8	Minnesota . . .	5	–
Virginia . . .	–	11	Iowa	11	–
West Virginia .	–	5	Nebraska . . .	3	–
North Carolina .	–	10	Kansas	5	–
South Carolina .	7	–	Colorado . . .	3	–
Georgia	–	11	Nevada	3	–
Florida	4	–	California . . .	6	–
Alabama . . .	–	10	Oregon	3	–
Mississippi . . .	–	8			
Louisiana . . .	8	–		185	184

Mr. Ferry thereupon declared Rutherford B. Hayes elected President, and William A. Wheeler Vice-President, of the United States. The decision was acquiesced in peaceably by the whole country, and by men of every party. But the Democrats have never ceased to denounce the whole affair as a fraud, and some newspapers have steadily refused to speak of Mr. Hayes as having ever been rightfully in possession of the presidential office. Their anger at the time was very great, and it was excusable, since they honestly believed that Mr. Tilden was fairly elected. It is to be hoped that the patriotism of the American people and their love of peace may never again be put to such a severe test as was that of 1876 and 1877.

XXV.

GARFIELD.

The disputed election of 1876 led to the introduction in Congress of a large number of propositions to amend the Constitution, and to supply constitutional omissions by law. Not one of these propositions has been passed upon by both Houses of Congress. Neither branch has even voted, since 1876, upon a resolution to amend the Constitution; and, although partial action has been taken upon one or two bills, the Constitution and the law remain precisely as they were in 1876. But it may be well to notice the suggestions which were made during Mr. Hayes's administration, — during the special session of Congress, October 15, 1877, and the regular session, which was a continuation of it.

Mr. Cravens of Arkansas offered a resolution of amendment to the Constitution, providing that the people should vote directly for President and Vice-President. Each State was to have a number of presidential votes equal to its electoral votes under the present system, which votes were to be apportioned in each State among the several candidates, in the proportion of the votes given to each; the legislature of each State was to direct the manner in which the presidential vote of that State was to be ascertained; on a day to be fixed by Congress, or, in case of disagreement between the two Houses, on a day to be named by the President, not less than fifteen nor more than thirty days before the 4th of March, a joint meeting of the two Houses was to be held, the President of the

345

Senate was to open the presidential votes, certified to by the governor of the State, and one list from each State was then to be counted under the direction of the two Houses; a majority of all the presidential votes was requisite to a choice. In case no choice had been made by such a majority, then the two houses, in joint convention, were to elect a president by *viva voce* vote, each senator and member having one vote, the choice being limited to the two highest on the list, unless two persons should have an equal number of votes next to the highest; one senator and a majority of the representatives from two thirds of the States were to constitute a quorum for the purposes of this election. In case no person should receive a majority of the Congress so voting, the President in office was to continue to be President until a choice was effected. The election of Vice-President was to be made in the same manner, and at the same time as that of President. Whenever the office of Vice-President became vacant, there was to be an election by joint convention of Congress, within ten days after the next meeting of Congress, or within twenty days if Congress should be in session at the time the vacancy occurred.

Mr. Springer of Illinois made a proposition, of which the leading features were: a presidential term of six years, the President not to be immediately re-eligible; each State to have a number of presidential votes equal to its electoral votes according to the present system, except that States having but one representative in Congress were to have but one presidential vote, and States having but two representatives were to have but three votes; a direct vote for President and Vice-President; a canvassing board in each State, with ministerial powers only, — consisting of the governor, secretary of state, and chief justice of the highest court, — to aggregate the votes, apportion to each candidate his proportional part of the presidential votes of the State, and to make return thereof to the President of the Senate; the two Houses to be in session on the third Monday of January after a presidential election, a joint meeting to be held, to be presided over by the President of the Senate, unless he should be a candidate for the office of President, and in that case by the Speaker of the House of Representatives, and if he were similarly disqualified, then by a presiding officer chosen by the joint convention; a plurality of votes to elect both the President and the Vice-President; the joint convention to be the judge of the returns and qualifications of the persons who shall be President and Vice-President. If no conclusion upon the returns should be reached by the second Monday in February, the convention was to vote *viva voce* upon the question who was constitutionally elected President, and who Vice-President,—a majority of those present to determine all questions.

Mr. Maish of Pennsylvania proposed a popular election of President, without the intervention of any electors. The votes were to be returned to the Secretary of State of each State, and to be by him opened in the presence of the governor and the chief justice of the highest court, and these three officers were to apportion electoral votes to each candidate in accordance with the returns. This proposition did not deal with the matter of a count of the votes.

Mr. Finley of Ohio proposed a direct vote of all the people for President and Vice-President, disregarding State lines altogether; a plurality of votes was to elect in each case, but if two persons had an equal and the highest number of votes, then the House of Representatives was to choose the President from those two; or, if the failure was in relation to the Vice-Presidency, then the Senate was to make the choice. In each case the voting was to be *viva voce*, and each member was to have one vote; the canvass of returns for President and Vice-President was to be made by Congress in a manner to be determined by joint rules or by law, and if the two Houses could not agree, the matter in dispute was to be referred to the Supreme Court for final decision.

Mr. Eaton of Connecticut proposed in the Senate an amendment constituting a tribunal for the decision of controverted questions arising out of the presidential election. Not less than twelve months before the occurrence of such an election, the governor of each State was to appoint, with the consent of the Senate of the State, five qualified persons, who were to hear and determine all questions of contests in relation to the choice of electors, and to transmit their report, sealed, to the President of the Senate.

A resolution offered by Mr. Riddle of Tennessee proposed a direct election by the people, a clear majority being required for a choice. In case such majority should not be obtained, then a second election was to be held within two months of the time of the first vote, when the choice should be limited to the two highest on the list. In case of no choice, by reason of a tie, on this second trial, the two Houses of Congress, in joint convention, each member having one vote, were to elect.

Mr. Sampson of Iowa proposed that the relative power of the States should be as it now is; that the people should vote directly for the executive; that the persons having a plurality for the offices of President and Vice-President in any State should receive the full presidential vote of that State, or, in case of a tie, that the votes should be equally divided among those having the highest number; and if no person received a majority of presidential votes, the choice of either President or Vice-President was to be made as the Constitution now provides for cases of no choice made by the electors.

In May, 1878, Mr. Southard of Ohio, from a committee of the House of Representatives, appointed for the purpose, reported a plan. It dispensed with electors altogether. Each State was to be entitled to as many presidential votes as it would have electors under the present system. The people having voted directly for President and Vice-President, the vote for each candidate in any State was to be ascertained by multiplying the number of votes given for any person by the number of presidential votes assigned to the State, and dividing the product by the whole number of votes cast; and the fractions were to be ascertained, to the third place of decimals. The returns were to be made to the Secretary of State of each State, who was to open them in the presence of the governor and the State auditor or controller; and the apportionment of presidential votes was to be made by them as a canvassing board. Contests as to an election might be passed upon by the highest judicial tribunal in each State, and the decision was to be sent to the President of the Senate at Washington. The votes were to be counted by the two Houses of Congress, assembled under the presidency of the President of the Senate, and all votes were to be counted unless the two Houses concurred in rejecting them; or, if there was a decision by the highest court of the State upon a contest, that decision was to stand unless the two Houses concurred in overruling it. If there were dual returns, or two decisions purporting to be by the highest court, that was to be accepted which the two Houses should decide to be the true return or the true decision. A plurality of votes was to elect the President, and in case of a tie the election was to be made in the manner now provided for the case of a failure to elect by the electors.   This proposition never came up for discussion.

A determined effort was made by the Senate, during the session of 1878–79, to amend the law relative to the count of votes, by a statute covering the whole subject. The bill was managed by Mr. Edmunds of Vermont. A brief account of its provisions only can be given. It changed the time for the appointment of electors in the several States to the first Tuesday of October in each fourth year. If a vacancy should occur in both the offices of President and Vice-President more than two months before the first Tuesday of October in any year other than that in which electors would be regularly appointed, a new election was to be held. The time for the meeting and voting of the electors was to be the second Monday in January following their appointment. The fourth section was as follows : —

> Each State may provide by law enacted prior to the day in this act named for the appointment of the electors, for the trial and determination of any controversy concerning the appointment of electors, before the time fixed for the meeting of the electors, in any manner it may deem expedient. Every such determination made pursuant to such law so enacted before said day, and made prior to the said time of meeting of the electors, shall be conclusive evidence of the lawful title of the electors who shall have been so determined to have been appointed, and shall govern in the counting of the electoral votes, as provided in the Constitution and as hereinafter regulated.

The provisions of the bill in relation to the count followed in general the custom of Congress under the twenty-second joint rule, with these exceptions: No vote from a State from which there was but one return could be rejected without a concurrent vote of the two Houses. If there were two or more returns, that only could be counted which was decided to be the true return in the manner provided in the section just quoted. If there were no such determination, or if there were two or more decisions purporting to have been made in accordance with a law passed in conformity with that section, that return, or that decision only, could be accepted which the two Houses acting separately should decide by affirmative vote to be in accordance with the Constitution and the laws. When the two Houses separated to consider objections to electoral votes, each member of either House might speak once only, for five minutes, and at the expiration of two hours it would become the duty of the presiding officer to put the main question. After several days of debate this bill was passed by the Senate, 35 to 26. The negative vote consisted entirely of Democrats; the majority was made up of Republicans, with the exception of Messrs. Bayard, Merrimon, and Morgan, Democrats, and Judge Davis of Illinois, Independent. It was referred in the House of Representatives to the select committee having the subject in charge, but no report was made upon it.

In May, 1880, the Democrats having a majority in the Senate, Mr. Morgan of Alabama reported from a select committee a joint rule for the government of the two Houses in counting the electoral votes. It differed from the rescinded twenty-second rule in several particulars. No vote from a State which sent but one return was to be rejected except by the affirmative action of both branches of Congress. If two or more returns should be offered, neither was to be counted unless the two Houses agreed in deciding that one of them was the true and correct return. Provision was also made for one hour's debate in each House upon objections, no member to speak more than once, or longer than ten minutes; and also for debate by unanimous consent in the joint meeting. It was further provided that an appeal might be taken from a decision by the presiding officer, which was to be overruled only by concurrent action of both Houses. This proposed rule was considered at length. Mr. Edmunds endeavored to have his bill, already summarized, with some changes, substituted for the rule. This was voted down, as were all other amendments, and the rule was adopted by the Senate, by a vote of 25 to 14, a party vote, except that Mr. Davis of Illinois voted with the Democrats. In the House, the Republicans endeavored to have the rule referred to a committee, but their motions having that object in view were voted down. Finally the matter was postponed until the first Monday in December, 1880. It was under consideration several times during the session, but the Republicans persistently opposed it, and on the last day that it was considered, Jan. 26, 1881, they filibustered successfully against its passage.

Early in February of the same year a resolution was adopted, which carried the conduct of the count back to the method so long in use before the twenty-second joint rule was adopted. It provided, however, for two tellers on the part of the Senate, which was an innovation introduced by the Electoral Commission Law of 1877. The second resolution directed that in case it should appear that the electoral vote of any State had been given on any other day than that fixed by law, the declaration of the result should be in the alternative form first introduced in 1821, with respect to the vote of Missouri. This rule was adopted by both Houses. In the Senate there was no division. In the House the second resolution was opposed by 77 members, of whom six were Democrats and three Greenbackers. The count of 1881 took place under that rule.

Mr. Hayes, immediately after his accession to the presidential office, reversed the policy of his predecessor in respect of the support of the Republican governments of South Carolina and Louisiana, and those governments were speedily overthrown by their Democratic rivals. This course eliminated the Southern question from national politics to a great extent, by the simple expedient of allowing those who threatened and proclaimed their purpose to rule, by violence if necessary, to have everything their own way. It made the South so far "solid," that in the Forty-sixth Congress, elected in 1878, there were but four Republican representatives from all the Southern States, against 102 Democrats. In the first half of Mr. Hayes's term the House was controlled by the Democrats, and the Senate by the Republicans, while from 1879 to 1881, each House was governed by a Democratic majority.

The events of this administration had far less influence upon the ensuing election than has usually been the case. The leading events, in a political sense, were: The silver agitation, which resulted in the passage of the act of Feb. 28, 1878, for the coinage of the standard silver dollar, after the bill had been returned by the President with his objections; the agitation for the repeal of the Resumption Act, which did not succeed, and the resumption of specie payments at the beginning of 1879; the attempt to revive the controversy over the "great fraud of 1877," by the formation of the Potter Committee; the passage, veto, and failure of a bill to restrict Chinese immigration; and finally the prolonged contests, first between the Senate and the House of Representatives, and then between the two Houses of Congress and the President, on the subject of attaching political legislation to appropriation bills. The purpose of the Democrats in

putting riders upon the appropriation bills, — to prohibit
the use of United States troops at the polls, to regulate
the impanelling of juries, and to prevent the appointment
of deputy marshals for elections in which representatives
were to be chosen, — was to force upon the President the
alternative of approving such political legislation or of
depriving the government of needed supplies. All these
controversies had for the most part died out before the
election of 1880 took place. It was seen, as that contest
drew near, that the Republicans were in much better
condition than they were four years earlier. Prosperity
had returned to the country with the resumption of
specie payments. The policy of the President had been
of a character to unite the party, partly because it had
forced the members of both wings to join in defence of
the legislation of the party, under the leadership of the
President, and partly because there had been no scandals,
or high official quarrels, after the first year of the administration. Mr. Hayes prepared the way for a fresh victory
of the Republicans, without attaching — possibly without
trying to attach — any considerable number of politicians
to his own personal fortunes.

Candidates for the succession were numerous. A movement was begun, supported by many persons who had been
strongly opposed to a third term for President Grant in
1876, to bring him forward again; and it was argued with
much plausibility that after an interval of four years between a second and a third election, the "third term" would
not be a breach of the unwritten Constitution. Mr. Blaine
was again prominent as a candidate in the West, and to a
greater or less extent in other parts of the country. Those
who were opposed to both Grant and Blaine favored, some
Mr. John Sherman, Secretary of the Treasury, and others
Senator George F. Edmunds. On the Democratic side

there was no concentration of opinion. It was in the early stages of the preliminary canvass universally conceded that Mr. Tilden would be nominated if he would accept the candidacy; but his health was known to be infirm, and, as he gave no indication of his intentions, his opponents worked secretly and successfully to secure delegates who were opposed to him.

The Republican convention met at Chicago on the 2d of June. Senator George F. Hoar of Massachusetts was the temporary and also the permanent president. Three days were occupied in preliminaries and in deciding cases of contesting delegates, of whom there were many. The opposition which the candidacy of General Grant encountered was significantly indicated by a resolution introduced by Senator Conkling, who managed the Grant canvass, as follows : —

Resolved, As the sense of this convention, that every member of it is bound in honor to support its nominee, whoever that nominee may be, and that no man should hold his seat here who is not ready so to agree.

After a brief debate, this resolution was passed by a vote of 716 to 3, — the latter being delegates from West Virginia. Mr. Conkling offered a resolution that those who had voted in the negative, " do not deserve and have forfeited their votes in this convention." To this summary way of disfranchising delegates there were numerous objections, and, in view of the possible rejection of the resolution, Mr. Conkling withdrew it.

On the fourth day General James A. Garfield reported from a committee a series of proposed rules. These were for the most part the rules of the convention of 1876, but one important amendment was made, to the effect that when the vote of any State should be announced by the chairman, if any exception should be taken to the announcement, " the president of the convention shall direct the roll of members of such delegation to be called, and the result recorded in accordance with the votes individually given." This was a direct and fatal blow at the " unit rule." A minority report was presented by General George H. Sharpe of New York, on behalf of himself and eight other members of the committee, recommending the retention of the rule as it had been adopted by the convention of 1876. The delegation from New York had been instructed to vote as a unit for General Grant, and the adoption of the new rule would allow several members of that delegation, who were not in favor of the ex-President's candidacy, to vote individually for the person whom they might prefer. The minority report was rejected without a division. An amendment having been adopted directing the national committee to prescribe a method for the election of delegates to the convention of 1884, the rules were adopted. The platform was then reported, as follows, by Mr. Edwards Pierrepont of New York: —

The Republican party in national convention assembled, at the end of twenty years since the Federal government was first committed to its charge, submits to the people of the United States this brief report of its administration. It suppressed the rebellion which had armed nearly a million of men to subvert the national authority. It reconstructed the Union of the States with freedom instead of slavery as its corner-stone. It transformed four millions of human beings from the likeness of things to the rank of citizens. It relieved Congress from the infamous work of hunting fugitive slaves, and charged it to see that slavery does not exist. It has raised the value of our paper currency from thirty-eight per cent to the par of gold. It has restored upon a solid basis payment in coin for all the national obligations, and has given us a currency absolutely good and equal in every part of our extended country. It has lifted the credit of the nation from the point where six per cent bonds sold at eighty-six per cent to that where four per cent bonds are eagerly sought at a premium. Under its administration railways have increased from thirty-one thousand miles in 1860 to more than eighty-two thousand miles in 1879. Our foreign trade has increased from seven hundred million dollars to one billion, one hundred and fifty million dollars in the same time, and our exports, which were twenty million dollars less than our imports in 1860, were two hundred and sixty-four million more than our imports in 1879. Without resorting to loans, it has, since the war closed, defrayed the ordinary expenses of government beside the accruing interest on the public debt, and has annually disbursed more than thirty million dollars for soldiers' pensions. It has paid eight hundred and eighty-eight million dollars of the public debt, and, by refunding the balance at lower rates, has reduced the annual interest charge from nearly one hundred and fifty-one million dollars to less than eighty-nine million dollars. All the industries of the country have revived, labor is in demand, wages have increased, and throughout the entire country there is evidence of a coming prosperity greater than we have ever enjoyed.

Upon this record the Republican party asks for the continued confidence and support of the people, and this convention submits for their approval the following statement of the principles and purposes which will continue to guide and inspire its efforts: —

1. We affirm that the work of the last twenty-one years has been such as to commend itself to the favor of the nation, and that the fruits of the costly victories which we have achieved through immense difficulties should be preserved; that the peace regained should be cherished; that the dissevered Union, now happily restored, should be perpetuated, and that the liberties secured to this generation should be transmitted undiminished to future generations; that the order established and the credit acquired should never be impaired; that the pensions promised should be extinguished by the full payment of every dollar thereof; that the reviving industries should be further promoted, and that the commerce, already so great, should be steadily encouraged.

2. The Constitution of the United States is a supreme law, and not a mere contract; out of confederated States it made a sovereign nation. Some powers are denied to the nation, while others are denied to the States; but the boundary between the powers delegated and those reserved is to be determined by the national, and not by the State tribunals.

3. The work of popular education is one left to the care of the several States, but is the duty of the national government to aid that

work to the extent of its constitutional duty. The intelligence of the nation is but the aggregate of the intelligence in the several States, and the destiny of the nation must be guided, not by the genius of any one State, but by the average genius of all.

4. The Constitution wisely forbids Congress to make any law respecting an establishment of religion, but it is idle to hope that the nation can be protected against the influences of sectarianism while each State is exposed to its domination. We therefore recommend that the Constitution be so amended as to lay the same prohibition upon the legislature of each State, and to forbid the appropriation of public funds to the support of sectarian schools.

5. We affirm the belief avowed in 1876, that the duties levied for the purpose of revenue should so discriminate as to favor American labor; that no further grant of the public domain should be made to any railway or other corporation; that, slavery having perished in the States, its twin barbarity, polygamy, must die in the Territories; that everywhere the protection accorded to citizens of American birth must be secured to citizens by American adoption ; and that we esteem it the duty of Congress to develop and improve our watercourses and harbors, but insist that further subsidies to private persons or corporations must cease; that the obligations of the Republic to the men who preserved its integrity in the hour of battle are undiminished by the lapse of the fifteen years since their final victory, — to do them perpetual honor is, and shall forever be, the grateful privilege and sacred duty of the American people.

6. Since the authority to regulate immigration and intercourse between the United States and foreign nations rests with Congress, or with the United States and its treaty-making powers, the Republican party, regarding the unrestricted immigration of the Chinese as an evil of great magnitude, invoke the exercise of those powers to restrain and limit that immigration by the enactment of such just, humane, and reasonable provisions as will produce that result.

7. That the purity and patriotism which characterized the earlier career of Rutherford B. Hayes in peace and war, and which guided the thoughts of our immediate predecessors to him for a presidential candidate, have continued to inspire him in his career as Chief Executive, and that history will accord to his administration the honors which are due to an efficient, just, and courteous discharge of the public business, and will honor his interposition between the people and proposed partisan laws.

We charge upon the Democratic party the habitual sacrifice of patriotism and justice to a supreme and insatiable lust of office and patronage; that to obtain possession of the national and State governments and the control of place and position they have obstructed all efforts to promote the purity and to conserve the freedom of suffrage, and have devised fraudulent certifications and returns; have labored to unseat lawfully elected members of Congress, to secure at all hazards the vote of a majority of the States in the House of Representatives; have endeavored to occupy by force and fraud the places of trust given to others by the people of Maine, and rescued by the courageous action of Maine's patriotic sons; have, by methods vicious in principle and tyrannical in practice, attached partisan legislation to appropriation bills, upon whose passage the very movements of the government depend, and have crushed the rights of individuals; have advocated the principles and sought the favor of rebellion against the nation, and have endeavored to obliterate the sacred memories of the war, and to overcome its inestimably valuable results of nationality, personal freedom, and individual equality.

The equal, steady, and complete enforcement of laws and the protection of all our citizens in the enjoyment of all privileges and immunities guaranteed by the Constitution, are the first duties of the nation. The dangers of a solid South can only be averted by a faithful performance of every promise which the nation has made to the citizen. The execution of the laws and the punishment of all those who violate them are the only safe methods by which an enduring peace can be secured and genuine prosperity established throughout the South. Whatever promises the nation makes, the nation must perform, and the nation cannot with safety delegate this duty to the States. The solid South must be divided by the peaceful agencies of the ballot, and all opinions must there find free expression, and to this end the honest voter must be protected against terrorism, violence, or fraud.

And we affirm it to be the duty and the purpose of the Republican party to use every legitimate means to restore all the States of this Union to the most perfect harmony that may be practicable; and we submit it to the practical, sensible people of the United States to say whether it would not be dangerous to the dearest interests of our country at this time to surrender the administration of the national government to the party which seeks to overthrow the existing policy under which we are so prosperous, and thus bring distrust and confusion where there are now order, confidence, and hope.

The platform was adopted unanimously, as was also the following resolution offered by Mr. J. M. Barker of Massachusetts : —

The Republican party, adhering to principles affirmed by its last national convention of respect for the constitutional rule covering appointments to office, adopts the declaration of President Hayes, that the reform of the civil service should be thorough, radical, and complete. To this end it demands the co-operation of the legislative with the executive department of the government, and that Congress shall so legislate that fitness, ascertained by proper, practical tests, shall admit to the public service.

The day's and the week's session was concluded with the formal presentation of the names of candidates. On Monday the voting began, and twenty-eight trials to nominate a candidate were made on that day. General Grant was the leading candidate, with 304 votes, and during that day his number fluctuated only between 302 and 309. Mr. Blaine came next, with 284 votes on the first ballot; his number varied on the first day from 285 the highest to 275 the lowest. Mr. Sherman began with 93 and ended with 91, having meanwhile dropped to 88 and risen to 97. Mr. Elihu B. Washburne of Illinois had 31 votes at the beginning, rose to 36, and had 35 on the twenty-eighth ballot. Senator Edmunds had 33 votes at the start, dropped to 32 on the second ballot, to 31 on the eighth, and held that number unchanged through twenty more ballots. Senator William Windom of Minnesota had ten votes, those of his own State, on every ballot. The number of votes necessary to a choice was in every case 378. The convention ended the day's voting without having made any progress towards a nomination.

On the morning of Tuesday there was a slight change. About twenty of the supporters of Mr. Edmunds, joined by a few others, transferred their votes to Mr. Sherman, giving him 116. His number rose to 120 on the thirtieth ballot; but, as not the slightest impression was made upon the Grant and Blaine forces, the movement came to nothing, and on the next trial his strength began to decline again. On the thirty-fourth ballot 17 votes were given to James A. Garfield. General Garfield had received one vote on the second ballot, the day before, and thereafter had received sometimes one vote, sometimes two votes, and sometimes none. He was present in the convention as a delegate and as the manager of Mr. Sherman's canvass, and had been a conspicuous figure in the proceedings of the convention. When he suddenly sprang into prominence on the thirty-fourth ballot, the idea of making him the candidate met with great favor. On the thirty-fifth ballot a number of Mr. Blaine's delegates transferred their votes to him, and gave him 50 votes. On the next trial, — the thirty-sixth, — he received 399, and was nominated. The history of the voting will be sufficiently exhibited by showing in a table the result of the 1st, the 28th, the 30th, the 34th, the 35th, and the 36th : —

	1st.	28th.	30th.	34th.	35th.	36th.
U. S. Grant.	304	307	306	312	313	306
J. G. Blaine	284	279	279	275	257	42
J. Sherman	93	91	120	107	99	3
G. F. Edmunds	33	31	11	11	11	–
E. B. Washburne	31	35	33	30	23	5
W. Windom	10	10	4	4	3	–
J. A. Garfield	–	2	2	17	50	399

The nomination was received with great enthusiasm by the most of the members of the convention, and with

great satisfaction throughout the country; but some of
the prominent leaders of the Grant movement were sullen
and discontented. A consultation took place between
politicians of the two wings, and the nomination of a
candidate for the Vice-Presidency was conceded to those
who had been upholding the cause of General Grant.
Senator Conkling, who was recognized as the chief
spokesman for the ex-President, named Mr. Chester A.
Arthur of New York. Mr. Arthur's only service in the
national government had been rendered as collector of
the port of New York, from which position he had been
removed by Mr. Hayes. The first ballot for a candidate
resulted as follows: For Chester A. Arthur, 468; Elihu
B. Washburne of Illinois, 199; Marshall Jewell of Connecticut, 43; Horace Maynard of Tennessee, 30; Edmund J. Davis of Texas, 20; Blanche K. Bruce of
Mississippi, 8; James L. Alcorn of Mississippi, 4; Thomas
Settle of Florida, 2; Stewart L. Woodford of New York,
1. The nomination of Mr. Arthur was made unanimous,
and the convention adjourned.

The selection of General Garfield was regarded, except
in very narrow circles, as an admirable one. That of Mr.
Arthur was looked upon in some quarters with dismay.
While the events of the past four years have greatly
modified public opinion, and have enabled Mr. Arthur to
deserve and to win universal respect, he was at that time
deemed by a very large section of the party unfitted, by
his political instincts and training, for a place on the
ticket. But those who were dissatisfied with that part of
the ticket were so well pleased with General Garfield,
that, after once giving vent to their feelings, they prepared to support both Garfield and Arthur with zeal.
Some of these who had set their hearts upon the nomination of General Grant were not, however, so easily
reconciled to the situation.

The next convention held was that of the Greenbackers. It met at Chicago on the 9th of June. The Rev.
Gilbert De La Matyr of Indiana was the temporary chairman, and Richard Trevellick of Michigan was the permanent president. On the second day the following platform
was reported and adopted: —

1. That the right to make and issue money is a sovereign power
to be maintained by the people for the common benefit. The delegation of this right to corporations is a surrender of the central
attribute of sovereignty, void of constitutional sanction, conferring
upon a subordinate irresponsible power absolute dominion over
industry and commerce. All money, whether metallic or paper,
should be issued and its volume controlled by the government, and
not by or through banking corporations, and, when so issued,
should be a full legal tender for all debts, public and private.

2. That the bonds of the United States should not be refunded,
but paid as rapidly as practicable, according to contract. To enable
the government to meet these obligations, legal tender currency
should be substituted for the notes of the national banks, the
national banking system abolished, and the unlimited coinage of
silver, as well as gold, established by law.

3. That labor should be so protected by national and State
authority as to equalize its burdens and ensure a just distribution
of its results; the eight-hour law of Congress should be enforced;
the sanitary condition of industrial establishments placed under
rigid control; the competition of contract labor abolished; a bureau
of labor statistics established; factories, mines, and workshops
inspected; the employment of children under fourteen years of
age forbidden; and wages paid in cash.

4. Slavery being simply cheap labor, and cheap labor being
simply slavery, the importation and presence of Chinese serfs
necessarily tends to brutalize and degrade American labor; therefore immediate steps should be taken to abrogate the Burlingame
treaty.

5. Railroad land grants forfeited by reason of non-fulfilment of
contract should be immediately reclaimed by government; and
henceforth the public domain reserved exclusively as homes for
actual settlers.

6. It is the duty of Congress to regulate interstate commerce.

All lines of communication and transportation should be brought under such legislative control as shall secure moderate, fair, and uniform rates for passenger and freight traffic.

7. We denounce, as destructive to prosperity and dangerous to liberty, the action of the old parties in fostering and sustaining gigantic land, railroad, and money corporations, invested with, and exercising, powers belonging to the government, and yet not responsible to it for the manner of their exercise.

8. That the Constitution, in giving Congress the power to borrow money, to declare war, to raise and support armies, to provide and maintain a navy, never intended that the men who loaned their money for an interest consideration should be preferred to the soldier and sailor who perilled their lives and shed their blood on land and sea in defence of their country; and we condemn the cruel class legislation of the Republican party, which, while professing great gratitude to the soldier, has most unjustly discriminated against him and in favor of the bondholder.

9. All property should bear its just proportion of taxation; and we demand a graduated income tax.

10. We denounce as most dangerous the efforts everywhere manifest to restrict the right of suffrage.

11. We are opposed to an increase of the standing army in time of peace, and the insidious scheme to establish an enormous military power under the guise of militia laws.

12. We demand absolute democratic rules for the government of Congress, placing all representatives of the people upon an equal footing, and taking away from committees a veto power greater than that of the President.

13. We demand a government of the people, by the people, and for the people, instead of a government of the bondholders, by the bondholders, and for the bondholders; and we denounce every attempt to stir up sectional strife as an effort to conceal monstrous crimes against the people.

14. In the furtherance of these ends we ask the co-operation of all fair-minded people. We have no quarrel with individuals, wage no war upon classes, but only against vicious institutions. We are not content to endure further discipline from our present actual rulers, who, having dominion over money, over transportation, over land and labor, and largely over the press and the machinery of government, wield unwarrantable power over our institutions, and over our life and property.

15. That every citizen of due age, sound mind, and not a felon, be fully enfranchised, and that this resolution be referred to the States, with recommendation for their favorable consideration.

An informal vote was taken for a candidate for President, with the following result: James B. Weaver of Iowa had 224½; Hendrick B. Wright of Pennsylvania, 126½; Stephen D. Dillaye of New York, 119; Benjamin F. Butler of Massachusetts, 95; Solon Chase of Maine, 89; Edward P. Allis of Wisconsin, 41; Alexander Campbell of Illinois, 21. The delegations began changing as soon as the strong lead of Mr. Weaver was known, and that gentleman was unanimously nominated. On a vote for a candidate for Vice-President, B. J. Chambers of Texas had 403 and Alanson M. West of Mississippi had 311. Mr. Chambers was thereupon unanimously nominated.

The Prohibitionists held a convention at Cleveland, Ohio, on the 17th of June. It attracted so little attention that no report of its proceedings was published in the leading newspapers of the country. Twelve States were represented by 142 delegates. A platform presenting the principles of the party, in much the same form as they were announced in 1876, was adopted. General Neal Dow of Maine was nominated for President, and A. M. Thompson of Ohio for Vice-President.

The series of national conventions was closed by that of the Democrats at Cincinnati on the 22d of June. What that convention would do was a matter of great uncertainty. Mr. Tilden had still not indicated what was his wish in respect to the nomination. It is probable that if he had frankly allowed it to be understood that he would be a candidate, he could have secured enough delegates to make him the nominee on the first ballot. But he neither encouraged nor discouraged his friends, and

left them in the dark as to his purposes; and the conse-
quence was that hardly a third of the delegates went to
Cincinnati for Tilden as their first choice. A great many
Southern members of the convention were in favor of
Senator Thomas F. Bayard of Delaware. General Hancock was brought forward by Pennsylvania, and had
strong support in other States. Ohio presented Senator
Thurman; and Mr. Hendricks, as well as other leaders of
the party, Mr. Henry B. Payne of Ohio, Speaker Samuel
J. Randall, and Judge Stephen J. Field, had their friends.
A movement was begun in favor of Mr. Horatio Seymour,
and it made not a little progress in a quiet way. Mr.
Seymour was captured by an "interviewer," and expressed himself in such terms that it was believed that he
really would not accept the nomination if it should be
tendered; and, though he received a few votes, there was
no opportunity to test his actual strength in the convention.

Simultaneously with the assembling of the convention
came a letter from Mr. Tilden, in which he "renounced"
the nomination. The letter was written in such a way
that it left room for both the friends and the opponents
of Mr. Tilden to say that he would not refuse the nomination if it should be tendered to him; but the prevailing
tendency of opinion was to take him at his word.

Mr. George Hoadly of Ohio was the temporary chairman of the convention, which did not effect its permanent organization until the second day, after the contested
seats had been passed upon. There were several cases of
contest. Two sets of delegates made their appearance
from Massachusetts, and the case was decided by admitting both sets, with a half vote for each delegate. A
more difficult case was that of New York. Here, too,
there were two full delegations, one chosen by the "regu-

lar" Democrats; the other, the "Tammany" delegation.
The attitude of the Tammany organization towards Mr.
Tilden in 1876, and the open declaration of Mr. John
Kelly and other members of the contesting delegation,
that if that candidate should be nominated again they
would not support him, did not give the delegation favor
in the eyes of the convention; and the committee on
credentials reported against giving them any recognition
whatever. A minority of the committee reported in
favor of granting their request to be allowed twenty of
the seventy votes of New York. After a debate the
minority report was rejected by a vote of yeas 205½;
nays 457, the New York delegation being excused from
voting at its own request. Thus Tammany was excluded
from the convention altogether.

Ex-Governor John W. Stevenson of Kentucky having
been chosen permanent president of the convention the
platform was reported by Mr. Henry Watterson of
Kentucky, and unanimously adopted. It was as follows: —

The Democrats of the United States, in convention assembled,
declare —

1. We pledge ourselves anew to the constitutional doctrines and
traditions of the Democratic party, as illustrated by the teachings
and example of a long line of Democratic statesmen and patriots,
and embodied in the platform of the last national convention of
the party.

2. Opposition to centralizationism and to that dangerous spirit
of encroachment which tends to consolidate the powers of all the
departments in one, and thus to create, whatever be the form of
government, a real despotism. No sumptuary laws; separation of
church and state for the good of each; common schools fostered
and protected.

3. Home rule; honest money, consisting of gold and silver, and
paper convertible into coin on demand; the strict maintenance of
the public faith, state and national; and a tariff for revenue only.

4. The subordination of the military to the civil power, and a
general and thorough reform of the civil service.

5. The right to a free ballot is the right preservative of all rights, and must and shall be maintained in every part of the United States.

6. The existing administration is the representative of conspiracy only, and its claim of right to surround the ballot-boxes with troops and deputy marshals, to intimidate and obstruct the electors, and the unprecedented use of the veto to maintain its corrupt and despotic power, insult the people and imperil their institutions.

7. The grand fraud of 1876–77, by which, upon a false count of the electoral votes of two States, the candidate defeated at the polls was declared to be President, and, for the first time in American history, the will of the people was set aside under a threat of military violence, struck a deadly blow at our system of representative government; the Democratic party, to preserve the country from a civil war, submitted for a time in firm and patriotic faith that the people would punish this crime in 1880; this issue precedes and dwarfs every other; it imposes a more sacred duty upon the people of the Union than ever addressed the conscience of a nation of freemen.

8. We execrate the course of this administration in making places in the civil service a reward for political crime, and demand a reform by statute which shall make it forever impossible for the defeated candidate to bribe his way to the seat of a usurper by billeting villains upon the people.

9. The resolution of Samuel J. Tilden not again to be a candidate for the exalted place to which he was elected by a majority of his countrymen, and from which he was excluded by the leaders of the Republican party, is received by the Democrats of the United States with sensibility, and they declare their confidence in his wisdom, patriotism, and integrity, unshaken by the assaults of a common enemy, and they further assure him that he is followed into the retirement he has chosen for himself by the sympathy and respect of his fellow-citizens, who regard him as one who, by elevating the standards of public morality, merits the lasting gratitude of his country and his party.

10. Free ships and a living chance for American commerce on the seas and on the land. No discrimination in favor of transportation lines, corporations, or monopolies.

11. Amendment of the Burlingame treaty. No more Chinese immigration, except for travel, education, and foreign commerce, and therein carefully guarded.

12. Public money and public credit for public purposes solely, and public land for actual settlers.

13. The Democratic party is the friend of labor and the laboring man, and pledges itself to protect him alike against the cormorant and the commune.

14. We congratulate the country upon the honesty and thrift of a Democratic Congress, which has reduced the public expenditure forty million dollars a year; upon the continuation of prosperity at home and the national honor abroad; and, above all, upon the promise of such a change in the administration of the government as shall insure us genuine and lasting reform in every department of the public service.

The business of the convention was transacted so expeditiously that the formal presentation of the candidates took place on the second day, and one ballot for a candidate for President was taken. It showed a slight lead for General Hancock over Mr. Bayard, but the combined vote for both these candidates did not constitute a majority of the convention. A second ballot was taken the next morning, when General Hancock gained nearly one hundred and fifty votes, and the delegations then began changing in his favor, and he was nominated. The hand of Mr. Tilden was detected, or rather suspected, in the voting, but if he had any part in the affair he suffered a defeat. The vote of New York was at first cast for Mr. Payne of Ohio, who was believed to be Mr. Tilden's heir; but, on the second ballot, New York and nearly all the recognized friends of Tilden voted for Mr. Randall, who was also supposed to be a favorite of Mr. Tilden. It was mentioned as a queer feature of the convention that none of the delegates seemed to be very enthusiastically in favor of their respective candidates, and it was said that those who voted at the beginning for General Hancock were ready to abandon him if any other gentleman should have a lead over him. Accordingly, although he had been named as a candidate and had received votes in the conventions of 1868 and 1876, and although he was so prominent prior to the convention of 1880, his nomination had all the effect of a surprise. The two ballots, the second as it stood originally and as it was when the changes had been made, were as follows:—

CANDIDATES.	1st.	2d.	After changes.
Winfield S. Hancock, Pennsylvania . .	171	320	705
Thomas F. Bayard, Delaware	153½	113	2
Henry B. Payne, Ohio	81	–	–
Allen G. Thurman, Ohio	68½	50	–
Stephen J. Field, California	65	65½	–
William R. Morrison, Illinois	62	–	–
Thomas A. Hendricks, Indiana . . .	53¼	31	30
Samuel J. Tilden, New York	38	6	1
Horatio Seymour, New York	8	–	–
Samuel J. Randall, Pennsylvania . .	–	128½	–
Scattering.	31	22	–

Two names were presented as candidates for the Vice-Presidency, that of William H. English of Indiana, and that of Richard M. Bishop of Ohio, "your uncle Dick," as he was termed by the delegate who nominated him, in an unsuccessful attempt to arouse enthusiasm. The preference for Mr. English was so strongly expressed as the voting proceeded, that Mr. Bishop's name was withdrawn, and Mr. English was nominated by acclamation.

The canvass of 1880 was a remarkable one in several ways. First, for the savage assaults that were made upon General Garfield by the Opposition. He was accused of numerous improprieties in his conduct as a member of the House of Representatives, of complicity in corrupt contracts, and of having been concerned in the Credit Mobilier, which had made a great sensation in Congress in the years 1872 and 1873. At one time the number "329" was painted, chalked and printed everywhere, on side-walks, doors and dead walls, and in the newspapers; that being the number of dollars he was alleged to have re-ceived as a Credit Mobilier dividend. At the very end of the canvass the famous "Morey Letter" was forged and scattered broadcast, particularly in the Pacific States. That letter, in which General Garfield's handwriting was counterfeited with some success, addressed to a mythical person named Morey, asserted principles on the Chinese question which, if they had been held by General Garfield, would have made him unpopular in California and the other States where "Chinese cheap labor" is regarded as a crying evil. It was lithographed and printed in vast numbers, and scattered among the voters in the Pacific States at a time when an effective denial of its authenti-city was impossible; and it had a great effect.

Another feature of the canvass was the sudden importa-tion of the tariff question into the political discussion a few weeks before the election. The Democratic platform had declared in favor of "a tariff for revenue only." Republican speakers seized upon this as an assertion of the baldest free-trade doctrine, and they denounced it with surprising vigor as assailing the interests of American industry. The Democrats could not make an effective reply, at least they did not; and they would not defend the phrase in its obvious meaning. No one really sup-posed that General Hancock was a free trader, but some unfortunate sentences which were written and spoken by him gave an opportunity to the Republicans to jeer at his supposed ignorance upon all tariff questions.

The canvass was also remarkable for the conspicuous absence of agitation upon Southern questions, which had less to do with the result than with that of any other election since the Abolitionists defeated Henry Clay in 1844, and this in spite of the fact that the South was still "solid" for the Democrats. Another fact was the utter failure of the Democrats to excite the interest of the people in the "fraud issue," meaning the result of the Electoral Commission law of 1877, which issue, the Democratic platform had said, "precedes and dwarfs every other." The canvass was, finally, singular for the discord and sullenness among the Grant men in the Republican party at the outset, followed, after a reverse in Maine in September, ·by a restoration of harmony and an increase of vigor which immediately thereafter gave energy to the canvass, carried Ohio and Indiana in October, and made General Garfield President. Reference must also be made to the scandals connected with the contributions of funds to the Republican treasury, which brought into unpleasant prominence the contributions of certain officials who were afterwards shown to have obtained their money by corrupt or otherwise improper acts.

General Garfield had but an insignificant plurality of the popular vote over Hancock, and very much less than a majority of all; but this was largely the result of abstention, voluntary or enforced, on the part of Republican voters in the South. Thirty-eight States took part in the election; in each the appointment of electors was by popular vote; and every electoral vote was counted as it was cast, — the two latter assertions can be made of no earlier election in the history of the country. The popular and electoral votes were as follows: —

STATES.	POPULAR VOTE.				ELECTORAL VOTE.	
	James A. Garfield, Ohio.	Winfield S. Hancock, Penn.	James B. Weaver, Iowa.	Neal Dow, Maine.	Garfield.	Hancock.
Maine	74,039	65,171*	4,408	93	7	–
New Hampshire, . .	44,852	40,794	528	180	5	–
Vermont	45,567	18,316	1,215	–	5	–
Massachusetts . .	165,205	111,960	4,548	682	13	–
Rhode Island. . . .	18,195	10,779	236	20	4	–
Connecticut	67,071	64,415	868	409	6	–
New York	555,544	534,511	12,373	1,517	35	–
New Jersey	120,555	122,565	2,617	191	–	9
Pennsylvania . . .	444,704	407,428	20,668	1,939	29	–
Delaware	14,133	15,275	120	–	–	3
Maryland	78,515	93,706	818	–	–	8
Virginia	84,020	128,586†	–	–	–	11
West Virginia . . .	46,243	57,391	9,079	–	–	5
North Carolina . .	115,874	124,208	1,126	–	–	10
South Carolina . .	58,071	112,312	566	–	–	7
Georgia	54,086	102,470	969	–	–	11
Florida	23,654	27,964	–	–	–	4
Alabama	56,221	91,185	4,642	–	–	10
Mississippi	34,854	75,750	5,797	–	–	8
Louisiana	38,637‡	65,067	439	–	–	8
Texas	57,893	156,428	27,405	–	–	8
Arkansas	42,436	60,775	4,079	–	–	6
Missouri	153,567	208,609	35,135	–	–	15
Tennessee	107,677	128,191	5,917	43	–	12
Kentucky	106,306	149,068	11,499	258	–	12
Ohio	375,048	340,821	6,456	2,616	22	–
Michigan	185,341	131,597	34,895	942	11	–
Indiana	232,164	225,522	12,986	–	15	–
Illinois	318,037	277,321	26,358	443	21	–
Wisconsin	144,400	114,649	7,986	69	10	–
Minnesota	93,903	53,315	3,267	286	5	–
Iowa	183,927	105,845	32,701	592	11	–
Nebraska	54,070	28,523	3,950	–	3	–
Kansas	121,549	59,801	19,851	25	5	–
Colorado	27,450	24,647	1,435	–	3	–
Nevada	8,732	9,613	–	–	–	3
California	80,348	80,426	3,392	–	1	5
Oregon	20,619	19,948	249	–	3	–
Totals	4,454,416	4,444,952	308,578	10,305	214	155

* Votes for a fusion electoral ticket, made up of three Democrats and four Greenbackers. A "straight" Greenback ticket was also voted for.
† Two Democratic tickets were voted for in Virginia. The regular ticket received 96,912, and was successful; the "Readjusters" polled 31,674 votes.
‡ Two Republican tickets were voted for.

The count of votes took place under the resolution already noticed. The electoral votes of Georgia were counted in the alternative manner first devised in 1821, as they had been cast on the second Wednesday of December. The vote was so close in California that one of the Republican electors was chosen by "split tickets." The electoral count was entirely devoid of incident, and General Garfield was duly proclaimed elected.

APPENDIX.

CONVENTIONS OF 1884.

The convention of the Anti-Monopoly party met in Chicago on May 14. Mr. A. J. Streeter of Illinois was the temporary chairman, and John F. Henry of New York the permanent president. General Benjamin F. Butler of Massachusetts was nominated for President, on the first ballot, by 122 votes to 7 for Allen G. Thurman of Ohio and 1 for Solon Chase of Maine. The nomination of a candidate for Vice-President was left to the national committee, who have adopted the candidate of the Greenback party, General Alanson M. West of Mississippi. The Anti-Monopoly platform was as follows: —

The Anti-Monopoly organization of the United States, in convention assembled, declares: —

1. That labor and capital should be allies; and we demand justice for both by protecting the rights of all against privileges for the few.

2. That corporations, the creatures of law, should be controlled by law.

3. That we propose the greatest reduction practicable in public expenses.

4. That in the enactment and vigorous execution of just laws, equality of rights, equality of burdens, equality of privileges, and equality of powers in all citizens, will be secured. To this end we declare —

5. That it is the duty of the government to immediately exercise its constitutional prerogative to regulate commerce among the States. The great instruments by which this commerce is carried

on arc transportation, money, and the transmission of intelligence. They are now mercilessly controlled by giant monopolies, to the impoverishment of labor, the crushing out of healthful competition, and the destruction of business security. We hold it, therefore, to be the imperative and immediate duty of Congress to pass all needful laws for the control and regulation of these great agents of commerce, in accordance with the oft-repeated decisions of the Supreme Court of the United States.

6. That these monopolies, which have exacted from enterprise such heavy tribute, have also inflicted countless wrongs upon the toiling millions of the United States; and no system of reform should commend itself to the support of the people which does not protect the man who earns his bread by the sweat of his face. Bureaus of labor-statistics must be established, both State and national; arbitration take the place of brute force in the settlement of disputes between employer and employed; the national eight-hour law be honestly enforced; the importation of foreign labor under contract be made illegal; and whatever practical reforms may be necessary for the protection of united labor must be granted, to the end that unto the toiler shall be given that proportion of the profits of the thing or value created which his labor bears to the cost of production.

7. That we approve and favor the passage of an inter-State commerce bill. Navigable waters should be improved by the government, and be free.

8. We demand the payment of the bonded debt as it falls due; the election of United States senators by the direct vote of the people of their respective States; a graduated income tax; and a tariff, which is a tax upon the people, that shall be so levied as to bear as lightly as possible upon necessaries. We denounce the present tariff as being largely in the interest of monopoly, and demand that it be speedily and radically reformed in the interest of labor, instead of capital.

9. That no further grants of public lands shall be made to corporations. All enactments granting lands to corporations should be strictly construed, and all land-grants should be forfeited where the terms upon which the grants were made have not been strictly complied with. The lands must be held for homes for actual settlers, and must not be subject to purchase or control by non-resident foreigners or other speculators.

10. That we deprecate the discrimination of American legisla-

tion against the greatest of American industries, — agriculture, by
which it has been deprived of nearly all beneficial legislation, while
forced to bear the brunt of taxation; and we demand for it the
fostering care of government, and the just recognition of its importance in the development and advancement of our land; and
we appeal to the American farmer to co-operate with us in our
endeavors to advance the national interests of the country and the
overthrow of monopoly in every shape, whenever and wherever
found.

The National, or Greenback, convention met at Indianapolis on the 28th of May. John Tyler of Florida was
the temporary chairman, and James B. Weaver of Iowa
the permanent President. The platform adopted was as
follows : —

Eight years ago our young party met in this city for the first
time, and proclaimed to the world its immortal principles, and
placed before the American people as a presidential candidate that
great philanthropist and spotless statesman, Peter Cooper. Since
that convention our party has organized all over the Union, and
through discussion and agitation has been educating the people to
a sense of their rights and duties to themselves and their country.
These labors have accomplished wonders. We now have a great,
harmonious party, and thousands who believe in our principles in
the ranks of other parties.

"We point with pride to our history." We forced the remone-
tization of the silver dollar; prevented the refunding of the public
debt into long-time bonds; secured the payment of the bonds, until
"the best banking system the world ever saw," for robbing the
producer, now totters because of its contracting foundation; we
have stopped the wholesale destruction of the greenback currency,
and secured a decision of the Supreme Court of the United States
establishing forever the right of the people to issue their own
money.

Notwithstanding all this, never in our history have the banks,
land-grant railroads, and other monopolies been more insolent in
their demands for further privileges — still more class legislation.
In this emergency the dominant parties are arrayed against the people, and are the abject tools of the corporate monopolies.

In the last Congress they repealed over twelve million dollars of annual taxes for the banks, throwing the burden upon the people to pay, or pay interest thereon.

Both old parties in the present Congress vie with each other in their efforts to further repeal taxes in order to stop the payment of the public debt and save the banks whose charters they have renewed for twenty years. Notwithstanding the distress of business, the shrinkage of wages, and panic, they persist in locking up, on various pretexts, four hundred million dollars of money, every dollar of which the people pay interest upon, and need, and most of which should be promptly applied to pay bonds now payable.

The old parties are united — as they cannot agree what taxes to repeal — in efforts to squander the income of the government upon every pretext rather than pay the debt.

A bill has already passed the United States Senate making the banks a present of over fifty million dollars more of the people's money, in order to enable them to levy a still greater burden of interest-taxes.

A joint effort is being made by the old party leaders to overthrow the sovereign constitutional power of the people to control their own financial affairs, and issue their own money, in order to forever enslave the masses to bankers and other business. The House of Representatives has passed bills reclaiming nearly one hundred million acres of lands granted to and forfeited by railroad companies. These bills have gone to the Senate, a body composed largely of aristocratic millionaires, who, according to their own party papers, generally purchased their elections in order to protect great monopolies which they represent. This body has thus far defied the people and the House, and refused to act upon these bills in the interest of the people.

Therefore we, the national party of the United States, in national convention assembled, this twenty-ninth day of May, A. D. 1884, declare: —

1. That we hold the late decision of the Supreme Court on the legal tender question to be a full vindication of the theory which our party has always advocated on the right and authority of Congress over the issue of legal tender notes, and we hereby pledge ourselves to uphold said decision, and to defend the Constitution against alterations or amendments intended to deprive the people of any rights or privileges conferred by that instrument. We demand the issue of such money in sufficient quantities to supply the

actual demand of trade and commerce, in accordance with the increase of population and the development of our industries. We demand the substitution of greenbacks for national bank notes, and the prompt payment of the public debt. We want that money which saved our country in time of war, and which has given it prosperity and happiness in peace. We condemn the retirement of the fractional currency and the small denomination of greenbacks, and demand their restoration. We demand the issue of the hoards of money now locked up in the United States Treasury, by applying them to the payment of the public debt now due.

2. We denounce, as dangerous to our republican institution, those methods and policies of the Democratic and Republican parties which have sanctioned or permitted the establishment of land, railroad, money, and other gigantic corporate monopolies; and we demand such governmental action as may be necessary to take from such monopolies the powers they have so corruptly and unjustly usurped, and restore them to the people, to whom they belong.

3. The public lands being the natural inheritance of the people, we denounce that policy which has granted to corporations vast tracts of land, and we demand that immediate and vigorous measures be taken to reclaim from such corporations, for the people's use and benefit, all such land grants as have been forfeited by reason of non-fulfilment of contract, or that may have been wrongfully acquired by corrupt legislation, and that such reclaimed lands and other public domain be henceforth held as a sacred trust, to be granted only to actual settlers in limited quantities; and we also demand that the alien ownership of land, individual or corporate, be prohibited.

4. We demand congressional regulation of inter-State commerce. We denounce "pooling," stock watering, and discrimination in rates and charges, and demand that Congress shall correct these abuses, even, if necessary, by the construction of national railroads. We also demand the establishment of a government postal telegraph system.

5. All private property, all forms of money and obligations to pay money, should bear their just proportion of the public taxes. We demand a graduated income tax.

6. We demand the amelioration of the condition of labor, by enforcing the sanitary laws in industrial establishments, by the abolition of the convict labor system, by a rigid inspection of mines and factories, by a reduction of the hours of labor in industrial estab-

lishments, by fostering educational institutions, and by abolishing child labor.

7. We condemn all importations of contracted labor, made with a view of reducing to starvation wages the workingmen of this country, and demand laws for its prevention.

8. We insist upon a constitutional amendment reducing the terms of United States senators.

9. We demand such rules for the government of Congress as shall place all representatives of the people upon an equal footing, and take away from committees a veto power greater than that of the President.

10. The question as to the amount of duties to be levied upon various articles of import has been agitated and quarrelled over, and has divided communities, for nearly a hundred years. It is not now, and never will be, settled, unless by the abolition of indirect taxation. It is a convenient issue, always raised when the people are excited over abuses in their midst. While we favor a wise revision of the tariff laws, with a view to raising a revenue from luxuries rather than necessities, we insist that, as an economic question, its importance is insignificant as compared with financial issues; for whereas we have suffered our worst panics under low and also under high tariffs, we have never suffered from a panic, nor seen our factories and workshops closed, while the volume of money in circulation was adequate to the needs of commerce. Give our farmers and manufacturers money as cheap as you now give it to our bankers, and they can pay high wages to labor, and compete with all the world.

11. For the purpose of testing the sense of the people upon the subject, we are in favor of submitting to a vote of the people an amendment to the Constitution in favor of suffrage regardless of sex, and also on the subject of the liquor traffic.

12. All disabled soldiers of the late war should be equitably pensioned, and we denounce the policy of keeping a small army of office-holders, whose only business is to prevent, on technical grounds, deserving soldiers from obtaining justice from the government they helped to save.

13. As our name indicates, we are a national party, knowing no East, no West, no North, no South. Having no sectional prejudices, we can properly place in nomination for the high offices of state as candidates men from any section of the Union.

14. We appeal to all people who believe in our principles to aid us by voice, pen, and votes.

General Benjamin F. Butler of Massachusetts was nominated as a candidate for President on the first ballot, receiving 322 votes, to 99 for Jesse Harper of Illinois, 2 for Solon Chase of Maine, 1 for Edward P. Allis of Wisconsin, and 1 for David Davis of Illinois. Alanson M. West of Mississippi was nominated by acclamation for Vice-President.

The Republican National Convention of 1884 was held at Chicago, June 3. John R. Lynch of Mississippi was the temporary chairman, and John B. Henderson of Missouri the permanent president. The platform adopted was as follows : —

1. The Republicans of the United States, in national convention assembled, renew their allegiance to the principles upon which they have triumphed in six successive presidential elections, and congratulate the American people on the attainment of so many results in legislation and administration by which the Republican party has, after saving the Union, done so much to render its institutions just, equal, and beneficent, the safeguard of liberty, and the embodiment of the best thought and highest purposes of our citizens. The Republican party has gained its strength by quick and faithful response to the demands of the people for the freedom and equality of all men; for a united nation, assuring the rights of all citizens; for the elevation of labor; for an honest currency; for purity in legislation; and for integrity and accountability in all departments of the government. And it accepts anew the duty of leading in the work of progress and reform.

2. We lament the death of President Garfield, whose sound statesmanship, long conspicuous in Congress, gave promise of a strong and successful administration, a promise fully realized during the short period of his office as President of the United States. His distinguished services in war and in peace have endeared him to the hearts of the American people.

3. In the administration of President Arthur we recognize a wise, conservative, and patriotic policy, under which the country has been blessed with remarkable prosperity; and we believe his eminent services are entitled to, and will receive, the hearty approval of every good citizen.

4. It is the first duty of a good government to protect the rights and promote the interests of its own people. The largest diversity of industry is most productive of general prosperity and of the comfort and independence of the people. We therefore demand that the imposition of duties on foreign imports shall be made, not for revenue only, but that, in raising the requisite revenues for the government, such duties shall be so levied as to afford security to our diversified industries and protection to the rights and wages of the laborers, to the end that active and intelligent labor, as well as capital, may have its just reward, and the laboring man his full share in the national prosperity.

5. Against the so-called economical system of the Democratic party, which would degrade our labor to the foreign standard, we enter our most earnest protest. The Democratic party has failed completely to relieve the people of the burden of unnecessary taxation by a wise reduction of the surplus.

6. The Republican party pledges itself to correct the irregularities of the tariff and to reduce the surplus, not by the vicious and indiscriminate process of horizontal reduction, but by such methods as will relieve the taxpayer without injuring the laborer or the great productive interests of the country.

7. We recognize the importance of sheep husbandry in the United States, the serious depression which it is now experiencing, and the danger threatening its future prosperity; and we therefore respect the demands of the representatives of this important agricultural interest for a readjustment of duties upon foreign wool, in order that such industry shall have full and adequate protection.

8. We have always recommended the best money known to the civilized world, and we urge that an effort be made to unite all commercial nations in the establishment of an international standard which shall fix for all the relative value of gold and silver coinage.

9. The regulation of commerce with foreign nations and between the States is one of the most important prerogatives of the general government, and the Republican party distinctly announces its purpose to support such legislation as will fully and efficiently carry out the constitutional power of Congress over inter-state commerce.

10. The principle of the public regulation of railway corporations is a wise and salutary one for the protection of all classes of the people, and we favor legislation that shall prevent unjust discrimination and excessive charges for transportation, and that shall

secure to the people and to the railways alike the fair and equal protection of the laws.

11. We favor the establishment of a national bureau of labor; the enforcement of the eight-hour law; a wise and judicious system of general education by adequate appropriation from the national revenues wherever the same is needed. We believe that everywhere the protection of a citizen of American birth must be secured to citizens by American adoption, and we favor the settlement of national differences by international arbitration.

12. The Republican party, having its birth in a hatred of slave labor, and in a desire that all men may be truly free and equal, is unalterably opposed to placing our workingmen in competition with any form of servile labor, whether at home or abroad. In this spirit we denounce the importation of contract labor, whether from Europe or Asia, as an offence against the spirit of American institutions, and we pledge ourselves to sustain the present law restricting Chinese immigration, and to provide such further legislation as is necessary to carry out its purposes.

13. Reform of the civil service, auspiciously begun under Republican administration, should be completed by the further extension of the reformed system already established by law to all the grades of the service to which it is applicable. The spirit and purpose of the reform should be observed in all executive appointments, and all laws at variance with the objects of existing reformed legislation should be repealed, to the end that the dangers to free institutions which lurk in the power of official patronage may be wisely and effectively avoided.

14. The public lands are a heritage of the people of the United States, and should be reserved, as far as possible, for small holdings by actual settlers. We are opposed to the acquisition of large tracts of these lands by corporations or individuals, especially where such holdings are in the hands of non-resident aliens, and we will endeavor to obtain such legislation as will tend to correct this evil. We demand of Congress the speedy forfeiture of all land-grants which have lapsed by reason of non-compliance with acts of incorporation, in all cases where there has been no attempt in good faith to perform the conditions of such grants.

15. The grateful thanks of the American people are due to the Union soldiers and sailors of the late war; and the Republican party stands pledged to suitable pensions for all who were disabled, and for the widows and orphans of those who died in the war. The

Republican party also pledges itself to the repeal of the limitation contained in the arrears act of 1879, so that all invalid soldiers shall share alike, and their pensions begin with the date of disability, and not with the date of the application.

16. The Republican party favors a policy which shall keep us from entangling alliances with foreign nations, and which gives us the right to expect that foreign nations shall refrain from meddling in American affairs, — the policy which seeks peace and trade with all powers, but especially with those of the western hemisphere.

17. We demand the restoration of our navy to its old-time strength and efficiency, that it may in any sea protect the rights of American citizens and the interests of American commerce. We call upon Congress to remove the burdens under which American shipping has been depressed, so that it may again be true that we have a commerce which leaves no sea unexplored, and a navy which takes no law from superior force.

18. That appointments by the President to offices in the Territories should be made from the *bona fide* citizens and residents of the Territories wherein they are to serve.

19. That it is the duty of Congress to enact such laws as shall promptly and effectually suppress the system of polygamy within our Territories, and divorce the political from the ecclesiastical power of the so-called Mormon Church, and that the law so enacted should be rigidly enforced by the civil authorities, if possible, and by the military, if need be.

20. The people of the United States, in their organized capacity, constitute a nation, and not a mere confederacy of States. The national government is supreme within the sphere of its national duties, but the States have reserved rights which should be faithfully maintained, and which should be guarded with jealous care, so that the harmony of our system of government may be preserved and the Union kept inviolate.

21. The perpetuity of our institutions rests upon the maintenance of a free ballot, an honest count, and correct return. We denounce the fraud and violence practised by the Democracy in Southern States, by which the will of the voter is defeated, as dangerous to the preservation of free institutions; and we solemnly arraign the Democratic party as being the guilty recipient of the fruits of such fraud and violence.

22. We extend to the Republicans of the South, regardless of their former party affiliations, our cordial sympathy, and pledge to

them our most earnest efforts to promote the passage of such legislation as will secure to every citizen, of whatever race and color, the full and complete recognition, possession, and exercise of all civil and political rights.

James G. Blaine of Maine was nominated as a candidate for President on the fourth ballot. The several votes were as follows: —

	1st.	2d.	3d.	4th.
James G. Blaine, Maine . .	334½	349	375	541
Chester A. Arthur, New York,	278	276	274	207
George F. Edmunds, Vermont,	93	85	69	41
John A. Logan, Illinois . .	63½	61	53	7
John Sherman, Ohio . . .	30	28	25	–
Joseph R. Hawley, Ct. . . .	13	13	13	15
Robert T. Lincoln, Illinois .	4	4	8	2
William T. Sherman, Mo. . .	2	2	2	–

John A. Logan of Illinois was nominated for Vice-President on the first ballot, receiving 779 votes, to 7 for Lucius Fairchild of Wisconsin, and 6 for Walter Q. Gresham of Indiana.

The Democratic Convention was held at Chicago, July 8. Richard D. Hubbard of Texas was the temporary chairman, and William F. Vilas of Wisconsin permanent president. The platform was as follows: —

The Democratic party of the Union, through its representatives in national convention assembled, recognizes that, as the nation grows older, new issues are born of time and progress, and old issues perish; but the fundamental principles of the Democracy, approved by the united voice of the people, remain, and will ever remain, as the best and only security for the continuance of free government. The preservation of personal rights; the equality of all citizens before the law; the reserved rights of the States; and the supremacy of the Federal government within the limits of the Constitution, will ever form the true basis of our liberties, and can never be surrendered without destroying that balance of rights and powers which enables a continent to be developed in peace, and social order to be maintained by means of local self-government. But it is indispensable for the practical application and enforcement of these fundamental principles that the government should not always be controlled by one political party. Frequent change of administration is as necessary as constant recurrence to the popular will. Otherwise abuses grow, and the government, instead of being carried on for the general welfare, becomes an instrumentality for imposing heavy burdens on the many who are governed for the benefit of the few who govern. Public servants thus become arbitrary rulers. This is now the condition of the country, hence a change is demanded.

The Republican party, so far as principle is concerned, is a reminiscence. In practice it is an organization for enriching those who control its machinery. The frauds and jobbery which have been brought to light in every department of the government are sufficient to have called for reform within the Republican party; yet those in authority, made reckless by the long possession of power, have succumbed to its corrupting influence, and have placed in nomination a ticket against which the independent portion of the party are in open revolt. Therefore a change is demanded. Such a change was alike necessary in 1876, but the will of the people was then defeated by a fraud which can never be forgotten nor condoned. Again, in 1880, the change demanded by the people was defeated by the lavish use of money contributed by unscrupulous contractors and shameless jobbers, who had bargained for unlawful profits or high office. The Republican party, during its legal, its stolen, and its bought tenures of power, has steadily decayed in moral character and political capacity. Its platform promises are now a list of its past failures. It demands the restoration of our navy; it has squandered hundreds of millions to create a navy that does not exist. It calls upon Congress to remove the burdens under which American shipping has been depressed; it imposed and has continued these burdens. It professes the policy of reserving the public lands for small holdings by actual settlers; it has given away the people's heritage, till now a few railroads and non-resident aliens, individual and corporate, possess a larger area than that of all our farms between the two seas. It professes a preference for free institutions; it organized and tried to legalize a control of State elections by Federal troops. It professes a desire to elevate labor; it subjected American working-men to the competition of convict and imported contract labor. It professes gratitude to all who were disabled or died in the war, leaving widows and orphans; it left to a Democratic House of Representatatives the first effort to equalize both bounties and pensions. It professes a pledge to correct the irregularities of our tariff; it created and has continued them. Its own tariff commission confessed the need of more than twenty per cent reduction; its Congress gave a reduction of less than four per cent. It professes the protection of American manufactures; it has subjected them to an increasing flood of manufactured goods and a hopeless competition with manufacturing nations, not one of which taxes raw materials. It professes to protect all American industries; it has impoverished many to subsidize a few. It professes the protection of American labor; it has depleted the returns of American agriculture, an industry followed by half our people. It professes the equality of all men before the law, attempting to fix the status of colored citizens; the acts of its Congress were overset by the decisions of its courts. It "accepts anew the duty of leading in the work of progress and reform;" its caught criminals are permitted to escape through contrived delays or actual connivance in the prosecution. Honeycombed with corruption, out-breaking exposures no longer shock its moral sense. Its honest members, its independent journals no longer maintain a successful contest for authority in its canvasses or a veto upon bad nominations. That change is necessary is proved by an existing surplus of more than $100,000,000, which has yearly been collected from a suffering people. Unnecessary taxation is unjust taxation. We denounce the Republican party for having failed to relieve the people from crushing war taxes, which have paralyzed business, crippled industry, and deprived labor of employment and of just reward.

The Democracy pledges itself to purify the administration from corruption, to restore economy, to revive respect for law, and to reduce taxation to the lowest limit consistent with due regard to the preservation of the faith of the nation to its creditors and pensioners. Knowing full well, however, that legislation affecting the occupations of the people should be cautious and conservative in method, not in advance of public opinion, but responsive to its demands, the Democratic party is pledged to revise the tariff in a spirit of fairness to all interests. But, in making reduction in taxes, it is not proposed to injure any domestic industries, but rather to promote their healthy growth. From the foundation of this government, taxes collected at the custom house have been the chief source of Federal revenue. Such they must continue to be. Moreover, many industries have come to rely upon legislation for successful continuance, so that any change of law must be at every step regardful of the labor and capital thus involved. The process of reform must be subject in the execution to this plain dictate of justice: all taxation shall be limited to the requirements of econom- ical government. The necessary reduction in taxation can and must be effected without depriving American labor of the ability to compete successfully with foreign labor, and without imposing lower rates of duty than will be ample to cover any increased cost of production which may exist in consequence of the higher rate of wages prevailing in this country. Sufficient revenue to pay all the expenses of the Federal government, economically administered, including pensions, interest and principal of the public debt, can be got under our present system of taxation from custom-house taxes on fewer imported articles, bearing heaviest on articles of luxury and bearing lightest on articles of necessity. We therefore denounce the abuses of the existing tariff; and, subject to the pre- ceding limitations, we demand that Federal taxation shall be exclu- sively for public purposes, and shall not exceed the needs of the government economically administered.

The system of direct taxation, known as the "internal revenue," is a war tax, and, so long as the law continues, the money derived therefrom should be sacredly devoted to the relief of the people from the remaining burdens of the war, and be made a fund to defray the expenses of the care and comfort of worthy soldiers disabled in the line of duty in the wars of the Republic, and for the payment of such pensions as Congress may from time to time grant to such soldiers, a like fund for the sailors having been already provided; and any surplus should be paid into the Treasury.

We favor an American continental policy, based upon more intimate commercial and political relations with the fifteen sister republics of North, Central, and South America, but entangling alliances with none.

We believe in honest money, the gold and silver coinage of the Constitution, and a circulating medium convertible into such money without loss.

Asserting the equality of all men before the law, we hold that

It is the duty of the government, in its dealings with the people, to mete out equal and exact justice to all citizens, of whatever nativity, race, color, or persuasion, religious or political.

We believe in a free ballot and a fair count; and we recall to the memory of the people the noble struggle of the Democrats in the Forty-fifth and Forty-sixth Congresses, by which a reluctant Republican opposition was compelled to assent to legislation making everywhere illegal the presence of troops at the polls, as the conclusive proof that a Democratic administration will preserve liberty with order.

The selection of Federal officers for the Territories should be restricted to citizens previously resident therein.

We oppose sumptuary laws, which vex the citizens and interfere with individual liberty.

We favor honest civil service reforms and the compensation of all United States officers by fixed salaries, the separation of Church and State, and the diffusion of free education by common schools, so that every child in the land may be taught the rights and duties of citizenship.

While we favor all legislation which will tend to the equitable distribution of property, to the prevention of monopoly and to the strict enforcement of individual rights against corporate abuses, we hold that the welfare of society depends upon a scrupulous regard for the rights of property as defined by law.

We believe that labor is best rewarded where it is freest and most enlightened. It should, therefore, be fostered and cherished. We favor the repeal of all laws restricting the free action of labor and the enactment of laws by which labor organizations may be incorporated, and of all such legislation as will tend to enlighten the people as to the true relation of capital and labor.

We believe that the public land ought, as far as possible, to be kept as homesteads for actual settlers; that all unearned lands heretofore improvidently granted to railroad corporations by the action of the Republican party should be restored to the public domain, and that no more grants of land shall be made to corporations or be allowed to fall into the ownership of alien absentees.

We are opposed to all propositions which, upon any pretext, would convert the general government into a machine for collecting taxes to be distributed among the States or the citizens thereof.

In reaffirming the declaration of the Democratic platform of

1856, that "the liberal principles embodied by Jefferson in the Declaration of Independence, and sanctioned in the Constitution, which make ours the land of liberty and the asylum of the oppressed of every nation, have ever been cardinal principles in the Democratic faith," we nevertheless do not sanction the importation of foreign labor or the admission of servile races unfitted by habits, training, religion or kindred, for absorption into the great body of our people, or for the citizenship which our laws confer. American civilization demands that against the immigration or importation of Mongolians to these shores our gates be closed.

The Democratic party insists that it is the duty of this government to protect with equal fidelity and vigilance the rights of its citizens, native and naturalized, at home and abroad; and, to the end that this protection may be assured, United States papers of naturalization, issued by courts of competent jurisdiction, must be respected by the executive and legislative departments of our own government and by all foreign powers. It is an imperative duty of this government to efficiently protect all the rights of persons and property of every American citizen in foreign lands, and demand and enforce full reparation for any invasion thereof. An American citizen is only responsible to his own government for any act done in his own country or under her flag, and can only be tried therefor on her own soil and according to her laws; and no power exists in this government to expatriate an American citizen to be tried in any foreign land for any such act.

This country has never had a well defined and executed foreign policy save under Democratic administration. That policy has ever been, in regard to foreign nations, so long as they do no act detrimental to the interests of the country or hurtful to our citizens, to let them alone. As the result of this policy, we recall the acquisition of Louisiana, Florida, California, and of the adjacent Mexican Territory by purchase alone, and contrast these grand acquisitions of Democratic statesmanship with the purchase of Alaska, the sole fruit of a Republican administration of nearly a quarter of a century.

The Federal government should care for and improve the Mississippi River and other great waterways of the republic, so as to secure for the interior States easy and cheap transportation to tide water.

Under a long period of Democratic rule and policy, our merchant marine was fast overtaking and on the point of outstripping that of Great Britain. Under twenty years of Republican rule and policy, our commerce has been left to British bottoms, and the American flag has almost been swept off the high seas. Instead of the Republican party's British policy, we demand for the people of the United States an American policy. Under Democratic rule and policy, our merchants and sailors, flying the Stars and Stripes in every port, successfully searched out a market for the various products of American industry; under a quarter of a century of Republican rule and policy, despite our manifest advantages over all other nations, in high paid labor, favorable climates, and teeming soils; despite freedom of trade among all these United States; despite their population by the foremost races of men, and an annual immigration of the young, thrifty, and adventurous of all nations; despite our freedom here from the inherited burdens of life and industry in Old World monarchies, their costly war navies, their vast tax-consuming, non-producing standing armies; despite twenty years of peace — that Republican rule and policy have managed to surrender to Great Britain, along with our commerce, the control of the markets of the world. Instead of the Republican party's British policy, we demand, in behalf of the American Democracy, an American policy. Instead of the Republican party's discredited scheme and false pretence of friendship for American labor, expressed by imposing taxes, we demand, in behalf of the Democracy, freedom for American labor by reducing taxes, to the end that these United States may compete with unhindered powers for the primacy among nations in all the arts of peace and fruits of liberty.

With profound regret we have been apprised by the venerable statesman, through whose person was struck that blow at the vital principle of republics, acquiescence in the will of the majority, that he cannot permit us again to place in his hands the leadership of the Democratic hosts, for the reason that the achievement of reform in the administration of the Federal government is an undertaking now too heavy for his age and failing strength. Rejoicing that his life has been prolonged until the general judgment of our fellow-countrymen is united in the wish that that wrong were righted in his person, for the Democracy of the United States we offer to him, in his withdrawal from public cares, not only our respectful sympathy and esteem, but also that best of homage of freemen, — the pledge of our devotion to the principles and the cause now inseparable in the history of this Republic from the labors and the name of Samuel J. Tilden.

With this statement of the hopes, principles, and purposes of the Democratic party, the great issue of reform and change in administration is submitted to the people in calm confidence that the popular voice will pronounce in favor of new men, and new and more favorable conditions for the growth of industry, the extension of trade, the employment and due reward of labor and of capital, and the general welfare of the whole country.

Grover Cleveland of New York was nominated as a candidate for President on the second ballot. The two ballots resulted as follows: —

	1st.	2d.
Grover Cleveland of New York	392	683
Thomas F. Bayard of Delaware	170	81½
Allen G. Thurman of Ohio	88	4
Samuel J. Randall of Pennsylvania. . .	78	4
Joseph E. McDonald of Indiana	56	2
John G. Carlisle of Kentucky	27	–
Roswell P. Flower of New York	4	–
George Hoadly of Ohio	3	–
Samuel J. Tilden of New York	1	–
Thomas A. Hendricks of Indiana . . .	–	145½

Thomas A. Hendricks of Indiana was unanimously nominated as a candidate for Vice-President on the first ballot.

The Prohibition party held its national convention at Pittsburg on July 23. William Daniel of Maryland was the temporary chairman, and Samuel Dickey of Michigan was the permanent president. The following platform was adopted: —

The Prohibition-Home-Protection party, in national convention assembled, acknowledge Almighty God as the rightful sovereign of all men, from whom the just powers of government are derived, and to whose laws human enactments should conform. Peace, prosperity, and happiness only can come to the people when the laws of their national and State governments are in accord with the divine will.

That the importation, manufacture, supply, and sale of alcoholic beverages, created and maintained by the laws of the national and State governments, during the entire history of such laws, is everywhere shown to be the promoting cause of intemperance, with resulting crime and pauperism; making large demands upon public and private charity; imposing large and unjust taxation and public burdens for penal and sheltering institutions upon thrift, industry, manufactures, and commerce; endangering the public peace; causing desecration of the Sabbath; corrupting our politics, legislation, and administration of the laws; shortening lives; impairing health; and diminishing productive industry; causing education to be neglected and despised; nullifying the teachings of the Bible, the church, and the school, the standards and guides of our fathers and their children in the founding and growth under God of our widely extended country; and, while imperilling the perpetuity of our civil and religious liberties, are baleful fruits by which we know that these laws are alike contrary to God's laws and contravene our happiness; and we call upon our fellow-citizens to aid in the repeal of these laws and in the legal suppression of this baneful liquor traffic.

The fact that, during the twenty-four years in which the Republican party has controlled the general government and that of many of the States, no effort has been made to change this policy; that Territories have been created from the national domain and governments from them established, and States admitted into the Union, in no instance in either of which has this traffic been forbidden, or the people of these Territories or States been permitted to prohibit it; that there are now over two hundred thousand distilleries, breweries, wholesale and retail dealers in these drinks, holding certificates and claiming the authority of government for the continuation of a business which is so destructive to the moral and material welfare of the people, together with the fact that they have turned a deaf ear to remonstrance and petition for the correction of this abuse of civil government, is conclusive that the Republican party is insensible to or impotent for the redress of those wrongs, and should no longer be entrusted with the powers and responsibilities of government; that although this party, in its late national convention, was silent on the liquor question, not so were its candidates, Messrs. Blaine and Logan. Within the year past Mr. Blaine has publicly recommended that the revenues derived from the liquor traffic shall be distributed among the States, and Senator Logan has by bill proposed to devote these revenues to the support of schools. Thus both virtually recommend the perpetuation of the traffic, and that the State and its citizens shall become partners in the liquor crime.

The fact that the Democratic party has, in its national deliverances of party policy, arrayed itself on the side of the drink makers and sellers by declaring against the policy of prohibition of such traffic under the false name of "sumptuary laws," and, when in power in some of the States, in refusing remedial legislation, and, in Congress, of refusing to permit the creation of a board of inquiry to investigate and report upon the effects of this traffic, proves that the Democratic party should not be entrusted with power or place.

There can be no greater peril to the nation than the existing competition of the Republican and Democratic parties for the liquor vote. Experience shows that any party not openly opposed to the traffic will engage in this competition, will court the favor of the criminal classes, will barter away the public morals, purity of the ballot, and every trust and object of good government, for party success; and patriots and good citizens should find in this practice sufficient cause for immediate withdrawal from all connection with their party.

That we favor reforms in the administration of the government, in the abolition of all sinecures, useless offices and officers, in the election by the people of officers of the government instead of appointment by the President. That competency, honesty, and sobriety are essential qualifications for holding civil office, and we oppose the removal of such persons from mere administrative offices, except so far as it may be absolutely necessary to secure effectiveness to the vital issues on which the general administration of the government has been entrusted to a party.

That the collection of revenue from alcohol, liquors, and tobacco should be abolished, as the vices of men are not a proper subject for taxation; that revenue for customs duties should be levied for the support of the government, economically administered; and when so levied, the fostering of American labor, manufactures, and industries should constantly be held in view.

That the public land should be held for homes for the people and not for gifts to corporations, or to be held in large bodies for speculation upon the needs of actual settlers.

That all money, coin and paper, shall be made, issued, and regulated by the general government, and shall be a legal tender for all debts, public and private.

That grateful care and support should be given to our soldiers and sailors, their dependent widows and orphans, disabled in the service of the country.

That we repudiate as un-American, contrary to and subversive of the principle of the Declaration of Independence, from which our government has grown to be the government of fifty-five millions of people, and a recognized power among nations, that any person or people shall or may be excluded from residence or citizenship with all others who may desire the benefits which our institutions confer upon the oppressed of all nations.

That while there are important reforms that are demanded for purity of administration and the welfare of the people, their importance sinks into insignificance when compared with the reform of the drink traffic, which annually wastes eight hundred million dollars of the wealth created by toil and thrift, and drags down thousands of families from comfort to poverty; which fills jails, penitentiaries, insane asylums, hospitals, and institutions for dependency; which destroys the health, saps industry, and causes loss of life and property to thousands in the land, lowers intellectual and physical vigor, dulls the cunning hand of the artisan, is the chief cause of bankruptcy, insolvency, and loss in trade, and by its corrupting power endangers the perpetuity of free institutions.

That Congress should exercise its undoubted power, and prohibit the manufacture and sale of intoxicating beverages in the District of Columbia, in the Territories of the United States, and in all places over which the government has exclusive jurisdiction; that hereafter no State shall be admitted into the Union until its constitution shall expressly prohibit polygamy and the manufacture and sale of intoxicating beverages.

We earnestly call the attention of the laborer and mechanic, the miner and manufacturer, and ask investigation of the baneful effects upon labor and industry caused by the needless liquor business, which will be found the robber who lessens wages and profits, the destroyer of happiness and the family welfare of the laboring man, and that labor and all legitimate industry demand deliverance from the taxation and loss which this traffic imposes, and that no tariff or other legislation can so healthily stimulate production or increase a demand for capital and labor, or produce so much of comfort and content, as the suppressing of this traffic would bring to the laboring man, mechanic, or employer of labor throughout our land.

That the activity and co-operation of the women of America for the promotion of temperance has in all the history of the past been a strength and encouragement which we gratefully acknowledge and record. In the later and present phase of the movement for the prohibition of the licensed traffic by the abolition of the drinking-saloon, the purity of purpose and method, the earnestness, zeal, intelligence, and devotion of the mothers and daughters of the Women's Christian Temperance Union has been eminently blessed by God. Kansas and Iowa have been given her as "sheaves of rejoicing;" and the education and arousing of the public mind, and the demand for constitutional amendment now prevailing, are largely the fruit of her prayers and labors, and we rejoice to have our Christian women unite with us in sharing the labor that shall bring the abolition of this traffic to the polls, she shall join in the grand "Praise God, from whom all blessings flow," when by law our boys and friends shall be free from legal drink temptation.

That we believe in the civil and political equality of the sexes, and that the ballot in the hand of woman is a right for her protection, and would prove a powerful ally for the abolition of the drink-saloon, the execution of law, the promotion of reform in civil affairs, and the removal of corruption in public life; and thus believing, we relegate the practical outworking of this reform to the discretion of the Prohibition party in the several States, according to the condition of public sentiment in those States; that gratefully we acknowledge and praise God for the presence of his Spirit, guiding our counsels and granting the success which has been vouchsafed in the progress of temperance reform, and looking to Him from whom all wisdom and help come, we ask the voters of the United States to make the principles of the above declaration a ruling principle in the government of the. nation and of the States.

Resolved, That henceforth the Prohibition-Home-Protection party shall be called by the name of the Prohibition party.

John P. St. John of Kansas was unanimously nominated as a candidate for President, and William Daniel of Maryland for Vice-President.

INDEX.